The Siren's Call

The Treasured Possession Duet

Tammy Bradley

Content Warnings

This book is strictly for readers over the age of eighteen, the content is also not for the faint hearted. It has graphically explained sex scenes, sex acts which also have BDSM aspects and blood play.

The book is set in a mafia world, so violence, torture and killings are throughout.

My main male character can be dominant, grumpy and an Alphahole by nature. My main female characters are feisty, strong but also have submissive tendencies in the bedroom. They can be territorial, aggressive, jealous and controlling, sometimes overly so.

I have graphic torture scenes, kidnapping, knife play and fight scenes. Characters are also killed or wounded.

There is also graphic language throughout this book.

If any of these things offend you in any way, please do not read on, I am also probably not the author for you as this is the style of the dark romance I write.

My book is also written in British-English.

If none of the above has bothered you, welcome

to my dark world of romance. I hope you enjoy my book and look forward to hearing what you think about it if you leave a review.

Acknowledgments

Firstly, I'd like to thank my Fiancé Craig; none of this would have been possible without you. You taught me I was able to love and be loved. You also gave me the support and confidence to finally chase my dreams.

I had kept my love of writing a secret from everyone, with no confidence and a low self-esteem. Even you didn't know I dreamt of being a writer until 25 years later. Yes, I know that was a big shock to everyone including you.

Our life together has been full of beautiful memories, love, and hope. But then we had the biggest tragedy any parent could have. We lost our beloved daughter Lexi. We cried, we broke, and we both very nearly didn't make it through. We have now come to the realisation that we will always be broken and none of our pieces will ever be put back together.

We have learned to adapt and live life for our 3 other precious daughters. They saved us with their smiles, love, and altogether craziness.

Thank you, Craig, for giving me 4 gorgeous girls, love and a home. Our story was never meant to be a bed of roses fairy tale. We were meant to be the hard-ass survivors who get to the end of our story with scars, bruises and bad hair.

I'm looking forward to the future with you and the girls. Our happily ever after is waiting for us, nobody can ever take that away from us. It's you and me until the end babe, love you forever and always.

To my children, my crazy girlies. I hope you are proud of your Momma even though you will probably never be allowed to read my books! I love you all more than life itself.

You saved me when I thought there was no hope when we lost Lexi. You showed me my biggest battle still lay ahead and gave me the strength to carry on.

I don't know what I did to deserve you all, but I thank the Gods for you every day. I'm never going to win any awards for best Mom, but know this my beautiful girlies. I will always love you with all my heart and soul.

You make me so proud. I hope all of your dreams and ambitions for your own futures come true. I'll be with you every step of the way.

To my precious Angel Lexi, I miss you so much every day my sweet angel, that it hurts to breathe. I know I was being unfair when I was begging for you to stay, I just didn't want you to be somewhere that I knew I couldn't follow.

Though your life was only a few short years

on this earth, you showed me what it's like to witness a true-life warrior. You fought so hard, defeated minimal odds, and always had a smile on your face while doing it. Oh, unless you had a nummy in your mouth or were snuggled in a blanket sleeping.

I was blessed to have you as my beautiful daughter and experience a life enriched by you. You were too precious for this earth. You had a far more important journey to fulfil. Your wings were ready, but Momma's heart wasn't!

Fly high sweet angel, fly high. Until we meet again, all my love always, Mom x

To my mom, what can I say Mom, but our journey has definitely been interesting. I hope I have been able to make you proud and I will always love you. Look after my Angel when it's time and make sure she knows how much I love her every day. You may have been called early but it's just your time to look after more than just us. You now have a higher purpose so do us proud.

Now, to my dear friends, that I've found along the way.

Kerry Morgan, my fellow nutter, PA, cheerleader and dearest friend. Thank you for all your support and patience with me whilst I was writing this book. You picked me up if I fell and kicked my arse when I doubted myself. Keep being you beautiful and I can't wait to read your first book when it's out. Love you babe.

Fiona Ferguson, you are an amazing friend and how much we have in common is scary. I'm so glad I met you and brought you to the Dark side. Keep smiling beautiful, and I love you.

Maggie Brown, Annalee Adams, Ashlie-Louise Pearson and Alyssha Glenn, I love you all dearly and thank you so much for everything you have done for me. You are always there when I need you and help me at the drop of a hat. My angel definitely sent you my way.

Open Eye Editing my Editors, who under a very restricted deadline edited and polished my book to perfection. I cannot thank you enough for everything you have done for me, and I look forward to working with you again on book 2.

My Alpha team, Kerry Morgan, Sharon Jackson and Raluca Butusina. To my Beta team and Arc team you are truly fantastic, thank you all for your help and support.

I'd lastly like to thank my fans for reading my books. Without you, I would never have been able to achieve my dreams. Thank you so much for all your love and support.

Chapter 1

Annabelle

Kim comes over and pinches my eyeliner as I touch up my Cherry Red lipstick.

"For fuck's sake Kim, that was new today, you better give me that back when you're done bitch. You're always running off with my stuff and never giving it back!" I scowl at her in the mirror and go back to add another layer of mascara.

"Chill your tits Belle, I'll give it back to you in a bit. What crawled up your arse today anyway?" Kim says, as she walks back to her dressing table in a black lacy thong. I think I've seen more of her body than the guests at the club have, but hey, this is what comes with dancing at a burlesque club I guess.

"I'm just pissed off with having to buy new stuff all the time because you pinch it! Remember to put it back this time." I look myself over and fluff my hair up more, giving it extra volume that it

1

doesn't need. I see Kim flip me off in my mirror and smile back at her.

Rose stands up from her own dresser and walks over to me. She's gorgeous, a tall platinum blonde, with a figure to die for and a huge pair of boobs. I've only been here for a short time, four months to be precise, but I would consider Rose one of my closest friends. I've missed having female friends.

"Are you okay Belle? You seem nervous tonight and that's unusual for you!" She puts her hand on my shoulder trying to comfort me.

"I'm just a bit on edge... as Pete said earlier the owner is in tonight!" I've never met the owner of the Club, as it was Pete the manager who hired me.

"Oh sweetie, don't worry about Kai! He'll be too busy in meetings or with some slut in the VIP lounge," she said, walking off to finish getting into her next outfit.

Everyone here is nice, but only if you don't get in their way of making money. A few of the girls are a bit upset though because I've been given the lucrative spotlight dance for the past two weeks.

We've already done four burlesque group routines tonight, then my spotlight freestyle and Crystal's pole dance, followed by some of the other girls' performances. My upcoming routine is my last dance of the night.

With a small sigh I get up to put on the costume for my dance. I had to be on stage in about ten minutes. I ran my hands over the outfit rail; all feathers, sequins and barely there ensembles.

I picked out my black lace see-through teddy that, as you can imagine, showed more of my body than it hid. Only my pussy was hidden by the elaborate ivy embroidered across it. I added thigh-high stockings and a pair of black stiletto heels. The finishing touch was my black lace gloves, and I was ready to go.

It didn't bother me to show my body off, as this was my way of rebelling against the life I'd been born into. This was my choice and if they didn't like it? Well; they could fuck off.

Dancing is my life. I've loved it from such a young age, even going to dance school three times a week. I fully intended to commit to it more if I was allowed, and eventually teach. Unfortunately, life took a vastly different turn at seventeen proving my life thus far was full of lies, deceit and betrayal. Shaking myself, I thought, 'enough of that.' The past is never a good place to go.

Sam, who looks after the dancers and is a regular mother hen to all of us, comes rushing in. She's stunning, with black hair and striking pale blue eyes. She used to dance, but then took to looking after the girls when she had a little girl about two years ago. So instead, she orders or makes all our costumes and does the set order every week.

"Belle you're up sweetie, it's packed out there! Show them what you're made of!" She gives me her megawatt smile and rushes off backstage. I take a deep breath and make my own way backstage to take my spot.

I stand there with my back to the curtains, right leg extended out and my hands clasped together in the air. The familiar sound of the curtains opening draws my attention to the audience. I have a quick peek and I've never seen it so full. The spotlight blinks to life and the audience disappears behind the glare. As the first bars of 'Under the influence' by Chris Brown spills out of the speakers, I take a breath and start to dance.

Running my hand down my left arm that is still suspended in the air, I shift my weight over to my right side and bend, gliding a hand up the length of my leg, giving everyone in the audience a generous view of my arse in the teddy thong. Lifting myself gracefully upright I spiral into a pirouette, turning to face the audience. Face down, my flaming red hair cascades down in waves to cover it.

The guys go crazy, calling out to me, whistling and cheering like an ocean roaring. I stand feet apart and lift my head slowly.

I continue on with my routine letting the music

carry me away, falling into the beat, running my hands over myself, allowing it to consume me. The tempo takes over my body as I lose myself to the dance.

The stage is wide and I walk gracefully over to the runway at its centre, which leads out into the middle of the club. Strolling seductively, I make my way down it, stopping halfway before dropping to my knees. Tipping my head back I begin rotating my hips, undulating them smoothly and, with each rotation, I open my knees. Dropping my bottom to the floor as though I'm riding a man, caressing my body with wandering hands. My hair brushes the curve of my arse in a sinful tease. Running my hands back up my body, I caress my breasts and move up to my throat.

As I'm lost in melodic ecstasy, a buzz of electricity sparks and prickles along my skin. I raise my head slowly and lock eyes with the most piercing ocean-blue eyes I've ever seen. The sight steals my breath. The spotlight isn't as bright here so I can see him fully.

Surveying the scene, I see he's sitting in the VIP lounge and his heated stare has me pinned. Captured by it, unable to tear my eyes away, I run my hands back over my body as I lower myself onto all fours and crawl further in his direction. Letting my gaze roam over him I finally notice the blonde, her face buried in his lap, giving him enthusiastic head. His hand is on the back of her head, pushing her down further on his cock at a rapid pace as I crawl toward him.

Bringing my gaze back to his, I find he hasn't looked away as he raises a mocking eyebrow at me.

Stopping at the end of the runway, directly in front of him, I quickly decided to answer his silent challenge. Let's see how long he lasts if I up the ante. I move to the beat once again; dropping my top half to the floor, I open my legs wider. Keeping my arse in the air, I pulse it up and down in a humping motion. In response he grabs the blonde's head on both sides and matches my movements. The audience is forgotten; I can't take my eyes off him. I'm enraptured in our game.

Rolling to my back, eyes on his, I tilt my head off the stage. Holding my legs pressed together, I lift them straight up in the air before spreading them wide. I repeat this a few times slowly, gradually easing them down to the floor again. Raising my knees I open them widely, caressing my hands over my breasts, while my hips are swivelling and thrusting to the music. Keeping my left hand on my breast I let my right hand roam down my body to my pussy. Rubbing over it a few times, I catch my clit which is throbbing for attention. Why is this man turning me on so much?

I lower my arse to the floor and flip onto my front. Easing back into the kneeling position, I spread my knees out wide. Bringing my fingers to my mouth tauntingly, my left hand goes back to my breast caressing it teasingly.

He stops his ministrations for a few seconds, gritting his teeth, and I know he's close. His pupils are dilated as his intense stare focuses on me and only me. I smile salaciously, putting two laced fingers in my mouth and sucking hard before removing them, placing my hand to my pussy yet again.

I gyrate against them, not quite touching, mimicking getting myself off right in front of him as I get lost once again in the music. He resumes his own rhythm to match mine as we clash in a battle of wills and lust. We both get more frenzied with our movements.

I'm not touching myself, but the intensity of the connection between us makes me feel like I want to come. The song is nearing its end and I know the moment will soon be lost.

His teeth grind down and his jaw strains, his hand presses the blonde's head hard to his lap and holds it there. His mouth opens and he tilts his head slightly back, his eyes never leaving mine. He tenses and I know he's coming; I throw my head back and tremble with need. Making it appear as if I too am in the throes of an orgasm.

The music stops and I lower my gaze to the floor, breaking the spell. Pushing myself up I pay him no attention, and turn my back, adding extra sway to my step as I sashay back to the main stage. Turning away, the audience goes wild. I let myself have one last look, and as he meets me with his own, I blow him a kiss and exit the stage out of view.

The adulation of the crowd follows behind me and I lean against the wall, my heart thundering in my chest as I try to compose myself. What the hell was I thinking? *Jesus Belle what the fuck.* My body is so hot and I'm so bloody horny it's unbelievable. *Get a grip, Belle!* I try to tell myself as I make my way back to the dressing rooms.

Sitting down at my dresser I take a few deep breaths of relief. Sam rushes in and calls to me.

"Belle, I don't know what the hell you just did on that stage, but the audience hasn't shut up yet. Bloody hell girl, you didn't dance it like that in rehearsal! My God I think I have a girl crush on you myself!" She starts fanning herself and I can't help but laugh.

We're both laughing when Adonis walks through the door, right into our dressing rooms. He looks directly at me and I start to feel a bit worried. He strolls over to us.

"The boss wants to speak to Little Red here!" he says to Sam, then looks at me.

"Of course, I'll send her over when she's dressed, Lev," Sam says, to which Lev leaves the room. I look at Sam with wide eyes, *what the hell would he want with me?*

"Get dressed quickly Belle and make sure you wear a nice dress from the rack. You don't want to keep Kai waiting!" Sam rushes out of the room. I quickly freshened up and chose a figure-hugging emerald silk dress with a high split to wear. I hesitantly walk out of the dressing room to meet up with Sam and find out my fate.

Kai

What a shit show today has been. Two shipments have been delayed and I can't get the answers. I need to find out why. This enrages me so I sent Misha and Pasha to sort it out because, if I go myself, I will end up killing them all with the mood I'm in. Add this to the meeting I've just had with one of my associates, which ended in me grabbing him around the throat and throwing him over the table to kick the shit out of him. Well, I'd say today has been a total shit show of a day.

"Do you want me to let the girl in Kai?" Lev asks from behind me in the VIP lounge of my club. I thought having the meeting here would have been a good idea but now, sitting in The Siren's Call- my burlesque club, I'm second-guessing my decisions.

"Send her in." I don't look around as I answer Lev, instead I continue to look at the stage, watching the show as the girls do their routine. A whiff of cheap perfume hits my senses and I already know this day is beyond saving. Suddenly Amy stands right in front of my view and goes to touch my face. I grab her wrist and squeeze it hard.

"You know what to do, now fucking kneel and get the fuck on with it!" Amy pouts but kneels and starts undoing my belt and pulling down my fly. My erection springs free, but it's going down by the second.

Amy starts to pump my cock and caress my balls. Which just fucking annoys me. I want to call an end to it, but I need to get off. I sit up and whip my belt off, grabbing Amy's hands and pinning them behind her back. I wrap my belt around them and fasten it in place so she can't use her hands on me again.

"Get my fucking cock in your mouth and stop pissing about," I spit with venom, lifting my cock and forcing it into her mouth. She looks at me with doe eyes, thinking I'm going to take pity on her. Fuck that! She's just a mouth to fuck. If she doesn't want to do it properly, I'll find someone that does.

She goes to town, trying to get my cock interested but it's at half-mast now and going down by the second. I put my hand on the back of her head and forced her down further, hitting the back of her throat. She gags and my cock finally pays attention. I keep on forcing her up and down on my cock.

I glance at the stage for inspiration. The curtains are just opening and the vision I see before me is mesmerising. A petite redhead stands with her back to us. She's in nothing but underwear and killer heels. Her red wavy locks hang temptingly down her back, nearly reaching to her voluptuous arse as the thong of her outfit disappears between her cheeks. She starts dancing and bends over to caress her hand from her feet upwards.

My cock goes rock fucking hard in seconds as I'm faced with her arse on full display. She stands and pirouettes to face me. Now I can see her lace-covered pussy begging for my attention. She has her head down, face covered by her hair so I can't see her features yet. My eyes rake down her breath-taking body starting with her ample lace-covered breasts. They are enticingly large for her frame. My eyes continue their leisurely journey, to her tiny waist and down to her voluptuous hips and thighs.

She has a perfect hourglass figure that I want to devour. I've not seen this girl here before, however, she will know who I am by the end of the night. Or my name is not Nikolai Filippov. If I want something I will have it, regardless of the repercussions. No one escapes me.

She lifts her head and I see the most beautiful sky-blue eyes I've ever seen. The little vixen continues with her routine, pressing nearer to me with every move. She's looking at everyone in the audience except for me, and it pisses me off. I keep moving Amy down on my cock, nearly forgetting that she needed to breathe.

The vixen on stage stops halfway and suddenly drops to her knees. She moves effortlessly and seems to let the music take control of her body. She tips her head back as she caresses her gorgeous body, and I can't fucking help it; I force Amy's head up and down on my cock imaging this Goddess on stage riding it instead.

I've never had a woman affect me like *this, ever.* I fuck them and get rid. I have no time for a woman. Never have, never will that's my number one rule. What the fuck is happening to me?

My Little Vixen on the stage brings her head back up and locks her eyes with mine. A shiver runs through my body and my cock's response is to thicken as my balls draw up. I'm so fucking turned on by this beauty that I know I will have to make her mine. That thought troubles me, so I choose to ignore it for now and go with the flow.

My Little Vixen looks down at my lap and watches me force Amy's head up and down on my engorged cock. Her eyes lock back with mine and I expect her to look away. But no, my vixen decides she wants to play, and the thrill that runs through my body is indescribable.

She comes to a stop right in front of me, at the end of the stage runway, continuing to dance erotically, her eyes never leaving mine. Dropping to the floor, she pushes her luscious tits into the stage with her delectable arse high in the air. Oh, how I want to get up on that stage and mark that arse with my hand. Maybe even with my belt. Fuck yeah, my stripes would look perfect on her porcelain skin. I'll bet I'll be able to see my marks on her for days.

Suddenly, she starts pumping her arse up and down like she's riding my cock again. I grab Amy's head, placing my hands on either side and pumping to the same rhythm as my vixen. Amy is gagging like hell, but do I give a fuck if she can't cope? Abso-fucking-lutely not. She can fuck right off.

My vixen flips over on her back and hangs her head over the stage, always keeping her eyes locked on mine. I wonder why she attracts my attention so much, as I always prefer a submissive by nature. One that would never dare to make eye contact and never push my boundaries like this little minx. I wonder if her brazenness is what is refreshing about her. Maybe? She carries on with her teasing and now she has her hand on her pussy, making me want to personally drag her off the stage.

My dominating nature is taking over now, and I want only my eyes to see her touching that pussy, making her get herself off before I clean up the mess she made with my tongue.

She's now on her knees, and I keep Amy's head steady on my cock. I'm ready to burst and I'm grinding my teeth to the point of pain. My vixen smiles at me and puts two lace-covered fingers in her mouth and sucks. I groan out loud before I can stop myself. The little minx is going to pay for that smile later. Amy moans for some fucking reason. I can bet she's happy with herself, thinking she's managed to get a reaction out of me because no woman ever has. What Amy will soon realise is that it's got fuck all to do with her.

My Little Vixen trails her wet fingers down to her pussy and starts to slowly rub over it. I match her, moving Amy's head at the same pace and our little game continues. I keep pace with her as she quickens her movements and her little pink tongue comes out to wet her lips, making me groan again. I can see her panting and a delectable flush in her cheeks tells me she's as fucking turned on as I am.

I try to grit my teeth again knowing any second I'm going to blow, but it's useless. I push Amy's head fully down on my cock so I'm now down her throat and come like I've never done before. I can feel Amy struggling to breathe but I don't fucking care. I tilt my head back with my mouth open in euphoria, keeping my eyes on my vixen who has her head thrown back as she mimics her own orgasmic reaction.

I'm pissed because she's broken eye contact and I want her attention back on me. I crave it, which is so fucking foreign to me. She finishes her display but keeps her head down, her eyes on the floor. I sit up, willing her to look at me, but she turns her back and saunters back towards the curtains on stage.

Finally my vixen turns her head towards me, making eye contact again and blowing me a kiss as she walks off stage. What the actual fuck? This little minx is in a whole heap of trouble now, mark my words.

I push Amy off me, putting my still erect cock back into my trousers and fastening them. Amy starts to smile at me from the floor and I've had enough. I grab her hands and unfasten my belt from around them. I thread it through my trousers abruptly refastening it.

"Get the fuck out. I don't want to see you again!" I

say venomously to her.

"But Kai, I made you feel good, didn't I?" Amy whines, looking up at me with a stricken look on her face.

"You did fuck all for me, you're so fucking useless. The Goddess on stage got me off. I SAID GET THE FUCK OUT!" I'm at the point that my rage will make itself known, but Lev acts before that can happen. He quickly removes a grovelling Amy from the floor and escorts her out of the room.

I run my hand through my hair and pace the room. *What the fuck just happened.* Lev comes back in, handing me a glass of vodka. I knock it back; it takes the edge off but it's not what I need right now.

"Go get me my redheaded vixen now Lev!" I bark. Lev smiles, going off to do as I wish.

I've known Lev all my life, he knows me better than I know myself. That is why he's my second in command and closest friend. He always gets the job done, but will express his concerns if he thinks I'm wrong… in private. He's priceless in our world. Loyalty always is.

I can't wait to get my Little Vixen in here and see which of her personas she brings. Will she be the vixen she portrayed or a meek little submissive? I don't know which one excites me more but I'm about to find out.

Chapter 2

Annabelle

I find Sam at the bar knocking back a tequila shot. A nervous energy I have never seen before emanates from her. I sit down on the stool next to her and she asks for two more shots of tequila.

She slides one over to me and turns to face me, a worried look on her face. The dread in the pool of my stomach threatens to boil over and the flight or fight feeling I'm familiar with encompasses me.

I grab hold of the bar to keep myself steady, so I don't run out of here like a bat out of hell. This is the only place I've felt comfortable in for the first time in three years, and I'm determined to keep hold of my new life for as long as I can.

"Belle. Look sweetie, you need to be careful now, I wouldn't normally be bothered that someone has drawn the attention of Kai. Plenty have come and gone in that department, believe me. The thing is they never last and he rarely ever goes back more than once. Some girls get heartbroken thinking they could have been his and end up leaving or they just end up bitter and twisted. You my girl are something special and I could tell that from the first moment you walked in through that door. You see, you have a beautiful soul that shines through those gorgeous sky-blue eyes of yours. There are the shadows I see when you think nobody is watching. I know you have demons that you are running from Belle, and I will never ask you about them I promise. Believe me, I have my own demons and they are locked away never to escape. I just don't want to lose you honey, so please be careful with that beautiful heart of yours, yeah!"

I sit there gobsmacked, my mouth slightly open for a beat too long as Sam reaches out and puts two fingers under my chin, closing my mouth for me with a loving smile on her face.

Normally I would have alarm bells ringing in my ears and an urge to run home to Luka and be on the next plane out of here. I mean we've done it plenty of times before but here? Here feels like the home I've never had.

Also, even though Sam isn't that much older than me. She reminds me so much of my mother that it hurts sometimes. Mama was not only stunningly beautiful, but also very intelligent. Above all else though, she had the kindest soul to ever brighten this godforsaken world. And I'd had a front-row seat when her beautiful soul was obliterated from this life. I have a scar so deep in my soul that I don't ever think it will stop aching from the pain.

I shake myself out of my thoughts, as I need to dig deep and reassure Sam that I'm tougher than I look.

"Sam, trust me, I'm fine, honestly. I'll go and see what Kai wants and come back out to see you before I go. Okay?" I tap her hand resting on the bar and go to leave, but she grabs my hand in a vice-like grip.

"Please be careful Belle, Kai is a very dangerous man!" She suddenly lets go of my hand and looks around in the mirrors of the bar to see if anybody overheard our conversation.

I feel like asking more about who Kai is but, with how edgy Sam is acting, I decide not to. You see, Sam doesn't know the sort of evil I've been subjected to in my life and hopefully, she never finds out.

"Please don't worry Sam, I won't be long I promise!" I get up from the bar and head over to the entrance for the VIP lounge.

I walk over to Greg and Peter who spot me and stand aside smiling at me. I give them my flirtiest smile back and wink at them as I saunter past. I head up the stairs and come face to face with Lev.

He's standing with another man, guarding the doorway that leads to the VIP lounge. When he sees me, his scowl turns into a panty-dropping smile that I'm sure impresses all the ladies. He's tall, very muscular and heavily tattooed from what I can see of the ink peeking from his unbuttoned shirt. Add gorgeous, and that smile to the equation, and I think my own pants might have just flown off, never to be seen again.

"Hello there Little Red!" he says, winking at me.

The other guard stands there like a silent sentinel at the door and I give him a once over. He's also well muscled and looks a little like a tank, with a mean looking edge to him. On closer inspection there is something else I can't quite determine. As I study his face, I realise what's holding my attention. His eyes. Although his demeanour is mean, his eyes are full of a sadness that calls to my own, so I address him.

"I don't think we've met Tank," I cajole amiably.

His stern expression flickers to amusement and back, so quickly I wasn't sure whether I had imagined it.

"This is Pasha," Lev chipped in.

"He doesn't say much, and he can be a mean sonofabitch," he adds.

Pasha inclines his head and steps to the side, allowing me access to the door.

"Are you ready to play with the big bad wolf today? Because my dear you have certainly riled him up good and proper!" Lev asks tauntingly.

I walk up to him and rest my hand on his chest, peering up at him through my lashes.

"Honey, I'll have him purring like a kitten by the time I'm out of here, so don't you worry that pretty little head of yours. Oh, and I might be small but don't underestimate this little pocket rocket! I like to bite!" I run my hand slightly down his chest and smirk at him before opening the door and entering the VIP lounge.

The VIP lounge is luxurious, lit with ambient blue lighting. Leather and plush velvet seating faces a balcony overlooking the entire club.

Kai stands with his back to me, his hands in his pockets as he looks over his kingdom. He's tall, blonde, 6ft5 at least and muscular if the pull of his shirt over his back is anything to go by.

His jacket is hanging over the back of a chair, discarded in favour of his sleeves rolled up to as far as they will go on his bulging forearms. The black silk shirt ripples across his body with every movement.

My attention is drawn to his glorious arse, oh my Lord I think I may be drooling. *'Oh my god woman, get a grip.'* I draw my attention away, with regret, from that peachy goodness and walk towards him.

"I believe you wanted to see me?" I say with my head held high and my shoulders back. *Come on Boss Man, let's continue our little game, let's see what you've got.*

"You, my Little Vixen, put on quite a show tonight. Pray, tell me was that all for my benefit? Did you want my attention, crave it maybe, or do you normally dance like that in my club?"

He isn't even looking at me and both that and his comment have me riled. Right Mr, my claws are coming out!

"I dance like that all the time, in your club as you put it! But believe me when I say that I do not want or crave your attention, Boss Man! If I draw a man's attention that's his problem not mine, I'm just doing the job you pay me to do. I consider you to be quite rude though, as a poor blonde was choking on your cock at the time! Your attention should have remained with her!"

I'm lying. In a way I did crave his attention, but I would never admit to it, and I will not be seen as an attention-seeking whore. I do what I do for me, a rebellion against my past life. Two fingers up at all the men who have tried to dictate and rule my life so far. I'll be fucked if I'll let another man think he can rule me again.

"Oh, but you see my Little Vixen, the blonde was irritating the fuck out of me until you came out on my stage. She served her purpose, as I imagined you sucking my dick up here, instead of what you imitated on my stage. You might want to lie to yourself Little Vixen but understand this. Don't ever fucking lie to me again, as you will not like the consequences!"

I swear that steam is coming out of my ears because I'm that mad. How fucking dare he! He's so fucking up himself that he's high off the fumes from his own bullshit!

To add insult to injury he hasn't even turned to grace me with his attention. Well, fuck you with a giant fucking strap-on!

"Well, I hope you enjoyed the show Boss Man because I know for a fact every other man and most of the women did too. So, if you want to believe I crave your attention you can fuck right off, you delusional arsehole!"

I turn and walk towards the door ready to get the fuck out of here and forget I ever met this arsehole. Urgh! I don't even hear him approaching, before I'm twisted and he's pressing me to the wall in two seconds flat.

His chest is heaving, and his eyes are piercing right down to my soul. His body is pinning me to the wall and his hand is gripping my throat. Not hard enough to choke me, but the grip is punishing.

I should be scared and a small part of me is, but the bigger part of me is on fire. As in oh my God this is fucking panty-wetting hot. He's so big, so angry and so fucking hot I nearly fucking forget he's an arsehole. Nearly!

"You need to keep that smart mouth of yours shut, my Little Vixen, because you are pushing your luck now. Do not mention any other man or woman in my presence again. I don't give a fuck what you say anymore but you have got my attention. The whole twisted fucking lot of it. And you will not be escaping so easily, do you hear me? I will punish that sexy fucking arse of yours until you confess you are lying and tell me how much you like my attention! With the marks on your delectable arse to prove it and remind you for days!"

I think I would be a puddle on the floor if he didn't have me pinned to the wall. Fucking hell that was hot, I'm burning up and blushing like mad. This man is so infuriating! He's such a dickhead, then he says things like that which turn me on. I'm so confused, my mind and my body are at war.

"If you think that I will admit to wanting your attention, let alone liking it, you're more of an idiot than I thought!" I spit, peering at him through my lashes.

"We shall see then won't we, my Little Vixen?" He's staring down at me, with the threat beating down on my body like a storm ready to engulf me. His eyes are flicking from my eyes to my lips. Suddenly, I'm nervous about what he's going to do.

"Bring it on Boss Man!" Shit, the words come out before I can stop them. I glance up at him and go to say something else. Hell, I don't know, maybe even *'sorry Mr Boss Man'* but I don't get a chance to do anything as his lips come crashing down on mine.

I'm so shocked I freeze; I can do absolutely nothing until his tongue licks across my bottom lip, demanding access. I must suddenly be beyond reasonable thinking, because I open to him, giving him all the permission he needs. He starts off the kiss so softly, caressing my tongue with his, encouraging me to participate.

What Kai doesn't know, what no one knows as a matter of fact, aside from my best friend and secret bodyguard Luka, is that I've never been touched by a man like this, or more than this. Not even so much as a kiss! There were rules to my previous life and if anybody had touched a hair on my head, they would have been killed.

Believe me, I've had plenty of chances since I left but I just haven't wanted to. I put on a good act as the "sexy vixen" Kai keeps on calling me, but it's all a front. A mask per se, but I feel as if that mask has been ripped off and shredded in one fell swoop.

I melt into Kai and start to respond to the kiss as best I can. This seems to be the response he was waiting for because suddenly, the kiss goes from slow and sensual to wild and animalistic in seconds. All I can do is hold on to his shirt in a tight grip and cling on for the ride.

Kai

I swear I think this woman in my arms, or should I say pinned to the wall, is who I was thinking about when I named this club. She has enticed me with her Siren's call, and I have no control whatsoever.

I don't kiss at all, it's one of my fucking rules. No kissing, no dates, no details. Fuck all personal. It's a fuck or a blow job then fuck off, but this woman has me ripping up my rule book and wanting, for the first time, to call somebody MINE! What the ever-loving fuck!

I was kissing her softly, trying to encourage her to respond but when she did? All bets were off. A flip switched in me, and my inner beast came to the forefront and said fuck this shit.

I'm now fucking her mouth with my tongue, clashing teeth and desperately trying to put my claim on this woman for everybody to see. To my surprise, she's giving back as much as I'm giving her.

She starts to writhe in my hold and lets out little whimpers which are sexy as fuck. I want to consume her, own her, and mark her so deep she will never be able to deny my claim again.

My cock has only been interested in her since I first saw her on stage, even after I blew my load in that bitches mouth. It wanted her then and it wants her now. It's as insatiable for her as I am.

I break the kiss sharply, ripping my lips away from her and she lets out a whine in protest which shoots directly to my balls. Fucking hell this woman will be the death of me.

I grab her waist and lift her higher on the wall, pinning her with my body again. She squeaks, but then wraps her legs around my waist. This position puts her hot, wet, little pussy directly against my aching cock.

Her dress has luckily opened due to the high split, giving me access to those glorious silky thighs. Looking down I run my hands from her knees up to the top of her thighs. Before sliding my hands underneath and squeezing in a punishing grip.

I put my forehead against hers and try to take a breath while my cock is throbbing against her wet panties. I look into her eyes and see that she is just as fucked as I am. If this was death, we both welcomed it with open arms.

I lift my right hand and push a finger underneath the flimsy little strap holding up the dress on her shoulder. I let it fall and it slips off, revealing her right breast. Her breasts are fucking unbelievable; voluptuous, and pert. She has tight rosebud nipples, begging to be sucked within an inch of their life.

I groan, grinding my cock against her pussy and her back arches, pushing her breasts out and up. I can't resist. I lower my mouth to her rosebud nipple and suck hard. She mews and writhes in my hold but there's no escape. I can't help myself and I bite down hard on her nipple.

"Oh, Oh, please, oh God Kai, argh, YES!" I smile around my mouthful and give her breast a quick kiss, then bring my head back slightly to blow gently on her wet nipple.

Her hands come up and wind themselves in my hair, scratching my scalp desperately with her nails, arching her back even more in an attempt to get me to put it back in my mouth.

"Oh, poor baby, is it a tease? Hmm… not getting the satisfaction that your body craves? You see, my beautiful Little Vixen, you have been a very naughty girl and naughty girls don't get rewarded. Naughty girls get punished, and if they are good girls taking it, they get rewarded."

To prove my point I grabbed her wet rosy nipple and twisted it hard. She screams and looks at me, panting with so much lust in her eyes it's beautiful. My Little Vixen likes pain with her pleasure. Fucking perfect.

I grip her under her thighs again and pull away from the wall, carrying her over to my chair, to sit down with her straddling my lap. She looks at me puzzled and starts to try and pull the strap back up on her dress. But I grab her wrist and squeeze slightly, raising my brow. She releases the strap, raising a brow in question back at me. I raise my finger and lightly circle her nipple. A whisper of touch to stimulate but leave her wanting more.

"Little Vixen, your performance earlier left me with quite a puzzling conclusion. If that performance were just for me in private it would have been appreciated greatly and rewarded accordingly. Both satisfactory to myself and you. As it is, you decided to give that little performance in front of the whole club. You let those men see what was meant for my eyes only and I can't let that misbehaviour go unpunished now, can I?"

Her brows crease and she seems to break out of the lust-filled bubble I had her in. She grabs my wrist to try and stop my touch on her. I grab her throat with my other hand and shake my head lightly, to tell her it's not going to happen.

"What the fuck are you on about Kai? It was a

dance, it's what you pay me for. I dance in your club, not just for you!" She attempts to get off my lap, but I tighten my grip on her throat. Her eyes widen and she tries to swallow past my grip.

"That there, honey, was not just your normal performance. Believe me, I have seen hundreds. You wanted to play with the devil, and you gained his attention well and truly. Now that you have my undivided attention there is no escape. You will be mine to do what I want to when I want to. I will guarantee you one thing though, my Little Vixen, you will love every single depraved moment of it and beg for more!"

Her eyes are dilated and she's breathing heavily. She's conflicted, I can tell by the way her brows are drawn together. My Little Vixen is going to be more of a challenge than I anticipated, her submission will be hard-won but oh-so-delicious when she gives it to me.

"My name is Annabelle, Belle to my friends, but you will never be one of those arsehole. One thing I can guarantee to you is that I will never be yours. No way in hell will a man own me, in this life or the next. You can go and get blondie back for round two because I'm not fucking interested!"

She tried again to get herself free from my grip, but she's got no chance. I'm not letting her go, and it's about time she learned; that when I've decided something, it's fucking final.

I flip her so quickly she doesn't have time to respond, so she's now lying across my lap. She's kicking and screaming profanities at me, which will only earn her more lashes on that delectable arse. I move my leg and trap both of her legs between mine, ripping her dress up as I do, to reveal her peachy arse in yet another thong. I growled deep from my chest, and tip her top half toward the floor, so she's forced to put her arms down to steady herself.

Undoing my belt buckle, I whip it out of my belt loops. She starts to renew her struggles as she must have heard the buckle being undone. No chance Little Vixen, you're mine now!

I put pressure on her lower back and lay my belt across her back. I start rubbing her arse cheeks and down the back of her thighs, then pick up my belt and double it over.

"Now my Little Vixen, each time I strike you with my belt you will count and thank me for your punishment. Then you will ask me nicely to have another. You will receive ten strikes, but only if you are a good girl and take your punishment correctly. If you misbehave or lose count, we will go back to the beginning and start again!"

She starts really struggling and screaming again. My Little Vixen is quite strong for her size and has so much feistiness, but all she's doing is delaying the inevitable.

"Argh, Kai, let me the fuck go you fucking lunatic. I swear I will punch you right in the fucking face if you dare raise that fucking belt to me. Argh KAI!"

I pin her with my legs and arm, then raise the belt and bring it right down on her left arse cheek, hard. She screamed and cried out for me to stop, but she isn't giving me the response I requested.

"I warned you before I started, Little Vixen, that I would not accept anything less than what I requested you to say. So shall we start again? If you want to be able to sit down in the next week, I suggest you think very carefully about your response after the next strike!"

She whimpers and struggles again but it will not deter me. I bring the next strike of my belt down hard on her left arse cheek. I was right before; her porcelain skin marks beautifully. My marks will last days for the world to see, which sends a flare of heat through my body. Mine!

"You better stop Kai or I will make sure you will regret every strike you bestow on me from now on!"

I strike her again, because she has a mouth on her that needs to be stopped. She just needs to utter the words I fucking need her to say.

"Argh, I don't really give a shit who you are Boss Man, I will walk into your room and slit your throat when you least expect it! Mark my words," she hisses at me.

Her response makes me want to bend her over the table, fist that beautiful red hair and fuck her raw from behind.

"Little Vixen, I have explained the response I require. I will not ask again; I will just carry on until I get my response!"

She is trembling in my arms, her anger seeping out in waves, which still doesn't deter me from my end game. I lick away any tears because I crave them. I bring the belt down again on the right arse cheek, just above the last mark.

"One, thank you for my punishment and please may I have another!" She says it so quietly I think I've imagined it, as she's also sniffling at the same time.

"Good girl, now louder next time and we can get your punishment over and get on to the pleasure!" I bring the belt down again on the other side.

"Two, thank you for my punishment and please may I have another!" She says it louder this time and with less venom in her voice.

I bring the belt down twice in quick succession on her sit spots, right under her arse cheeks. She screams and wriggles, crying for a moment.

"Three, Four, thank you for my punishment and please may I have another!" I let out a loud growl and grip my belt tighter. I'm just about hanging on to my discipline here, as I just want to lift her up and place her on my throbbing cock. The pain of my erection against my fly is the best kind of agony.

I carry on the spanking and get the correct response every time. By the time we get to eight she lets out a moan.

"Does my Little Vixen enjoy my belt? I wonder, if I felt your pussy would it be soaked for me, Hmm? Shall I see?"

She moaned again and I draped my belt on her reddened arse. I ran my hand down her arse cheek slowly and dipped my fingers under her panties. I push my digits through her pussy lips and directly to her clit. Fucking hell, she's soaked. I laugh and continue, running small circles around her clit, not quite giving her any relief.

"Good girl, such a good girl for me. I think my Little Vixen likes my type of punishment. So I think that, if you are naughty in the future, I'll have to think up a different type of punishment for you!"

My Little Vixen lets out an agitated whine and tries to wriggle her pussy slightly to get me exactly where she wants relief. *Not yet baby, soon*. I remove my fingers from her pussy and put them in my mouth. Fucking hell, she tastes amazing. The sweetest nectar I've ever tasted and now I just want her to sit on my face.

I hear her groan and look down to find her head slightly turned, watching me. I lick my fingers clean and pick up my belt again, giving her the last two strikes halfway down her thighs.

I quickly pick her up and place her straddling my lap again, she won't be able to sit properly for a while. I rub her arse and knead it occasionally, which makes her arch her back with a mix of pain and pleasure.

"Such a good girl, you are such a good fucking girl. I need to fuck you baby; I need to fuck your pussy right here and now!"

I move my hand around and dip my fingers into her pussy lips again. She moans and I move further back, towards her tight little hole. As I'm about to push in she grabs my hand and stops me. I look up and her face has gone from euphoria to worry in two seconds flat!

"What's wrong Annabelle?" I frown, looking directly into her eyes.

"I..." She tries to look away, but I grab her jaw and make sure she's looking straight into my eyes.

"Tell me what's the matter now, Annabelle!" She starts to blush and looks down.

"I can't Kai, I just can't!" She's got tears in her eyes and I'm starting to get worried now, and a little mad. She will fucking answer me.

"Answer me now, Little Vixen, or I will be forced to punish you in another way which will be far less pleasurable for you I promise!"

Her teary eyes shoot to mine.

"I'm a fucking virgin you arsehole! Are you happy now?" She looks down again.

I'm fucking gobsmacked, that's the last thing I expected to come out of her mouth. Fucking hell, she's the sexiest fucking virgin I've ever met. All my thoughts race and I can see she's going further, back into her head. Fuck that!

"Fucking hell baby, you're so fucking hot it's unbelievable! You're coming home with me now!" I stand up with her in my arms and chuck her over my shoulder.

"Kai, what are you doing? Put me down right now!" She starts thumping my back.

"Baby, you're going nowhere except my fucking bed! There's no escape for you now, my Little Vixen!"

Chapter 3

Annabelle

"Put me down Kai, you can't carry me through the club like this! You fucking neanderthal, let me go!"

I scream and pound at his back with my fists. He will not carry me, like a stricken damsel in distress over his shoulder, like a prize he's won! I'm so mad right now, he better watch out if he lets me go at any point. I will show him who he's messing with.

He walks out the VIP lounge door and passes Lev. I lift my head up to find Lev smirking at me and following behind us.

"Lev, why the fuck are you amused? Will you tell him he's being ridiculous carrying me through the club like this!"

"I thought you were going to have him purring like a kitten Little Red, what's the matter? Did you deny him his cream?"

Lev tips his head back, chuckling, as I stick my swivel finger up at him, smiling maniacally.

"Okay Lev, you have now put yourself on my shit list. I'm going to enjoy kicking you in the balls once I'm free!"

Why the hell did I think Lev would help me? He's loyal to Kai and how can I really blame him for that? Luka will always have my back and has done since I was a kid. Oh my God, Luka is going to flip his lid if I don't return tonight, I need to contact him but what the fuck am I going to tell him?

"Oh, I'm shaking in my boots Little Red. Can you see me shaking?" Lev chuckled, his smile breath-taking and sadistic at the same time. It's how it kicks up slightly further on the right-hand side than the left. The dimples deepen in his cheeks, giving him that lovable rogue look but his eyes show me his true self.

"Fuck you arsehole!"

We descend the stairs and Kai carries me past Greg and Peter, out into the main club. I look up at them both and Greg goes to step forward to do something, but Peter grabs his arm and pulls him back. All I see is their heated argument as I'm carried further into the main club.

As we pass the bar. I see Sam and her face is stricken. She runs up to Lev as we pass and they start arguing. Sam is a little firecracker, she's much smaller than Lev but is on her tiptoes trying to get in his face. Lev just grabs her hair and pulls her head back bending down to put them face to face. Sam seems to melt in his hold as he says something to her that I can't hear. Interesting!

Kai is still making his way out with me and I'm running out of time now. It looks like I'm not going to get any help. I start trying to kidney punch Kai to escape, but he's so bloody tall that I can't quite get an effective strike.

"Let me the fuck down, you psycho!"

I scream at the top of my lungs, hitting and kicking him as much as his hold on my thighs allows. He suddenly stops smack bang in the middle of the club and everyone is staring at us, waiting to see what's going to happen.

I start to think he's going to let me go and then I feel an almighty slap on my arse. It's like I've been electrocuted. The shock is astounding. My arse was painful enough with his lash marks still throbbing. This has ignited not only the pain of that experience, but also sent a bolt to my traitorous pussy.

"You will behave and be a good girl now Annabelle, or do you want to meet my belt again? Believe me, my Little Vixen, I will not hesitate to place you across my knee and paint your arse with more of my marks right here in the middle of my club!"

He's silent, awaiting my answer, as I expect the whole room is. I wouldn't know because I haven't lifted my head since he spanked me. I'm in a haze of embarrassment, lust, and confusion. I hate this man so much in this moment. He's so damn annoying, but I can't deny the way he makes me feel.

He takes my silence as my answer and starts to make his way out of the club again. I go limp in his hold. Let him think I've given up but I'm just saving my energy.

We make it outside and I shiver from the cold. Come on, it's Birmingham in the middle of March, it's freezing. At least it's not raining though.

Kai puts me down and grabs my arm, turning me to a car that's ready and waiting at the curb. Lev appears and opens the back door for us to enter. I've had enough of this shit now, so I go full attack mode and show these fuckers I'm not to be messed with.

Kai releases his hold on me and slips his arm around my waist to steer me into the back seat. As I get close enough to Lev, I strike as fast as I can. Grinning, I twist and knee Lev right in his bollocks, hard. He goes down to his knees, cupping his bollocks and I twist quickly to Kai. Who's staring at me in a mixture of astonishment and lust, but fuck you arsehole.

People have underestimated me all my life. I'm used to it. Kai goes to grab me, but I drop to the floor and avoid his reach. I flip my shoes off and kick out with my right leg to sweep his legs out from beneath him. The trouble is he's massive, and I was really fooling myself if I thought I was going to drop him on his arse. His knees give a little but he stays standing, staring at me with amusement until someone grabs me from behind.

I'm dragged up and pinned in a punishing hold by the arms. I look at Kai and the murderous look on his face scares me for the first time since I've been in his presence. He isn't looking at me though, he's looking at the person holding me.

"Lev, if you do not take your hands off her now, I'll put a fucking bullet in your brain!"

What the fuck? I'm so shocked at what Kai's just said, but the more worrying feeling is why I think it was so bloody hot. I'm panting and hot, and my pussy seems hotwired to the man in front of me. I should be trying to escape or plead for my release but I'm frozen, pulled in by the force of this man's orbit.

"Chill Kai, I'm taking my hands off her now!"

Lev releases my arms and I turn to face him and start stepping back slowly, putting distance between us. What I forget though is I'm backing myself straight into the devil himself until it's too late. My back collides into a wall of muscle and Kai's hand comes up to grab me around my throat.

Lev has his hands up in surrender, his eyes following Kai with concern. Kai's breath is ragged at my back and his body is pulsing with brutal energy. His anger is whirling around us all, threatening to engulf us and leave nobody in its wake.

Luckily, Sam decides at this precise moment to run out from the club with my bag gripped in her arms. She comes to a sudden stop, looking from me and Kai to Lev. She looks worried and unsure whether to approach.

"It's okay Sam, come here sweetheart!" Lev says, not taking his eyes off Kai.

Kai's body seems to relax a bit behind me, but he doesn't release the punishing grip he has on my throat. He lowers his mouth down to my ear.

"Oh, my Little Vixen, you will pay for that little display, you really do love my punishments don't you baby? I will take it easier on you though because that was so fucking hot. I was thinking of tying you to my bed because I think you will look delectable, bound and gagged, waiting for my attention. I have now decided that I much prefer that fire and fight I just witnessed. When I get you into my bed Annabelle, I need you to give me your worst baby, show me your inner monster. I swear Little Vixen, we will have such a euphoric experience burning together on our way down to hell!"

I gasp and shudder as Kai straightens back up and pushes his engorged erection into my back. If I was on fire before I'm self-combusting now. He seems to have a hold over me that no other man has ever had. Not even my arsehole of a Papa.

I'm watching as Lev and Sam have yet another heated whispered discussion, and Lev tries to calm her by putting two fingers under her chin and raising her face to his. He's now forgotten about Kai's threat and is solely focused on Sam.

Kai turns me to face him, and I lift my eyes to his face automatically. He brushes my cheek with his palm and places a soft kiss on my forehead.

"Good girl, now I'm going to get you in the car, and I want you to be on your best behaviour. Lev will bring your bag from Sam, okay?"

"I'll come with you Kai, just don't hurt Sam, please!"

Sam has a little girl, and I don't want her getting hurt for interfering and trying to save me.

"Nobody will hurt anyone Annabelle, just get in the car okay!"

Kai opens the door and I get in, sinking into the

luxurious seats. Kai shuts the door, goes around the other side and lowers himself into the seat next to me in the back.

I'm filled with nervous energy and worry. I look out the window to check on Sam. She's now standing hugging herself as Lev walks toward the car we're in. She averts her eyes from watching Lev's retreating figure to looking at me. We lock eyes and I give her a smile which I hope reassures her that I'm fine. She smiles tightly, but I know I'm not kidding her at all.

Lev gets in the front passenger seat and the car drives off from the club. It's set in the city centre of Birmingham, so the streets are full of the usual drunk partygoers. Who are either going to the next club, off to land a kebab or trying to hail a taxi back home.

I watch the hustle and bustle out of the car, until we go onto the expressways and head into the richer part of the city. I must keep my wits about me and follow the direction we're heading. Luka has a tracker fitted into my phone which I'm hoping will lead him to me, if I need him to.

The scenery changes from clubs and bars to five-star hotels, high-end cocktail bars and Gentlemen's clubs. The car pulls into a beautiful hotel called Enigma Hotel and Spa. It's probably the poshest hotel in Birmingham.

The staff immediately rush to approach the car

but Lev steps out and they stop in their tracks, retreating back to the doors. When they have returned to a safe distance Lev opens my door. He puts out a hand to help me out but I ignore it, stepping out and standing to the side so he can close the door.

I look up at the Hotel which is at least thirty floors high with floor-to-ceiling windows. The building is luxurious and screams money. Expensive décor and, would you believe it, a fountain smack bang in the middle of the driveway.

Kai puts his hand on the small of my back and I turn to look at him. Is this what he does with all his women, brings them to a high-class hotel to impress them? Sorry honey that won't work for me.

I'm surprised to see at least another three cars surrounding ours when I look back, with guards observing and alert. This looks a bit overkill for a burlesque club owner, but I don't have much time to mull it over as Kai moves us toward the reception of the hotel.

All the staff in reception stare at us when we pass, or should I say they stare at Kai. Well, I don't blame them really. If I worked here, I'd be drooling as he passed every day too.

We get to the lifts, but we don't go to the ones for guests to use. We head to a lift all on its own, labelled 'Private.' Kai steps up to the pad located next to the lift and presses his palm to a scanner situated to the left. It opens immediately and we all enter.

There are only three buttons on the panel, which is weird as I counted at least thirty floors. There is LG I'm assuming for the lower ground floor, maybe it's an underground parking garage, G for the ground floor which we've just come from and then P... Oh my god we're going to the penthouse suite.

Kai slips his arm around my waist, pulling me into his side, his big palm hugging my hip and his thumb lazily rubbing up and down my waist. He reaches over to the panel, presses the P, and we start the ascent up. Lev is standing in front of us, facing the doors.

When the lift comes to a gentle stop and the doors open, Lev steps out and nods to two other burly guards posted inside the penthouse. He stands aside as Kai steers me into the apartment. The guards then skirt around the side of the room and leave via the lift. I look over to Lev and find him disappearing down a hallway to the left.

The room must be at least the width of the full hotel at the front, with floor-to-ceiling windows. It's astonishing. The space is decorated with a minimalistic feel, but everything in here screams wealth. God, he must pay a bomb to stay here.

A massive dining table that must seat at least twenty sits in the middle of the room, with fresh-cut Calla Lilies in a crystal vase as the centrepiece. Modern art is hanging on several internal walls and when I look over to the left-hand side, I have to hide a gasp as there is a huge sunken seating area. The seating looks like Italian leather, and it has several plush cushions and throws scattered along the three sides. Up on the wall, facing the seating area is a huge flat screen TV. It must be at least one hundred inches, if not more.

"Would you like a drink my Little Vixen?" Kai whispers in my ear, making me nearly jump out of my skin. I turn my face to respond but he's still so close to me that our noses rub against each other as I look into his eyes. My heart thumps against my ribcage, trying to escape as I stare into those gorgeous ocean-blue eyes. They're mainly an intoxicating, piercing blue which seems to sparkle with mischief, and there were flecks of alluring emerald green which lure you to drown in this man's depths.

"Baby?" Kai whispers, stroking my cheek with his palm as I stand hypnotised by his eyes, probably looking like every other woman he's ever looked at. This thought shakes me out of his lure.

"Bacardi and Coke if you have it, please!"

He kisses my forehead and goes over to the bar I hadn't seen in my quick scan of the room before. I walk over to look out of the windows, to try and focus myself and not look like a love-sick puppy. *Bloody hell, what is this man doing to me?*

The view is spectacular, with panoramic views out over the city. People are still mulling about in and out of establishments, going home or loitering on the streets. I look further out and can even see green fields, hills and unspoilt land, free from the taint of man. It's as far from where I used to live as you could get and maybe that's why it feels like home so much.

Kai comes to join me overlooking the city and hands me my drink. I accept it with a nod and go back to looking out at the view, taking a small sip of my drink. Just as I like it, double Bacardi with a splash of coke. Heaven.

"How do you like the view my Little Vixen?"

"It's quite beautiful, Kai, but if you think this grand tour will get me into your bed and stroke your ego? You are very much mistaken!"

I take another sip of my drink but nearly choke when I hear Kai start laughing. I mean come on, this man is the epitome of a domineering arsehole, why does he also look so God damn gorgeous when he laughs as well? I bet he shits skittles too. Urgh!

"Annabelle my dear, I would never try to lull you

into my bed, my beautiful Little Vixen. The only thing you will be stroking tonight is my cock, I have never needed to have my ego stroked. As I said to you earlier, I want you and only you to come to my bed, so I can treat you like the goddess you are. I want to be gentle with you at first, but I cannot promise that I will be able to hold back after that. I'm not a good man Annabelle, far from it, but I'm a monster in the bedroom. The choice is yours my Little Vixen, do you want to join me on the dark side?"

Kai knocks his vodka back in one and looks at me with a raised brow and a sinful promise in his eyes. Good Lord, this man irritates the fuck out of me but that doesn't stop me from wanting to climb him like a tree.

I think of what my virginity has been to me all this time; a commodity that vicious men thought they could barter for and sell. As though it belonged to them in the first place. It's time to take back what is only mine to give away and what better way than to give it away willingly? I also know that at least Kai will make it enjoyable and then we can part ways and I can forget about one of the things that has been nothing but a burden.

"You know I'm a virgin Kai, why are you at all interested in me? You could have brought a multitude of women back here instead of me!"

I finish off my drink and Kai takes it from me, going to put both empty glasses back at the bar. He comes back to me and lifts my face to his, using his fingers under my chin. I look between his eyes trying to gauge what his response is going to be. My stupid heart is beating ten to the dozen, giving away how much his response really matters to me.

"Let's just set one thing straight here and now before we go on my Little Vixen. I have never brought anyone back to my home, ever. It's not something I do. I fuck and leave. Now you Annabelle may be a virgin and think that it's a flaw, but I can assure you that it is nothing but a precious gift. As I've said I can't promise I'll be able to control myself, but I will try to be gentle at the beginning. You have demanded my full attention from the moment I first saw you, that's never happened before. You are an enigma that I fully intend to consume and make you mine by the end of the night!"

Well fuck me, I don't know what I was expecting Kai to say, but it certainly wasn't that. My mind and body are at war as to what to make of his declaration. I will never belong to a man as long as I live. I won't have what happened to Mama happen to me, I can't.

My heart, though, is trying to beat through my chest and pour its innards over the floor at the declaration he's just made to me. It's like my heart wants me to stop thinking for once and try just letting go.

Now, my pussy? That bloody hussy needs to calm herself down, because she just wants to suffocate him by sitting on his face to stop him from talking. She wants action not words and now she's acting like a dick-starved porno star.

Fuck this shit, it's about time I lived my life for me and if Kai is my biggest mistake so be it. I'll deal with whatever happens tomorrow. Come what may.

"Kai, I'm yours for one night and one night only. Now shut the fuck up and show me what it means to be yours. Not what other women get, I want the no holds barred version of you. Worship me like I'm a goddess but fuck me like I'm your whore!"

Kai's eyes dilated and he full-on growled, yes growled, tossing me over his shoulder. He takes me off down the right-hand side of the penthouse where I assume his bedroom is.

Have I done the right thing, or have I just handed myself to the Devil with no holds barred? Well, I'm down the rabbit hole, let's see if I come out whole or tainted by making the worst decision of my life so far!

Chapter 4

Annabelle

I swear if this man keeps on carrying me over his shoulder, I'm going to have no blood left in my body, it's all going to be in my head. I'm currently clinging to his shirt like a spider monkey as he walks down the corridor on his way to his bedroom.

He suddenly stops in front of double doors at the end of the corridor and throws them open. He strides through, leaving the doors to ricochet off the wall and the furniture on either side of them. I jump a mile at the noise they make and I'm sure they will be dented or damaged by the impact.

I'm so engrossed in thinking how much damage he's just caused that I don't realise we've stopped, and I'm currently being catapulted onto the bed. I must've bounced several times before finally landing in a heap, for fuck's sake. I know I didn't really ask for romance, but the room spinning is not a good mood setting. I lay my head back on the pillows and try to compose myself.

Kai walks back to the doors, slams them shut and locks them. What the actual fuck, seriously? He turns to look at me lying on his bed and devours my body with his eyes. They seem to take in every dip and curve of my body. I squirm at his perusal and try to not be affected.

Kai walks to the drawers that are positioned at the side of the room and I watch as he empties all his pockets of his belongings in the top drawer, adding the key that he used to lock the doors.

He turns to face me, and I gulp at the immense heat in his eyes. I feel myself blushing red under his heated gaze. What the hell was I thinking, giving my first time to a man like Kai? I'm so inexperienced and he's like a man whore, Jesus!

"That blush is so adorable painting your porcelain skin Annabelle, I wonder what you'll look like when I'm well and truly fucking you into oblivion. Will you beg for me Little Vixen, cry or scream my name? I can't wait to find out every little reaction you will have for me. But first, wait exactly where you are and do not move an inch. I'll be back soon!"

Kai walks through a door to the left and I hear the shower come on. What the hell is he doing? Why would he leave me here to have a shower? I'm starting to get mad, ready to get up and try to leave when it suddenly hits me. He was having a blowjob. He must be washing the blonde off him. My anger starts to subside because would all men like him think of that before they go with someone else? Maybe, but I can't help finding it endearing.

I lay back down and look around the bedroom as I sink into the opulent comfort of his bed. Well, I say bed but I'm sure I and most of the girls from the club could sleep on here comfortably, it's that big. The sheets must be Egyptian cotton one thousand thread, they are so soft and luxurious. The headboard is solid oak with funny metal hooks added to the sides of the bed.

The rest of the room is the same as the rest of the penthouse, minimalist with another door off to the right. As I'm wondering what lies behind that door, I hear the shower switch off. Oh, fuck!

Kai walks out of the bathroom and I swear I stop breathing. He's only got a towel tied loosely, hanging low on his hips. This is the first glimpse of his body I've had, and Wow!

He stands at the bottom of the bed looking at me and I don't give a fuck, but I ogle his body like it's my favourite obsession because it may as well be. Holy hell!

I look him over, he's so tall I'd guess 6ft5, I can see the body the clothes had hidden until this moment, God it's a masterpiece. He's huge, muscles on top of muscles, all well-defined. His shoulders are broad, and he has huge muscular pecs, a fucking eight pack and one of those v's that everyone raves about lately. There must not be an ounce of fat on him.

His body is covered in tattoos, several on his chest. He must have a huge one covering his back that I'm desperate to see. I can only make out what appears to be tips of wings wrapping around his ribs, as though hugging him on both sides.

I slowly bring my gaze back up from his towel to study his face. He's smirking at me, knowing I'm unashamedly ogling him, but I don't care. I'm going to take my fill while I can.

He's gorgeous, with blonde hair cut close at the sides and longer on top, enough for me to grab hold of and I can't wait. He has high cheekbones and an angular jaw with a hint of stubble which I can't wait to feel on my body. I rub my thighs together at the thought. Those deep ocean eyes and full kissable lips... I'm utterly fucked, hook line and sinker.

"It's time to strip for me, my Little Vixen. I'll give you the option on how you do it this time. When you have finished, I want nothing left on your delectable body!"

Kai turns and sits on the bottom of the bed facing away from me. I gasp as I now see the Angel that covers his back and disappears under his towel. It's absolutely beautiful and seems to calm me slightly. I take a few breaths and decide to go all out. Hey, why not? You only lose your virginity once!

"Have you got any music in here Kai?"

Kai turns his head to smile at me and my lord it's glorious. His face looks younger with his pearly white teeth and panty-wetting smile gracing his gorgeous face. He gets up and goes over, retrieving his phone from the drawers. He taps a few buttons and music starts to flood through speakers hidden somewhere in the room.

I recognise the song straight away, 'Love is a Bitch' by Two Feet. It's the slowed down version. The song is so sensual my body wants to move to the beat immediately. Good music always gets a hold of me and makes me relax. Who knew Kai had such good taste?

I crawl slowly to the end of the bed towards Kai and sensually climb off so I'm standing. Kai goes and sits on the bed, so his back is against the pillows and headboard, with his left leg stretched out in front of him and his right leg bent slightly. How his towel hangs on for dear life I will never know, but I'm kind of getting jealous of it.

He folds his hands behind his head, his huge muscular arms on full display, and I think my mouth is watering at the sight in front of me. He starts to smirk, and I know he's caught me yet again ogling him.

"Strip my Little Vixen, I do not like to be kept waiting!"

Okay, big boy, you asked for it. I step back nearly halfway to the doors so he can see my full body and start swaying sensually to the music. Slowly, I start to run my hands down my body while very slowly moving my hips in sexy circles.

My whole body is compelled by the beat of the music and it's not too dissimilar to the movement of a snake. As my hips go left, my shoulders go right, in slow hypnotic, sexual movements to tempt Kai with the forbidden fruit. Quite fitting in my emerald green dress, with my red hair and lipstick.

Leisurely I bring my hands back up my body, caressing my hips and breasts on the way and raise them above my head, keeping my body enticing his gaze.

Kai's eyes are roaming my body with a lazy perusal, the only way I know he's affected is the slight tightening of his jaw and the occasional flex of his forearms. Holy hell this man is fucking hot.

I twist slowly away, eventually facing the doors and, as I turn my head slightly to look at him through my lashes, I grasp my zip at the bottom of my back. The dress is totally opened back so the zip is situated at the base of it. I pull it down excruciatingly slowly and watch his eyes follow the movement. He doesn't yet know I'm seeing his every reaction in the full-length mirror by the wardrobes.

Turning back to him I put my fingers in my dress strap, gently teasing it off my shoulder and letting it go. It falls and exposes my left breast to his perusal. Never stopping the sensual sway of my body, I do the same with the right strap which exposes my right breast and my dress ends up pooled on the floor like a rippled puddle of silk.

I'm left in my black lace thong and high heels, manipulating my body in a sultry rhythm making sure his eyes are always on me. I twirl away, and as my hips are swaying, I exaggerate the movement even more and slip my fingers in the sides of my thong.

Kai's eyes are dilated and following the movements of my hands; his mouth is slightly open and he licks his lips slightly. I peer at the towel through my lashes and holy hell he's massive everywhere if the tent between his legs is anything to go by.

I pull all my inner strength together and temptingly begin to tease my thong over my hips and arse. I start bending down and pull my thong down my legs, giving him a totally unhindered view of my arse and pussy. As I peer at Kai through my legs and he's now sitting up straight, fisting the sheets in his massive hands. Staring directly at my pussy with possessiveness and lust. This gives me the strength to do my next move.

I straighten and kick off my heels. Turning back to Kai I saunter to the bed. I climb up and leisurely crawl towards him, keeping my movements sensual. When I get to him, I crawl to his lap and make sure none of my body connects with him. With my knees apart on either side of his hips, I'm right there in front of his eyes and above him, totally naked and unashamed. Temptation personified, yet only ever touched by the man in front of me.

Kai reaches out to grab my hips but I knock his hands away, shaking my head at him. I go back to slowly and sensually teasing him with the movements of my body, pressing my body as near as I can to his without touching it.

Reaching up, I put my hands in my hair, which in turn pushes my boobs right up in front of his face. I exaggerate the rotation of my hips and arse just over his groin in the towel. Watching his reactions through my lashes I can tell he's close to losing his patience with me as his breaths become sharp and ragged.

I decide it's time to start moving my little tease on a bit further, so I slowly lower my hands from my hair and caress my breasts right in front of his face. Suddenly he growls, my eyes widen and then I'm grabbed by his huge hands. I'm on my back with his big body encasing mine on the bed in two seconds flat.

We're both panting and staring at each other, just taking a moment to steady ourselves. After a few seconds he crushes his lips to mine and proceeds to devour me whole as though he's a starved man. Lips bruising, teeth clashing and tongues in a war I think neither of us wants to lose.

I grab onto him and can't resist dragging my nails down his back. Kai's body shudders under my fingertips and he breaks the kiss with a growl. He looks at me with lust, possessiveness and another emotion I'm yet to decipher. His look seems to scorch my soul with the intensity of it.

He lowers his head to my neck and starts kissing his way down towards my pulse point. His touch is so erotic I can't help pressing my pelvis to his, desperate to feel more of him.

Kai growls against my skin and bites down on my neck hard. I cry out in pain and ecstasy at the feelings this man provokes in me. I never thought someone biting you could be so fucking hot, my inexperience making me feel suddenly vulnerable, I tentatively explore the feeling. Kai sucks on the same spot he's bitten and kisses it gently. He then trails his tongue down over my collarbone softly.

My body seems to have a mind of its own; my back arches towards him and my legs wrap around his still towel-clad waist. I let out a noise I've never made in my life and I blush fifty shades of red, closing my eyes a little embarrassed by my wanton reactions to this man. I mean who the fuck makes those noises? It sounded like a mixture between a needy whine and horny fox. *For fuck's sake Annabelle get a fucking grip!*

"Eyes on me Annabelle. I want those eyes and those sexy as fuck noises you are making. Let yourself go my Little Vixen. I've got you. All you need to do is feel."

Kai must have sensed my discomfort and I melt at his words. What the hell is this man doing to me? I open my eyes just in time to see his mouth close around my nipple and his piercing ocean eyes lock with my gaze, drawing me in until I'm drowning in their depths, demanding my attention. My back arches again pushing my breast further into his mouth as he caresses my nipple with his tongue.

I let out another keening sound and tighten my legs around his waist and arse. I tip my head back and close my eyes as my arousal hits a new peak before he bites down hard on my nipple. I scream and automatically look down at him.

"I will not warn you again, my Little Vixen, eyes on me!"

Holy hell, my breaths become shallow and my body heats. My pussy is so wet that my juices weep down my inner thighs, which would be mortifying if I were not so drunk with desire. My nipple fucking hurts, but the pain is weirdly turning me on more. Kai puts his mouth back on my nipple, soothing the pain of his bite, always keeping his eyes on me.

If I'm like this now, how the hell am I going to survive the night? Kai goes on to my other nipple giving it the same treatment as the other one, only the bite to my nipple is not as hard this time, which strangely disappoints me. Is it weird that I preferred the first bite better?

He trails his tongue down my stomach and around my belly button which makes me laugh like a schoolgirl as it tickles. I try to lift my pelvis and wriggle away from him, but he grabs my hips with his hands and holds me securely in place. He smirks, blowing lightly on my lower stomach and his head has a direct view of my pussy.

I think I stop breathing, as he sears me with a devilish look of intent and blows on my pussy. I gasp at the sensation and when he continues, I arch my back again.

Kai lowers his mouth to my pussy and with a

growl, devours it like he was kissing me earlier, roughly sucking my clit, biting it occasionally and then consuming me like a man possessed.

I mean I've seen pornos with men doing this to women before, but I thought those women were exaggerating the noises and pleasure they were getting. If the men are anything like Kai, my view on pornos has totally changed. God, this man knows how to provoke pleasure in a woman.

I'm tightening my thighs around Kai's head, suffocating him at the same time. He growls against my clit so no, he's still in the land of the living. I sink my fingers into the longer hair on Kai's head and tug on it.

Now I'm chasing the intense orgasm I can feel building while I'm grinding my pussy into Kai's face, watching his eyes darken with desire. The noises he's making while devouring me are sinfully erotic.

Kai moves one hand off my hips and I feel his fingers at my pussy. He pushes one finger in gently and must put two in the next time because I start to feel full. He doesn't penetrate deeply but I feel his fingers curl inside me, finding my sweet spot while sucking on my clit.

"Oh! God! Kai! Fuck yeah! Oh my fucking God!... Yes! Yes! There baby! Please don't stop! Oh fuck! I'm going to... KAI!!!"

Kai bites down softly on my clit and I feel like I'm

combusting from the inside out. My whole body spasms, and his name is ripped from my lips like a blessing and a curse. I have never felt anything like this in my life, the intensity of my orgasm scattering my thoughts and blowing my mind.

I'm slowly coming down from the intoxicating high and look down at Kai, he's gently blowing on my pulsating pussy then lifts his face to look at me. He smirks at me and licks his lips which are covered in my release. Oh, my fucking God! He looks carnal. I've never seen a man look so sinfully delicious in my life. He proceeds to lick me from my arse to clit. His face covered in my juices, he dips his tongue in my pussy licking me clean.

I'm sensitive now so I try to pull his head away by pulling his hair harder, and this seems to aggravate him further. His eyes narrow and he lifts his head slightly.

"This pussy is mine. Do you understand me, my Little Vixen? You will give me another orgasm and you will not disturb me until I'm finished."

"Kai, I can't. I'm so sensitive, please stop."

I try to wriggle away but Kai grabs my arse cheeks in his hands squeezing slightly and goes back to ravaging my pussy. My efforts are futile as Kai seems determined in his mission to kill me off with another mind-blowing orgasm. What a way to go!

Kai

Fuck, I can't remember the last time I ate a woman's pussy, but let's just say it's been a long fucking time. But Holy Hell, my Little Vixen's pussy is delicious, a nectar so sweet I am already addicted. I want more so I continue devouring her, taking her to the heights of pain and pleasure.

My need to take her unyielding little pussy is so great but my cock is fucking huge, and my vixen's pussy is untouched and so fucking tight. I need her dripping for me so much that I feel her juices coating my balls when I fuck her. Fucking hell, to hear that no one has ever even fucking kissed her, it's driving me wild with possession, lust, and obsession.

Tonight, I will make sure I've imprinted myself so deep within her that she'll crave me just as much as I crave her. I've never had these thoughts about a woman before which makes it worrying but for some reason, so goddamn right. She just calls to me, like a moth to a flame, threatening to burn my world as I know it to the ground.

As I ravage her pussy with my mouth, I squeeze her arse cheeks which should give her the bite of pain I've learnt she likes. It will still be sensitive from her earlier spanking with my belt. From the way she's moaning and writhing in my hold, it's having the desired effect. That and she is obviously sensitive from her previous orgasm.

My Little Vixen is so sexy in her ecstasy and those noises she's making go straight to my fucking cock. Shit, they are so sexy. I can see her trying to stifle them, her vulnerability making her uncomfortable, but I will make sure she knows how fucking hot they are.

Annabelle arches her back again and lets out another whimper, so I know she's getting close. I put two fingers back in her pussy again; this time though I scissor them inside her to try and loosen her up for my cock. She tips her head back, her eyes drifting closed and lets out a husky moan. I stop, immediately.

"This is the last warning you will have my Little Vixen, eyes on me or I will stop. I want you to see and feel every last little bit of pleasure I give you. Your only focus in my bed is me, and only me, and in return I'll grant that same respect to you. I want your undivided attention, those sexy as fuck noises you make and your passion go straight to my cock. Trust your body, Annabelle!"

"Oh God, Kai please don't stop!"

Now her eyes are back on me. I go back to building her orgasm back up again. I have a good mind to deny her as a punishment, but I needed her dripping.

Her eyes start to dilate again as I'm sucking on her clit and fingering her pussy, so I start licking her clit instead, gently on purpose to keep her orgasm there but to not take her over the edge yet.

She squeezes my head between those delicious thick thighs of hers and grabs fists full of my hair trying to get me to devour her pussy again. My Little Vixen needs to know who's in charge in my bed. I want her wildness. I crave it, but I will dominate her in my bed which she will soon come to realise.

"Kai, please baby, I'm so close, fuck. KAI!!"

My Little Vixen is getting mad as she digs her nails into my scalp and tightens her thighs, trying to grind her pussy on my face. Holy hell, fuck it. I just can't resist this fucking woman. I suck her clit into my mouth and bite hard, evoking a scream out of her and I devour her, sucking and licking her clit like a condemned man with his last meal. It may well be my last with how tight her thighs are crushing my head. What a fucking wonderful way to go, having a face full of pussy.

I stop my scissor action in her pussy and go back to rubbing her g-spot harder this time. Annabelle groans and her legs start to tense up, she arches her back and screams out my name again and again and again, whilst I usher her through the effects of this second orgasm.

I lick all of her release from her pussy lips, but purposely leave the rest for lubrication to ease my way. She's so fucking gorgeous lying there, blushing, with messy hair and that sexy orgasmic glow.

Hearing my name coming from her lips is satisfying but it also brings out the possessive side of me. In time this woman will be mine, by whatever means necessary. Although in vain, she will be fighting against me tooth and nail.

I kiss her pussy gently one last time and rise to my knees, putting my hands on the bed on either side of her. I slowly prowl over her body. Annabelle's eyes suddenly widen and she seems to start coming out of her orgasmic bliss. I raise my brow and smirk at her, as I'm sure she can see the devious look in my eyes.

She goes to say something, but I claim her lips before she can get a word out. She moans into my mouth as I suck on her tongue and thoroughly make her breathless with my kiss.

Her little talons go dragging and digging themselves into my shoulders and back, making me end the kiss with a growl. Fuck this woman is spectacular. Normally women touching me is a big turn-off. I usually tie them up and fuck them, because if they touch me, they tend to think they have a claim on me. Fuck that! But Annabelle, fuck, she can touch me as much as she fucking wants.

"God, you taste divine my Little Vixen. Can you taste yourself on my lips, hmm? Taste your sweet nectar from when I was devouring your delectable pussy?"

I lean my head down to her ear and nibble on her lobe, whispering gently in her ear.

"Are you ready for me, baby? Are you ready to be fucked so hard that you will never be able to extract the feeling of me from inside of you? Ready to be worshipped as my queen, then fucked like my whore? That is what you requested isn't it, my Little Vixen?"

She gasps and lets out an adorable little whimper as I kiss down her throat and bite down on her flesh when she doesn't give me my answer.

"Yes, fuck yes! I'm ready Kai, give me your worst. Never underestimate me, Kai. Because I'll always surprise you. You will learn soon enough that I always give back more than I ever take!"

With that, my Little Vixen rears up fast, sinking her teeth into my neck hard while grabbing the back of my head and digging her nails in deep. Fuck, yes, this woman is magnificent. I growl and grab a fist full of hair pulling her head back, making her release my neck. She's got a malicious smile on her lips which makes me smirk and kiss the fuck out of her.

I release her and she drops back onto the bed, panting. I kneel in between her legs and grab my towel. Her eyes widen and her smile disappears as I pull it from around my hips and throw it across the room. She looks down at my cock and her eyes nearly pop out of her head. God, she's adorable.

"Fuck Kai. What the fuck is that thing? That's not a dick it's a fucking deadly weapon and there's no bloody chance in hell that thing is going to fit in me. Fuck no, ehh ehh, no chance Mr horse dick!"

I can't help it and I burst out laughing, fuck she's funny. She starts to try and wiggle out from under me which soon ends my laughter as there is no way my Little Vixen is going anywhere.

Dragging her back to me, I cage her in with my body. My God, she's so small compared to me but totally makes up for it with that sassy attitude of hers.

"You my Little Vixen are going nowhere! I will fit, I assure you. I know I'm big, but you will be absolutely fine. It will hurt at first as you already know but once you get used to me, I will fuck you so hard baby. You will forget about the pain and only be able to concentrate on the immeasurable pleasure you feel. I will possess that delicious body of yours and invade your mind and soul.

Don't forget to always keep your eyes on me. Don't be afraid at any time to tell me how you feel or if you are in pain as I will stop and help you through it. You are mine to fuck, cherish and devour. So, stop thinking and just feel for me, baby."

I cradle her face with my palm and gently stroke my thumb over her cheek. She's still wide-eyed and I know she's panicking. She just needs to trust me enough to look after her. My heart is beating so fucking fast because I don't know what I will do if she decides not to carry on.

"Okay Kai, I trust you. I don't know why but I do. Please don't make me regret it!"

Thank fuck for that. God, nothing has ever felt so important to me in my life. This little red-headed vixen walks into my life and turns it upside down in one night. I don't say anything else, there's nothing left to say. I reach down with my hand, grabbing her arse and tilting her pelvis for me. I start rubbing my engorged cock over her clit, trying to relax her and gain some much-needed lubrication.

I watch her intently, gauging the changes in her body, her little pussy lips getting wetter. Her eyes dilating and getting half-lidded, those beautiful sky eyes peeking at me from under her lashes and her delectable little whimpers breaking their way through. A fucking symphony to my depraved soul. What a gift for this devil indeed.

There is no way I'm going to be able to do this without causing her some pain, so I reach down and line my cock up with her pussy. I capture her lips in a soul-searing kiss, she melts into, and I thrust into her pussy hard and fast.

Annabelle breaks from the kiss and screams my name, arching her back and panting. She's in pain I can tell, and her pussy is trying to adjust, pulsating around my cock trying to strangle it and eject it at the same time. Fuck! She's so fucking tight, I'm having to grind my teeth to keep still and not fuck her senseless.

She feels like heaven, and I should never be allowed to enter. She's trying to wash away the sins of my tainted life. How the hell this woman walked into my life is unknown, but I will thank whichever beings sent her to me forevermore.

Her pussy is starting to adjust, and the pulsating is slowing. I lean down and suck on her neck making her writhe in my arms. I move to her ear and whisper. "Such a good girl for me, you're doing brilliantly Annabelle. I'm halfway in so I'm going to start fucking you now. Let's see if your sweet little pussy can take me balls deep. No one has managed to so far, my sweet Little Vixen. Let's see if you are the exception, shall we?"

I kiss down her neck and slowly make my way to her delectable breasts. I suck her rosebud nipple into my mouth, and she arches her back pushing her nipple further in.

"What the fuck, Kai? Why didn't you tell me before we started that nobody has been able to take all of your dick. Holy hell! That's kind of important information here, you fucking prick. No, don't bother telling the virgin that you have a monster fucking dick that no fucking woman has taken fully. And bear in mind, more than half of those women have probably had more dick than I've had hot meals. If you break my fucking pussy Kai, I will cut your balls off and fucking feed them to you, you bastard!"

Fuck, this woman is so hilarious and that feistiness that pours out of her mouth goes straight to my cock. I grab her hair in my fist and wind it around my hand, while the other hand still holds on to her arse, keeping her tight little pussy exactly where I want it. I pull her head back and tilt my head to the side raising a brow at the same time.

"You, my sassy Little Vixen are going to take my cock and fucking love it. Now all you need to do is shut the fuck up and be a good girl. You are fucking mine; do you fucking understand me? MINE!"

I keep her in the hold I have and slowly pull my cock out until only the tip is left in before I drive it back in, harder and deeper. Her mouth opens and she lets out a feral groan. I do it again, going harder and deeper each time. Our faces are inches apart and her legs wrap around my hips which puts about three-quarters of my dick in her juicy little pussy.

"Fuck Kai, shit! I can't take it anymore. Fuck, your dick's going to come out my mouth in a bit. Jesus Christ. Argh!"

I start ramping up the speed of my thrusts, looking into her eyes. She's glorious, a true goddess in the flesh, the sweetest temptation a man could ever know.

Her hands find my back again and her little claws come out to play, my back is going to be covered in her marks tomorrow. I'm more than surprised that this is something that excites me. My Little Vixen, leaving her marks on me. Her hands travel down my back and she grips my arse in her little hands.

Fuck, it's like a switch is flipped and I can't hold back any longer. I power into her, thrusting my cock in and out of her pussy; driving her into the mattress. Her cries are feeding my monster. He wants to devour, conquer, and possess her. I move my hand from her delectable arse and put it on the bed ready to take my full weight. I release her hair from my grip and move my hand to her throat. I squeeze tightly, not enough to choke her but enough to withhold some air.

I fucking let loose. I can't help it, seeing my hand around her throat. Her mouth opens in a silent gasp and her eyes are burning with so much lust. I fuck her so hard the headboard is banging off the wall, as the bed is moving so much. I ramp up the speed and try to go deeper.

Her tight little pussy has no chance, it's pulsating and fluttering all over the place. Her juices are coating my cock, spilling out onto the bed. The noises she makes are so fucking erotic, my balls start to tighten and I'm fighting myself for the first time in years not to come like I'm a fucking teenager again. These are the feelings she provokes in me, what a fucking gift.

I growl and squeeze her neck tighter, thrusting even faster and deeper when she just explodes like a fucking bomb around me. Her pussy clamps down on my cock so hard I think it might cut it off if her pussy doesn't release me.

She shudders and screams my name so fucking loud my eardrums are throbbing. Her thighs are squeezing me so hard she's slowly cutting off the circulation to my legs. I fight my release as I'm determined to have her in more positions before our first time is over. She finally relents and I thrust hard and deep. Her pussy gives up the fight and I get to visit a paradise I've never experienced before, gifted to me by this sweet little virgin before me.

I'm balls deep and it's that fucking surprising, I release my hold on her throat and rear back to look at where we are joined, to see something I never thought possible. I groan down at the sight, grabbing hold of her hips and thrusting into her hard and fast.

"MINE!" I roar out like a fucking savage animal as I fuck my Little Vixen into the bed. Her hands are gripping onto my wrists for dear life.

"Kai," Annabelle shouts and then whimpers. Making me go harder and faster, I lower my hand to her clit stroking it with my thumb.

"Come for me baby, show me who owns this little juicy pussy. Whose pussy is this, Annabelle?"

"It's my pussy, nobody else will ever own it!"

Fuck that, she will tell me that her pussy, and more importantly, she herself is mine by the end of the night. I stop everything and pull out of her pussy fully. I watch her juices and some blood seep out over her arse and onto the bed. It's such a beautiful sight. The proof of her virginity is also all over my cock. I reach for her and flip her over onto her front. She starts to try and struggle and complain. But before she can even get a word out, I push her head down into the bed keeping my hand there. I raise her hips and ass up and thrust into her once again.

I fuck her hard and fast; pushing her head into the mattress as I fuck her senseless. She will give me the answer I want. She will be mine. The sound of our flesh slapping together echoes around the room, mingling with her muffled whimpers. It's so damn erotic, I tip my head back groaning out loud and lose myself in her. In a frenzy of feeling and fucking. At finally being able to be me with a woman. Of maybe feeling for the first time since I was a child. Fuck, maybe ever!

My hold on her head slips and I grab her hair in my fist, pulling her head to arch her back. I fuck her hard, loving her screams and moans. I spank her arse hard with my other hand leaving her with a lovely red handprint.

"Now tell me my sexy little vixen, who owns this fuckable little pussy?"

"Me, I own it. You fucking dickhead!" Annabelle shouts out and does something that shocks the fuck out of me. She starts riding my fucking dick like it's her favourite new toy, this feisty little vixen. I keep still and watch her ride my cock with vigour. Fuck me, this woman is magnificent. Holy hell!

I spank her arse hard twice and lean my body over hers to growl in her ear.

"WHOSE. PUSSY. IS. THIS?" Insinuating each word with a hard punishing thrust.

"Mine!" She shouts again with venom.

"Wrong fucking answer Annabelle."

She will learn, I cup both of my hands around the front of her throat bringing her up off the bed so she can't rest her hands on the bed and fuck her savagely.

The sweat is glistening on our bodies, the slapping of our flesh meeting echoing in the room and our lust-drunk moans and gasps filling the air. This woman evokes me to want to own her, possess her but to worship at her feet at the same time. I fuck her like this until I feel both of our bodies are at the brink of self-destruction, and exhilaration overtakes me, making my nerve endings spark like a live wire before consuming everything in its wake.

I lean over her body again and remove one of my hands from around her neck to grab her chin turning her face to me. "Whose pussy is this, Annabelle?"

"Yours Kai. Its fucking yours!"

I slam my mouth down on hers and fuck her mouth at the same rhythm as I'm fucking her pussy. My heart is thumping so fast in my chest I think it's going to explode. Finally, she's mine! I'm fucking ecstatic and soon she will learn what belonging to me entails. Now that she's my feisty little Queen!

I lean back on my heels and bring Annabelle with me still kissing the fuck out of her and powering into her from below. Her tight little pussy starts to spasm, and she breaks the kiss with a scream. She detonates into such a powerful orgasm I have no choice but to follow along with her. I grab her hips bringing her down, shuddering on my cock at a rapid speed and I tip my head back and roar my release to the ceiling. Fuck me, I've never experienced an orgasm like it. It's so powerful, I'm lost for what feels like ages but could only be seconds.

We both collapse to the bed, me on top of her at first, sweating and breathless. I finally manage to roll us over and bring her to me, nestling her onto my chest and wrapping my arms protectively around my Queen. I bring the covers over us and just lie there as peace settles over me, soothing my dark, tainted soul.

Chapter 5

Annabelle

I'm shocked out of the most blissful sleep I've had in ages, by shouting and angry voices coming from what I assume is the living room of the penthouse. I pull up the sheets to cover myself and rub my eyes to clear them. I'm still half asleep and trying to get my bearings. I'm sore in the most delicious way but nevertheless, I'm still very tender. I suppose that's what you get when you tempt a man like Kai to take your virginity. I never imagined in my wildest dreams he would be that big; but my God he's huge, not only in length but girth as well. I was not kidding when I referred to him as Mr horse dick but damn, I really did expect to be split in half.

The voices grew even more irate, and I think it was time for me to make my move. If I leave now hopefully, Kai will be too occupied with what he's obviously dealing with at the moment to be bothered.

lifting the sheet I put my legs over the side of the bed to stand up and I feel our combined release escaping from my pussy. I look down and find a bit of blood there too. I turn to look at the bed and I'm mortified to find some on the sheets as well.

I run to the ensuite; cleaning myself up and relieving my bladder while I'm there. I look in the mirror and I'm so shocked at my reflection, that I burst out laughing. My hair looks like I've been dragged through a hedge backwards, my mascara has run around my eyes and my lipstick is smudged beyond repair. I assess the rest of my body and find I have bite marks and a love bite on my neck. I turn around and look at my sore arse and sure enough I still have Kai's belt marks all over my bum cheeks and the backs of my thighs. I'm startled by the realisation that I liked seeing his marks on me. Well fuck!

I wash my face to clean it of makeup and put some toothpaste on my finger in an attempt to freshen up my mouth.

Once I'm finished cleaning myself up, I return to the bedroom and try to find my clothes. I search the bedroom high and low but can only find my dress. My thong has disappeared, so it looks like I'm going bare.

I get dressed quickly and grab my heels; I don't put them on yet because I'm hoping to find my bag and disappear without them taking much notice of me. I rummage through Kai's top draw before I leave, taking a little memento of my own. He has my knickers, I have this.

Putting my ear to the door I listen to the commotion down the hall. They're still arguing so I open the door quietly and start to creep down the corridor towards them, keeping my back to the wall. Then I hear a voice that makes my body freeze just before I come to the end of the corridor.

"I will not ask you again. What the fuck have you done with Annabelle? Where the fuck is she?"

Oh, my fucking God, Luka has tracked me down and he sounds so angry. I should have made sure I got a message to him, letting him know I was safe. That I wouldn't be home until the morning. I can understand why he's angry. Luka has been my bodyguard since I was fifteen, but now he is also my flatmate and best friend. He also helped me escape my previous hell and has been my protector ever since.

I creep to the end of the wall I'm hidden by and peep around the corner to assess the situation. I have to swallow my gasp at what's before me but it's hard because my heart is in my throat. Luka is on his knees with Lev's gun positioned at the back of his head and he's facing Kai who also has his gun aimed at Luka's head too. Pasha is leaning against the wall casually like the leaning tower of fucking pisa, one brick wall to another.

Fuck this shit, nobody threatens my friends with a gun and fucking gets away with it. *'Time to bring your A game, Annabelle!'* I take a deep breath and retrieve the memento I stole. Since Kai obviously thinks it's okay to steal my knickers, I took my own souvenir.

A familiar feeling of déjà vu invades me as I enter the room as though the scene before me was not out of the ordinary, which it most definitely wasn't given my hellish past. I also try to pretend that I don't look like I've been thoroughly fucked and that I can't actually walk properly. I drop my heels on the floor as I walk over to Kai. It's a risky move seeing as everyone is pointing a gun at my friend and could just shoot him dead. When I'm halfway across the room, I smile at Luka while holding out two fingers on my left hand quickly. It's our secret code that I'm okay and not to worry or interfere.

I continue my journey to Kai. I stand right in front of him and put my left hand on his chest. I reach up and cup his neck. I pull his lips down to mine as I raise up on my tiptoes, crashing my lips to his in a clit tingling kiss.

Kai must be shocked at first because he freezes, but he soon takes over the kiss in his domineering way, as I knew he would. I placed all of my cards on it so he will be oblivious to the move I'm making as he's distracted by fucking my mouth with his tongue.

I raise my fisted right hand up and when I know it's four inches under Kai's chin, I press the release button on my stolen memento. I break from the kiss and plaster a sinister smile on my face. I wink at Kai while keeping my grip on the back of his neck, with his own flick knife under his chin.

"I suggest you take your guns off of my friend and put them away right fucking now. I do not take kindly to my friends being hurt or threatened. We will leave immediately, and you will never have to see us again. Do not fuck with me. I told you both this when I met you and now all you are doing is pissing me the fuck off!"

Kai's eyes are dilated and full of lust. Kinky fuck must be getting off on me holding a knife to his head. He smiles down at me and I feel him put his gun in the back of his joggers. *Did I forget to mention that he is only in a pair of hot as fuck grey joggers, bare chest, and feet?* His hair looks no better than mine, it's messed from where I was pulling on it last night. Fuck, this man is hot as hell, like sin personified.

"Fucking hell, my Little Vixen, you are fucking perfect for me in every way. You have no fear in holding my own blade to my throat, growling up at me like an angry little kitten. You have more balls on you than most of my associates combined. I promise you this though, you will pay for it with more of my belt marks on that fuckable arse of yours. How is my delicious pussy now, is it still dripping with my seed?"

I stick his blade in further under his chin drawing blood this time and watching in fascination as it drips down the blade to my hand.

"You mistake me for someone that actually gives a shit, Kai. You fucked me and took the virginity that has been a noose around my neck for what feels like a lifetime. But make no mistake Kai, my pussy will never belong to any man and neither will I. So, take your vulgar words and horse dick and go stick them up your arse! You fucking arsehole!"

I hear Lev snort and try to cover it up with a cough, Pasha gives a scary grin... Kai looks at his men before he does a double take at Pasha.

"I didn't know you had teeth, my friend," Kai mutters, shaking his head slightly and refocusing. He finds my gaze, his eyes narrow and he arches a brow at me, gracing me with a wicked smile.

"Oh, Annabelle, my adorable Little Vixen. You are seriously mistaken if you think you can deny my claim on you. You and that luscious little pussy belong to me now, you're mine and always will be. You will make for a very vicious Queen to reign by my side, with a formidable temper to match. I don't care one bit whether you are willing or reluctant as you have no choice in the matter. You will not be leaving my side from here on out and will face punishments for any bad behaviour!"

What the actual fuck is he on about, me being his Queen? He owns businesses including the Siren's Call which is where I work, but that in no way makes him a King... does it? I'm so confused and, Kai is obviously lost in the feelings of his grandeur. I just need to hurry up and get myself and Luka out of here. It's a shame but I think now we may have overstayed our welcome in Birmingham and it's time to move on, yet again.

"Seriously, Kai, I think you're very fucking delusional. Now, Henry and I," I begin looking at Luka and using his alias "will be on our way. We'll leave you to get on with your day. As I assume 'Kings' are very busy running their empires. I would also make a crap 'Queen' because, as I've already stated, I have a problem with male tyrants!"

Shit, I really fucked up this time listening to my hussy fucking pussy, all she ever seems to do is get me in trouble. Now I've got to leave the home I love and some really lovely friends.

I'm fucking tired of running and being scared,

it's fucking draining, but the alternative is so much worse. I have no choice because if they ever find me, I will be beaten, likely imprisoned or worse still murdered. Luka will be slaughtered instantly for his betrayal, and I can't have that on my conscience. I will not have him killed, or die trying to protect me.

While I'm distracted by my inner meltdown, I miss Kai's movements as he grabs my hand with the knife and twists me around before I have a chance to react. He grips my throat with one hand and twists my wrist holding the knife with the other, making me release it.

Kai pulls me into his chest and leans down to whisper in my ear, and I shiver in his hold and close my eyes.

"I love this new side you've shown me, my Little Vixen, your feistiness is hot as fuck. Who knew I would be so turned on by knife play? Well, we will definitely be exploring this new kink of ours soon, my Queen. I saw your eyes dilate with lust as my blood ran down my knife and onto your hand. Let's see that sexy little pussy quiver on my cock as I'm fucking you with my knife at your throat."

I'm unable to hold back the moan or the shiver that steals down my spine at Kai's filthy words. He's right though I was so fucking turned on by his blood seeping down his knife and onto my hand. What the fuck was wrong with me? Why does my pussy contract at the thought of him fucking me with a knife at my throat? Fuck. I think I need serious help.

"Please let me go, Kai!"

"As I've told you before my Little Vixen, you are going nowhere. Now tell me who the fuck is this Henry of yours and why would a friend come armed to rescue you. I know he's not your lover as I still have your sweet virgin blood covering my cock but he's more than a friend. So, tell me my Queen, who the fuck is he?"

I take a deep breath and open my eyes looking at Luka with questioning eyes, he knows I'm asking him how the fuck we're going to get out of this one. He's worried, I can tell and all because I've fucked up and brought Kai into our messed-up life. God, what else will I drag this poor man into? I bet he wishes he had never met me. I attempt to reply to Kai, but Luka beats me to it.

"When Annabelle didn't come home on time I went to the club and asked around to see if anybody knew where she was. I was worried as you can imagine that something had happened to her. I'd never forgive myself if something did and I hadn't tried to help. She never stays out, so it was unusual. I tracked her to this address and got as far as asking for you. Then your men grabbed me and brought me up here."

I was hoping this would be enough of an explanation for Kai, but I should have known. Nothing was going to get me out of my predicament with Kai. He saw me as his and nothing was going to change his mind. All I could hope for was that he'd let Luka go and I would get a chance to escape soon. All our lives would be in jeopardy if I were found here. Everyone would die at those bastards' hands and, no matter how much Kai annoyed me, I could not let that happen.

Kai

I knew both Annabelle and Henry were lying to me, I'd already seen a dozen signs and their body language that indicated they weren't telling me the truth. I've never been known for my patience, far from it, but when it now concerns my Little Vixen I didn't like it one bit.

She was mine and I would be the one to look after her. She would also soon learn that she would be punished if she lied to me because it was something I would not tolerate at all from her. She was to be my Queen, my wife, my lover, and eventually the mother of my children.

I was a possessive bastard by nature, but with Annabelle it seemed to consume me. From the moment I first saw her I knew she was mine, and nothing and no one was going to stop me from claiming her, least of all Annabelle herself. She would soon come round, but if she needed to be kept here as my Little Vixen then so be it. She would soon find out that what I wanted I always got; maybe with a lot of blood spilled along the way but she will be mine in the end.

"See Henry, if that's your real name, I know you're both lying to me and I would suggest you both start telling me the truth immediately. There is no way any of my staff would have given you my home address, let alone tell you that I had taken Annabelle with me. Now, are you going to tell me one of my staff has betrayed me, or are you going to tell me the truth? Also, bear in mind you have a Russian accent when you are mad. It's slight but I noticed it considering I'm also Russian. So, who the fuck sent you? And who are you to my Vixen?"

Henry's eyes widened in shock at my observations and information about my nationality; few people could tell when meeting me, as I'd had a privileged upbringing and was taught perfect English. I had been encouraged to use the language all the time as my position here was always certain. I was supposed to expand our reign and take out our opposition in England while I was at it. So I was given the tools to achieve this goal; education, money and power.

Annabelle goes rigid in my hold and begins to tremble a little which starts to worry me. What part of the information I have just given would make her react like that? Is she worried I'll kill Henry? Or is it someone at the club she's worried about?

I stroke my thumb on her throat and whisper in her ear. "Calm yourself, my Little Vixen, I will not harm you. You are too precious to me. Now, I'm not saying you will not be punished, but you are not in danger from me at all."

If I thought my words of reassurance would calm my Little Vixen, I was clearly mistaken. It seemed to enrage her because she thrashed in my hold and tried several self-defence moves to free herself. I'm astounded by her skill and the power she has considering how small she is compared to me. I'm 6ft5 and she must be no more than 5ft4 at the most. If I had considered that a weakness, in this moment I would've re-evaluated that stance.

Annabelle manages to get an elbow to my solar plexus, and she brings her head back just missing headbutting my nose. Regardless of how big she is, she would have definitely broken it had she connected with my face. I have no choice but to restrain her in a harsh hold, but I need her to stop attacking me and possibly hurting herself.

Holy hell, my Little Vixen is so fucking hot when

she fights me, she turns me on like no other. This is so surprising to me as I've always gone with submissive women and never had a relationship. Yet with this woman in my arms, I would gladly burn the world for her and enjoy her being right by my side watching it burn.

Regardless of my obsession with her though, something I've said has set her off. I look to Lev and Henry and see that Lev has also had to restrain him as he must have tried to aid Annabelle. Lev gives me a nod that he has the situation handled and I mull over my next move by going over what has been said in my head.

The precise moment that seemed to ignite a reaction in her was when I mentioned that I was Russian. Why the hell that would set her off I have no idea. After all her friend Henry, if that is actually who he is, is Russian too. No, my Little Vixen couldn't be, could she?

"кто ты, черт возьми? Ты дикхед!"

I direct the question at Henry but it's Annabelle's reactions I'm focused on. My heart races in my chest in anticipation and my Little Vixen falls right into my trap and reacts instantly to confirm that she understands Russian. My biggest question yet is, was my Little Vixen Russian?

A weird sensation encompasses me, it doesn't matter in the slightest to me but what are the chances a little Russian red headed vixen has managed to infiltrate my heart? I thought I didn't have one, but Annabelle proves that my assumptions were wrong. That cold organ in my chest has come back to life with a vengeance and it's because of the woman in my arms.

Nobody answers my question and I'm growing impatient with the need to discover the truth she is trying so hard to hide from me. If she thinks she can keep anything from me, she is sorely mistaken. I will know everything about her before the day is out because I will have no secrets between us. Ever.

I lean down again and bite her neck over my mark from yesterday. She whimpers then groans when I soothe it with my tongue. I whisper in her ear.

"Tell me, my Little Vixen, are you Russian? A truly glorious gift presented to me by the fates, to make sure our paths crossed when they did. They believe as do I that we are destined for each other. What is your real name, my Королева?"

She shudders in my arms, and I nuzzle her neck taking a deep breath of her scent which drives me crazy. That hint of chamomile that I've detected before now comes to the forefront and reminds me of home. The subtle signs were there for the taking but I never followed them through.

"Don't tell him anything, Annabelle, Trust…"

Lev cuts off Henry's response by covering his mouth with his hand. He kidney punches him which makes him bend over coughing. He doesn't show any pain which is surprising and a little impressive because I often spar with Lev, and he has a mean punch.

There is so much more to this situation, and the fact that they are trying to keep it from me only pisses me off more.

"I will tell you nothing, you fucking asshole, and Lev, if you hurt Henry again, believe me, a knee in the balls is the least of your fucking worries. Kai, you better let me the fuck go now before I show you how truly fucking crazy I am!"

I sigh as I know my Little Vixen's willpower is strong, but if she thinks I'm giving up on finding the truth she is wrong.

"You will tell me right now or I will have Lev kill your precious Henry."

On reflection this likely wasn't the wisest thing to say to her because she reacts with such voracity, I'm shocked and in awe at the same time. She fights my hold, she kicks her legs, throws punches and elbows and thrusts her head wildly to connect with any weaknesses that can be found in my grasp, trying everything to escape.

She seems well trained in combat, and appears to know which vulnerable areas to aim her blows. She lands some well timed hits before I finally snap, grappling her over to the windows and ensnaring her hands above her head by her dainty wrists with one of my large unforgiving ones. My other curls around her slender throat to secure her. Both of us are breathing heavily with the exertion and I lean my weight against her, crushing her glorious legs with my own more muscular ones, incapacitating her with my large frame.

I can feel my lip swelling where she caught me with an elbow, and my ribs are also sore. None of it matters though because it only adds to the carnal lust I have for this woman, which I know she can feel pressing against her stomach. At this moment I just want to take her back to my bed and let us both take out our frustrations with each other in the best way possible, because I know it would be the best sex either of us have ever known.

"Calm down my Little Vixen, no harm will come to your friend if you just tell me the truth!"

Annabelle closes her eyes and then opens them, and I'm stunned to see unshed tears in her eyes. My body is overcome with a feeling that I've never experienced before. Guilt. I've clearly distressed her. I need to put this right, but I can only do that if she lets me in.

"I can't tell you, Kai. I wish I could, but I can't drag anybody else into my fucked-up life. Please just let me and Henry go. I swear we will disappear, and you will never see us again. I'm begging you Kai, please?"

I stare into her beseeching eyes, ones that are driving a knife into my heart because she's asking me to let her go. She will learn though that I will do anything to protect her; she is yet to find out the power I possess but she will soon. Therefore, I need her to tell me what is going on because I need to eliminate any possible dangers that are posing a threat to my Queen.

"We need to get one thing clear, Annabelle. You are not going anywhere. You are mine now and I protect what is mine. I will explain to you the power I possess soon enough but I just need you to tell me the truth. Trust me, I will burn the world for you and fuck you in the ashes. Believe me when I say you are safe here with me and I will let nothing and no one hurt you, ever. Do you hear me?"

Annabelle closes her eyes again and whimpers as the tears she was holding back escape the hold she had on them. She's trying to be strong, but she needs to understand that she doesn't need to be anymore. That's what I'm for. I will be her strength, her defender, and her King all in one. Don't get me wrong I love her strength and courage, but she's not on her own anymore.

"Kai, you don't understand that the people I'm running from are extremely powerful and deadly. I know you think you're powerful, but you don't understand the world I come from."

What kind of trouble has my Little Vixen gotten herself into? Fucking hell, she's scared shitless, and I need to put a stop to this right now. I will not have my woman constantly running and looking over her shoulder.

"You're starting to piss me off with your lack of faith in me, my Queen. Just tell me your name and I'll find the rest out for myself!"

Now, if you could have told me I would be stunned to silence with the next words out of my Little Vixen's mouth, I would have told you to fuck off, but they did.

You may think a name means nothing as it's easily changed or erased. That may be true in a normal life but in our life, our world, your name means everything. Especially the name I was about to hear, for Annabelle wasn't just some sexy dancer who entranced me. No, she was fucking Bratva royalty. A princess who very much on the run from some immensely powerful people and, most surprising of all, my family's most hated enemy.

"My name is Valentina Ivanov!"

Chapter 6

Kai

Hearing that name gracing my Queen's lips shook me to my core, causing me to break my hold on her and stagger back a few steps. That look of hurt she gave me at my knee-jerk reaction was heart-breaking and gut-wrenching. I couldn't help it though because his name was like a bullet to my newly found heart. How could my Little Vixen be the spawn of such evil? Mikhail Ivanov is her father. Fuck!

I turn my back to her and run my hands through my hair grabbing it by the roots and then roaring to the ceiling in rage. "FUCK!"

I hear her whimper behind me, but when I manage to calm my rage slightly and cast her a lethal glare over my shoulder, she steels her spine and schools her features, giving me her best 'I don't give a fuck' face.

"I will ask you a question now and if I sense you

are lying to me, I will not hesitate to kill you both!"

Valentina's eyes fill with unshed tears again, ones I know she is desperate to retain as she sees them as a weakness. She bites her plump bottom lip and nods her reply.

"Was this all a façade, planned by your family? Pretend the little Princess is on the run for years, then she suddenly gets a job at my Burlesque club of all places. Infiltrate my establishment with the hopes of catching my eye um? I bet you couldn't believe your luck hey, Princess Valentina. What a glorious job you did for Papa, tricking the dumb fuck Prince so fucking easily. What was the plan? Make me love you and then break my heart and put a bullet in my head for good measure. What a fucking fool I've been. So easily tricked by your virginal pussy. Bravo, Princess Valentina. Bravo."

Her face is puzzled at first by my outburst, trying to piece together all I have accused her of. She looks over to Henry who is looking as puzzled as she is. Valentina looks at me again, she has so much hurt and betrayal in her eyes I start to doubt myself, but I don't lose my composure. This just can't be a coincidence though, can it?

"Firstly, who the fuck are you? Also, how do you know my family?"

Does she think I'm fucking stupid?

"Don't play dumb with me, Printsessa. Don't try

and pretend you have no clue who I am. The game is up and now I'm growing impatient. Also, very trigger happy."

There she is; my Little Vixen's eyes are raging with anger. She marches over to me with no concern for her safety at all, as she stabs her finger in my chest and looks up at me with what I can only describe as pure hatred.

"Fuck you, arsehole! If you think I would do anything for my Papa other than spit on his dead corpse, you are sorely mistaken. That bastard ripped my world from me and destroyed anything good I ever had in my life. He sold me and killed the most precious thing in the world to me. If it weren't for Luka, I would have been raped numerous times, or killed myself by now. Take your pick, but do not think I would ever do anything for that monster. Ever! Now, I have not got a clue who the fuck you are, other than tonight at the club when I learned your name. I didn't know the owner was even Russian or I would never have worked there. Shit. You even fucked me, and I didn't even know or sense you were Russian until you spoke it just now."

Fucking hell, I'm so confused. I'm torn between her venom and obvious hatred for her Papa. But my own conclusion of the plot they have conspired against me is still raging in my mind, refusing to let me listen to anything she has to say. At least I knew both their real names now.

I need to sort my head out and push these feelings I have for her right the fuck out of my head, as they are clouding my judgment. But first I need to see one more reaction.

"Very well. We will play your little games for a bit longer, Princess. Let me introduce myself, where are my manners in front of such royalty? My name is Nikolai Viktorovich Filippov. Heir to the family throne of one of the deadliest Bratva empires. But you haven't heard the best part yet, Princess. I swear you'll love it so much it will make your sweet little cunt flutter. My family is your family's sworn enemy."

My heart was pumping so hard that I thought it was going to explode out of my chest. I waited, anticipating her reaction to my name as it meant more to me than I care to admit. I was expecting disappointment at her reacting to my name but there was no recognition at all. The only part of my whole speech that affected her was to realise that we were her family's sworn enemy. Valentina's eyes widened in shock and then horror at the predicament she now found herself in.

She looked over at the man I now knew as Luka and not Henry with a panicked expression on her face, but he looked as shocked as she was by the news. Luka, though, had reacted to the mention of my family name. I scrutinised them both while they processed this new information.

Luka's face drained of colour and a flash of regret crossed his face that puzzled me.

"I'm so sorry, Valentina, I've failed you," Luka pleaded to Valentina. What the fuck had he done, had he tricked her into this? Knowingly feeding her to the lions? I'd fucking kill him now if he has.

"What the fuck are you sorry for?" I shouted.

Luka didn't break eye contact with Valentina though.

"I should have checked your new job out, to make sure I knew who was involved in the business. I've become complacent, and I take all the blame. I'm so sorry. I have made such a grave error in protecting you. I'm so sorry, sweetheart."

Luka drops his head in shame and Valentina lets out a quiet sob, quickly stifling it with her hand. She straightens her spine, lifts her chin, and schools her features once more. What a Bratva Queen this woman is meant to be, more balls than most of the men I deal with daily.

Luka's words irk me though, I'm so infuriated with him for not taking more care of Valentina. I can also gauge the close friendship they have with each other. His endearment toward her makes me want to shoot him dead where he stands. Seems like learning we are adversaries hasn't quelled the possessiveness I have for her.

He's about our age, mid-thirties, whereas Valentina is in her early twenties, and I'm guessing from his words to Valentina that he is her bodyguard. It must be the only way she was able to escape her family, if her story is to be believed.

If he is her bodyguard, he's brought a death sentence upon himself for aiding her escape. I'm still undecided, I think an interrogation of them both is in order to ascertain the facts of the dilemma we find ourselves in. Only then will I make the call to my father to explain the situation.

Valentina turns to face me again. Her eyes are red, and I can see some tears have managed to escape the death grip she had on them. Her features and posture though are calm and controlled, no doubt from years of practice in the family she comes from.

"This is the first and only time I will ever do this Kai, so please make the most of it. I'm begging you. Please will you let Luka go, I have brought enough misery to his life. I don't want or wish to be responsible for his death. I will not be able to live with that on my conscience. I'll stay and you can do anything you wish to do with me. I have not lied to you though. I didn't know who you were, it's not some trick, or plans to deceive you. If you wish to hand me over to your family to kill, do so but understand this; it will not hurt my Papa as he is incapable of love. It will however hurt his pride that his possession has been taken."

"NO, LENA! Please, sweetheart, do not do this!" Luka pleads to Valentina, making me clench my fist when he uses what is likely his pet name for her.

"You've sacrificed too much protecting me, Luka, it's time for me to repay your loyalty. I will not allow you to be affected anymore by your association with me. I wish to free you of your obligation to me so you can try and live a normal life. Go Luka, and forget you ever knew me, please. Find someone to love and try to have a happy life for me, my friend!"

"No, Lena, I won't leave you, ever. We will find a way; we always do, you know that sweetheart. If you stay, I will stay and whatever my fate is, so be it. But please don't ask me to leave because it will never happen."

Valentina sighs and shakes her head, already knowing that she will not win the argument with Luka. It reminds me so much of my relationship with Lev, as I know he would do exactly the same as Luka is doing now, for me. True loyalty is extremely hard to find in our lives so when you do find it, it becomes that much more precious.

"Nobody is going anywhere! You will both be

staying here until I decide what to do with you. Lev, take Luka to a spare room and lock him in. You know which one to use, and make sure to secure him so we might speak of this matter in more depth. Pasha…" I pause, momentarily at a loss. I shrug and continue… "go and find something useful to do. I don't know, figure it out."

Pasha gives a cheeky salute and a mocking finger wave before leaving the room.

Lev pulls Luka up by his arms and follows behind him to lead Luka to our interrogation room down his wing of the penthouse. It's soundproofed and has some special little tools that get people talking rather fast. While he is making the arrangements for Luka I will get Valentina settled, or should I say fastened in, to await my personal method of torture. From what I've seen though, I think my Little Vixen will like it a bit too much.

"Come, Princess, let's get you acquainted with one of my favourite little toys. I have not had a chance to test them out yet and to say I am excited is an understatement.

Valentina

I gasp in astonishment at Kai's words. I should

be afraid after all; now that I've found out we're enemies, but I can't help feeling turned on. What the hell is wrong with me? Don't misunderstand me I'm scared for Luka, really fucking worried that they will kill him. They will try to torture him for information, but they will never succeed. They don't know Luka as I do, he'd die before he would reveal anything I didn't wish to be divulged; he is that loyal.

I need to try and persuade Kai to release Luka or at least not torture him. I need to divert his attention so I can formulate an exit strategy for us both.

Kai gives me one of his trademark sinister smirks and starts to walk toward his bedroom. He doesn't even look back to see if I'm following him, because what choice do I have? So I follow Kai, like an obedient puppy. Let him underestimate me again. They will all find out who I really am soon enough.

I have not given my all in any fight I've had with them yet. There has always been someone there that I've not wanted to get hurt for me. Sam, back at the club and now Luka here. I'll bide my time and attack when they least expect it.

As I follow Kai, I can't help but admire his hot as fuck body. This man is built for sin. A giant amongst men, with a wide frame of hard rippling muscles, a slim waist, and that edible arse. Fuck, I like a good arse and this man has a perfectly proportioned one, which leads to sinfully thick thighs like tree trunks. This man has never missed a leg day in his life that's for sure. Urgh, why are the most mouth-watering men off-limits?

I enter Kai's bedroom and walk towards the bed, unsure of what he has planned for me. Kai closes the door and locks it, walking over to his dresser and placing the key there. He turns to survey me, crossing his arms over his chest, making his biceps bulge and the veins in his forearms swell. I hope I'm not drooling. Why are men's forearms so fucking sexy? *Shit, concentrate Valentina, he's the enemy.*

"Strip!"

One word, just one fucking word. Does he think I'm a dog that will sit and beg for him? No, fuck that.

"Who the fuck do you think you are? I'm not one of your whores at the club, Kai, I will be remaining dressed. Now tell me what you wish to discuss?"

"As I recall" he replies derisively. "You were all but begging me to make you my whore not too long ago. Maybe I do not wish to discuss anything at all. Perhaps we should start by refreshing your memory. Now, FUCKING STRIP. VALENTINA! Before I cut that fucking dress right off you. I will not ask you again."

Stupid treacherous pussy, why the hell are you fluttering like a hummingbird locked in a cage. Looks like I can't rely on my body to hide my reactions to this son of a bitch. Give my pussy a bit of dick and she becomes a cock whore. Fuck!

"Go screw yourself." I smile and cross my own arms over my chest. Not just to portray my fuck you stance but to also hide my hard-as-glass fucking nipples. I ache to rub my thighs together but that would just be an obvious signal to my aroused state.

Before I can even react, Kai races towards me. I didn't even notice him move but he's on me in seconds. *How can a man that big move so fucking fast?*

He grabs me and flings me over his shoulder and I begin kicking and screaming. He walks to the top of the bed and throws me down unceremoniously. I bounce a few times. My teeth smash together with the force of the fall, so much so that I'm lucky I didn't bite my tongue.

I give Kai a seething look and get ready to give a vicious onslaught of how much of a prick he is, but I'm stopped when he leans down to the side of the bed and presses something. There's a clinking noise and movement on the ceiling. I look up and to say I'm stunned at what I see is an understatement.

"What the fuck?" I whisper.

I watch in both horror and confusion as two holes open in the ceiling and two lengths of chains are lowered. I feel a thud on the bed and jump in shock. I look down and see four padded leather handcuffs thrown down beside me. I look at Kai with defiance and he graces me with a knowing smirk. Oh, hell to the no!

I try to leap off the bed only to be snagged around the waist by Kai's iron-gripped arm. I throw my head back, hoping I connect with his nose but hit his rock-hard chest instead. Jesus that hurts!

We scuffle, me trying to kick out or scratch the fuckers' eyes out. Kai doesn't try to attack. I notice that all he does is deflect my assaults until he successfully manages to restrain me on the bed with his immense weight. He's straddling my stomach and has also managed to pin both my arms above my head.

"Fucking let me go Kai, for God's sake you prick. I swear I'm going to kill you for this," I seethe.

"I'm going to castrate you and force feed your balls to Lev and make your stupid ass watch. Then I'm going to beat the shit out of you and see if I can't knock some of that fucking dumb right out of you and that thick skull of yours!"

I thrash my pelvis and legs trying to get out of his hold, but it doesn't fucking work. *Fuck. Think Valentina, think.* I try to think back to my classes with Vladimir, my Systema trainer. I try not to panic and then have a brain wave. I bring my legs up quickly, crossing my calves over each other and in front of Kai's neck. I have now effectively trapped his head in my legs so I can try a choke hold or maybe just snap his neck. Why does that last thought pains me so much? *Soft, Valentina, you're going soft. Focus!*

Squeezing my legs tighter I pull them down trying to choke him, Kai releases my arms and grabs at my legs, trying to get out of my choke hold. I reach up trying to claw at his face, to stop him from escaping my death grip. I manage to mark his face scratching him, but not before he manages to prise my legs apart with his powerful arms. I try to clamp my legs more, but he is far more powerful than I am. So instead I release my leg hold and quickly push forward, managing to head-butt him, hard, directly on his nose. Shit, that hurt!

Kai's nose is bleeding but not gushing as I'd hoped. His face is covered in scratch marks, making him look like he'd a fight with an alley cat. He wipes his nose with the back of his hand and looks down at the blood, then back at me with a smirk. Bastard!

"Valentina, Valentina, Valentina, all this foreplay is just getting me hard. Now be a good little girl and behave while I put my cuffs on you, or I'll just give the order to kill Luka immediately!"

"You may kill Luka but know this, you will gain your own damnation right along with it," I spit, through barred teeth. "I know you already see me as your enemy, but if you do that you will find out what being one of my enemies is like. I will hunt you down like vermin and I will not stop until I destroy you, sending your twisted black soul back to Hell. You will welcome hell when I'm done with you, I promise you that!"

Kai grabs me around the throat hard and lowers his face inches from mine. I do not cower or look away. I keep my eyes intently on his, keeping my breathing as steady as I can. If these men sense weakness they capitalise on it and bleed it dry.

I know Kai knows that Luka is my weakness but as for any other, he is yet to find out. He will soon realise I have none, although maybe that has changed, as Kai is fast becoming a weakness I can't afford to have, especially if my Papa finds out.

"If you are a good girl and behave, I will promise not to hurt your precious Luka. How's that for a promise? I think it's pretty generous on my part actually."

I sigh and contemplate his offer. Does he think I was born yesterday? These men think that if you are born with a vagina, it somehow makes you incapable of understanding their games.

"Okay, re-word your proposal and I will accept

your offer."

"Valentina, you are pushing your luck my Little Vixen!"

"Promise me Luka will not be harmed or killed by you or any of your men. He will also be allowed to guard me still."

"Fuck, Valentina, do you really think you are in a position to negotiate? Also, do you think Luka has done an excellent job at protecting you so far, hmm? He did, after all, allow you to fall into the Lion's den, quite literally."

"Those are my terms, take them or leave them, Kai!"

Kai tips his head back and laughs, and he looks so fucking beautiful. It's almost as though he's forgotten our predicament... almost. He locks those piercing ocean-blue eyes on me, and they are glittering with mischief and lust. I raise my brows in question. What the fuck is he up to now?

"Okay, my Little Vixen. Say I agree to your proposal, what is it you are offering me in return? Because what you have proposed is worth far more than I'm willing to agree to without anything in return."

I take a deep breath and really consider what I'm about to offer Kai. Can I do this? Am I brave enough to go through with it? Although, on the other hand, what options do I have? I lick my lips and take my last breath of freedom. I've fought this for what feels like a lifetime, but this seems to be the lesser of two evils. I just hope I'm making the right decision.

"Me Kai, you will get me! I will be yours to do whatever you wish to, for however long you want."

Kai's eyes flare with lust and shock. I don't think he predicted I would offer myself. I know he thought it was the last thing I would do. Shit, I've even surprised myself; that is the most stupid thing I could have done. But what is the saying 'Keep your friends close and your enemies closer,' well this is what I'm about to do. Let's see how these bastards fare with a viper in their nest.

"Accepted, my Little Vixen. In exchange for your friend Luka's life and safety, you will offer yourself to me. No holes barred, please mind the pun. What you don't realise is that by offering yourself to me completely you will now have one week to organise our wedding. Saturday will be our wedding day and you will become my wife and queen."

"What the actual fuck? I didn't agree to marriage Kai. Why the hell would you want to marry your enemy, as you so put it? Are you fucking crazy?"

"Far from it, my sweet little vixen. You want your

friend's life; I want yours in return. That is my proposal."

There must be something I'm missing, why would Kai want to marry me? He could have any number of women, why me? My Papa, of course. He wants to rub it in my Papa's face. The fact that he has me, the daughter of his worst enemy. For fucks sake, men are so fucking predictable.

A dick-swinging contest is the last thing I wish to be in the middle of, but what choice do I have? I have to save Luka. We'll figure a plan out before the wedding and escape.

"Okay, Kai you win, I accept your proposal."

Kai smiles down at me and squeezes my throat tighter, and he surprises me by kissing me with so much passion. The kiss goes on for what seems like a lifetime, and I can't help getting swept away in it. I kiss Kai back, giving him as much intensity as he's giving me, until he breaks the kiss and silently pulls back.

He grabs the discarded leather cuffs and attaches one to each of my wrists. Then he places the chains through the cuffs and padlocks them securely. I lie there unmoving just watching Kai as he threads the chains through the hooks attached to the headboard.

Oh, so that's what they're for.

When both of my wrists are secured, he leans

down and presses a button on the side of the bed. He keeps his finger on it and suddenly the chains are pulling my wrists up and pulling my arms to the point of discomfort. He releases the button when he is satisfied.

He does the same with my ankles, but instead of being attached to chains from the ceiling, he pulls my legs apart, so I'm now spread-eagled; then pulls chains from under the bed and attaches the cuffs to those. He tightens them as he did with my arms. I'm totally at his mercy and should be scared but I'm not, I'm aroused and horny as fuck.

Well, who knew?

Kai surveys the bindings and, when he's happy, he rakes his gaze over my body. I feel scorched by his intense perusal of me, and I'm still in my dress so he can't fully see all of my body.

Without making eye contact with me, Kai turns his back on me and goes to his dresser. He gets his key and goes to the door, opening it and leaving the room without a word. Fuck, is he just going to leave me here alone all day? My mind goes into overdrive with what is going to happen to me, and I go into panic mode pulling at my restraints to no avail.

I'm just about to start screaming bloody murder when Kai enters the room again, closing the door and locking it behind him. He puts the key in his dresser again and then comes to stand at the foot of the bed. He lifts his head and the look on his face is sinister, making me gulp.

Oh, fuck!

"Shall we play a little game, Valentina? I think you have introduced me to something I wish to explore and who better to explore it with than my wife-to-be? You have been up close and personal with my favourite toy before, but not as close as you're going to be in a moment. As you will find out, Valentina, I'm a sadist so if you don't like what I'm doing to you, well? I don't quite give a fuck."

I'm puzzled by what he's said and to be truthful, I'm unsure what he means by saying he's a sadist. I haven't got a clue and my brows draw together in a questioning look. Kai's smirk is ever-present as he reaches into his jogging bottoms and pulls something out. I gasp in shock, OH.MY.FUCKING.GOD!

Kai pulled out his flick knife.

Chapter 7

Kai

I have such a foreign feeling flooding through my body, I can't decide whether it's joy or excitement. I've managed to secure Valentina as my wife and Queen, a lot faster than I'd thought it would take me. I have still got a lot of things to iron out, my father's reaction to my decision being the main one.

This I will resolve tomorrow though, as now I have to teach my Little Vixen a lesson; one she will remember for a long time to come. I also need to get the information clear on her relationship with her Papa. All in good time though, as I intend to test my soon-to-be wife's limits and I plan on taking my time doing it.

Collecting my Grandfather's knife that my Little Vixen has seemingly taken a fancy to. I go and inform Lev that we will not be interrogating Luka, much to his dismay. He argued the point, much to my irritation, but finally stalked off in a foul mood. I asked him to watch over Luka until I finished with Valentina, before I walked back to my room.

I don't know why Lev is in such a sulk lately, but I've a feeling it has something to do with Sam. Another thing I'll have to resolve tomorrow as I need my second-in-command on top form, especially with the revelation of Valentina's parentage.

Now I stand at the foot of my bed admiring my handy work; Valentina looks glorious in my chains. I had them installed before I even moved in, ready for my use, but I wasn't lying to Valentina when I said that I have never brought another woman here.

I can't even remember the last time I actually spent time with another woman. Fucked, yes. Countless blow jobs, yes. But that was all a means to an end. Me coming and them leaving as soon as I could get rid of them, end of story. Valentina though has surprised me. She's intoxicating and demands my time and attention, while being the most beautiful woman I've ever seen. She has this aura that captivates me and that fire she exudes with every bite of that sharp as fuck tongue is glorious.

The beast that resides inside me craves death, destruction, and power. I have never been satisfied, always wanting more. Nothing has ever calmed me until Valentina.

I want to own her and devour her, yet I do not wish to destroy her. I want to keep that fire. I want her spirit to challenge me every day until it obliterates us both.

What a spectacular way to go.

She will make a magnificent Queen, but will she stand by my side wearing our crown, or will she stab me in the back and wear her own family's crown? I'm still undecided.

Valentina is currently pulling at her chains, panting with anger and desire. She knows she shouldn't be turned on by my chains and my knife, she still believes she is a good girl. Yet I can see her erect nipples trying to escape her dress, the flush of arousal in her face and knew if I felt between those luscious thighs of hers, she would be dripping wet.

Once I'm on the bed I prowl over her body, straddling her stomach but making sure not to put all my weight on her, as compared to me she's tiny. I flick out my knife and lock my eyes with her shimmering sky-blue eyes, as she trembles before me, exuding lust, passion and fury.

I move the blade to the top of her dress, not taking my eyes off her for a second. Her eyes fix on the blade, and she licks her lips absently, watching my next move with nervousness. We both watch, enthralled as my knife cuts through the front of her dress like butter and the tattered remnants pools onto the bed revealing her delectable body for my perusal.

Valentina's body still displays my bite marks and if I flipped her over, her arse would still bear my belt marks. My dick is aching with a need I have never felt; until my Little Vixen succumbs to me, luckily, I have room in my joggers to accommodate it.

I slowly glide my knife from her collarbone and carve a path through her heaving breasts. I'm careful not to break the skin, yet press just hard enough that my blade leaves a red mark as I go on my journey.

Valentina whimpers causing me to smile, I mean I really fucking smile. I can't remember the last time I truly smiled like this. My journey continues, guiding my blade down her stomach before pausing at my destination; her deliciously wet pussy.

"Valentina, I will explain the rules to you once and once only. If you do not do as I have instructed there will be punishments of my choosing. So, it's in your best interests to concentrate and be a good girl. Do you understand me?"

"Screw you, arsehole! You can't handle me loose, can you? You have to chain me up to get me to comply. Oh and you also know if I were free, I would scratch your fucking eyes out." Valentina is seething as she spits her venom at me.

Why does that filthy disobedient mouth of hers get me so fucking hard? It's as though I'm mentally begging her to disobey me, so I can use it for much better things. I tut at her, purposely blowing on her wet pussy, making her whimper and try to clench her thighs together.

"Only good girls get rewards, Valentina. You do want a reward, don't you?"

To insinuate my point, I glide my tongue from her arse to her clit lightly, teasing her with what she could have if she were good. But also, what I can take away in an instant.

"Answer me, Valentina, do you understand?"

"Yes!"

"Yes, what Valentina?"

"Yes, I understand, you prick!"

It's sudden and it's shocking; her reaction is priceless as I slap her pussy hard. The teasing causes her to scream and thrash around in her binds, gulping for breath in an intoxicating blend of pleasure and pain. It was in that moment that I could tell she was trying to figure out which of her reactions was winning the battle, so I slapped her pussy again with the same pressure. She throws her head back with a scream that turns into a guttural moan. Her pussy is glistening with her juices and is now so red and raw, that I have to hold myself back from just burying my face in there and devouring her.

"Answer me correctly, Valentina."

"I understand, Kai."

"Perfect. Good girl. Now, I will ask you a question and you will answer it straight away, and truthfully. You will then be rewarded accordingly. But if that sexy little mouth of yours spits venom at me once more, or if I think you are trying to deceive me, well I shall punish you as I see fit. Now believe me Valentina, you will not enjoy my punishments. Do you understand the rules?"

"Yes Kai, I understand."

"Good girl. The first question is, are you working with your Papa to deceive me?"

"I would rather die than work with that monster," Valentina spits with venom.

As with any other interrogation I do, I am always watching the suspect intensely, to gauge their reactions and look for any tell-tale signs they are lying. I have done thousands of interrogations and always get the answers I require, but I have never done one like this before.

She's telling the truth which isn't a surprise but it's reassuring to have the confirmation. Now, time for my Little Vixen's reward.

"Such a good girl! Time for your reward but one more rule, do not come."

"What the fuck does that me…"

I don't give her the chance to finish her sentence before I lower my face and start devouring her delicious pussy. Valentina pulls on her chains, groaning and arching her body as much as she can. I eat her pussy like a starved man, flicking her clit with my tongue at a maddening pace, and sucking it hard in my mouth.

"Oh my God! Fuck! Yes Kai, please… let me come. Oh yes."

Valentina's legs start to shake, and I know she's close, so I move my mouth from her pussy to the top of her inner thigh. I nibble at her thigh and suck on it, smiling because it looks like she will carry a lot more of my marks by the time we are through.

"Fuck Kai, why did you stop?"

"I told you Valentina, not to come. You will not come until or if I allow it. If you do come without my permission, you will incur my punishment. So shall we try again?"

Valentina nods as she pants and shoots me a venomous look, but she's learning as she keeps her delectable mouth shut. I know she's dying to verbally assault me, I can feel the tension emanating from her body. I, on the other hand, want her to slip up because even though she will not enjoy her punishment, I will.

"Second question. Who did your Papa sell you to?"

She flinches at this question as though I've slapped her. I can't blame her, it's an insensitive question, but I need to know who else I'm up against. She gasps and turns her head to the side, denying me eye contact. Valentina is trying to shut me out but I'm afraid that will not work with me... ever. And my Little Vixen needs to learn that, starting now.

I reach up cupping her jaw with my hand. I've only just realised how big my hands look compared to her petite frame. Gripping her jaw slightly tighter, I turn her head back toward me. Her eyes are glistening with unshed tears, but she refuses to release them.

"Tell me, my Queen. I need to know who your father sold you to." Absently I rub my thumb soothingly against her jaw, showing a compassionate touch I never thought I possessed. She closes her eyes briefly and leans into my comforting touch.

Only minutes pass in our blissfully stolen moment. In this time we are not enemies, not under the pressures and requirements of our families. We are both content to enjoy a peaceful respite we would very rarely get in the world we live in. Our moment is shattered though with her next whispered words.

"Isaak Volkov"

As if this mess couldn't get any worse, she had to name yet another one of our family's enemies. This one though hits me harder, as his Papa was responsible for the murder of my Mama. We killed his Papa in retaliation, hence how Isaak became head of his family.

My papa is going to be furious with my news tomorrow. Our world is about to blow up and we will need to be prepared for the war we are about to start.

"Good girl Valentina, you have done me proud. Now the last question I have for you. Are you ready baby?"

"Yes Kai."

"Okay. Who did your Papa take off you, that hurt you so much?"

"Kai, that's such an unfair question. Why do you want to know anyway? To use it against me?"

"No, never Valentina. I just want to know why you hate him so much. I want to know what he did to hurt you?"

"So, you think selling your own daughter isn't enough of a reason?"

"Of course I do Valentina, but I also know the person he took from you hurt you more. So, who was it?"

"He didn't just take the only person I ever loved from me, Kai. He took my world. He broke me when I refused to agree to be sold and to marry Isaak. My Mama defended me and started to argue with Papa. She slapped him when he called me an ungrateful worthless whore. Then Papa shot her in the head, right there in front of me. He told me it was my fault and if I didn't marry Isaak the same would happen to me."

Valentina

"Valentina, I'm so sorry this happened to you, but I promise you that I will never let him, or Isaak, hurt you again. You are safe with me. Nobody will be able to hurt you from now on."

If only that was true, I really want to believe Kai, but nobody can stop the inevitable from happening. When my Papa finds out where I am, he will come for me. Despite what Kai thinks, nobody will be able to stop him. Then he will make me pay for running from him with my life or my soul.

"Sorry Kai, but as soon as my Papa finds out that you have me, he will stop at nothing to get me back."

"Then let him try Valentina, because I vow to kill him myself for how much hurt he has caused my Queen!"

The only people in my life that have protected me are my Mama, Bear and Luka, so it's hard for me to trust people so easily. Kai also has me chained to his bed with a knife ready to do God knows what. Don't get me wrong, it's hot as fuck. I mean come on, who wouldn't want to be in my exact position right now. Kai is the epitome of a sex god and he's slowly getting me addicted. I've just got to remember to protect my heart in all this.

"If that's all your questions Kai, are you going to release me?"

"Never, my Little Vixen, I'll keep you chained here for as long as I want. You see, now we have the questions over and done with; we have unfinished business left that I wish to explore. So be a good girl and do not come until I give you permission."

Is he serious? I've just had to dredge the mess of my life up. Does he really think I'm in the mood for sex right now? I need to check on Luka and I'm in dire need of a cup of tea.

"Look, Kai, I'm not in the mood for this shit anymore. Unchain me, please."

"Valentina, if you open your mouth for anything

other than my cock again, I will force-feed you it, until you choke. Do not test me, you will not like my punishments. You have already been warned."

"Fuck you, Kai! If you think me meek you have made a grave error. I will not be some submissive body for you to use and discard. Now release me, please."

Kai doesn't answer me but gives me a smirk as though I've just fallen right into his trap. I can't help thinking maybe I have because I can't release myself from the chains he has me in. God, he's totally insane, what the hell have I gotten myself into now? I wonder as Kai gets off the bed and pushes his joggers off, kicking them to the side. He's totally naked now and my eyes ogle his body. He's magnificent and huge everywhere, with tattoos and muscle upon muscle. I may trick him one day and chain him to the bed so I can lick every inch of his body. Maybe pay back the torture I know he is going to inflict on me now. Is he really expecting me not to come when he's licking my pussy?

Hell no!

He prowls over my body with the grace of a leopard, a predatory look on his face. I'm in trouble, I can tell from the glint in his eyes.

Shit.

I try to kick my knee out to catch his balls on the

way up, but I can't move an inch. Fuck! I rattle at the chains, but I don't know what I think I'll achieve because they're padlocked.

Kai's face is directly in front of mine now, his ocean-blue eyes calculating my every move... not that I can make any. He licks his lips slowly and sensually, then lowers his head and bites my bottom lip hard. I try to hold back any reaction, but can't help letting out a pitiful whine when he bites even harder. Shit, now my pussy is getting ideas, the fucking floozy. I release an obscene amount of juices that coat my inner thighs, and it's totally fucking embarrassing.

He releases my lip and licks it a few times, how the fuck does he think licking it is going to help. I've probably got teeth marks on my lips, if not blood. He lifts his head slowly with his tongue still out and... is that my blood on his tongue? Fucker.

He licks his own lips and closes his eyes, moaning. He straightens up and now his cock is directly in front of my face. Absently I lick my lips, as I stare at the veins and the swollen head leaking a bit of pre-cum. I have to give him his due. He has a gorgeous cock.

I remember myself and look up to see Kai smirking at me, smarmy bastard. He reaches around and grabs a handful of my hair pulling my head back, then stares down at me as he caresses my lips with his thumb, all while his intense focus is on my mouth.

He pushes his thumb past my lips, and I suck it into my mouth. All of my protests have abandoned me, and my body seems to have decided for me; it wants what Kai is offering.

Fucking traitor.

He pulls his thumb out slowly, dragging my bottom lip down as he goes. He grabs his cock and slowly jerks off right in front of my face. I make the mistake of gasping at his action, and he force-feeds me his cock. I don't know how the hell he thinks it's going to fit in there, but I can't help licking it to see what he tastes like. Kai throws his head back and groans, looking absolutely glorious in his pleasure. A thrum of pride pulses through me that I've made him feel that way.

Kai looks back down at me and all the gentleness has fled, his eyes seem to have changed, and his pupils have dilated to nearly swallow all of the blue. He grips my hair tighter at the roots and reaches underneath himself to grab my throat. He squeezes tight and starts to fuck my mouth hard, slowly forcing himself further and further into my mouth.

I'm choking and start gagging when the head of his cock hits the back of my throat. All this causes Kai to do though is to grip my throat tighter and moan in ecstasy, pumping faster and deeper until he's down the back of my throat. I can feel my spit leaking down my chin and my eyes are watering with all the gagging. I grip the chains in a panicked state because now I'm finding it hard to breathe. I bite down on his cock, but this only makes him fuck my throat harder, throwing his head back and groaning. I give in to the feelings pulsing through my body. My nipples are hard, and my pussy is pulsating as though I'm going to come any second.

He fucks my mouth in a frenzied state. My body arches and I come just from sucking his cock. I've had no stimulation at all. What the fuck is wrong with me?

While I come down from my orgasm, Kai roars looking at me so intently I'm shocked. His mouth starts to gape slightly and then his cum is flooding my throat. It's thick and creamy but there is just too much. I try to swallow as much as I can, but I can feel it dripping down my chin.

"Fucking hell, Valentina, you are magnificent. Such a good girl for me."

Am I blushing? I think I am. Fuck.

Why is it so hot when he praises me? It makes me want to be a good girl for him all the time to receive praise constantly. Shit, what am I thinking? *Focus Valentina!*

Kai releases his hold on my hair and throat. He

trails his fingers in his cum and my spit that has dribbled down my chin and starts to rub it all into my chest and neck.

"What are you doing, Kai?"

"Marking you as mine, my sweet Little Vixen. All fucking mine!"

Well, alrighty then. I can't help but feel both delighted and scared about that statement. My emotions are all over the place and, until he releases me and I put some distance between us, they will not settle. It's the effect he has over me. He seems to enchant my senses and captivate my body; it's a feeling that is euphoric and unnerving at the same time.

Kai slowly moves back down my body, blowing on my overly sensitive skin as he goes. I swear he loves just teasing me.

I try to arch toward his mouth but to no avail. His head goes back to his starting position directly over my pussy and he continues blowing on my aching flesh. I swear if I could move my fucking legs, I would use them to lock his head down there and see how he likes to suffocate on my pussy.

Fair's fair, right?

"Kai, either eat my fucking pussy or stop the clit teasing and release me."

He chuckles at me and I'm just about to give

him another piece of my mind, but he stops me in my tracks when he starts sucking on my clit as though it's his favourite meal, before adding three of his massive fingers into my pussy and finger fucks me hard. I'm so overwhelmed, going from aching for his touch to a sensation overload. I swear, I'm going to come in two seconds flat as I can feel the orgasm cresting already.

I'm just about to tip over the edge when I feel a sharp slice on my right inner thigh. I gasp and look down, opening my eyes to see what happened. Kai starts sucking on the spot and pain radiates through my system.

"Oh, shit Kai, what the fuck happened?"

He doesn't answer but I feel his lips release my thigh, and his tongue probes the spot making it pulsate again. I watch him as he watches my reaction to what he's doing too.

I can see what he's done now. He's cut a shallow line on my inner thigh and the sight of him sucking my blood sends my body into overload. The pleasure and pain from the cut are so conflicting, but the sight of Kai licking and sucking my blood tips the balance to pleasure.

Kai continues teasing the cut and starts finger fucking me again.

"Yes! OH. FUCK. KAI. ARGH! Please let me come, oh God, I really need to come!"

The bastard just stops everything and looks up at me with a sinister smile, he has my blood dripping down his chin. He's so fucking hot but such a fucking tease at the same time. He gets on his knees, lifts my hips with one hand and positions his cock at my entrance. He reaches behind me and grabs a fist full of hair again, then slams his cock so hard into my pussy that I'm sure he's split me in half. I scream and he pistons his cock so fast and hard that the chains rattle and the bed slams against the wall.

He doesn't stop, he goes on for what feels like a lifetime, fucking me like an animal. A primal need has overtaken him and his body is dripping with sweat. I'm pushed over the edge into a spine-tingling orgasm, as my body shudders and pulsates. I scream and cry out and still, Kai keeps up his onslaught fucking me throughout, never stopping.

My mind is a muddled mess, and my body is so caught up in getting over the last orgasm I don't realise the next one is upon me until it hits, but this time when I orgasm, Kai presses his thumb into the wound he made on my thigh. When he does, I seem to go into a never-ending orgasm. My body shakes, my back arches pulling at my binds and I feel an awful lot of juices flood out of my pussy.

I would worry that I'd wet myself if I weren't so consumed with having about three orgasms in one and seeing dots in front of my eyes.

When I've finally started to come out of the mind-blowing orgasms, I start making sense of my surroundings again. Kai is still fucking me at the same speed, staring at me with an intensity I've never experienced in my life. He reaches down to the bed to retrieve the knife. This time when he lowers it, he makes a shallow cut along the underneath of my left breast. He lowers his head and sucks my breast into his mouth.

Kai moves both his hands and cups the underneath of my shoulders to carry on his onslaught on my body, using his grip to get more leverage to fuck me into oblivion. All while he is sucking and licking my breast.

He bites down, hard, on my breast and sends me careening into another orgasm. Fuck, I'm going to pass out at any second, I don't think I can take any more orgasms.

"Oh, please Kai, I can't come anymore, please, oh god, Kai!"

"Your body will cope, Valentina, you're being such a good girl for me, just hold in there, my Little Vixen. Just a little bit longer baby, yes baby, That's it, such a good girl!"

Kai makes a slice down the side of his throat and makes an identical one on the opposite side of my own. He lowers his neck to my mouth. He wants me to suck his blood while he sucks mine. It's so fucking erotic that my pussy starts pulsating on his cock that's still thrusting like mad inside me.

I place my lips over his throat where the cut is and start to suck, he groans so loud, and his thrusting goes out of sync as his movements stutter. He grabs my arse cheek with one hand and then grabs my hair with the other and starts to suck at the cut on my neck. We both groan in unison, and it seems to set off some primal need in our bodies. He's fucking me again, hard and fast, and I'm trying to fuck him back as much as I can move.

We're sucking each other's necks as though our lives depend on it, our bodies are covered in sweat and blood, mostly mine but I couldn't care less. This is another level of emotions and carnal need. I know I'm not experienced but this just seems euphoric, primal and erotic.

The room is full of the indecent noises of our fucking. Chains are rattling and the headboard is banging off the wall so hard I think the plaster is going to fall on us any minute now. The slapping noises of our bodies meeting in a frenzy and I'm ashamed to say a sloppy wet sound is coming from my pussy. Then there are our muffled groans into each other's necks. It's a scandalous symphony of animalist behaviour and I wouldn't change any of it.

I'm going into yet another mind-altering orgasm and I feel like my head is somewhere else floating in the air. I release Kai's neck and scream so loud I think I will lose my voice. My body is in a full body shudder and Kai is roaring out his own release.

His body is pulsating along with mine and we are both in a world of our own in our orgasmic bliss. Kai slams his mouth down on mine and gives me the most scandalous kiss. Fucking my mouth with his tongue and sucking my lips and tongue into his mouth.

When we both stop trembling and our orgasms slip away, Kai's weight falls on top of me. We're panting and are both beyond exhausted. We lie there, just trying to catch our breaths and recover our bodily functions.

This moment is for us; no thinking, no talking, nobody else, just me and Kai. It's a moment I want to remember for the rest of my life, but can it last?

Chapter 8

Kai

"Nikolai."

"Papa."

"To what do I owe the pleasure of a telephone conversation with my prodigal son?"

"I have something important to tell you and it warranted a call."

"Well then get on with it, time is money as you well know Nikolai. Also, I have some palms to grease as your dipshit of a brother has been up to his usual tricks."

"What has Dimitri done now?"

"Oh, just leaked a sex tape of him fucking the chief of police's wife online, which has now gone viral as you can imagine. So I've got your sister dealing with it and I'm greasing the palm of our friend the police commissioner. I tell you Nikolai, it's a good job we have him in our pockets. Anyway, what have you got to tell me as I have a meeting in an hour with him at the club?"

"I need you all here on Friday and to stay over the weekend, no exceptions!"

"Do you forget who you are talking to Nikolai? I do not take kindly to orders, especially from my own heir. Why do you need us all there anyway?"

"I'm to be married Papa, and I would like you all there. Is that too much to ask?"

"What the hell are you talking about Nikolai, you cannot get married. I haven't even started to look for possible alliance matches for you yet. This is unacceptable, you know this. You are my heir, you have to marry accordingly!"

"Enough Papa!" I growl down the phone.

"You will not disobey me on this Nikolai!" my Papa growls back.

"I will and I am. Now, this is going to happen with or without your presence, but I would love for you all to be there for me. On Friday you will all get to know my soon-to-be wife at a dinner I have planned for us all. Then we will marry on Saturday. I will send you all the details via email when they are confirmed. Can you please make sure Dimitri and Isadora are in attendance? And I need you to bring Mama's engagement ring with you."

"You know the protocols, Nikolai, I cannot let you do this. Who are you trying to marry anyway, some lap-dancing whore who has tempted you with her skills in blowjobs? Come on son, do not be fooled."

"I said enough Papa! I will not live by these antiquated rules. My job has always been about our future. A future that is free from all these stagnant beliefs and protocols as you put them. I will not be forced to marry someone full stop, and I hope that stands for Dimitri and Isadora too. We are the future of our family Papa, do not make us the enemy!"

"It is the way it has worked for centuries Nikolai, and it has worked well for a reason."

"For the benefit of men, father, not women; you were lucky that Mama loved you. I really need your approval on this Papa, we need to move forward and grow, not stay in the past. My future bride is a testament to that, and I wish the same for my siblings."

"Okay, I'm listening."

"I will be marrying Valentina Ivanov on Saturday, Papa!"

The phone line was silent for such a long time that I looked at my phone screen to make sure the call hadn't dropped. I knew this would be a shock to my Papa, so I let him have his time to process the fact that I was marrying the daughter of our enemy.

"Please tell me this is some sick joke of yours Nikolai! Besides, I thought she was missing anyway?"

"I am deadly serious Papa. I'm marrying her Saturday. It's a long story and I'll fully update you when you are here, but it's definitely Valentina."

"Maybe it's not a bad idea after all, we can use her to rub it in his face. That his daughter is your new whore and will be used and discarded accordingly. The more I think about your plan, the more ingenious it is. He will hate the fact you own his daughter; it will drive him to the point of madness."

I have to take a few deep breaths to control my anger at hearing my father talking about Valentina like that. The trouble is, it would have been my precise reaction to the situation before I actually met her. I would have used her as a whore and discarded her, maybe even sent her Papa footage of all the deprived things I did to her. But hearing him talk about my Little Vixen like that now makes me want to fucking strangle him. Valentina is mine and will always be.

"I will not have you talk about Valentina in that way Papa! There is no plan, and no ill-treatment of Valentina will be tolerated by you or any of the family. She is to be my wife and she will be the Mama of my children. Her Papa's sins will not be passed onto her. I actually think you will all get on with her swimmingly as she hates her Papa as much as we do. I will however take great pleasure in the fact that it will drive the old bastard to the point of madness that I am marrying his daughter."

"Have you checked everything out Nikolai, this is not some elaborate plan to double-cross you? I can get Isadora to check everything for you, scan her emails and phone conversations?"

"Do you take me for some kind of fool Papa? Do you not remember who has gotten information from people for you for years? You know there is nobody that can withstand my form of interrogation. After all, torture is an old friend of mine Papa. Wouldn't you agree?"

"I meant no ill will, Nikolai, I just wanted to make sure you have checked everything out. Some women have the gift of the sirens. They lure you in and before you know it, you're drowning. I just want you to be safe."

"Everything is under control Papa, I assure you. Just make sure everything is in order over there and I'll see you all on Friday. I'll forward you all the details and don't forget the ring. Stay safe and see you soon."

"Stay safe Nikolai, and we'll see you soon."

I sat in my office for a while just mulling over the conversation with my Papa. I'd had my own doubts about Valentina and Luka, but I thought that I had laid them to bed last night. Speaking to my Papa has brought them back to the forefront again, I pick up my phone and dial Isadora.

"Privet Nikki, please don't tell me you have been sticking your dick where you shouldn't too. I have enough to do covering Dimitri's ass, let alone having to see my other brat's dick on the same fucking day. He's a freaky fuck Nikki, I think I may need to wash my eyes out."

I laugh out loud which I think startles us both because I rarely do, and I quickly fire off a text to Lev to bring me Valentina's bag.

"Papa told me you were busy clearing up Dimitri's mess again, I think he needs to come and have some more training in much more suitable intel gathering strategy techniques. Married women are a volatile species and if his dick doesn't drop off, he may just get it chopped off by a possessive husband."

"Chance would be a fine thing, it would take a load off my heavy work schedule if it did drop off, ha. Anyway, why are you calling Papa, and what can I do for you?"

"Papa will inform you later about what I called him for but in the meantime, I need a favour. I need you to keep it discreet and only come back to me with your findings. Da?"

"You know me, Nikki, for the right price I can

get you any information you want, and my discretion is my honour as always. Who's the mark?"

I sigh and there's a knock on the door, "Da?" I call and Lev enters with Valentina's bag.

"Did you find a phone?" I say to Lev.

"Da, boss."

Lev rummages around in the bag again and hands me a battered phone with a cracked screen.

"Did you do this damage?" I ask Lev with irritation as the phone is fit only for the bin. I hear Isadora tapping at a hundred miles a minute as is her normal speed when she's on her laptop. She's mumbling about men and them being ignorant.

"Net, it was in that condition when I looked at it, Boss."

"Fuck" I say and signal Lev to leave, he nods and exits the room.

I swipe the phone and find that she doesn't even have a pin code or lock on the screen. Shit, my girl needs to be taught how to protect her belongings. I browse the phone and find her number. I jot it down to enter in my phone until I get a replacement for her.

"Her name is Valentina Ivanov, I've just messaged you, her number. I need you to do a full investigation. I need the answers in two days. Da?"

"What the fuck are you up to Nikki? Why do you want information on that slut for? Hasn't she done a disappearing act, run off with her bodyguard the last I heard? Probably fucked him and stuck a knife in his back the crazy bitch."

"Just get me the information I need Isadora, the quicker the better. What is your price?"

"Well, for information on that crazy bitch the price has just gone up tenfold. I need a backup rig and I have my eye on several pairs of Docs. Considering you are in England and these are one-off pieces, you can obtain them for me. I'll send you the information over and one mil should be enough to cover the rig I will need."

"Done, I'll transfer the money now. Oh, and remember discretion, Isadora."

"Da, Nikki."

She cuts the call and I slump back in my chair. I have the craziest feeling getting Isadora involved is going to come back and bite me in the arse. However, it's a risk I am willing to take as I need to be sure every base is covered. My Little Vixen needs to be safe, but I also have my family coming and I'm not willing to take any risks with their safety.

Sighing, I place Valentina's phone back in her

bag and put it in my bottom drawer. I retrieve a burner phone and put it in my pocket. I get up and leave the room, ready to find my Little Vixen. She has planning to do and a tight schedule to keep.

Valentina

Waking up for the second time and finding Kai absent from the bed is annoying. Is he some early fucking bird or just an insomniac who doesn't sleep, who the fuck knows?

I roll out of bed and grab some clean clothes out of the drawers. I attempt to roll up the joggers and pull the drawstring on them tying it around my waist and they're still nearly falling off. I give up and kick them off just leaving his t-shirt on. Which fits me like a dress anyway. I finger comb my hair, brush my teeth with my finger again, then leave the room in search of some much-needed tea.

I walk into the main room to find Luka sitting at the dining table nursing a coffee. I run over to him and chuck myself at him, catching him off guard and nearly spilling his coffee on the table. I hug him so tightly I'm not sure whether he can breathe or not. He laughs and hugs me back with the same intensity.

"I'm so glad you're okay Luka, I hate the price you always have to pay in being my friend. It isn't fair but I don't know what I would do without you. I love you; you know that don't you?"

"I do Lena and I love you too. I'm fine, just worried about you, did he hurt you at all?"

Luka pulls back and takes my face in his hands studying it before his eyes trace my frame to check for any injuries. I know he can see the marks on my wrists from the chain cuffs and the bite marks and knife wound on my neck. His expression turns stony, and I can feel the anger building in him.

"It's okay Luka, nothing happened that I didn't consent to. I promise I would tell you if it did. Kai didn't harm me in any way."

"She's telling the truth; now get you're fucking hands off my soon-to-be wife! If I see you touch her again, I'll cut them fucking off."

I scramble up off Luka's lap and his hands fall away. Luka looks at me with so much hurt in his expression it kills me.

"What have you done, Lena?"

I go to answer him, God knows what I'm going to say to him, but it doesn't matter because Kai gets there before me.

"Valentina has agreed to be my wife and you are

to be her guard when you can be trusted with her safety. Until then you will always be monitored by my team, any signs of betrayal of trust from either of you will result in punishments. Do I make myself clear?"

"Da" Luka responds stoically.

"Fucking crystal" I spit at Kai, giving him my best 'fuck you' face. He may have gotten my agreement to marry him in exchange for my friend's safety, but it doesn't mean I will be a docile woman.

Kai goes into one of his pockets and pulls out a phone, which he slides across the table to me. I put my hand out to stop it from sliding off the table, and look down at the latest iPhone in disgust.

"What the fuck is this?"

"What does it look like my Little Vixen, it's your new phone and you will always keep it on you. If you are not in mine or Lev's presence, I want hourly updates on what you are doing. You can either text or phone, our numbers are already programmed in as those are all the numbers you will need. Now, I have dress fitters, caterers, and the best wedding planners available coming in two hours. Make yourself presentable and I'll have Lev order breakfast for an hour's time. You'll find an outfit for you in our walk-in wardrobe."

"I don't need a new phone, I have a perfectly good one of my own thank you, that also has all the numbers I need. Also, can't you just get one of your many women to sort the wedding out as I'm going to go back to sleep for a few hours before I'm due at work tonight? Thanks for the offer though."

I get up, blowing Luka a kiss to which he just smirks and start to make my way around the table to exit the room again, leaving the phone on the table. Before I get a chance to walk away from the table Kai grabs my arm and spins me around. He grabs the back of my neck and pins my head on the table, pinning my arms at my back at the same time.

"What the fuck? Let her go!" Luka roars and goes to get up and come to my rescue. Then I hear a thud and see a knife sticking out of the table right by Luka's hand. Luka freezes with a pained expression, and I look to see Lev at the doorway to the kitchen.

"Sit the fuck down Luka because I'll make sure the next one doesn't miss." Lev spits.

I know Luka though; he won't worry about his own safety when it comes to mine. I need to defuse the situation quickly because they will always use my friend against me.

"It's okay Luka, I promise. Sit down, please."

Luka grits his teeth angrily, but does as I ask and

sits back down. Lev comes over to the table and retrieves his knife, tossing it up in the air and catching it with skill before putting it back in its sheath. He retreats to lean against the wall, crossing his arms against his chest and smirking at me. Fucker!

Kai leans over me. He uses the hand he was pinning my neck down with to grab a handful of hair instead. He runs his nose up and down my neck. I try not to shiver at the contact, but my body seems to have a mind of its own where Kai is concerned and betrays me. How can I hate him so vehemently, when my body seems to crave him like crack? I suppose that's the art of addiction. It buries itself so deep you have no choice but to submit, or cut it out and lose part of yourself in the process.

"Did you think I was giving you an option on what you were doing today, my Little Vixen? Now, you will do as I've asked and take your new phone with you. I expect to see you dressed and back here ready for breakfast in an hour. Do not test me on this Valentina, or you will not like the punishment you get in front of your friend. Da?" Kai whispers in my ear.

"Yes Kai, I understand." I grit out staring at Lev still because I can't look Luka in the eye. I can see in my peripheral vision though that he's looking towards the elevator with his jaw gritted and his hands balled into fists straining with how tightly he's squeezing them.

"Good girl," Kai whispers, placing a gentle kiss just below my ear. Then he releases his hold on me, sits back down and starts to read the morning paper as though none of that shit even happened. I straighten myself up and grab the phone off the table, before I march toward Kai's bedroom seething. I hear Kai instruct Lev to give Luka a phone and to tell him what the security measures are regarding my care.

By the time I get to Kai's room, my anger needs an outlet, so I open the doors roughly and make sure to slam them behind me. I hate when men, especially in families like ours, treat women as though they are weak. That we need looking after and are unable to do anything but look pretty and suck their cocks. After a while, they even get bored of that and visit their whores instead.

I really feel like throwing a big paddy, screaming and shouting. Maybe throw a few things around the room, but I doubt it will do anything but make me angrier.

Instead I opt to strip off, just dumping his t-shirt on the floor and stepping into the shower. I turn the water on and feel it go warm with my hand before stepping under the spray. I stand there for about ten minutes feeling so overwhelmed by my situation that I fall to the floor and let the tears flow. I silently purge my emotions, building them up and using them as ever-present walls around my heart and soul. I don't see crying as a weakness as long as you don't do it in front of people who will use it against you. They find the things that you hold dear or freedoms you want, and they obliterate them, standing in the wake smiling. So cry, but only show your tears to the worthy as they are the only ones who are capable of protecting a broken heart and shattered soul.

As I feel time slipping from my grasp I stand, washing my body and hair on autopilot. Getting out of the shower, I walk over to the double sinks to brush my hair, thinking about all the shit Kai is going to get me to do and cringe.

What the fuck does he think I know about weddings anyway? I despise weddings. In our world all they are is a show of power or money or, in most cases, showing off your newly bought possession. The woman you will defile, torture and discard when she is of no use and a young new addition comes along.

I rinse my mouth out and brush my hair, then go into the bedroom. I get changed into the clothes that have been left out for me. An emerald green, wrap-around, knee-length dress and shoes to match. At least I have underwear on, a matching white lace bra and knickers.

Taking a deep breath, I leave the room and walk

straight over to the table with my head held high. Kai stands and pulls out the seat next to him at the head of the table. So, I end up seated on the left of him and Lev is sitting opposite me on his right-hand side. Luka is seated next to Lev looking over some paperwork and files he must have been given in my absence.

Luka looks up at me and gives me a smile that doesn't reach his eyes. He knows we must tread carefully until they trust us and then maybe we can escape, disappearing forever. We need to be clever though as I know we will only get one chance and if it fails, I have no doubt Luka will pay with his life.

A flurry of staff arrives bringing in breakfast and drinks for us all. There's full English breakfast options, to a full continental breakfast spread, and even fresh exotic fruit salads. They also offer a variety of drinks to us too; tea, coffee, and orange juice to name a few. I'm not that hungry so I just accept tea from the staff when they ask and sit drinking it silently.

Kai doesn't seem happy with this and picks up my plate adding bacon, scrambled eggs, and tomatoes to it, before placing it in front of me. Everybody else then helps themselves, Luka and Lev eat as though they have never been fed before, inhaling the food rather than eating it, whereas Kai eats with the finesse and control he has at all times.

"Eat, Valentina. We have a long day ahead of us today, all the plans must be finalised today so everything can be organised in time. You will need your energy."

"I have to be at work by five for rehearsals, and Luka has to be at work soon too. We can't just not turn up Kai, we have rent and bills to pay."

"Luka has quit his job and is now working for me. He read his contract and signed it while you were getting ready. As for the flat, we have paid off any debts and are emptying it as we speak. All your personal possessions will be brought to you both by my men, Luka explained the flat was furnished so everything is sorted already."

"What the fuck! Why was I not consulted on any of this?" I shout.

I slam my cutlery down and stare straight at Luka. What the fuck is he thinking, how could he do this behind my back? Give up our home and quit his job to start working for Kai. He stares at me but doesn't say anything.

"Luka knows a good thing when he sees it Valentina, he is going to be very well-paid and has the knowledge that you will be safe. He knows this is the best option for the safety of you both."

"What about my job, I'm still due there and if I'm not mistaken, I already work for you so you can't give me another contract!"

"You are to be my wife, Valentina. You no longer work for me. Sam has been informed of the change by Lev and has changed the sets to compensate."

"What the fuck!" I scream. "You have no right to stop me from dancing. If I wish to dance, that is my right, not yours. I also want to earn my own money. I will not be a kept woman until you tire of me. How dare you take my freedom from me!" I roar.

"NO WIFE OF MINE WILL DANCE FOR ANYBODY ELSE BUT ME. DO YOU FUCKING UNDERSTAND ME, VALENTINA!" Kai growls back at me.

"Argh!" I scream at the top of my lungs and pick up my tea and throw it at the wall. I start picking up random things and chuck them too. Nobody has the right to take my freedom from me. I'm dancing not stripping, for fuck's sake. Even if I were, he met me while I was doing that so what gives him the idea I'd ever give it up.

Kai grabs me, twists me around and throws me over his shoulder. I'm kicking and screaming trying to land a hit on him that hurts. He ignores me and just spanks my arse hard as he continues to walk toward his room.

"I will not give up my dancing for you, you overgrown neanderthal. You have no right at all to quit my job for me. I'll fucking cut your bollocks off in your sleep for this Kai. I swear, you fucking arsehole!"

Kai just sniggers and gets to his room, closing the doors behind him. If he thinks he's chaining me up again he can fuck right off!

Chapter 9

Valentina

I sit with my legs tucked underneath me, sulking like a five-year-old who's been told she can't have a pony. My reason for sulking though is a red raw arse, after Kai has yet again punished me with his fucking belt. The arsehole has also told me I can no longer dance at his club. If the fucker thinks he can stop me dancing, he has another thing coming.

He is currently sitting next to me on his phone, talking or messaging people, while a six-women team is fussing around us trying to show us a selection of wedding attire. I couldn't give a fuck if I wear a bin bag, to be honest, and am currently ignoring everyone.

That is until two of the women are whispering away in the corner. So far they have taken every opportunity to flash their tits at Kai. Now, one pushes her luck a bit too far. She runs her hand up Kai's arm and rests it on his shoulder, trying to whisper something seductively in his ear, and I've had enough. I reach over Kai and grab the hand she has on his shoulder, bending it back to the point of snapping. She squeals in agony and the room goes silent instantly, but I couldn't give a fuck. Kai ends his call abruptly and stares at me.

"Do you normally flirt with all the grooms? Try and flash your fake tits at them in hopes of a quicky in the bathroom. Well, you picked the wrong groom today bitch. For disrespecting me I should snap your scrawny fucking neck but instead, I'll give you ten seconds to get your arse out of here. Tick Tock bitch."

I release her hand.

"I wasn't…"

I slap her so hard around the face it echoes through the room and she staggers back, holding her face. Luka sniggers and Lev's mouth is agape. I still haven't looked at Kai's reaction, I couldn't care less. It was me she was disrespecting.

"Ten, nine…"

She runs out of the penthouse crying, still holding her cheek. I turn to the other prick tease with a malevolent grin on my face, and she cowers.

"Bitch I suggest you leave too, before I make you."

She bolts out of the door after her friend. I sit back down positioning my sore arse gently on the seat. I look to the remaining team and smile demurely as though I have not just slapped their colleague.

"You may continue if it will hurry things along a bit. I want a simple gown, with a small trail in ivory. Mr Filippov will have a blue suit, white shirt and brown shoes; whilst you're at it, make matching suits for Luka and Lev. We will also forward you the details for his father and brother. Have two pale blue bridesmaid dresses selected, one in a size twelve for Sam and we will also forward the size for Kai's sister. They will come for a fitting Friday afternoon, make sure any alterations to the dresses or suits are completed by the night and the suits sent to our apartment. Chop chop ladies."

I sit back with a smile on my face when they scurry around trying to get what I've asked for. I get up to go and grab myself a drink and Kai grasps my wrist, pulling me onto his lap in the process.

"Where are you going my Little Vixen?"

"I was just going to get a drink."

"Lev, can you organise some drinks for me and Valentina? Also, call Misha while you're there and tell him I want him and Pasha here in an hour."

"Of course, boss."

Lev leaves the room smirking, while Luka smiles at me and sends me a wink. I hide my smile and try to remove myself from Kai's lap. He doesn't seem to like that though, and tightens his grip on my waist. I sigh and try to make myself a bit more comfortable on his lap. I also try to ignore his raging erection that is currently digging into my very sore arse.

"Miss Ivanov, could we get you to try this dress on behind the screen please." The dressmaker asks.

I get up from Kai's lap and this time there is no argument from him; he releases me with a hard slap on my arse. I look back at him with an icy glare and he has the audacity to smirk at me. I sigh heavily and retreat behind the screen, to see what dress they have chosen for my fake wedding. What a waste of money and time when we could have just hired an official to come here to marry us.

When I look at the dress hanging in front of me, I gasp and put my hand over my mouth too late. Everyone has heard me and Kai is instantly on alert.

"What's the matter, Valentina?"

"Um, nothing. I just stubbed my toe."

Fuck! Why the hell did I say that? Jesus, how

stupid did I sound? Kai doesn't say anything else, so I assume I've gotten away with it, and go back to my perusal of the breathtaking dress hanging in front of me.

The dress is an ivory silk gown that will cling to my every curve. It's embroidered with an intricate lace bodice that will keep my girls up and in nicely, which stops just above my waist but continues around the hem of the trail. It's the most beautiful dress I've ever seen, so wasted for this sham of a wedding but I might as well go to the lion's den dressed in style.

I get undressed and shimmy myself into the dress, but the bodice ties with ribbons at the back. I have to regretfully call for assistance to help me fasten and tighten the dress. After feeling like I'm going to pass out several times or rip the poor dress maker's hair out, I'm finally securely in the dress.

I'm then left alone to stare at my reflection. The dress is spectacular. I look just how I dreamt I'd look on my wedding day. My eyes fill with unshed tears for a future lost and a child's fantasy shattered beyond repair. I get caught up in my perusal and mourning when Kai calls for me.

"My Little Vixen, are you going to come out and show me the dress?"

I take a deep breath to settle my emotions and

take one last look in the mirror. There is no way I'm not going to be able to show Kai the dress, but I'm really scared of his reaction. It scares me that he will not like me in the dress and shatter my heart completely. The thing that scares me the most is how much I really care about his reactions to me.

I have unhealthy emotions regarding Kai; I want his desire, his care, his devotion and above all his love. I want him to look at me as though I'm the only woman in the world. I want him to need me more than the air he breathes. I need him to give me the love I lost and never thought I would be lucky enough to get back when I lost my Mama.

But I'm not a child anymore, and after living in our world nearly all of my life I know better than to dream the impossible. Mafia men do not love, it's a sign of weakness to them. They see women as commodities or possessions, to use and abuse until they have had their fill. They either pass their unwanted present onto some other sadistic fucker or just dispose of the rubbish. After, they get another new shiny plaything and rinse and repeat. They are not loyal to their wives either, as they have several mistresses or fuck toys.

Now, do I expect Kai to be any different? Hell no, so these stupid feelings I have for him have to stop. I can't let him have any power over me at all, and to give Kai my heart would be one of the biggest mistakes of my life. It's time to show these bigoted Mafia men how dangerous a Queen can be once she has been crowned. Believe me I'll burn their worlds down to the ground and stand laughing in the ashes of their kingdoms.

I step out from behind the screen where the makeshift changing room is situated as a huge man enters the room. I stop, frozen in place, locked in a memory long forgotten in my past.

I was running through the woods near our estate chasing butterflies. I thought I was a lost fairy princess back then, if only life was still so simple. No fairy prince would ever come to save me though. I was destined for a gilded gold cage for all eternity, that was until I ran into the chest of a giant of a boy. The force of the collision made me fall back and land flat on my arse.

I cry out in pain and go silent in shock as I look at the boy in front of me. I know I'm small as I'm only eight, but this boy must be at least 6ft. He is bigger than most of my Papa's guards, with muscles I've never seen on a boy before. He's also scowling at me as though he's annoyed with my presence.

"Who are you?" I ask, unable to hide the trepidation in my voice.

"Why do you want to know, going to tell your Papa on me? Um?" He growls angrily at me. His voice is so deep and gravely I wonder to myself as to whether I hit my head in my fall, and if this is all a dream. I pinch myself to test the theory, but no. It's real.

"Why would I tell my Papa about you? Why are you here?"

"It's none of your business why I'm here, go back to your entitled existence Princess."

I watch him walk back from where he was coming from, confused by what he's said. I'm not a Princess, far from it, and why would I tell my Papa about him? My Papa is cruel to my Mama, especially if she disturbs him in his office. No, I stay clear of him at all costs. I'm still pondering his words as he disappears further into the woods, and I get angry because how dare he speak to me like that.

I get up and march after him ready to give him a piece of my mind, not worried in the slightest for my safety. I'm marching deeper into the woods for about 10 minutes when I stop, stunned by the sight I see before me.

The boy is grappling with a deer. He seems to have it in a choke hold, trying to suffocate it to death. I think about going over to stop him, to rescue the deer somehow, but for some reason, I decided to hide behind a tree instead. The deer stops moving. I don't think I will ever get the noises it made whilst struggling to survive out of my head. The boy loosens his hold and bows his head; I'm sure I heard a quiet sob escape from him. He runs his hand over the deer and stands up, quietly composing himself.

I'm unsure why I do what I do next. Thinking back now it was rather stupid of me, an eight-year-old girl, but I did it anyway. I step out of my hiding place and slowly walk toward them. The woodland floor is not a quiet place, so as I'm walking toward him a twig snaps under my feet. The boy whips around, staring at me like a predator on alert.

"What the hell are you doing here, have you followed me? I knew you were going to be trouble, haven't you got any sense in that little head of yours? I guess not when you follow strangers into the woods, You're lucky it's just me, little girl," the boy growls at me.

"I was following you to give you a piece of my mind, you big...Bear you. I don't appreciate the way you spoke to me back there, what gives you the right to judge me. I'm not a princess actually, far from it, and I would not tell my Papa about you because that would also get me into trouble for being here in the first place."

"You're telling me that your own Papa doesn't even know where his precious princess is? Being the man he is, I very much doubt it, Red."

"What do you mean? The man he is?"

"Do you not know Red? That your Papa is the Bratva boss in this area, that in turn makes you a Bratva princess, Red. A Kingdom built on blood and bones, but a Kingdom nonetheless. So, I very much doubt your Papa doesn't know where you are Red."

"I... So, my Papa kills people too?"

"Yes Red. Sorry but your Papa is an awfully bad man. Now, I need to go before they come in search of you and catch me with a deer from your estate. I'll be dead if they do."

"They would kill you for killing a deer. Why do you need it anyway?"

"To sell to the butcher in town so I have money to live and eat."

"What about your family?"

"I have none... Red I am homeless, born to a prostitute who is long dead so I escaped before they could sell me to the clients. Some of the other prostitutes helped me."

"Oh... I'm sorry... It must be really hard to live on the streets."

"I get by doing things like this and the money also helps me pay for some of my fights too."

"What fights?"

"Cage fighting Red, I earn enough to keep me going. Now, I have to get going."

"Will I see you again?"

"Why would you want to see me?"

"I've never had a friend."

"I don't think your Papa would approve of me, Red."

"I don't care what he thinks, I would like to be friends with you Bear."

"My name isn't Bear."

"My name isn't Red either so I'm calling you Bear and that's that."

"Okay Red, I'll see you Friday. Come to the woods at the same time and I'll find you."

"Okay Bear, see you Friday."

"Yeah, Friday Red."

Bear reaches down and hauls the deer onto his back. He strolls off into the woods, not looking back once.

I snap out of my memory and run into Bear's arms, squeezing him so tight he starts chuckling at me. I can't believe he's safe, when he didn't turn up after a close encounter with my Papa's men. The last time we had met, about three years after our first encounter, I was sure they had caught him. Maybe even killed him, because Bear wouldn't leave me like that.

"Bear, I'm so glad you're alive." I sob into his huge chest, while he runs his huge hand gently over my hair.

"Red, you don't know how glad I am to see you again. I had to flee after the last time we met but I never forgot my promise. I came back for you, but you had vanished, people were saying you were missing but I thought he had actually killed you. I was heartbroken and blamed myself for not coming back sooner."

He squeezes me really tight, and I let out a squeal

because it's too tight.

"Sorry Red, still don't know my own strength," he says, releasing me and chuckling down at me.

"I thought he had caught and killed you, my god, I sobbed for days."

"What the fuck is going on here? Misha take your goddamn hands off my future wife."

Bear and I pull away from each other and I look over to Kai. He looks like he's going to kill Bear and I can't have that. I pat Bear on the chest and saunter over to Kai. I run my hands down his chest and I can feel the anger radiating from him like a geyser about to explode. I go onto my tip toes and Kai responds by leaning his head down to my height.

"Do you not like the dress, Kai? I was hoping you would. I love it but maybe it doesn't look as good on me as I thought. You see, I pictured you untying my corset and the dress falling to a puddle on the floor. Of course I wouldn't have any underwear on, so I would be naked, ready for your sadistic desires."

I lower myself to the ground and go to turn and walk away, but Kai is quicker grabbing me in a tight grip around my neck. He positions my head so I'm looking directly at him then smiles sadistically at me.

"I want to rip that fucking dress right off you

my Little Vixen, you have no idea how utterly beautiful you are. You look so fucking sexy I want to gouge every man's eyes out in this room for seeing you in this dress. You are mine do you fucking understand, FUCKING MINE!"

I have no clue why his violent words turn me on, but they do. This is Kai's form of desire and I wanted that, didn't I? I slam my lips to his in a wanton show of lust. I want him to want me, but I know he will never love me. I suppose until I find a way out, I will have to put up with that knowledge. Kai deepens the kiss as he usually does by fucking my mouth with his tongue. Damn, this man knows how to kiss. Kai breaks the kiss and I whimper in protest.

"Go and get changed, my Little Vixen. This is the dress, I do not need to see any more. Misha, you and Pasha go to my office now and wait for me there. Lev go with them and Luka, you see our guests out, all the others will come for their fittings and alterations Friday."

"There are some alterations I need to make to Miss Ivanov's gown so I can get everything ready for Friday. I also need to take the measurements for all of the men here, Mr Filippov."

"I'll give you ten minutes to get everything you need, start with me and the men first, then you can do Valentina's alterations under Luka's supervision. Luka, I trust you to keep my woman safe and to make sure everyone is gone."

Kai

All the women start scurrying around taking all our measurements as quickly as they can. I ordered Lev's and my measurements to be taken first because I need to find out what connection Misha has to Valentina. It's driving me insane. I can feel anger building to the point I may just kill everyone in the room any second now.

Finally, with our measurements done, I leave Valentina in Luka's care. This is the first test I will be giving him, as I have security cameras in my office so I will see if he tries to aid her escape.

I open the door and take a seat behind my desk, glaring at Misha sat in the seat opposite me with Pasha seated beside him. Lev leans up against the wall, lighting up a cigarette and taking a deep drag.

I open my drawer and take out my own cigarettes, lighting one and relishing the hit of nicotine which calms me slightly.

"Lev, sort us some drinks, will you? I fucking need one after all that shit, I thought at one point they would measure my cock. For fucks sake, I have suits tailor-fitted all the time, they don't do that shit."

"I'm only glad Valentina didn't witness them measuring you, I think she may have just kicked their arses and then cut your bollocks off for good measure. She's a proper hellion, that one, I know first-hand. My bollocks are still sore from my first encounter with her," Lev winces.

"Shit, my woman is hot when she is angry. I've always wanted women to do as I tell them, then fuck them off but Valentina... she's addictive."

"Are you just using Valentina to get one over on her Papa or do you really love her and want her as your wife?" Misha asked.

"What the fuck has it got to do with you if I'm using her or not? I suggest you keep your fucking mouth shut where my woman is concerned. How do you know her anyway?"

"It's got everything to do with me Kai, I respect you and appreciate you, you are the boss. But I'm not going to let Valentina get hurt, she's like a little sister to me, so having one yourself you should know how I feel. I failed her once before and I've never forgiven myself for that, she's the only family I have. Nobody is going to hurt her as her Papa and his men did, I'll fucking fight to the death for her!"

Misha was out of breath and the aggression radiating from him was immense. I'd never seen Misha show his emotions, he has always been an emotionless killing machine. An excellent negotiator and torture expert, hence why at his age he was my third. And, his size scared most people instantly.

He said Valentina was like a sister, which calmed me slightly as he had no interest in her sexually. Good fucking job because that would have been one hell of a fight with him. Bear, as Valentina called him, is a very suitable name for him.

"She is to be my wife and I do not intend to hurt a single hair on her head. You have my promise on that, Luka is her bodyguard now. Though if you want, I can also put you on her protection unless I need to pull you off for something else. On the wedding day though you will be protecting Valentina alongside Luka until she arrives at the church."

"I will protect her with my life Boss, you have my word."

"Good that's settled, now tell me what happened with my shipments. Who needs killing and when am I getting them back?"

"Well, I don't think you'll be happy with the answer boss, especially considering who he is."

"Just fucking tell me, Misha."

"Isaak Volkov boss. He ambushed the ship on the way here. They killed all the men on board about twenty miles out. Luckily, our contacts had found the ship and contacted the clean-up team, and everything has been taken care of," Misha reports.

"We have notified all the families and given your regards. I offered them the usual compensation and lifetime protection of the Filippov family," Pasha begins to report before pausing, "maybe we could make that into a catchy logo... we kill em you compensate 'em." Catching my unimpressed look he mumbles, "Tough crowd" before he continues. "I have the tech team running through the traffic cameras and CCTV footage to track the shipments or vehicles involved," Pasha reports.

"I want him found and I want him alive, I think this is going to be a family torture session and killing all rolled into one. Put the usual contract out and set the price at five million pounds, that should be a tasty prize. I'll contact my Papa tonight after the club and meeting with Polish. I need you both there as with the mood I'm in, they will not fare well if they do not agree to our terms."

"Da Boss," all of them say in unison.

"Good, now Misha, Pasha, go to the club and make sure everything is ready for our arrival. Lev, you go downstairs and sort the men out for our departure. I'll be taking Valentina and Luka tonight, so I want everything to go smoothly. Valentina is annoyed enough that I'll not let her dance anymore, so I want her watched closely. Understood?"

"Da Boss," all of them reply.

"Brilliant, now I have a woman to sort out, so fuck off."

They all leave my office laughing at me, I don't blame them as I value my balls where they are. Valentina has an attraction to rearranging balls on men.

Seeing her in her wedding dress is enough incentive for me to leave my office and go in search of my Little Vixen though. She looked sensational in her dress, a true goddess here on earth. Never mind the wedding night, I will be fucking her in the dress on the way to the reception. She will spend all of our reception talking to our guests with my cum dripping from her pussy. Everyone will know who owns her. Me, Nikolai Filippov! God help any man who tries to touch what belongs to me.

Chapter 10

Valentina

I'm standing in the V.I.P. area of The Siren's Call, watching the other girls do their burlesque routines. I'm so envious of them, I belong on that stage, and I worked hard to earn my spot.

My favourite dances are 'Seven Nation Army' (the New Orleans version of the song,) it's a slow sultry group dance. Then 'Tough Lover' by Christina Aguilera, another group routine. 'Fever' by Peggy Lee is the epitome of sex, and our routine is phenomenal.

Kai is discussing the coordination of his meeting with Lev, Misha and Pasha. It looks like Misha will be sitting in on the meeting, Lev and Pasha being the guard dog's on the door and Luka will be babysitting me at the bar. Fuck my life.

I'm currently ignoring them all because it's either that or I may just chop off all their bollocks in a tantrum of epic proportions. Maybe that's the right way to go though, as it might get my anger out and release it with violence instead of dancing. I wonder whether Kai would consider employing me as an assassin instead of a dancer.

"Little Vixen, it is time for you to go now, I'll message Luka when it's time for you to be brought back to me. Behave yourself or you know how you will spend the rest of the night. Your delectable arse sore and no release will be granted."

"Fuck you arsehole, I'd rather spend the night listening to Lev's tantalising conversation than go anywhere near you."

With that, I turn around and walk toward the door, followed closely by Luka. I can hear Misha and Pasha laugh as I leave, while Kai and Lev are mumbling under their breaths.

I go to the bar and Luka orders us a drink, my usual Bacardi and Coke. Luka just has a Coke.

"Why are you not drinking Luka? Has the big boss told you that you're not allowed?"

"I wouldn't drink anyway protecting you Lena, you know that. You need to stop sulking and understand all this is to protect you. I had to take Kai's offer when you told him who we were. I will not have anything happen to you Lena. You are like my little sister and with Kai knowing, I had to make sure he was involved in protecting you too. Once your Papa finds out where you are, he will come for you Lena and there is only one of me. I need to make sure if anything happens to me, you are protected."

"Nothing's going to happen to you, Luka I'll kill anyone that tries."

"Your Papa will bring an army Lena, you know that. I'm only one man and you are a badass bitch but like me, there is only one of you. At least with Kai and the Filippov's family protection, I know we have a chance at keeping you safe. Please don't make this any harder than it already is Lena. If there was another way, I would have taken it, and you know that's the truth."

"I do Luka, you know I trust you. I'm just pissed because I can't dance anymore, you know how much my dancing means to me. I'll get over it eventually but until then I'm allowed my hissy fit, okay? It's a girl's prerogative."

"Believe me, in all the time I've spent with you Lena, I know better than to get in the way of you and your hissy fits. It's the only form of torture that would ever get me to spill all my secrets. I even feel sorry for Kai having to put up with them."

I give Luka my best impression of a death ray coming out of my eyes and totally obliterating him. When he just cracks up laughing at me, I jab him in the arm which has the opposite effect than I intended. He laughs even more. I must be losing my touch. We sit, there drinking and having a laugh for about half an hour. I've had enough though and need some female company.

"Come on arsehole, if Kai thinks I'm sitting at the bar all night he's got another thing coming. When have I ever been obedient? I'm going to the changing rooms to speak to the girls and Sam."

Luka has a scan around the area before he and Pasha follow me into the staff-only entrance to the offices and changing room. I pass Sam's office and she isn't there, so I go into the changing room and I'm immediately pounced on by at least five half-naked women. I'm not tall so two pairs of tits are crushing my face and the other girls are hugging us all.

I mean as deaths go, suffocation by tits doesn't sound that bad really, but it's not something I'd like on my epitaph. I try to get my head free from said tits and, with a struggle, I finally manage.

Luka stays close, whilst Pasha does his best impression of a gargoyle by the door.

"God girls I've only been gone a couple of days, anybody would have thought I was dead."

"Well as far as we knew you were, after you were all but kidnapped out of here by Kai. Then Sam told us you weren't dancing here anymore, girl I thought I would never see you again," Rose worriedly said.

"I'm okay honey, honestly. He's just a controlling neanderthal of a man, with a superiority complex. Chucking small women over his shoulder obviously gets him off."

"I wasn't worried about you in the slightest. To be honest, I was glad you were gone. I finally got my spot back, so don't think coming back now is going to mean you'll be getting it back, bitch," Kim says from her dressing table giving me a cheeky wink in the mirror as she adds more mascara to her false lashes.

"Love you too bitch, nice to see you haven't lost that sunny disposition while I was away," I say, smirking at her as she smiles back at me in the mirror.

"Never mind that bitch, where have you been and are you back for good?" Rose says hopefully.

I look at all my girls, mostly naked as their tits and arses are on full display. To anybody else, this would be the strangest conversation of their lives but, I'm used to it.

"Okay, I've been with Kai. I will also not be dancing anymore so no need to worry Kim. I am not going to steal the spotlight again, so put those claws away."

"What the hell, you've been with Kai for the whole time? Also, what do you mean you aren't bloody dancing here anymore, dancing is your life, Belle?"

"Right, firstly yes, I've been with Kai this whole time. Secondly, Kai fired me, so I'm not allowed to dance here anymore."

"WHAT?!" Rose all but screeched, nearly deafening me in the process.

All the other girls were looking at me in shock and dismay too.

"I was with Kai, I shouldn't have to spell out to you guys what we were up to, should I?"

"You were having a fuck feast with our hot as fuck bosses' boss and you didn't think to pick up the phone to let one of us know you were okay."

"Well, I didn't have my phone on me until just now. I knew we were coming to the club, so I thought it was better to explain in person."

"We've all been worried sick, and you were having the time of your life or probably in a sex coma. What the hell did the prick fire you for?" Rose asked angrily.

God this woman always has my back, no matter what. It was so refreshing to have so many people looking out for me after years of nobody.

"Isn't it obvious Rose, he doesn't want his new piece of arse dancing for other men. She'll be back with us when he tires of her," Stacey sniped.

"Shut your mouth bitch before I rip your fake extensions out." Rose spat at Stacey.

"Well Amy hasn't got fired, yes the others did, but she's still here for now," Kim said.

"Yes, she's with him now that's why, obviously his time with Belle hasn't satisfied him enough. She left about 10 minutes ago," Stacey said, smiling like a Cheshire cat.

I try to not let my emotions show on my face, but I'm devastated. I knew Kai wouldn't be loyal but to actually know it's happening right now is like a knife to the gut. I feel my eyes tearing up a bit and know I need to have a moment on my own to let my emotions out. I can't let Kai see me like this, he obviously doesn't care about me. So why should I care about him?

I turn and head out the door, I see the sad look on Luka's face, but I don't want his pity; I truly can't cope with it. I walk out the door and go to pass Sam's office, the door is partially ajar but I'm not emotionally stable enough to talk to her right now. I'll catch up with her later.

As I reach the door, I note that Pasha has disappeared from its entrance, no doubt scaring some poor unsuspecting victim somewhere else, so I go through and the voice I hear makes me stop in my tracks.

"Please baby, I need you. Fuck, I don't want to fuck anybody else. Why do you make us suffer like this? You know you want me too, if I put my hand on your pussy right now, you know it would be dripping for me," Lev drooled.

"I can't Lev, you know I can't. Go fuck one of your other women, I can't give in again; it was a mistake the last time," Sam replied breathlessly.

"What last time, you know there's been more than one time, baby. Your pussy aches for me, just as much as my cock aches for you. We were both made for each other, I don't know why you fight it so much, baby."

"Your cock aches for any woman's pussy, God it's been in enough. Need I remind you I have a daughter, so my pussy doesn't just weep for you either," Sam seethes.

"They were just a fuck, a release because you kept on denying this chemistry we have. I don't care if you fucked someone else and had that gorgeous daughter of yours. I'll take care of her, just the same as I will her mama. You belong with me, now let me show you why baby," Lev cooed.

I hear Sam moan and then Lev groans. Fuck, I need to stop being a voyeur at the door; not that I can see. My imagination is so much better so I slowly walk past the door as quietly as I can, slipping into the toilets.

I sit on the toilet and let the floodgates open, I let myself cry for my broken heart yet again. I just think I'm never destined to find love. I think it's a myth from fairy tales. Something that existed long ago but gets lost as the generations lose the skill.

I go to the toilet, flushing it before I leave the cubicle to wash my hands. With that done I look at my reflection. Thanking God for waterproof mascara, I assess myself in the mirror. My eyes look a bit red and puffy but at least I don't have panda eyes.

Luka knocks on the door, making me jump in the process.

"Lena, Kai has just messaged that he wants to see you."

I walk out of the door, look up at Luka and smile.

"Let's go and see his majesty, we don't want to keep him waiting, do we?"

"Don't go off on one Lena, try keeping calm and listen to what he has to say."

"I'm calm Luka, I don't give two shits who he's fucking. I'm just a chess piece he's playing and another hole he's fucking. I'll just bide my time and find a way to escape. Then they will regret ever crossing me, the lot of them. None of them know how dangerous I really am, let them underestimate me. All of them will pay for the wrong's they've done to me!"

"I think he cares Lena, honestly."

"Well, I don't, so fuck him."

I march off, down the hall and out of the private

entrance. Men are shouting and hollering at Crystal swinging around the pole. I storm past them on my way to the V.I.P entrance, which is guarded by Greg and Peter. Greg goes to speak but I just pass him by without saying a word. I feel bad, but I've got to keep calm and Greg being nice to me might set me off again. As I ascend the stairs to the V.I.P lounge I just catch Misha dragging Amy away from the door.

Pasha notices me as I reach the top of the stairs with Luka just behind me. He taps Misha on the shoulder who pushes Amy away and she turns to see me, she smiles sadistically and walks over to me.

"You obviously don't satisfy him in the bedroom honey but don't worry, I've just sorted him out for you. Just remember that's my pussy you will be tasting when you suck his cock," Amy sniped.

"Keep moving Flora," Pasha bites out with quiet menace, through barred teeth.

"Flora?" Misha gives Pasha a questioning side eye.

"Yeah, you know, cos she spreads easily," he explains quietly to Misha, while he rolls his eyes like he's humouring a 5-year-old.

"Man, if that's the sort of joke you make when you talk, I think I prefer you to stay silent…" Misha says, wincing.

"You're only saying that cos you were too dumb to get it," Pasha mocks.

Whilst the guys continue to insult each other in the background, Amy tuts and goes to walk past me pouting, but I grab her arm and pull her back. Misha and Pasha stop fucking around and Misha goes to say something, but I put my hand up to silence him and he crosses his arms over his chest smiling.

"Do you think I'm worried about a two-bit whore like you? He fucks loads of women daily. You are but one of many skanks he has collected. Oh, and he's summoned me now, so I better not keep him waiting," I answered back.

"Oh, he's also told me he's marrying you, but I need to be on call for when he needs me, something about setting me up in an apartment as his mistress."

At this I just see fucking red. I don't even think she's talking a load of bullshit or go to ask Kai the truth. To be honest, I would have rather not known if he was fucking other women. Amy though had to get a rise out of me by throwing it in my face.

I bring back my right hand and smash her right in the face. I hear her nose crack, feeling it shatter under my fist. She squeals, putting her hands over her face and fucked up nose, blood pouring down her face and on her hands. I smile in satisfaction, turning around and descending the stairs just as Lev is coming up them.

Luka catches up with me at the bottom of the stairs and I exit into the main room. I see Sam at the bar, so I march over to her. Luka tries to grab me, but I shrug him off.

"You better leave me the fuck alone, Luka. I'm warning you."

He backs off and as I finally reach Sam. I also see another blonde woman at the bar, on a laptop of all things. She looks up when I reach Sam and gives me a venomous look. She looks far from Kai's type as she has doc martens on, combat trousers and a cropped ripped band t-shirt. Her blonde hair is in two buns, situated on the top of her head. She also has tattoos and piercings.

I'm not in the mood to get into it with another blondie today so I ignore her.

"Sam, I need my spot. Get me the hottest guy in the club and put him at centre stage on a chair. Play me 'I See Red by Everybody Loves an Outlaw.' I'll be out in 5 minutes."

"Belle…" Sam goes to say, but I'm in no mood to talk.

"Just do it, Sam" I say as I walk off to the private entrance. I'll show you, Kai Filippov, if it's good for the goose it's good for the gander.

Chapter 11

Kai

I've just finished my meeting with the Polish. It went surprisingly well, which is good considering all the shit that's been happening lately. I still have no news on Isaak which is grating on my last nerve, then Amy comes storming in without knocking, followed quickly by Misha.

"What the fuck are you doing here? Couldn't you two manage to stop the little bitch? Do I have to get replacements for you both?"

"Sorry Boss, she was adamant you called for her," Bear replies.

"I didn't but I'll sort it, now fuck off."

"Da Boss."

I go and pour myself a drink, then sit down in my chair surveying the crowd. I feel Amy's hands on my shoulders and immediately sit forward making them drop away.

"Don't be like that Kai, you know I make you feel good. I always do," Amy says sultrily coming around to stand in front of me. I look up at her and smile at her sadistically.

"You've never satisfied me Amy. I don't know where you got that impression from. Fuck off before Valentina gets here."

"Who the fuck is Valentina?"

"My Fiancé. Or, as you know her, Annabelle."

"You can't be marrying that bitch, surely."

"I can and I will, so fuck off now before I drag you out by your hair."

"Kai, be reasonable. Even if you are marrying that slut, you can still have your other women. I know you are Mafia. You can still have me as a mistress, put me up in a flat and I'll be there when you need me."

I slump back in my chair, staring out to the stage where Crystal is finishing off her pole routine before she leaves the stage. I glare at Amy when she kneels between my spread legs. She places her palms on my thighs, edging her hands higher and higher. She gets to her destination and tries to unzip the fly on my trousers.

I move so fast that she gasps when my hands painfully grip her wrists, stopping them from touching any part of me. I look at her with the disgust I feel, how I could have ever let her touch me I have no clue. But I cannot, and will not, have her disrespecting my future Queen.

"Amy, if I hear you say one more word about Valentina, I will not hesitate to shoot you in the fucking head. Are we clear?"

"I…"

I don't give her a chance to say anything because I've had enough. I grab a handful of hair and drag her to her feet. Once standing I tower over her, snarling at her in disdain.

"Get the fuck out of here, you are no longer employed here. You are not even allowed to enter the premises at all."

I drag her to the door, open it with my free hand and chuck her out to Misha and Pasha. They're standing there smirking as she stumbles and falls on her arse. She squeals and looks at me in horror. Yes bitch, fuck with my woman and you will pay. Pasha looks at me with an assessing gaze before speaking.

"Would you like us to take out the trash boss?"

I give him a sharp nod in agreement. "Get that bitch off my premises immediately, if I have to tell you your jobs again, I'll set Valentina on you. Understand me?"

Pasha lifts one eyebrow but otherwise remains stoic, but Misha tips his head back and a full, deep, bellowing belly laugh comes out of him. I've never heard Misha laugh in all the years he's worked for me, ever. He raises his hands up in surrender and now looks at me, still laughing slightly.

"Please no boss, anything but Valentina. That girl has a temper to rival Lilith herself, she also tends to go for the bollocks."

He cups his balls protectively, pulling a face that cracks me. I chuckle as I close the door, leaving them to deal with Amy. I walk over and collect my glass then refill it, walking back over to sit back down. I light up a cigarette, take a deep drag and message Luka to bring me Valentina.

I message my Papa to make sure all the arrangements have been made for them to come over for the wedding. I also message my jeweller to make sure my custom piece will be ready for the night before the wedding. It's a present for Valentina for our wedding day, but it's also a clear sign to everybody of my ownership. A clear 'touch her and you die,' literally.

I hear a commotion outside the door and Amy squealing, but I ignore it, letting Misha and Pasha do their jobs and get rid of the rubbish. I hope they get their acts together because the last thing I want is Valentina running into her.

Ten minutes go by and now I'm getting annoyed. Luka comes in the door along with Misha and

Pasha. They aren't looking happy and now I'm on edge, Valentina better not have done a runner.

I go to ask them what's wrong when suddenly the lights go totally off. Throwing the whole club into darkness I look around, alert to a possible attack but then a guitar rift starts playing and a spotlight appears on the stage. Sitting on a chair is a man with his back to the audience.

I recognise the song, it's 'I See Red' by Everyone loves an Outlaw, but my pulse shoots through the roof as I see Valentina walking into the spotlight. I dig my nails into my palms with how much I am clenching my fists. My teeth fare no better as I grind them together.

Valentina is wearing a red lace thong and matching balcony bra with red fishnet hold ups, teamed with red stilettos that are so high I have no clue how she walks in them, let alone dances. Her flame-red hair is loose and falling in waves to her arse, her mesmerising sky-blue eyes sparkling brightly in the spotlight.

The trouble is her focus is not on me, it's on the soon to be fucking dead man in the chair. If my Little Vixen thinks this is the way to get back at me for not letting her dance in the club, she'll be sorely mistaken. She'll pay for this stunt with way more than a sore arse.

She stands in front of the dickhead in the chair and raises her head to lock her gaze with mine.

The smile she aims at me doesn't reach her eyes, I can see the turmoil and sorrow in them as she tries to display a totally different persona to everyone else. My Little Vixen forgets that I know all of her tells now, just in our brief time together they are ingrained in my soul.

Valentina breaks eye contact and walks around the man in the chair, her hand caressing his arms and shoulders. He's looking at her in awe like he's witnessing the once-in-a-lifetime gift of seeing a real-life Siren. True to their nature Valentina is luring him in under her mesmerising spell, ensuring there is no escape. He will be forever spellbound to her and all to his downfall; though instead of drowning the unsuspecting victim, his death will be at my hands and the enjoyment I will get out of it will do nothing to quell the rage pulsing through my veins threatening to erupt at any second.

She arrives back in front of him and lowers herself to his lap, straddling him while resting her hands on his shoulders. She looks down at him smiling then starts grinding herself into his lap. She tips her head back as though she's in ecstasy, speeding up the rotation of her hips while she grabs his hair at the back pulling his head back.

Valentina leans forward continuing to grind herself into his erection because any man in here would have one, even without her sitting on their lap. She then starts to lick his neck. That's it, my rage can't be contained any longer.

"ARGH!" I roar so loud I see even Misha jump back slightly.

Picking up the closest table I throw it against the wall, narrowly avoiding Lev's head. Chairs, tables, and anything not secured to the floor will get destroyed in my rampage. I see blood dripping down my hands but ignore it in my fury, although destruction of the V.I.P lounge does nothing to contain my dismay.

I walk toward the door ripping it open as I take my gun out of its holster, taking the clip out making sure it is full and ramming it back in. I leave the safety on and return it to its holster. It's my favourite Makarov, the first gun given to me by my Papa for my first killing. Only apt that it's used to kill the first dickhead dumb enough to touch what's mine.

"Kai, wait up. You need to know what happened first," Lev shouts.

I couldn't give two shits what's happened, my woman shouldn't be giving any fucker a lap dance. She'll be lucky if I don't kill her for this stunt, or maybe she'll wish she were dead by the time I'm finished with her. I nearly rip the hinges off the private door separating me from the main seating area and stage. Peter and Greg jump at the sound of the door smashing against the wall.

They choose the right course of action though and step back out of my way.

As I'm marching towards the stage, people get out of my way or stare at me with worried looks on their faces. I must look menacing, but I couldn't care one bit. This is my club, my city, my fucking Queen currently rubbing herself on some prick's dick.

Misha's hand falls on my shoulder this time and I've had enough. I grab his hand and turn to punch him in the face for thinking he can stop me in my pursuit of punishing my Queen. He's a big fucker but I manage to split his lip.

Not stopping, I march up the stairs as my heart races and my body pulsates with a feeling I've never felt before. It feels as though my heart is being ripped out of my chest the closer I get to them. Neither of them is aware of my presence as they both have their eyes closed.

I reach the chair and stand at the side, pulling out my gun I point it directly at the fucker's head. People start to scream and rush when getting out of their seats. Valentina's eyes fly open and sharply focus on my gun, digging into the unsuspecting prick's temple. Her eyes quickly look up to mine which stops all her body movements, though instead of looking scared she looks enraged. What the fuck has she got to be pissed about?

The music cuts off, people are rushing to exit the club and the staff are helping them. The prick hasn't moved but his hands, that were holding Valentina's arse while she gave him a lap dance, have slipped down to his sides. He looks like he is going to piss himself at any second and is looking hopelessly at Valentina for help.

I've had enough. I grab Valentina's hair at her nape and drag her off the fucker's lap. He goes to bolt but I kick the chair with him still in it across the stage.

"Take that prick to the basement, I'll deal with him after I've finished with my Little Vixen here. Send the staff home and make sure the club is empty," I growl at Lev, Misha and Pasha.

"Let me go you dickhead!" Valentina shouts trying to claw at my hands.

"Tame yourself little kotehok, save your claws for later as you will need them for what I have planned for you."

I drag her backstage with her screaming and shouting in all her magnificent glory. Every hit or move she makes to try and dislodge herself from my grip on her hair, I deflect.

When I slam the door open to the changing room all the girls scream and turn in shock when they see me holding a red-faced Valentina by her hair. They look between us, unsure of what to do.

"Get the fuck out, now!" I roar.

I drag Valentina in, and the girls scramble to grab their clothes and rush out of the room. Rose goes to say something, but I feel Valentina shake her head in a warning not to. My clever girl hasn't lost all her marbles tonight then. Rose still gives me a furious look, but exits the room like the others.

I lock the door behind them and undo my belt with my free hand, ripping it out through the belt loops of my trousers. I push Valentina's head against the door and finally release my grip on her hair. She starts to struggle and tries to push away from the door.

"Kai, fucking let me go now. I'm going to kick your arse all around this club. Aren't you busy anyway with all your mistresses to bother with boring old me? The virginal pussy is conquered now, so go back to your whores and stop clit blocking me. If you have women, I sure as fuck am having any fucking man I want."

Her words hit me in the gut like a knife. The fuck is she fucking other men. Over my dead body and all of theirs. I grab her hands and hold them together in a punishing grip, making her squeal. I wrap my belt around her hands and tighten it far tighter than it needs to be. She will not be able to escape and will re-enact every minute of the lesson I am about to teach her now, whenever she sees the mark adorning her wrists.

I whip her body around to face me and grab her tightly around her throat, squeezing forcefully enjoying the fear laced into her delicate features. She's bold though my Little Vixen, she defiantly glares back at me, goading me to act. I look at my hands covered in my own blood, then I wipe the blood on her face, smearing it over her cheeks.

"You listen and you listen good Valentina, if I so much as hear or see another man sniffing around you, let alone touching you, he dies. No man or woman touches what's mine, you hear. NOBODY!" I roar out the last part of the statement in her face, squeezing harder on her throat.

"Fuck you, Wanker." Valentina seethes right back at me, then she spits right in my face.

I'm in shock for a few seconds then fury takes over. I spin her body back around, grab her hair and slam her head back against the door. I lean right in her face silent for a few moments, our erratic breaths the only noise in the room.

"First blood, then spitting Valentina. Tut tut, what other kinky little fuckery are you holding back from me, um? Believe me, Valentina, I will find out every sordid little secret in that beautiful head of yours. As for now my Little Vixen, it's time for you to pay your penance to the devil you awoke."

"You just fucked Amy, I've every right to fuck any man I like. So, you can stick your punishment up your arse, prick."

I'm taken aback for a moment as to why the hell she thinks I fucked Amy. Did she see Misha and Pasha taking her away?

"I have not been near a woman since I met you Valentina and I have no intention of doing so. Do you hear me? Oh, and talking about arses I think I might have to introduce my cock to yours."

"She bragged about it Kai, right outside the V.I.P lounge. Told me I'd be sucking off her skanky pussy juices from your cock."

"You played right into her hands Valentina. You didn't think though, did you? Didn't stop your actions to ask Misha maybe or even ask me, no you just acted as usual. You ground MY PUSSY on some worthless prick's cock."

"Oh, so pointing a gun at said prick's head in a packed-out club was any better Kai?"

"Fuck yes, he has worse coming, and I couldn't give a fuck about anyone seeing. You. Are. Mine!"

I've had enough of this shit now, it's time for action. My little minx's mouth is running away with her, and I need to shut it the fuck up. I have no desire to have it bitten off though, so stuffing my cock in it is a no-go.

I unfasten my belt from around her wrists

bringing her hands to place them in front of her, replacing the belt securely in place again. I raise her hands above her head and hook her bound wrists on the coat hook. I test the sturdiness of it and pat myself on the back for my expensive tastes. Solid brass fitting, no expense spared on any fixtures together with solid oak doors.

Stepping back, I take Valentina in. She's trying to struggle but balancing slightly on her tiptoes she soon gives up. Good girl, her body now stretched out awaiting my punishment. *Um, what to do?*

Firstly, that vicious mouth needs a gag. I ponder my choices and then find exactly what I'm looking for. Slipping my fingers in the straps of the red-laced thong resting on her luscious hips, I slip it down over her voluptuous arse. I can't resist biting down hard on her left arse cheek, evoking a squeal from Valentina. I lick over my bite mark loving the shiver that runs down her spine at my touch. My blood coats her skin tainting her porcelain perfection with streaks of crimson delight.

No matter what my Little Vixen says, she is affected just as much as I am, our chemistry is phenomenal. Our bodies call out for each other's touch, just as much as our souls cry out for each other's love.

I lift each of her feet up to take off the thong, rising back up and pushing my body into hers.

Pressing my cheek against hers I bring the wet thong up to my nose, taking in the aroused scent of her pussy. Valentina moans and I growl, fuck her pussy smells divine. I grab her cheek, squeezing slightly so her mouth opens and stuff her thong in her mouth.

I walk over to the closest dressing table and pick up some tit tape, walk back over to Valentina and use it to tape her mouth shut slightly so she can't spit my makeshift gag out.

Perfect.

I step back and pull her arse back a bit which naturally arches her back even more. She isn't going to be able to stay like this for long as she's on her tiptoes in fuck me heels. Time for my punishment.

I grip her arse cheeks in my palms and squeeze them savagely, digging my fingertips into her arse so hard she will bear my prints for at least a week. Valentina's muffled screams fill the room like a ballad to my twisted soul. I tip my head back, closing my eyes and squeezing even harder. Maybe next time she will think before grinding this glorious arse in some prick's lap. Releasing her from my punishing grip, I watch her erratic breathing as it slows slightly.

I grab a fist full of her hair and yank her head back, then I bring my palm down on her arse cheek full force. Valentina screams and yanks on the coat hook, she slumps slightly but I keep her in place by her hair. I do another four spanks on the same spot in quick succession, all the time Valentina is screaming and writhing in my hold. This is nothing compared to what she is going to endure now.

My hand moves to her sit spots just beneath the crease of her arse cheeks hitting them with the same savage brutalness. Then the middle of her thighs gets the same treatment, fifteen spanks in total on her right-side. Time for her other side.

Valentina's screams have turned into wails and her chest is heaving at a rapid pace, I can't blame her though most women would have passed out from the pain by now. My Little Vixen is a warrior that's for sure, her tears balm my tortured soul. I swap the hand holding her hair and lean in whispering.

"That's it my Little Vixen, cry for me; let me hear your suffering. Maybe next time you decide to show your claws and let another man touch what's mine, you will think back to this punishment."

Valentina keeps sobbing and I lick some of her tears from her cheek. Umm, how delicious the taste of remorse is on my tongue. I repeat the spanking on her left side, five spanks in each spot, arse cheek, sit spot and thighs.

By the time I have finished my own palms are

throbbing with the most delicious pain. Pushing Valentina forward I unhook her from the coat hook and turn her to face me. She tries to hide her head, but I put two fingers under her chin to force her to look at me.

"Taken like the true Queen you are Valentina, don't cross me again my little kotehok. Next time will cost you more than not being able to sit for days, understood?"

Valentina nods her head slightly still sobbing and whimpering. I raise her bound wrists again and lift them, attaching them to the coat hook again. I pull the lace cups down that hide her succulent breasts from me. Giving each nipple a nibble and sucking them hard into my mouth. Valentina's sobs slowly turn into moans.

Freeing my throbbing cock from my trousers, I grab Valentina's arse cheeks and lift her up. She automatically wraps her legs around my waist, her fuck me heels digging deliciously into my arse. I ram my cock into her dripping pussy, slamming her body into the door.

Every time I slam my cock into her, the door bangs with the force of my thrusts. I rip the tape off her mouth and pull her thong out, stuffing it in my pocket. Another pair for my collection. I claim Valentina's mouth like a starved man. Fucking her mouth with the savagery built up in me from the moment she walked onto that stage.

I pick my pace up, fucking her like I'm possessed, which I am. I'm done for, ruined by the little spitfire in front of me.

I rip my mouth away and release her arse to place both hands around her throat. Squeezing her throat to restrict her breathing slightly, I fuck her so hard I think the door is going to give in at any second. I couldn't give two fucks though, she will go away from this knowing I own her. Mind, body and soul.

"Who. Do. You. Belong. To?" I punctuate each word with my thrusts.

"You, Kai. Only you," she rasps.

"What a clever girl you are, such a good girl."

I place my face in her neck, sucking on her flesh. The sweat is pouring off us both, but I make no effort to slow down. I bite down on her neck, and she shatters gloriously on my cock, screaming so loud I may be deaf in my right ear after we finish.

How tightly her snug little pussy squeezes me and flutters all over my cock, it tips me over the edge. I rear back, tipping my head back and roar my release as my cum floods Valentina's pussy. Good, I want my cum dripping down her thighs for everyone still here to see who she belongs to.

With my cock still pulsating in her pussy and her pussy still contracting around my throbbing cock, I capture her lips again. Biting savagely down on her bottom lip, then soothing it with my tongue. Valentina moans and I take the opportunity to slip my tongue in her mouth.

This kiss is slow, languid, and passionate. The hunger is still there but, with both of us sated, we take the time to explore each other. I suck on her tongue holding it prisoner, feeling her pussy pulsates with each suck or nip on her tongue.

Valentina bites down on my bottom lip, digging her pearly white teeth in hard. If her little claws were free, I have no doubt they would be clawing at my skin, stating her desire and claim over me. What she doesn't realise though is she needs to place no claim whatsoever. I'm ensnared, captured by her allure, destined to worship at her feet for an eternity.

Reaching up, I unfasten my belt and throw it to the floor. I rub the harsh red welts blooming on her wrists, then bring each one to my lips to pepper kisses along the marks. I glimpse up at Valentina to see her watching me with unshed tears in her eyes, her bottom lip trembling.

"No more tears my Little Vixen, what a good girl you've been. Although I delight in seeing you weep for me, the lesson is over. Go get dressed and be back here in five minutes ready to leave. Do not wash or shower as I want my cum dripping down your thighs until we get home."

I lift her up off my still erect, dripping cock and

lower her to the ground. Slapping her arse, I send her off on her way, while I tuck myself away and replace my belt.

I fire off a quick text to Lev telling him to get the cars ready for when we leave. I fire off another text to Misha telling him to make sure the prick in the basement is ready for my arrival.

Hearing Valentina's heels clicking on the floor signalling her arrival, I turn to see her in a green silk, wraparound dress. It's modest and falls to her knees hiding my marks underneath. Teamed up with green stilettos and her hair falling to her arse she looks almost angelic. Shame she chose the devil to corrupt her, now she's in my gilded cage with no chance of escaping.

"Come beautiful, it's time for you to leave, Luka and Lev will take you home. I will be back later tonight, make sure you shower and ready yourself for my arrival."

"Why? aren't you coming home with me Kai?"

"Um, finally you are calling it home. It's music to my ears my Little Vixen. I have unfinished business that doesn't concern you, once it's taken care of, I'll be home."

"Fuck Kai, I'm not stupid. Do you forget where I grew up, don't treat me like a damsel in distress all the time. If you aren't going, neither am I. What are you up to?"

"I can never forget the place and family you grew up in kotehok, lucky for me though I think you inherited all your genes from your Mama. I have to teach someone the consequences of touching my woman. So, no arguments, it's time for you to leave."

"You can fuck right off Kai, it was my fault he got into this. He doesn't know who I am, he just thought he was the lucky one to get a lap dance. You will not harm him at all, do you hear?"

"He's lucky I didn't kill him instantly, Valentina."

"I don't give a shit Kai, he doesn't know either of us. It's not his fault. What are you going to do next, put pictures up in all your establishments saying, 'She's my woman if you touch her, you're dead?' Be real Kai."

"Actually, I think you're onto something there my Little Vixen."

"Fucking hell I can't believe you Kai, get out of my way now."

My little hellcat pushes me away from the door and marches off down the hallway. Swinging the door open, she continues towards Luka and Lev who are standing talking to Isadora of all people. Fuck, why is she here so soon?

I quicken my pace as Valentina has already reached them, Isadora has already turned and given Valentina a scowl. Valentina ignores her though and starts arguing with Lev and Luka.

"Will you two talk some sense into him please, he's going to kill that man. It was my fault, not his, he shouldn't be punished for my mistake," Valentina whines.

"Maybe you should have thought of the consequences of your actions before you carried them out. I can't think of many men who would stand by and let their soon-to-be wives grind their pussies on another man's cock. Let alone my..."

"Who the fuck asked you bitch, and what the fuck are you still doing here anyway. I thought the rubbish had been kicked out earlier."

"You better shut your mouth bitch, before I shut it for you."

"You wish. I'll wipe the floor with your skanky little arse."

Lev has to grab Isadora and I restrain Valentina. I think it would have been a fair fight though and very entertaining to watch, but it's unfair on Valentina as she obviously doesn't recognise my sister.

Isadora shrugs Lev off, and he steps back with his hands raised in surrender. Pussy. He knows what my sister's like when she's upset. God help anybody who gets on the wrong side of her.

"I've done a thorough search and she's clean,

mores the fucking pity. Thanks for the Docs. Oh, Papa thought you may wish to have this early so sent me over. I thought I'd kill two birds with one stone, didn't actually think I'd end up killing your future bride though.

"You wish bitch, I'd snap your neck before you even got a hit."

"Shut the fuck up both of you, you're giving me a headache."

Isadora slams the ring box in my right hand and a file in my left hand. Before I have a chance to pass the file to Lev, Valentina swipes it out of my hands and opens it. She scans the report and looks at me with venom. I put the ring away and get ready for the atom bomb that is Valentina about to go off.

"You did a background check on me and all my technology, so you still don't trust me Kai even after everything I've told you. How could you and who is this bitch anyway?"

"This "bitch" is his sister and the next time you fuck my brother about I'll slit your throat, understood?"

"What? You got your own sister to do a background check on me? I can't believe you Kai."

"Lev take my sister to your place and for God's sake keep her there until I've sorted this shit out. Luka go and tell Misha to kick that prick out of here and tell him to never come the fuck back. Fuck, why do women cause me the most trouble in my life?"

Luka goes off to do as ordered and, after giving me a look that could kill most people, Isadora walks off with Lev. I face Valentina and fuck my life; tonight isn't going to go as intended. When I was back at home after knocking ten tons of shit out of that prick, I wanted to introduce Valentina to my Den. At this rate, I'll be lucky if she comes home at all.

Chapter 12

Valentina

I'm consumed by anger. How dare he get his sister to investigate me and as for his sister, well we get along swimmingly, don't we? Never mind a wedding taking place, I think Isadora and I will be planning to assassinate each other well before then. Thinking of that though, we only have three days until I have to marry Kai. Shit, I need to get out of this and fast.

"Valentina I can see those clogs working overtime in that pretty head of yours. You need to calm down and think rationally about all of this because we've both just witnessed what happens when you go off on one."

"What do I need to think about Kai? You've just made me even more of an enemy than I was before with your family. Not only have you given them reason to not trust me, but you've told them that you don't either."

Kai sighs and runs his hand through his hair. It's a frustrated tell that he has, I've noticed.

"What do you want me to say? If I could assure my family in any way that you are not part of some elaborate plan to kill us, it was to let my sister run a no holds barred check on you. I had my doubts as well Valentina, you know this. Wouldn't you if it were the other way round?"

I actually stop and think about this whole messed-up situation we are both in. If we knew who each other were when we met, we wouldn't have touched each other with a ten-foot barge pole as they say here. Kai would have probably killed me instantly to get one over on my Papa. Don't get me wrong, I would have given him a good fight. If there is anything my Papa did right in his sordid existence, it was to make sure I was trained to fight.

The thing Kai doesn't realise though, or maybe he does, is that my Papa would have had him killed the instant he found out. If I were on the run with Luka when we met and Luka had known who owned the club, we would have been on a plane out of Birmingham within the hour. So yes, I can understand Kai checking my intentions out, he would be a fool not to. And the man I know is far from a fool. He oozes a shrewd intuition and has an omniscient nature; what he doesn't know already, he will torture the required information out of you within no time at all.

"All right, I'll admit that you were in the right to do the check, but couldn't you have gotten anyone else other than your sister? Fuck's sake Kai, I thought I was a bitch, but she's a Harley Quinn computer nerd! All I need to see now is the Joker pop out from the V.I.P. Lounge and maybe Deadpool fall in from the skylight."

"You're calling my sister a nerd and yet you're naming DC AND[1][2] Marvel characters? My Little Vixen, I definitely have so much to learn about you, which is what I intend to do over the next few weeks. To answer your question, Isadora is the best hacker, or computer nerd as you call her, that we know. She's family, so can be trusted with this confidential information, including that I have the missing Russian Bratva Princess, Valentina Ivanov in my possession. As you can understand this is sensitive information that, if it fell into the wrong hands, would be catastrophic."

"I give up!" I say throwing my hands up into the air.

"You'll be fine Valentina I promise, Isadora is a sweetheart really. She has a temper that rivals your own, but I think you both have a lot in common. Give it time and I think you'll be the best of friends. I promise!"

"I think you're definitely delusional if you think

that's ever going to happen. Anyway, can we go home now? I'm tired and I desperately need a shower, I'm covered in your blood and spunk."

"Just the way I like you my Little Vixen. Misha will be taking us home shortly, and I have some business to take care of so I will be leaving you with Misha and Luka."

"Won't you need Misha with you? Did the meeting not go as planned?"

"It went better than expected, that's what I don't trust. I need to do some checks while my sister is here, so I will head over to Lev's. I'll be taking Pasha with me so don't worry. Don't wait up as this may take a while. I also have some more surveillance I wish Isadora to do as well. I need to give her the venues for the wedding to do a full security check."

"Do you think my Papa knows I'm here Kai?"

"He might have heard whispers, but you don't need to worry my Little Vixen, I will keep you safe. Trust me, okay."

"I trust no one, Kai, so don't ask me to. It's the safest way to be, so your heart doesn't get broken. It's the best way to ensure I'm not killed or betrayed, the one person I trusted in my life died because of me. It won't happen again."

"You'll learn in time Valentina; I will stop at nothing to protect what's mine."

I want to reply but I'm too exhausted to get into any more arguments. That's all Kai sees me as, his prized possession to show to all the Mafia world. The daughter of the enemy, meek and obedient. I'm tired of being someone's trophy or pawn to play on the chessboard.

I always look to the best possible example of how valuable women are. The lioness stalks, hunts, and kills their prey. She feeds the King, her Lion. She looks after her pups and her Kingdom but above all her King. In return he protects her and his cubs, that's the King I want.

All I want is a King who finds me valuable and lets me fight by his side. A man who finds my mind as valuable as my body and loves me with all his heart. A true King and Queen ruling their empire together, side by side. I don't just want to be a King's treasured possession; I want to be his world as he would be mine.

If my Papa knows I'm here, he'll be coming for me. I'd like to believe Kai will be able to protect me and Luka; but I know my Papa. He'll stop at nothing to teach me a lesson for the embarrassment I've caused him. Death will be a blessing compared to what he has planned for me.

Misha walks in with Pasha and Luka; I look straight at Misha's blood covered hands, and my stomach drops, yet another person suffers for my actions. Why do I keep on doing this? Will I never learn that my actions can cause people around me to be killed or injured. Misha notices my incessant glare at his hands and excuses himself.

Kai's arm goes around my waist, and he pulls my body against his.

"Are you ready to leave Valentina?"

"Yes, I'm exhausted."

"You'll be able to rest when you are home, don't forget to shower though."

"No shit Sherlock, I'm covered in blood Kai."

"Less of that feisty little mouth of yours or I'll have to think of better uses for it. Maybe I'll have to keep you permanently gagged to keep that sharp tongue of yours confined."

"I'd like to see you try Kai; I'll guarantee you'll be missing some fingers if you do."

"See there's my feisty little kotehok, so delicious in her anger."

"Fuck off Kai."

Kai, Pasha and Luka start laughing at me, just as Misha comes back into the main room, minus the blood over his hands.

"Come on guys let's get Valentina back home. I'm scared for our balls if we don't."

They all laugh at Kai's comment, and I can't help smiling a little. I'm getting quite the name for myself lately where men's balls are concerned. Misha and Pasha scope outside the club to make sure it's safe to leave; before they usher us out and into Misha's Range Rover SV. Kai and I are in the back and Luka gets into the passenger seat, Misha gets into the driver's seat, and we take off at breakneck speed. Pasha follows in another car with several men that must have been waiting.

After being in Lev's Bentley Flying Spur, I didn't expect the luxury feel inside the Range Rover but it's no less extravagant in its features. I have yet to see the car Kai drives himself, but knowing him it will match his persona to a T.

Kai is typing away on his mobile, as I look out at the city and its people passing me by. Women are clambering about on sky-scraper heels traversing the cobbled pathways, some have given up altogether and are carrying them in their hands. Men are eyeing up the ladies or laughing with their pals, no treacherous heels for them. All they have to do is stay up straight.

I've always felt envious of men, they shower, stick on their best clothes and style their hair. Spray on some aftershave or cologne and there you have it, they are ready to go out. Ladies have a long list of tasks throughout the day to get ready for a night out. Shower and shave every body part you can think of. Dry and either curl or straighten their hair, then next make-up. The last task is what they are wearing; this task normally involves stripping out the entirety of their wardrobes to find they have nothing suitable at all. The other option is to spend two hours trying on every item of clothing, to end up choosing the first dress you tried on.

In no time at all we made it back to the hotel. Luka and Misha exit first. Misha opens Kai's door, letting him exit, while Luka opens my door and helps me out of my side. Kai joins me and puts his hand at the base of my spine, ushering me in the hotel with Misha in front of us and Luka behind. Pasha and the other men stay with the cars.

We all enter the private lift and ascend to the penthouse; I walk off down the corridor to Kai's room. I enter the bedroom and start untying my green wraparound dress as I simultaneously kick off my heels. As I'm wearing nothing underneath the dress I head straight for the bathroom.

Walking to the shower I turn it on, testing the heat of the shower with my hand; finding it lovely and warm. I stand under the shower lowering my head, so the cascading stream of water pelts over my hair, my face and down my back. I place my hands on the tiles in front of me, staying there in total bliss, finally feeling my body relax and my mind calm for a moment.

I sense Kai entering the shower. His scent encompasses me, lulling my body to react and my treacherous pussy to pulsate. My nails are trying to grip the smooth tiles but can't find any traction, my body wants him like its next breath. My mind knows we shouldn't though. Wanting the devil will only bring me more heartbreak.

Kai's hands slowly encompass my waist, then caress my stomach as he leans his huge frame over me. He kisses my neck and the sensitive part just behind my ear, then whispers in it. "Calm yourself my Little Vixen, just let me take care of you. Then we will settle you in bed."

"I…"

"Give me this Valentina, please."

I don't answer, I really don't know what to say. Hearing Kai say please is a shock that I'm completely unprepared for. I try to calm my breathing and relax my body.

Kai moves over to the glass shelves which before had housed all of his things, such as shampoo, conditioner, and body wash. Now though, it houses an array of women's items too. I notice a shampoo and conditioner that looks similar to mine but far more expensive. Hopefully, it will do a much better job of containing my naturally curly locks. The most shocking thing is the scent though. How did Kai know I love Chamomile?

He picks up the shampoo, squeezes a liberal amount into his palm and walks back over to me. Kai starts to massage it into my hair, massaging my scalp at the same time. I'm too late to stop the moan that comes out. Well, I say moan it's more like a mixture of a cat in heat and a porn stars award winning orgasm.

"That's it my little kotehok, let me hear you purr for me."

"I'll do more than purr for you if you keep doing that to me Kai. Fuck."

"Um, interesting. My Little Vixen likes me to pet her. Noted."

"Fuck off Kai, now shut up and continue."

Kai chuckles and continues turning me to mush with his hands. He turns me around to wash the shampoo off and then conditions my hair, running his fingers through my hair, which I'm amazed he can do as it's normally knotty as hell. He washes that off, going to grab the body wash from the shelf.

"Face the wall and put your hands flat against the tiles. Be a good girl Valentina I think you've been punished enough tonight, don't you?"

"What are you doing Kai?"

"I'm washing you; Valentina, I like dirty girls but only in the right way. Hands against the wall and spread your legs apart."

I bite my tongue to stop me from giving the reply that's on the tip of it. I do as he requests and bow my head, awaiting whatever Kai has in store for me. No matter how much I try to tell myself I'm not falling for him it's hopeless, I'm only kidding myself.

Witnessing this softer side of Kai is my downfall, I never expected this from him. He's showing a tenderness that is unheard of in our world, especially for a man of his stature.

Kai runs his soapy hands over my back in a soft caress but when he feels any kinks in my muscles, he kneads the area until they have gone. He continues manipulating my body, just as he is my mind. Legs, arse, stomach, tits, every inch of my body. When it comes to my pussy, I think it's going to become sexual and my pussy starts to weep. My clit is pulsating at the lightest graze of his fingers. But Kai continues his gentle caress, not paying any attention to my needy clit or my pussy.

Once he's finished cleaning me, he moves away and grabs his own shampoo. I don't know what possesses me, but I go over to him and grab the bottle.

"Let me, Kai."

"I don't expect anything back from you Valentina, I did this because I wanted to not because I had to."

"I want to Kai, please."

His ocean-blue eyes scrutinise me, trying to gauge any lies in my statement. When he finds nothing, he smiles at me and it's breathtakingly beautiful. I've only ever seen him smirk or laugh but when he's smiling like this, I feel ecstatic. I've created this reaction, an exceedingly rare vision that I will truly treasure. He looks younger, more carefree, and panty-dropping hot.

I can't resist but smile back at him, and I think it's the first real smile I've given someone in a long time. We stay in this moment for what seems like hours just smiling at each other, showing our true selves for once and neither of us wishes for this to end.

Kai goes over to the other end of the shower and picks up the wooden bench like it weighs nothing, before he pads back over and places it up against the glass just behind the shower head. I squeal as he turns to me next, sweeping me from my feet and standing me on the bench.

"Don't worry little vixen, it's only so you can reach my hair."

"Are you calling me a short arse Kai?"

"Never."

"Um hum, I believe you. Now turn around so I can wash your hair."

"Yes, my Queen."

He bows to me, and I laugh as he turns around and places himself close enough for me to start washing his hair. I squeeze some shampoo onto my palm and hand him the bottle. I start to run my fingers through his hair, then begin to massage it in, lathering it up with my movements. I drag my nails against his scalp and Kai growls... I love how his body responds to my touch, maybe a little too much.

"There, all done, you wash that out and I'll get the bodywash."

I step down off the bench and pick up his body wash, flipping the lid and smelling it, closing my eyes as I do. It smells like the woodlands I used to play in as a child, hints of Russian sage and peppermint are there in its essence. No wonder Kai's scent always encompasses me and makes me feel calm. I turn around ready to walk over to Kai but, as I look at him washing the shampoo out of his hair, I'm dumbstruck.

His blonde hair glistens in the water as his huge hands run through it. His eyes are currently closed, and his face is free from all its usual hardness. His high cheekbones are to die for and his full kissable lips surrounded in blonde stubble that I yearn to feel between my legs.

As I finally walk over to him, I watch his muscles ripple in his huge back and bulging biceps. His body is a true work of art, along with the tattoos adorning his skin. I run my fingers over the tattoos on his chest, wondering about the origins of them as I go. On his left pec is a verse of writing from a book I assume, whilst on his right pec is what looks like a family crest.

I see the tips of the wings on his rib cage, so I go around the back of him to investigate the Angel that covers his back in more detail. I've seen all his tattoos before, but not really studied them. The Angel is so intricate it looks real and covers his whole back, the feathers of the wings reaching to just above his arse. The clouds above the angel are actually angel wings themselves, with sun rays beaming from them. I drag my hands over the tattoo, arriving back in front of Kai again. His huge erection stands proud and unashamed; I look up into his eyes full of desire.

I grab his erection, pumping it slowly, but Kai's hands stop my motions and he leans down kissing my forehead.

"Just clean my Little Vixen, nothing sexual needs to happen. You're exhausted and need to sleep."

I dump some more body wash in my hand, smiling at Kai and grabbing his erection again, soaping it up and washing his balls with my other hand. He tips his head back into the shower stream and moans. It's so deep and full of lust and I just love it, that I end up giggling a bit. Kai's head lowers again and his hand snaps out to stop my movements.

"Naughty kotehok, you have problems with rules, don't you? I haven't got time to teach you at the moment, but you will learn. Also, I think your arse has suffered enough tonight. Go and get dry, I'll finish cleaning myself."

I pout up at Kai and start to walk off. My actions always seem to cause a reaction in Kai though; he slaps my arse before I move far enough away from him and it bloody stings. I give him a dirty look but scuttle out of the shower, holding my arse before he can smack it again. Wrapping a huge fluffy towel around me I can't hide my smile as I exit the bathroom and, for the first time in ages, I don't want to.

Kai

As I finish cleaning myself off, I can't help but chuckle, I definitely have my work cut out for me with my Little Vixen. I always expected a virgin to be meek and shy in the matter of their sexuality, but Valentina has always been the total opposite. Maybe it's her dancing or maybe it's just her defiant attitude to life, always wanting to be in control of her own.

I wanted to introduce her to my Den tonight, but things totally took a different turn, including the appearance of my sestra. I now need to sort that shit storm out and use her to my advantage as well. Security definitely needs tightening, amongst other things. I also need her to investigate the Polish, something is fishy there and doesn't sit quite right.

I stop the shower, grab a towel from the rack and give my hair a quick ruffle to dry it slightly. Wrapping it around my waist and leaving the bathroom, I find Valentina rifling through my t-shirt drawer. I ogle the view of her bent over, with her pussy and arse on full display, then go to my walk-in to get dressed. I put some boxers on, plus a pair of beige jeans, and teamed it with a khaki coloured long-sleeve top before I pulled on my army boots.

As I walk out of the walk-in wardrobe, Valentina is pulling on my Guns and Roses band t-shirt. Fuck, I love seeing her in my t-shirts. She looks delicious and, with her red locks against the black t-shirt my fucking god, she's sexy.

"Do you want something to eat Valentina, you haven't eaten properly in days? I can get the guys to order a pizza in."

"Yes, that would be nice, I'll have pepperoni please. I'll just put some bottoms on, and I'll be out."

"Good."

I leave Valentina to sort herself out and exit our room to go and update the guys. I find Misha standing, looking out of the floor to ceiling windows, Luka and Pasha sitting at the table having a conversation. They both look up as I enter and Luka gets up from his seat.

"Is she alright Boss?" Misha asks, looking concerned.

"She's fine Misha, she's showered and is just getting dressed at the moment. She wishes to have a pepperoni pizza so can you sort that? Also eat yourselves, I don't know how long this is going to take."

"I'll sort it Boss, are you sure she's okay with the blood and everything, she looked quite pale when she saw it."

"She's absolutely fine with blood Misha, trust me. She's seen so much in her life it's unbelievable. The training her Papa made her do in her adolescence also sorted out any issue with blood. I couldn't keep up with the number of broken noses she caused or other wounds with her knives," Luka says.

"What the fuck are you telling me? Men were fighting with her? Were they using weapons as well?" I ask, annoyed beyond belief.

"Trust me Kai, I feared far more for the men than I did for Valentina. Vladimir fully trained her, he was her Systema coach, you just haven't seen her in action yet. Every soldier that ended up fighting her came off worse, even the arseholes that managed to get hits in. Nikon was a mean motherfucker; he had a history of beating women up and even scarring one horrendously. Valentina also knew this and, the first time her Papa made her fight the guards, she called him out for a personal fight." Luka says.

"It's Boss to you prick! What the fuck was Valentina thinking?"

"Sorry... Valentina never cared about getting hurt, she wanted to teach this idiot a lesson. I said one of us could do it, but she refused. She said the only way for the bastard to learn was to be taught the lesson by a woman. So, when she picked him to fight her, he was ecstatic. He didn't like Valentina, just saw her as a rich Bratva princess; he jumped into the fighting ring while the other soldiers egged him on. It was a chance to hurt her without repercussions from her Papa," Luka continues.

"Fuck me, what was she thinking? I knew she was crazy, but this was suicidal! How old was she?" I say, gritting my teeth in anger.

"She was fifteen when she fought Nikon, after only three years training. She had to start training shortly after she was caught in the woods by her house. I think it was her sadistic bastard of a Papa's way of punishing her, along with stopping her dancing lessons." Luka says.

Misha runs his hands through his hair, pulling slightly as his face screws up in anger.

"I knew he'd hurt her, I tried to get back to

her, but I couldn't get enough men willing to go against Mikhail at the time. That's why when you spotted me at that fight, I agreed to join your ranks. I worked my way up and I borrowed some of Dimitri's men and tried to rescue her. She was gone by that time, and I feared she was dead. Fuck I should have acted quicker," Misha rages.

"Why didn't you tell me, Misha, did Dimitri sanction your actions?" I seethe.

"She was your enemy Boss; you all hated the family with a vengeance. I didn't think you'd be interested, and no, Dimitri knew nothing of the rescue mission."

I look at Misha seething, but I know that back then I would have probably told him he wasn't allowed to rescue her. I would have told him to leave her to rot. This sickens me to the bone now. I'm so angry with myself, even though I didn't know her. My hatred was born from lessons taught and inherited from the anger between the two families.

"She had her protectors, Misha, we all did our best to protect her. And I finally managed to get her out of there with the help of a few of my fellow soldiers. The fights and training were things we couldn't get involved in, it would have given us away and ruined any hope of our escape," Luka says.

"Not fucking soon enough, anyway what

happened?" I say angrily.

"Well, she had gotten Vlad to get specially commissioned fighting knives made for her. The Spetsnaz knives have a bladed edge on each side; one serrated and the other a cleaner blade edge. Hers also had a guard on the handle so she can keep her grip when using the blade in either direction. She still has them today, along with her set of ten Strij throwing knives."

"Fuck me, they are fucking lethal knives," Misha says with a proud look on his face.

"Deadly. Anyway, she has the Strij's attached to her combat belts and each of her Spetsnaz fighting knives in her hands when she enters the ring. Nikon is skipping about it, egging his fellow soldiers on. They were leering at Valentina and cheering for him. Her Papa sits in a chair opposite the ring, on a raised platform so he can see the fight unhindered. Nikon turns and sees Valentina with her knives, he laughed and made fun of her. Valentina just stands there calm and with no expression on her face.

"Her Papa shouts the order for the fight to begin. Nikon raises his knife in front of himself and charges Valentina. He's expecting his weight and height to scare Valentina, or knock her to the ground so he can jump on her. But Valentina just stands there and, at the last moment, swerves to the side out of his way. At the same time, she brings her left hand up and across his chest, whilst bringing her right hand up and across his back. Nikon roars in pain and looks down, seeing a gaping slice across his chest, and we can see the matching one on his back. He looks at Valentina in disbelief but she just smiles at him, wiping his blood off her knives on her trousers," Luka pauses, shaking his head at the memory.

"Nikon charges her again in his anger but this time, Valentina runs at him too and slides through his legs, catching the inside of his thighs with both her knives. The cuts she has inflicted on Nixon are not meant to kill; believe me she knew how to inflict such wounds. No, Valentina is bleeding him slowly, wearing him down and making him slower. She didn't have any intention of killing him, she had totally different motives as we soon found out," Luka wipes his hand down his face.

"This time Valentina runs at Nikon, making her first mistake. He turns and ends up elbowing her in the face; she's knocked to the ground by the force. There was blood everywhere, both Nikon's and now Valentina's. I was going to go in the ring to stop it, but other soldiers held me back. Mikhail had noticed my reaction, so I had to hide my anger. The bastard was sitting there smiling about the fact that his daughter was injured and was going to get a beating as she still hadn't got up." Luka walks over to the windows lost in his memories.

"The sick bastard. I swear when I manage to get my hands on him, I will make his death last days." I feel tremendous rage, I can't believe someone would do that to their own daughter.

"Sick is not the word for that man. Nikon then climbs on top of Valentina who we all believe is unconscious as she hasn't moved at all. But we underestimated her cunning, Nikon most of all, a mistake that would be his last. He brings his blade to her body and runs it up her chest whispering to her as he does. To this day I don't know what he said to her." He shook his head. "Then he runs it against her neck, starting to draw blood, ready to mark her. That's when her legs come up, locking around his body, and she slices his wrist—the one he was holding his knife in—which he drops immediately. She tips his body backwards, flipping herself at the same time, ending up on top of him. Nikon tries to bring his legs up to get to her, but ends up roaring in pain as she's got him pinned down with her knees. The cuts she inflicted inhibited his movements and he was unable to remove her. His inability was his undoing. That's when he lies there cold, staring at her, as she smiles at him with blood running down her nose and over her face." He took a long breath.

"What happened next?"

"Well, I remember her talking to him. She'd said that she heard he likes to cut women up, and that he liked how it felt to scar their pretty faces."

I nodded, eager to hear more.

"Then she cut three big slashes across his face, one on his forehead, the other across his nose through to his right eye, and the last from his lip to his cheek."

My eyes widened.

"Nikon howled in anguish, even trying in his lethargic state to flip her off him but failed."

"Once Valentina had finished the final cut, she stepped off him and he lay motionless on the floor of the ring."

I couldn't help but feel proud of her.

"She looked up at her father in disgust and then left the ring," Luka finished, staring absently out of the window.

I'm astounded. My Little Vixen is a true warrior. I knew she was a fighter, but to be fighting her Papa's soldiers at such a young age? My God she's amazing and so strong.

"He told me, 'Your face is such a pretty canvas for my work and you will remember my face every time you look in the mirror'." Valentina says.

We all whip around at the sound of her speaking and just stare at her. She ignores us all and walks over to the sunken sofas, sitting down and picking up the remote, turning the TV on.

"How long is the pizza going to be, I'm starving," she shouts.

We all just look at each other dumbstruck. I have no clue how long she was there to hear Luka telling the story, but it must have been a while for her to know Luka didn't know what Nikon said to her.

I nod to Misha. He and Pasha go off to order the pizza, Luka goes into the kitchen and I make my way over to her. I sit next to her as she sits with her legs tucked underneath her. I grab one of the fur blankets and place it over her lap. She looks at me and smiles, going back to choose a movie to watch.

"Valentina, I can't believe what that prick made you do; I swear when I get my hands on him..."

"Luka had no right in telling you my past Kai. My past is the past and it needs to stay that way. I've had to make my peace with it and so does everyone else. I don't want anyone's pity or remorse; I lived it, that's enough. I also survived and managed to escape. It's my fight, it will always be."

"I'm here for you now Valentina, don't you understand that."

"I do Kai, and I thank you for that. I don't think

you quite understand though, if my Papa finds me, he will stop at nothing to get me back."

"Well, you're mine now so he will have a fight on his hands. He will never take you away from me!"

"I hope you're right Kai, I really do."

Valentina chooses 'Underworld' and snuggles down onto the sofa to watch it. Luka comes out of the kitchen with a hot chocolate for her and hands it to her with a smile. She looks at the cup and, noticing the small marshmallow's floating on top, she beams back at him. He takes a seat to the right of her, looking at the film she has chosen.

"Not this again Lena, you must have seen it about 50 times already."

"You know it's one of my favourites Luka, now shut up and watch it."

He chuckles and shuts up to watch the film. A flash of jealousy washes over me with the ease they have in each other's company. I contemplate staying, having pizza and watching the movie with her, but I know I need to speak to Ida. Especially if I wish to keep my promise to Valentina about keeping her safe. I need to be that person who doesn't let her down, the person she can trust and rely on.

"I'm going now Valentina, don't wait up, I'll be late. Okay?"

"I won't. I'm watching this and eating my pizza then I'll be going to bed. Be safe Kai."

"I will, my Little Vixen."

I kiss her forehead and squeeze her hand, then leave her to watch her film. I nod at Misha who is by the lift as I enter and he nods back. I gesture to Pasha and he stands to follow me, then turns as I press the button to go down and, as the doors close, I see her staring at me. I sigh, rubbing my hand down my face. This is going to be a long night.

"She's quite something, your woman." Pasha's voice breaks the silence.

"She isn't just something, my friend, she is everything," I replied.

"For as long as I've known you, I have never seen a woman get under your skin. It's kind of a relief that you are human like the rest of us." Pasha quips.

"She isn't just some woman, Pasha, she's destined to be mine, my family, the mother of my future children, the very breath I take," I state quietly, turning towards him. He stiffens suddenly, as though stung, before a sadness permeates from him and he goes quiet and thoughtful. I turn away again, believing the exchange over before I hear him whisper, to me or to himself, I don't know.

"I understand boss, family is everything…"

Chapter 13

Kai

As I enter Lev's apartment, I hear my sister's voice straight away. She's nagging Lev about Valentina. When I enter the living room she's sitting at the table, rambling on ten miles a minute while her fingers are flying across the keyboard of her laptop. She also has two monitors and computer towers spread over the table. On one monitor is my hotel and on the other is Lev's apartment. She's already logged into all the internal cameras and traffic cams, as well as all external CCTV footage of the surrounding areas of both buildings.

"I've already told you Ida, you probably know more than me. All I know is Kai's smitten, so good luck with that one."

"Well, we need to change his mind then don't we, I don't trust her Lev. How can the spawn of that Devil be anything other than pure evil in a

G-string? She has a good pair of tits, I'll give her that, but I'll bet Kai has teeth marks on his dick from that treacherous pussy of hers."

"I wouldn't let him hear you talking like that Ida, he threatened to kill me for grabbing her when she tried to attack him. So, believe me when I say, he's definitely smitten."

"Too fucking late, you pair of old washerwomen, haven't you got anything better to talk about like security for my imminent wedding? You're a bitch Ida, because you would have seen me arriving on the cameras, so why are you running your mouth?" I announce as I make myself known.

"Thank fuck for that. I'm off out for a cigarette because Ida has been doing my head in for hours. What took you so long Kai? Can you please remember I'm not a babysitting service for the psychotic women in your life. I have enough trouble in that department myself," Lev mutters to me as he goes to leave.

"I heard that, arse wipe. I'm not psychotic, I'm just morally challenged. Are you still pining after Sam? You fucking drip. I would think having a child by another man would be a sure sign that she is well over you. Get over her Lev, your dick isn't as fantastic as you thought," Isadora shouts from her seat.

"Fuck you Ida, that was a fucking low blow. You

know fuck all about Sam and me, so shut the fuck up," Lev shouts angrily, then slams the door.

"God, Ida. Who pissed in your Cheerio's today and what the fuck's up with you?"

"I'm absolutely fandabidozi. It's you lovesick puppies, being led around by your dick's, is what worries me the most. Good job I'm here now to sort all of you out, kick some sense into your batshit brains. Have I got to worry about Misha as well, or is it just you two dipshits?"

"Misha only has his fuck buddies. Lev and I are fine, so leave it the fuck alone. You need to concentrate on the security for us all; all of the venues need to be secured and monitored."

"What does it look like I'm doing now, idiot? I've secured here and your hotel. Lev has already forwarded me the venue details and I'm covering the route as we speak. Though, if my plan works, there will be no wedding and we can all go back to normal. All this is going to bring us, Nikki, is a whole heap of shit. You need to knock this infatuation on the head and just shoot the bitch. If you haven't got the balls, I'll do it for you. Call it a wedding present for your future, more appropriate bride."

"I swear Ida, if you harm a single hair on Valentina's head, you'll regret it. I'm trying to talk Papa out of arranged marriages for us all and it's hopefully working. If you harm Valentina though, I'll make sure you're married off to the most vicious bastard I know."

"Come on Nikki, that's child play for me, you should know this by now. I'll have the fucker eating out of my hand in hours. No fucker can control me unless I allow it. But I'll leave your precious Princess alone. Fuck Nikki, you're more fucked than I thought. What is it about her?"

"She's mine, that's all you need to know. I protect what's mine, even from you Ida. Don't get in my way on this, promise me."

"Okay, okay, jeez! But don't say I didn't warn you Nikki. Trust me, a viper senses a fellow viper. She'll be your downfall; but I'll always be there to kill any fuckers that try to kill you though. Nikki, you know I love you Brat."

"I know and I love you too, Sestra. Valentina isn't like how you make her out to be, I promise. I've learnt a lot about her during this time. Luka even told us some of the vicious things her Papa has made her do. It's sickening Ida, I swear. Also, did you know Misha knew Valentina when he was younger, just before he joined our ranks?"

"Fuck no, that big bear gives fuck all away. He did once borrow some of Dimitri's soldiers to go on a mission to his hometown, but I just thought it was a vengeance mission after what happened to his Mama, so I didn't inform any of you. Is he involved with her romantically Nikki?"

"No, I questioned him as soon as I found out they knew each other. He sees her as family, his only family. He blames himself for letting her down. When he went on that mission and when he couldn't find her, he thought her Papa had killed her."

"Fuck, that explains a lot. No wonder he's so fucking moody."

"God Ida. Do you ever feel any empathy?"

"Fuck that shit, everybody suffers Nikki. I'm just here to keep you fuckers safe, you guys are the only thing that matters to me. Everything else can go fuck itself."

"God, what happened to my sweet little sestra?"

"Life Nikki. Life. Is there anything else you need me to do because, as you can see, I'm busy as fuck trying to keep you pricks alive."

"I do, I've got a hit out on Isaak Volkov. He ambushed…"

"Yes, yes. Misha has the tech team on it. I always keep an eye on you Nikki. I've already set up programmes and worms to track them, which I'm going to check on in a bit. Then my babies will be set to scour the digital footage and any footprints they may have left. If there is anything to find, my babies will find them. Anything else?"

"Shit Ida, I'm starting to worry about you. Calling

your worms babies, do you get out at all?"

"I would if you and Dimitri would stop dicking about and give me a bit of free fucking time. Team that with keeping an eye on Papa and wherever he's sticking his dick lately? I'm maxed out; looking after you three idiots is fucking exhausting. I have no time to suck a dick, let alone ride one."

"Too much information Ida, way too much. Fuck, I need to wash my ears out."

"How do you think I feel, my eyeballs are sore after the number of times I've washed them out seeing all of your dicks. None of you are bothered where you stick them, it's a wonder they haven't all dropped off by now. Maybe I could get time for a dick or two myself then."

I laugh at Isadora, she's funny as fuck but such a little brat. I feel sorry for the fucker that ends up married to her. At least I won't have to worry about her, I know she can give far more than she will get and then some.

"Anyway, I need you to look into the Polish. I've just had a meeting with them, and I have a feeling I can't shake about them. They agreed far too fast to all our propositions."

"Already done!"

"What the fuck, who told you about the meeting?"

"Nobody, my babies check your phone records daily. Keywords and uncommonly used ones are reported immediately to my phone. Also, if you think you can stop me Nikki, by getting a new phone or number, don't waste your money."

"God, it's like having a stalker."

"I'd love to have a stalker, there's this amazing book with my favourite psychotic fuckable stalker…"

"Stop right there. God, Ida you're so fucking strange. What did you find out about the Polish?"

"Spoilsport! The Polish may be in a bit of bother with the Irish. They know that working with you also brings an alliance of sorts. I think they are waging on this deterring the Irish from acting. You are, after all, the biggest fish in this pond Nikki."

"What have they done to attract the Irish's attention?"

"Oh, just one of the brothers may have dipped his dick in an Irish pussy he shouldn't have. Liam and Lorcan are not happy at all! Sloane is their cousin and now has a bun in the oven."

"Fuck me, what a fucking mess. The last people you want after you are those psychotic Irish twins. Which brother?"

"Jakub. Aleksander and Szymon are furious with him. They sent him into hiding months ago with their two sisters. So, I suspect that's why Aleksander has agreed to your terms so easily."

"Shit, I'd say. Thanks for the intel. I'm going to need you to keep an eye on the Irish and Polish for me. I'm a man of my word, so the agreement still stands and they have an army. I'm going to need extra men if I'm to take on Isaak and Mikhail. Are you any nearer to finding them?"

"Like I said before, I'm tracking Isaak as we speak. Once I have a location, you'll be the first to know. Mikhail is still at his mansion, but he deployed a big influx of soldiers yesterday. Last I checked they were on their way to the airport. I'm tracking the flight logs as we speak. The Irish and Polish are my next big job, so if you would just fuck off, I will be able to get on with it. I might even have time to sleep for an hour or two."

"Are you sure I can leave you with Lev, without you two killing each other?"

"Isn't that the excitement of it all, not knowing whether you'll have a best friend when you wake up in the morning?"

"Leave him alone Ida, for fuck's sake. What is the matter with you, I need him on top form so don't wind him up over Sam will you? Just try to be nice to people while you're here, it's only for a short time. Oh and you are due at a fitting on Friday for your bridesmaid dress with us, along with Sam and Valentina. Papa and Dimitri will be meeting us there and then we'll have a meal for just the family, to introduce Valentina before the wedding."

"Oh, how exciting... not. What the fuck do you think you are doing trying to put me in a dress Kai? That's a big fat no from me, but the meal might be fun. I can't wait for Papa and Dimitri's reaction to Valentina."

"Everyone will be on their best behaviour, do you understand? I'm not having this shit; I've got enough on my plate. Oh, and you will be wearing a dress, Ida."

"We'll see. Now fuck off, I'm busy."

"It's been lovely speaking to you too, Ida."

"Yeah, yeah."

I leave Lev's apartment with somewhat of a weight lifted, as I know Ida will be working flat out on the security. I also now know what is plaguing the Polish and I'm not going to be wondering why two enraged Irishmen arrive in my city. The amount of shit piling up on my plate at the moment is diabolical. Here's me, planning on whisking Valentina away for a honeymoon. At this rate I'll be lucky if I get a chance to spend any time with her at all.

Pasha is waiting in the car, ready to take me back and Lev is outside the apartments on his phone when I get outside. He looks angry and ends the call when I reach him.

"What's up with your face?"

"What do you think, it's Sam and her mixed messages again. She's driving me crazy Kai; I can't keep doing this with her. Maybe it's time to give up and cut my losses, like Ida says. She's over me, right? Why the hell do I keep chasing her?"

"You know as well as I do Lev, you'll never stop chasing Sam. You need to sit down with her and talk this through. Don't tell me you've fucked her again."

"Yes." Lev sighs.

"Lev you need to talk to her, not fuck her. No wonder you never sort out your relationship if all you do is get your dick wet instead of talking things through."

"It just happens Kai, I can't help it. When I manage to get her alone, I want to be inside her. She pushes me away so much I just want our connection back. It's killing me."

"I know Lev, but it isn't going to get any better if you just keep on having sex instead of talking. She'll think that's all you want her for, just to dip your dick in. Sort your shit out Lev, I need everyone focused. The Polish may be getting some heat off the Irish, so we'll have the nutty Irish twins arriving in my city soon. Plus we have Mikhail and Isaak to contend with. Ida will give you an update when you go back up."

"Well, that's something to look forward to. A scintillating conversation with Ida. Shit, Kai can't you have her at yours?"

"No, and I've told her to behave. Just try and last a couple of days, yeah? That's all I ask. I've got to get back to Valentina now, I'll call you later."

"Make sure you answer your phone, Kai, I may have to make an S.O.S call. Why did that sweet little kid we knew have to grow up?"

Lev walks back to his building shaking his head in dismay. Poor fucker, I don't envy his situation. I climb back into my car and head back to the hotel. I hope there's some pizza left; I'm starved.

Valentina

As I watch the lift doors close on Kai, I can't help but wish he would have stayed. It's silly, I know, but we just haven't had any normal moments together. Just to chill and watch a movie, eat a pizza and cuddle on the sofa. What do I expect though, he has a Bratva empire to run, he doesn't have the time to just chill with me.

"What's up Lena?"

"Nothing Luka, only tired, that's all. It's been a hell of a night and I'm also hangry."

"When are you never hangry? The pizza will be here soon. Misha just ordered it, with chicken strips and chips as well. So, not to worry, your hangry monster will be well fed."

Luka laughs as I punch him in the arm, cheeky bugger. I snuggle into his side and settle down to watch the film, drinking my hot chocolate. Misha joins us shortly after, settling down on the other side of me. He has a bottle of Bud in his hand and is looking at the TV with a slightly puzzled look on his face.

"What's up with your face Bear?" I ask.

"What the fuck are you watching Red? Vampires and werewolves? Shit babe, what happened to you? Although, I have to say, that suit she is wearing is fucking hot."

"Don't diss my kink Bear. And it's Lycans actually. Vampires and Lycans are hot full stop and Selene is sexy as fuck. She's a badass, a vampire and all in a latex suit."

"Whatever floats your boat Red. Do we get to see her out of the suit?"

"Typical bloke, just shut up and watch it."

"How many times have you seen this?"

"She's watched the whole series about 50 times," Luka answered for me.

"What the fuck? How can you watch a film that many times?"

"Because it's my favourite series duh. Will you two just shut up and watch it."

"Fuck's sake Red, you're so bloody bossy."

"She's hangry, get used to it," Luka mutters.

"What the fuck is hangry?" Misha asks, puzzled.

"Oh my God, you don't know what hangry is? Have you never had a girlfriend say she's hangry?" I ask.

"I don't do girlfriends, Red."

"What never?"

"Never fucking ever."

"What? So you're a virgin?"

"Fuck off, of course not! I have fuck buddies that's it. I fuck'em and leave."

"Well hello Romeo, I bet they are queuing up around the block for you and your charm. Jesus wept!"

"They are actually Red. But it's not the charm that they are after, it's my dick. They get my dick and then I leave. See? Everyone is happy."

"What the hell, you need some training on how to treat a woman right. Don't worry Bear, I've got you."

"I don't need any help Red, I'm perfectly fine the way I am. Now, what the fuck is hangry?"

"It's when a woman is angry because she is hungry, hence hangry. It's a scientifically proven fact."

"Fuck right off Red, it's just another excuse for you all to be brats. Any excuse and you all jump on it; you just need a firm hand."

"Says you Mr Casanova. Just remind me how many relationships you've had? Oh, that's right, a big fat zero."

"I don't need a relationship to know when a woman needs a firm hand because she's being a brat."

I'm just about to give another bratty reply when Misha's phone rings.

"Saved by the bell," Misha laughs, getting up and heading to the lift.

Arsehole, I'll get him back for that one. He enters the lift and smiles at me when the doors are closing. A couple of minutes later the lift doors open with Misha and another one of Kai's guards hauling in a load of pizza boxes over to the table. I pause the film and head over, followed by Luka.

I'm not even joking, there must be ten pizza boxes on the table, five chicken strip boxes and five boxes of chips. Plus different flavours of fizzy pop.

"Bloody Hell, is this for the other soldiers as well?" I ask, bewildered at the amount of food in front of me.

"Fuck no, those fuckers can eat when they clock off. This is for us, and I ordered the boss his usual as well."

"What's that?"

"He has two meat feast pizzas."

"Two extra-large meat feast pizzas to himself?" I asked, shocked.

"Yeah, Red. He's a big man, do you think a couple of slices would be enough?"

"Well, no, but two whole pizzas? My lord."

"Here's yours Luka. A meat feast with extra cheese, chips and chicken strips." Misha says as he passes Luka's food to him.

I watch as Luka settles down at the table to eat his food, looking back to see Misha carrying two pizzas, a box of fries and chicken strips and placing them on the kitchen counter. He comes back and gives me my pepperoni pizza. I sit down ready to have a couple of slices and look bewildered at Misha when he picks up five pizza boxes and starts tucking in.

"Holy hell, are you really going to eat five pizzas?"

"Yeah, no problem. I'll probably eat these before you finish your measly three slices," Misha laughs.

I just smile at him thinking, yeah right. As I'm opening my pizza box I look over to Luka and see he's already eaten two slices of his pizza. These men, I honestly don't know where they put it all. As I tuck into my first slice of Pepperoni heaven and moan. God I was hungry.

"See told you she was hangry, once she's eaten that slice, she'll stop moaning," Luka says around a mouthful of his pizza.

"Thank God for that. If Kai comes in and hears her moaning like that, he'll shoot us both in the head and ask questions later," Misha states.

"Fuck off both of you, and let me enjoy my pizza. I haven't eaten properly in days and you're ruining my moment," I say trying to enjoy my food.

"It's easy for you to say, you won't get your head shot off. That would definitely ruin my dinner," Misha grouses.

"Now, you're being dramatic. Kai wouldn't shoot you for such a stupid thing."

"You wanna bet? If he hears you moaning like that and it's only us two here, what do you believe he's going to think? Oh, it's okay she's just moaning over a pizza or she's getting dicked? I'm a red-blooded male Red, he'd shoot us."

"Fine. And you men call us dramatic. I'll try to stop moaning, okay?" I roll my eyes at him making sure he sees me, before I get another bite from this slice of heaven.

"He has a point, Lena, just put yourself in Kai's position. If you walked in and he was moaning like that, you wouldn't think it was because of pizza, would you? You just broke someone's nose, then had to be pulled off her, all of that for her just running her mouth. Then you caused even more shit by giving some dickhead a lap dance. You're both as bad as each other," Luka states.

I go quiet and continue eating my slice of pizza while mulling over what Luka just said. I suppose he's right, we both tend to overreact where the other is concerned. So, I consciously try to continue with my dinner without any moaning.

About three slices in, a couple of chicken strips and some chips down, I'm stuffed. I look at the guys and Luka has finished everything and is scrolling on his phone. Misha has eaten every bit of his food and is sitting there with a smirk on his face. Fucker! I give him the middle finger and pour some more coke into my glass.

I go back over to the sofa and settle back into my blanket. Misha and Luka come and join me as I press play on the film. I get about two-thirds into the film and can feel my eyes dropping. I try so hard to keep them open but fail and drift off.

The next thing I know, huge arms are lifting me up and bringing me to a muscled chest. I take a breath and intuitively know it's Kai from his Hugo boss cologne. I snuggle in and wrap my arms around his neck.

"Have you managed to eat, Kai?"

"Don't worry, my Little Vixen, I've eaten my food. Now sleep, I've got you; I'm just taking you to bed."

Kai places me in his bed and strips my pants and leggings off, leaving me just in his shirt, then covers me with the duvet. I hear him closing the doors; he must have also gone to get undressed. His side of the bed dips and he pulls me closer to him. I snuggle into him and his arm stays wrapped around my waist. His big body cocoons me, making me feel safe and secure. I drift back off to sleep, hoping we can stay like this forever. The thing is though; tomorrow always comes, whether we are ready for it or not.

Chapter 14

Kai

I wake up with Valentina spread over my chest. Her hair is covering my face, which is most likely what has woken me. It's tickling my nose and I think I've inhaled some of it. I rub my nose and try to spit out her hair, fuck this. If I cough a fur ball up later, she's going to get a reddened arse tonight.

I won't tell her though, because to wake up with her small delicate body spread over mine is glorious. It's not something I expected to want, need or crave, because I hated when women tried to touch me. Firm rules have always been in place. Some have tried, and their hands have been bound straight away. Valentina though has triggered a different reaction in me from the start. I crave her; her time, her touch, her body and her fight.

As I manage to get the last of her hair from my

mouth, I try to untangle my legs from hers, but she's like a baby monkey the way she's clinging on to me. She moans in her sleep and clings on harder. That sound goes right to my dick. Her moans are so fucking delicious; even in her sleep I'm tempted to flip her over and eat her delectable pussy out until she wakes. But, I know I have far too much to do today if I wish to spend any time with her tonight.

I grapple with her clinging limbs and manage to free myself from her grasp; she huffs and ends up turning over, hugging onto her own pillow and snuggling back down with a contented hum. I look disgustedly at the pillow, now nestled between her breasts and thighs. What did it come to that I'm now envious of a fucking pillow. Fuck me! I need a coffee. I place the duvet back over her and leave her to sleep.

I shower and do the rest of my morning routine, then dress in my custom Savile Row suit, black shirt, and my bespoke Gaziano and Girling shoes. I take a last look at Valentina as I fix my cufflinks and fasten my watch, placing my gun in its holster and my knives in their custom sleeves.

I close the doors to our room and head towards the kitchen to get my much-needed coffee fix. Lev and Misha are looking at several files on the dining table as I arrive; they greet me and go back to the file. They know better than to talk to me before coffee. Luka is making some and, when I arrive, he places one in front of me.

"Double espresso shot; I'll do your cortado now Boss." Luka greets.

I nod and shoot back my espresso in one go. I head over to the fridge and grab a bottle of mineral water, opening it and taking a few swigs as I get back to the table where Lev and Misha are having a disagreement about something.

"Keep it fucking down, Valentina is still sleeping!" I grumble.

"Sorry Boss." Misha grumbles

"Oh, I'm sorry that Princess Pea is still having her beauty sleep. We, on the other hand, are trying to keep your precious princess and the rest of us a-fucking-live." Lev spits.

"Fucking wind your neck in arsehole. Also insult Valentina again and I'll kill you myself. Now, what's the update from the security team and has Ida been in touch?"

"Ida says that Mikhail's soldiers have landed at Heathrow, private flight number 243-567. She's tracking their vehicles, but it definitely looks like they are heading to the midlands. The security teams at all of our venues are on high alert and I've called more reinforcements in. Ida has informed your Papa of the developments and he's taken the necessary precautions with the family home, businesses and his flight arrangements." Lev states.

"So why isn't Ida here with you, who's with her now?" I ask, getting more aggravated by the minute.

"She was tracking them and putting all the security measures into place. She sent me over to make you aware. Our main security squad was with her when I left... and she was laying into Pasha. He was looking at her like he may just resort to shooting himself in the head," Lev grumbles.

"Well, I'll go and bring them here. Shit I've got enough crap to sort out today without all this added to it. Tell Valentina when she wakes that I want her ready when I arrive back. We'll be heading out to The Siren's Call tonight. Tell her I'll message her the details." I mutter as I grab my keys and start to head out.

"Kai I'll come with you; you shouldn't be heading out unguarded with all this going on!" Lev shouts.

"Like fuck you will, you need to stay here with Valentina. I want hourly updates on her."

"Kai, she has a thirty-guard security team plus Misha and Luka. I think she's got enough security. I'm coming with you."

"I said stay the fuck here Lev, that's a fucking order. If anything happens, I want Luka and

Misha to hunker down here with Valentina. You, Lev, need to get to the roof. Take the fuckers out from your nest, I want Valentina unharmed do you all understand?" I look at all of them, making sure everyone is clear on their orders.

"Da Boss!" Misha answers immediately.

"You do understand that Valentina won't just stand back and wait for you to come for her, right? She's not the damsel in distress type, we'll be lucky if we will be able to keep her here," Luka argues.

"Are you telling me you and Misha aren't up for the job Luka?" I question angrily.

"I'm saying you don't know Valentina if you think she will just stay here!" Luka snaps back angrily.

This is the final straw with this idiot. I don't, and have never, liked the relationship he has with Valentina. I flip out and grab him by the neck, pinning him to the table in a matter of seconds. I lean down and shout in his face as he struggles against me.

"Are you telling me you know my Queen better than me prick? Do you think I'm such a cunt that I'd allow you to fuck me over like that? I will fucking end you right here…"

"Kai, let Luka go dear. I need my morning tea before I can cope with the amount of testosterone in this room. I was having a lovely sleep before you lot started having a cock slinging contest. Morning Bear, babe," Valentina says as she wanders towards the kitchen.

"Morning Red!" Misha replies, smiling at her.

"Am I just invisible here?" Lev gripes.

"No such luck arsehole, you always linger like a bad smell!" Valentina replies.

Misha sniggers and I can't help but smile at the shit she always gives Lev; I release Luka with a shove, making my way toward the kitchen. She's making her tea when I get there and wrap my arms around her waist.

"I'm sorry we woke you, Little Vixen, I had meant to be back for when you awoke."

"Don't worry Kai, I need to do some exercise anyway this morning, not training and dancing will take its toll on me."

I spin her around so she's facing me, gripping her throat as I stare down at her.

"Are you saying you will be dancing in front of my men while I'm gone?"

"No Kai, I'm not in the mood to dance. I'll be training with them instead."

"What the fuck Valentina, are you stupid? They are trained bratva soldiers."

I don't have time to think about the stupidity of

my own question before Valentina strikes. She knees me straight in my bollocks before I can react to the move. I groan and fall to my knees on the kitchen floor, cupping my battered balls.

"You men have a very obvious weakness that I love to exploit. You always forget about those dangling assets between your legs" Valentina says, as she circles me kneeling at her feet. She puts her fingers under my chin, lifting my eyes to hers. "Don't ever underestimate me Kai. I may seem weak but I'm far from it. I've been fighting soldiers since I was a child, I think I can handle your men. I hate it when men forget the strength a woman truly possesses. Just because we choose to submit sometimes, doesn't mean we don't have the ability to bring a man to his knees when we choose."

Valentina places a soft kiss on my nose and saunters off into the living room, leaving me to recover from her attack. Fuck, that woman undoes me in ways I've never imagined. I manage to overcome the excruciating pain any man gets from a well-aimed hit to his crown jewels and stand. I dust my suit off and walk towards the living room with a slight limp to my walk. I think I may have to invest in some groin guards for me and my men.

As I enter the living room, Misha sniggers at my walk and Lev is looking moody with his arms crossed, shooting daggers at Valentina who is calmly sitting at the table scanning the files. As she slowly sips her tea, she flips the reports Ida has sent over and examines the pictures of the soldiers her Papa has sent over.

"Band two and three of his soldiers, he means business Kai. I gather they are on their way to us now?" Valentina says.

"Yes, I'm going to collect Ida and we have adjusted security accordingly!" I reply, intrigued by her knowledge.

"Band two is his specialist attack soldiers. Not all of them are here, about half are missing, I guess the rest are guarding him. Konstantin and Borislav are in the group though, they are in his elite forces," Valentina continues.

"If we can capture either one of these two alive, we may get some information about what else he intends to do," Lev comments.

"If you think you'll be able to capture these two without them killing you first, you're dumber than I thought. If you do manage to capture them, they will not give you any information no matter the torture methods you use." Valentina replies.

Lev glares at Valentina again and starts to sulk. I smile at the way Valentina seems to not give a fuck about what people think of her.

"They   haven't   experienced   the   torture techniques Kai and I have created!" Misha states.

"Trust me Bear, you will never get anything out of these two or Alik, Savin, Sasha or Miron. You'd be best hoping Yakov and Shura know something, but I doubt it. He only has a select few soldiers that are allowed in his elite faction and for good reason. As you know Bratva soldiers would rather die than give any information out," she replies.

"I wonder why he's sent Band three out Lena; they normally always stay to defend him, Alik and Savin never normally go out on missions!" Luka says.

"We've been away for three years Luka, a lot can change in that time. It is worrying though, as he has sent over fifty specialist soldiers. Even 2356 is in the group. Shit, he's a fucker if I ever met one," Valentina replies.

"Who is he?" I ask.

"Papa's favourite sniper, nobody knows his name, only his number. I did learn his sniper name though!" Valentina replies with a concerned look.

"Which is?" Lev asks.

Valentina looks at me, then Luka, before finally looking at Lev.

"His sniper alias is 'Steel Eye;' he's in the top five deadliest snipers. He's going to be a big problem for us. Only one other sniper is more deadly and that's Karma Calling," Valentina replies.

Lev looks at me with a glint in his eye, I know what he's thinking and I know how long he's been after Steel Eye. They have a very personal vendetta with each other. I also know there is nothing I can do to stop him going after his nemesis. I nod, to give him the okay to do what he wishes and to blow the cover on his secret identity.

"Well, it's a good job you have him here then, isn't it? Don't worry Little Red, he will not be a problem!" Lev states, with a sinister smile.

"What do you mean we have him here?" Valentina says in shock, staring at us all with a questioning look.

I can see the excitement in her eyes at meeting the elusive sniper. I'm hoping this is a way for my best friend and Queen to fix their differences.

"I'm Karma Calling, Valentina. And I've been waiting for my chance to kill Steel Eye for an exceptionally long time. He has been elusive until now but you, Little Red, have just given him his death sentence. I can't thank you enough for that," Lev replies and nods to Valentina, placing his hand over his heart in a sign of respect for her.

"No fucking way, Oh my God! You're a God damned legend. Your hit ratio and distance kills are phenomenal. I've got so many questions; I've heard you use your Papa's sniper rifle, that was handed down to you. What was his alias? Please tell me it was the Preacher. He was the best sniper ever, you're close to breaking his record but my God he was phenomenal!" Valentina replies.

She's so excited I think she's going to topple her chair with how she's bouncing up and down on it. I didn't know how bloodthirsty she was until the last couple of days, but there's definitely more to her than meets the eye. I love how passionate she is about the things she loves. She's constantly surprising me.

"Enough questions for now my Little Vixen, we have too much to prepare for and I need to collect Ida. The guys are staying with you until I return and then we will be going to the club later. Behave, my Little Vixen!" I warn Valentina.

"Who me? Misbehave? Never. Oh, why aren't you taking any of your men with you?" she replies, coyly at first then she turns worried.

"I am perfectly capable of looking after myself, Valentina. My men are staying here with you, they have their orders. Do not fight me on this Valentina," I warn.

"This isn't the time to act all Rambo on me Kai. You need backup with you to collect Ida, just in case my Papa's forces attack you on the journey.

These soldiers are not just cannon fodder, intended to just kill a small number of people but not present much danger. These are my Papa's elite and for a good reason. They don't just run in and attack, they always have a strategy of attacking unexpectedly."

"I'll be fine Valentina and I'll hear no more of it. The guys will stay with you. I won't be that long, and Ida has eyes on the vehicles so she will know when the attack is imminent. We'll pack up Ida and the men guarding her then head back with Ida monitoring everything on the way. Ida is a wildcat herself, Valentina, she's very capable of fighting."

"So am I Kai, fuck I've been doing it all my life. I've asked you to not underestimate me."

"I'm not underestimating you Valentina, I'm protecting you. They will attack here first. I know they will and I need you protected. Lev will scope out from his nest to try and detect Steel Eye, then he will pick off any threats to us on the ground. Misha and Luka will protect you, as well as the rest of my guards. We have an influx of guards coming in as we speak and several other teams meeting me at Lev's apartment."

"It's pointless trying to change his mind, Red. He's as stubborn as you. You're well suited actually." Misha states.

We both reply in unison with "Fuck off" and

"Fuck you Bear."

Luka, Misha, and Lev all burst out laughing, while Valentina and I stare at them all and I can't help but smile when she starts giggling. Holy hell she looks even more beautiful when she lets her guard down like this. I love her feistiness, I always have, but this side of her doesn't appear very often. I need to make it my goal to see more of this.

I hate to break the moment, but I must leave as soon as I can to ensure I'm back before the attack. I message Ida to tell her I'm on my way and to start packing her stuff up.

"I have to go now Valentina; I won't be long I promise. Please behave and be gentle on the guys."

I walk over to Valentina, placing a gentle kiss on her forehead, then start walking to the door. I hear them start trying to decipher the bomb I've just dropped; I would feel sorry for them, but I start to laugh instead.

"What does he mean Lena? What are you up to?" Luka asks.

"Yes Red, if you think you are getting me involved you have another thing coming," Misha gripes.

"What the fuck is everyone on about? Can someone let me in on the inside joke?" Lev asks.

"Well, I need to do some exercise this morning as I'm no longer allowed to dance at the club." Valentina says innocently in reply.

"Hell, fuck no, I'm not dancing. You can do whatever you want but no fucking way am I getting involved," Lev shouts.

"Come on Red, Lev's got a point. None of us are dancing material. You can dance and we'll all sort out a plan for guarding you, okay?" Misha says.

"Guys you have it all wrong she doesn't want us to dance, but I'll tell you now you may wish she had," Luka announces.

The last thing I hear as the lift closes is Lev's raised voice and Misha groaning. *'Good luck guys you'll need it'* I think to myself and chuckle as the lift descends down to the basement.

Chapter 15

Valentina

As I watch the door closing on the lift, I feel an uneasy dread in my stomach that won't shift. I'm worried for Kai and even though I don't like his sister much, I'm worried for her too.

"What the fuck is that supposed to mean? Luka stop speaking in riddles and spit it out," Lev growls.

"Oh crap!" Misha groans.

"Oh crap, what? Will someone tell me what the hell is going on?" Lev growls again.

I smile at him and put my hands demurely under my chin, waiting a few extra moments before I put Lev out of his misery.

"I am going to change into my gym gear, and I expect you all to be ready for when I have finished. I'll be easy on you as I haven't got my knives at hand. Which reminds me Lev, where have all our things from the flat gone?"

"They're all boxed up in the room next to mine. What fucking knives are you talking about and easy on us how?" Lev replies, confused.

"Combat training, wrestling, anything goes really. My throwing knives and combat knives. Oh and my special made garter straps should be there as well for my throwing knives."

I stand up and start walking back to Kai's room as Lev is cursing at the lads; nothing like a good fight to get the blood pumping. Luka has seen me fight, but Kai's men have yet to witness it.

Grabbing a quick shower and brushing my teeth, I tie my hair in two braids and put them in buns at the bottom of my head. People tend to grab hold of my hair when fighting, that's a lesson I learnt years ago. I dress in black leggings and a tight vest top, containing the girls securely. I don't bother with any footwear, as bare feet grip Kai's flooring better. I leave Kai's room and head back into the living room to find everyone still there arguing.

"Is everyone ready? I am!" I announce.

"No way I'm fighting you Red, this is ridiculous!" Misha says.

"What's the matter Bear, are you scared of little old me?" I tease.

"Fuck off, I don't want to hurt you!" Misha says.

"Come on Bear, it'll be fun! I promise not to hurt you too much." I taunt again.

"I've said no, Red, stop trying to rile me. It's not going to work." Misha bites out angrily.

"You're no fun Bear!" I say, pouting sulkily at him.

"Luka, Lev, are either of you up to the challenge?" I say, turning to them both.

Lev is smiling at me and Luka is shaking his head.

"I've had enough punishment training with you Lena, give Lev a go!" Luka says.

"Chicken shit!" I say, smiling at him.

"Let's make this a bit more interesting, shall we Lev? If you win you get whatever you want from me. If I win, I get whatever I want from you. How's that sound for a sweetener?" I offer.

"Um, that's quite appealing. Obviously, it can't be sexual because babe? I just don't see you that way. I also prefer to be alive, so I think I can come up with something. I'll take you on Valentina. It will be my pleasure and payback for the knee in the balls the first night we met," Lev replies with a smirk.

He takes off his leather jacket, slinging it over a dining room chair, which leaves him in a tight white t-shirt and black skinny jeans. He also removes his shoes and socks and starts to do stretches to warm up.

"I know exactly what I want you to do, so I hope you're a good kisser." I taunt.

"I'm not kissing you, Valentina," he replies, looking a bit worried now.

"Oh, shit man. You know Kai is going to kill you for this if you lose Lev!" Misha says, shaking his head.

"Nice knowing you Lev!" Luka says laughing.

"It's fine. She won't win anyway, what do you take me for? Don't make it too easy for me babe," Lev taunts, rotating his arms.

"It's okay baby, the big bad sniper must be able to beat the itty bitty girl, mustn't he? If he doesn't then what would that mean for his reputation?" I snipe back.

"You wish babe, bring it on!" Lev states.

"Okay, old man!" I say, sauntering towards the table.

"Fuck off, I'm Kai's age so don't give me the shit about being an old man when you're fucking one!" Lev says.

"We'll see. Luka and Misha, can you move the table to give us some more room please?" I ask.

The guys move the table across towards the floor-to-ceiling windows, which gives us a good amount of room to fight in. I turn to Lev who has followed me, and I start stretching out my shoulders and neck. I get into my fighting stance and keep myself nimble as well as stable.

Fighting a man that has a clear advantage over you is all about tactics. Men are taller and heavier. They have a farther reach, with longer arms and if they catch you with a head butt or punch, they can knock you out in seconds. These are also the things that will work against them in the end and the things you need to take advantage of. Stay nimble, make them do all the work and tire them out, all the while giving strategic hits to the body. While doing all of this you also need to try and avoid a hit by them in the process.

I look at Lev and blow him an air kiss smiling at him. He smiles back and then runs at me. He goes to grab me and I slide in between his legs, getting up quickly to face him again. He turns, still smiling, and goes for me again. This time though, as I try to sidestep him, he manages to grab me, squeezing me tightly against his body. He's trying to restrict my air and wear me out with the struggle to escape. So, I bring my right leg up and slam my heel down hard on his foot. This encourages him to bring his weight forward as he tries to move his foot out of my way; exactly what I was waiting for. I relax in his arms giving him my dead weight to hold which, with him being off balance, topples him forward. He has to release me to put his arms out to save himself as he falls forward.

Standing up, and catching my breath after the hold he had on me, I watch as he gets back up. Lev rose, looking at me with what seems to be admiration. I don't think he expected me to be able to look after myself, being a Bratva princess and all. I call him on with my hands again and he comes at me, this time slower. He tries to grab me around the waist leaving himself wide open, so I pummel him with punches to his abdomen, then bring my elbow up and into the side of his head. He pushes me away and shakes his head, looking a bit shocked.

I run at him this time, jumping up and wrapping my legs around his neck locking my knees at the back of his head. I flip my body back down, flipping him over onto his back as I release my legs and end up face down. I get up on all fours and pounce on him; he's winded and a bit disorientated but manages to get an elbow into the side of my face. It knocks me for six for a bit, and as I wipe my hand over my mouth; it comes away with blood on it.

This still doesn't deter me though as I flip onto my back. I grab the top of his arm in between my legs and bend his wrist back in my hands, holding on with all my might. He can't get out of the hold and, if he doesn't submit soon, either his wrist or arm will break. Which is a travesty, after just finding out who he is.

He struggles a bit more as his pride takes a battering, but then he taps my leg as he curses to himself. I release him instantly and get up, holding my hand out for his and helping him up too. Once he's back up, he looks down at me with a smirk on his face.

"Okay, Little Red. What do you want from me as a reward for winning? You're a right little spitfire, aren't you? God, you remind me so much of Ida," Lev says.

"I hope I'm nothing like her but hey; life's a bitch and then you meet one. Anyway, like I said I hope you're good at kissing."

"I'm not kissing you Valentina. I don't fancy dying at Kai's hands today," Lev groans at me.

"You will do as I ask, I won the fight fair and square Lev. So, get on your hands and knees at my feet now," I demand.

"Oh, my fucking God! Hold on, I've got to film this to show Kai." Misha laughs as he takes his phone out of his pocket and starts to film my plan playing out.

Luka winks at me with a huge smirk on his face and I look at Misha, who is now filming, to address Kai.

"Hey Baby, I always told you men should stop underestimating me. Looks like you're just in time to see Lev pay the price. I asked him before we fought if he was good at kissing, shall we see how good?" I say towards Misha's phone.

I look at Lev and smile at him, signalling towards the floor with my finger pointing to my feet. Lev looks at me weirdly and then gets on his knees at my feet. I pat him on the head like a dog and look down at him.

"That's a good boy, now kiss my feet!" I demand.

Lev looks at me with astonishment but takes it better than I thought. Which both annoys me and makes me relieved at the same time. He's been a right pain in the arse since I met Kai, so maybe this and finding out who he is will help us develop a better relationship. He gets down on all fours and kisses both my feet in turn. As he gets up, I smile at him and put out my hand for him to shake. He grabs my hand but doesn't shake it. He kisses the back of it.

"You will make a great Queen and it will be a privilege to serve you," he says and bows his head.

He releases my hand leaving me in shock still looking after him as he walks away towards his room here. I look over at Misha and he stops filming with a big goofy smile on his face. Luka is standing there smiling at me too. I'm flabbergasted. Truly and utterly shocked by Lev's statement. I have never really thought about being a Queen. Bratva men don't usually let their wives have anything to do with ruling, so I didn't imagine that Kai would be any different. I'm sure he'll have enough of me anyway, once my Papa is dead and he no longer needs to protect me.

"Did that just really happen?" I ask in shock.

"Yes Red, Kai's best friend and second in command just gave you one of the greatest honours a Bratva man can give. I would also say it's well deserved, you truly have a warrior's heart, Valentina," Misha states.

"I don't know what to say, I'm shocked. We've never really got on!" I reply.

"I think you've found out something about each other today that has given you both a newfound respect for one another. You have a lot of good people on your side Valentina, who respect and trust you. Now, all that's left is for you to believe in yourself Red, and to also trust in every one of us to help keep you safe. That, my lovely, will be the time you become our true Queen," Misha says.

"Lena, Kai says he wants you ready for the club when he gets back. I don't think he'll be much longer. While you go and get ready, we'll clean the room and get ready as well," Luka says, smiling at me.

"Okay," I reply.

I don't know what else to say so I walk away to Kai's room to shower and get ready. Today has been such a day of revelations and enlightening events and it's not over yet. My Papa's soldiers are on the way to cause havoc and God knows what else. I'm exhausted but there's no way I'm not getting involved in this fight. Papa's made one very vital error. He made his daughter into a lethal weapon, one who knows far too much about his methods of war.

I jump in the shower, washing my hair and shaving everything. I decide to leave my hair to dry naturally into its curls. It's become a lot less frizzy since I've started using the conditioner Kai bought me. I apply a light layer of make-up, focusing on my smoky-eyes, eyeliner and mascara. The last thing I apply is a layer of my favourite cherry red lipstick, before having one final look in the mirror as I walk to the walk-in wardrobe.

I pick out a black lace, strapless bra, with matching thong, and put them on then search for some thigh-high hold ups. I finally find some with a matching garter belt; when I pull them on, the stockings feel like silk. They are definitely a new addition made by Kai. Strapping my garter belt to them, I go in search of a dress. I see numerous hangers of new dresses and clothes, my own scattered amongst them. As I'm perusing the new dresses, I find a beautiful black Valentino couture dress. I try it on and it fits like a glove. I give myself a once over in the wall mirror and I'm stunned. The dress is short, just covering my arse which means my stockings and garter straps are on full show. The silver diamanté edging around my bust line brings everyone's attention to my girls. Kai is going to have a total fit when he sees me, even though he brought it for me. I add black strappy sandals and head out into the living room.

Lev, Misha and Luka are sitting at the table looking over the files. It seems as though Luka is giving them details on each of the soldiers pictured. As I get close to the table, they all look up. Lev chokes, Misha just stares at me and Luka shakes his head.

"What's the matter with you lot?" I ask.

"I think you forgot to put your dress on Red," Misha gripes, looking away hastily.

"Oh God, he's going to kill us when he sees her," Lev whines.

"He brought me the damn dress, so I'm wearing it," I snap back.

"He may have paid for it but he didn't choose it personally. I also don't think he would think you'd look like that in it either," Lev replies.

"Look like what?" I ask.

"Like every man's wet dream, okay? Don't say I

didn't warn you," Lev says.

I'm about to reply when his phone rings. He takes it out of his pocket, looking at the name and answers it straight away. His face is stern as he listens to the person on the other end.

"How long Ida?"

"Is it both groups?"

"Have you got enough back-up?"

He holds the phone away from his ear as I can hear Isadora shouting from where I'm standing. He puts the phone back to his ear then replies.

"I know you're capable Ida, will you just answer the fucking question?"

"Thank you, where are you now?"

"Rough ETA."

"I'm nesting in ten. Misha and Luka will be protecting Valentina as instructed. I'll put 'extreme' in action now."

He listens a few more seconds then ends the call. He types out a message and puts his phone back in his pocket, standing up from the table.

"'Extreme' is in action with immediate effect. ETA of forces fifteen minutes, ETA of Crown twenty minutes. Your objective; to protect Vixen. Arm up and the radios stay on channel five," Lev orders walking off towards his room.

Misha heads towards Kai's office and I run after

him, looking for answers.

"What's going on Bear? Are they here?" I question.

"Not yet, we've got fifteen minutes," he answers.

He goes to the far wall and pushes the bookcase out of the way, revealing a hidden door. He keys in the code and the door pops open, revealing a treasure trove of weapons. I'm so engrossed, staring at the array of Makarov's, Kalashnikov's, grenades, etcetera, that I don't see Bear throw the bullet proof vest at me. It hits me in the chest and falls to the floor. I look down at it then look at Bear.

"Put it on Red, I'm not arguing about this. Pick out any weapons you require. Luka stock up, additional weapon belts are over there," he instructs.

Luka straps on his bulletproof vest and adds some weapon belts to strap several guns to. I look around while I fasten my vest on and can't really find anything that takes my fancy. I strap a weapons belt on and add a few Makarovs to it and some ammo, then make my way over to Bear who's picking up some smoke grenades.

"Bear, where are our things from the flat stored?"

"Second room after the lift to the right of the penthouse, why?"

"I won't be long," I say, walking out of the

weapons room in Kai's office.

I reach the room he indicated and open the door. I take in the small number of boxes that signify mine and Luka's worldly possessions. It's pitiful really, but you have to travel light while on the run.

Rummaging through a few I finally find what I'm after. My god I've missed my knives. Pulling them out of the box I place them on the table and pull out my specialist made thigh straps and chest straps. I attach the custom straps to each thigh and add three of my throwing knives to each. Then secure the remaining four to the chest straps along with my fighting knives.

I head back to Kai's bedroom, going into the walk-in wardrobe. I take off my sandals and replace them with my army boots. I also grab my hooded cloak, putting it on as I walk back to the office. Misha and Luka are walking out, armed to the hilt as I arrive.

"Bloody Hell Red, you're like something out of Assassin's Creed," he says, eyeing me up and down.

"I aim to please, so what's the plan?" I ask, not beating about the bush.

"Protect you, nothing more, nothing less. So don't get any silly ideas in that crazy head of yours," Misha replies.

"Fuck that shit, I'm not waiting up here while Kai and his men fight. I'm not Rapunzel waiting in my tower for the prince to rescue me. So, you can either be with me or not." I state.

"It's more than my life's worth Red, Kai gave explicit instructions for you to stay here. We are to keep you here, using any force necessary," Misha warns.

"I'd like to see you try and I don't care what Kai says, these are my Papa's men. Luka and I are valuable assets in this fight. I asked Kai not to underestimate me Bear, I expected more from you," I reply, hurt.

"We're trying to keep you safe Valentina, not underestimate you. Now I've found you again, I'll do anything I can to protect you. You're like the little annoying sister I never had, I don't want to lose you, okay?" Misha begs.

"That's so sweet Bear, you're like the annoying older brother I never had. So, with that in mind, know I will not behave and what's the plan?" I reply.

"Fucking hell, Red. If I manage not to die in this fight saving your arse, Kai will kill me when he sees you down there." Misha whines.

"You'll be fine Bear; I'll protect you, don't worry. Now, have you got a plan, or do you want me to take the lead?" I inquire, grinning savagely.

"Fucking hell, are you sure I haven't fallen asleep watching one of your film's? Please tell me I'm dreaming, and I'll wake up any second." Misha pleads.

"No, this is Valentina: the uncut version I'm afraid, Misha. Best just hold on for the ride because it's about to get bumpy," Luka voices.

I give him a dirty look and then pinch Misha. He doesn't even flinch, but I get my point over.

"See, not dreaming big guy, we only have a short amount of time left. I say we attack them from the lift side with the soldiers guarding the reception area. We can keep them at bay and try to force them back outside so Kai and the other forces can take them out from there. They will have no escape from our ambush," I explain.

Misha looks at me like I've grown a second head.

"You're full of surprises Red, that just might work. You must stay behind us though Valentina. Do you understand?" He orders.

"Of course," I say smiling.

I have no intentions of staying behind them, but I'll agree for now. Luka is looking at me. Knowing full well I won't, he shakes his head in dismay.

Misha gets a call to say Papa's soldiers have arrived via Isadora, who's monitoring their moves. She relays that they are only a couple of minutes away due to Kai's erratic driving.

We head towards the lift and when we step in, I pull my hood over my hair. Pulling the guns from my belt, I take a deep breath and ready myself for the fight. As I watch the number on the dial go down, a shiver runs down my body in anticipation. It's always like this when I fight, I think I'm a blood thirsty bitch at heart.

Chapter 16

Kai

I'm pushing my Bentley Gt Continental to its limits as Isadora is scanning footage on her laptop in the passenger seat. At the moment she's tracking Mikhail's forces and also deploying her drones to locations outside of the hotel. Pasha is trying to keep up with us, with the rest of my men in pursuit. We're about five minutes away when Isadora's Laptop starts bleeping.

"They just arrived at the Enigma. Nikki, your men are ready in the reception area, and I've just sent them a warning. Lev's just going to nest and assures me your little princess is safe with Misha and Luka."

"Good we're about five minutes max away now, have you put the safety measures in place on the hotel?"

"I have initiated all safety measures. The soundproofing has activated in every hotel room, doors are all locked so no guests can leave. The staff have given the protocol message to all the hotel guests, telling them they must stay in their rooms. The guests have also had complimentary food and beverages. The windows are all now replaying the past hours footage, so we don't have to worry about onlookers. The roads have been blocked off by our men. Just in case any guests arrive, and my Idabots have just arrived."

"Good, the sooner we get this under control the better. I'll have to contact Victoria at Star Press to get a handle on any reports. She'll have to put a spin on it for us and overshadow any stories. What the fuck are your Idabots Ida?"

"I'm glad you listened to my advice in buying a press office, they definitely come in handy. Doesn't Victoria normally ask for a fuck in return for her services Nikki? I can't see Valentina liking that, can you? Oh, my Idabots are my drone's, dickhead, they have certain modifications that have turned them into right little deadly fuckers."

"Victoria will do as she's instructed, or she will be disposed of. Plenty of people are willing to do her job if she doesn't like it. I fucked her because it was convenient, now it's not. I don't even want to ask you what you've done to your drone's, just make sure the little fuckers don't kill us or my men."

"I have programmed them with facial recognition and uploaded all Mikhail's men's images into them. Don't worry, my little hellions will behave. What do you take me for Nikki?"

"The psychotic bitch you are, Ida! We're a couple of minutes off now."

"Perfect. Everything's set up and ready, my phone will control my Idabots, so I'll press the button when we need them. Did you k... Oh shit!"

"What? What the fuck's up Ida?"

"The penthouse lifts just activated, it's on its way down to ground level. I'm logging into the reception camera's now, maybe it's Misha on his way down."

"What the fuck, he was instructed to stop with Valentina. Why the fuck does nobody do as they are told anymore?"

"Looks like your control is slipping Nikki, you best get that shit fixed fast."

"Fuck off Ida, we're here. Now sort your shit out."

We both check our weapons as I pull up just a short way from the Enigma. We get out and start to make our way forward but have to retreat slightly as a bullet hits the branch directly above my head. Pasha and the rest of my men pull up and form a bullet proof barrier with their Range Rover SV's.

As my men exit their vehicles, we all gather

behind them as I wait for confirmation from Lev that Steel Eye has been terminated. I'm just about to ask Ida for a sit-rep of inside the hotel when several bullets rain down on us again. Pasha dives on me and covers me, using his body as a shield. I manage to see another one of my men has done the same for Ida. Pasha grunts, but the gun fire abruptly stops. Pasha rolls off me, holding his side with a pained look on his face. I help him up and assess his side; he's taken a bullet for me.

"You're going to have to step out of this battle my friend, I'll leave some of the men here with you. Once we clear the hotel, I'll come back for you." I reassure.

"It's just a scratch Boss, I'll be fine. I'll get it sorted out once we have the hotel back under control," Pasha says, and he grunts when I help him to stand.

"You took a bullet for me, it's not just a scratch. I owe you a debt, I won't forget that," I praise.

"It's nothing Boss, I will just add it to all your other debts... you know you're racking up quite the bill. Do I need to send out some heavies to collect?" Pasha mocks cheekily.

"Nah," I chuckle, amused despite the fucked up situation we're caught in.

"Now, shall we show these fucker's why they shouldn't mess with the Filippov's or are you gonna start writing me love letters?" Pasha replies.

"Fuck off, you stubborn bastard. Let's show them what a true Bratva army is made of and try not to die, yeah?" I reply.

"You say such sweet things to me, boss!" He jokes and gives me a wink.

I flip him off and turn to survey the front of the hotel as all hell breaks loose in the reception area. There's rapid gun fire and Mikhail's men, who were trying to infiltrate the reception area, start to retreat out.

"Oh, sweet lord of mine! I think I may have just come!" Isadora announces, while sitting on the floor watching her phone.

"For fuck's sake Ida, are you watching porn in the middle of this shit show?" I shout.

"Well, if there's such a thing as a lady boner, I've definitely got one. Fuck, that's sexy as fuck." Isadora replies, still engrossed in her phone.

"Stop fucking about and sort your shit out Ida. What's going on in the reception area? Mikhail's men are starting to retreat?" I ask.

"Just watch the doors and you'll see. Fuck Nikki, I might just have to steal your woman for myself," Isadora announces.

I scowl down at her, ready to give her what for, when I get the message I've been waiting for. Lev sends me confirmation that Steel Eye is terminated.

"Pasha. Sniper down, attack from both sides but watch gun fire because our men are in there. Go!" I instruct.

Pasha and my men split up and head to entrap Mikhail's men. I take my jacket off, throwing it on the ground as I pull out my guns.

"Come on Ida, time for action or are you staying to watch your porn?"

"Three, two, one... look at the doors Nikki!"

I look over to the reception doors of my hotel to see Misha and Luka heading out of them. Fucking hell where's Valentina, I'll kill those fucker's if they left her on her own. Then I see a cloaked figure stepping out behind them and my jaw drops. Literally drops. As the hood falls, I see her flaming red hair as she throws two knives at the same time. One hitting its target on the left, straight into its mark's forehead. The other gets a man who's just about to fire a shot at Misha.

Now I know why Ida was so immersed in her screen. Fuck me sideways! Valentina is wearing a full-length hooded clock, army boots and the Valentino dress I purchased for her. The dress barely covers her arse but that isn't my main concern at the moment. The fact that she has teamed the dress with a suspender belt and silk thigh highs is. Fuck me! She looks like a walking wet dream, a mixture between Jessica Rabbit, Kassandra from Assassin's Creed and Lara Croft, all mixed into one sexy as fuck, kick ass creature. I want to strangle her as much as fuck her for daring to come out fighting in that outfit. My possessive nature wants to kill every man dead for seeing such a sight.

Misha and Luka are shooting a pathway, but some of Mikhail's men are getting too close. I start forward, not taking my eyes off Valentina as I see her take some more knives out. She doesn't falter and kicks the man to the right of her, jumping on him when he falls and stabbing him repeatedly in the chest. The other man grabs her, wrapping his arm tight around her neck and I see red. I shoot and his head explodes all over Valentina.

She immediately looks in my direction and when she makes eye contact with me, my world stops. Her smile is breath-taking. Even with all the blood and brain matter splattered all over her, it doesn't distract from her beauty. She stands and starts running towards me. Ida runs past me, firing at anybody posing an attack at us.

Valentina finally reaches me and jumps on me, wrapping her legs around my hips. My arms immediately wrap around her waist, holding her to me. She looks me over for any injuries and then grabs my head slamming her lips to mine.

As she kisses me with the passion and fire only she can ignite, she consumes me like no other. I let my ferocious little kitten take her fill, slipping her delicate little tongue over mine as she takes little nibbles on my bottom lip. Her nails are digging deliciously into my shoulders and she starts to rub her pussy over my hardening cock, tented in my trousers.

I'm just about to slam her against the nearest wall when she pulls away, looking at me with so much desire. Gunshots, yells and death surrounds us, but we're both too consumed in each other to care. That is until she reaches down to her stockings and pulls out one of her Strij throwing knives. Still staring into my eyes, she throws it slightly to the left of my head. I hear a thud and look back to see one of Mikhail's men lying on the floor, eyes wide open but lifeless and Valentina's knife is right between his eyes. I have no clue how she spotted the man approaching behind me.

"How the fuck did you see him, you were looking straight at me?"

"Peripheral vision baby, I think you better let me down so we can finish this."

I shake my head at her, chuckling slightly as I let her body slide down mine. This woman is going to be the death of me, I'm sure of it. I should be sorting this threat out and all I can think about is her.

We part and I go to push her behind me, but she knocks my hand away. I have no time to discipline her, but the punishments are piling up. My stubborn little brat needs to learn that I will put her back in her place once I get her home. I take in our surroundings and notice at least ten of my men lie injured or dead. Ida has someone pinned to the floor as she's laughing down at them. She has his head in a tight grip then, with a quick violent twist, she snaps his neck. With all the men dead outside, we head into the reception area.

Misha and Luka are currently checking that all of Mikhail's men are dead. Pasha is checking on our men.

The lift doors open and Lev steps out with his sniper rifle strapped to his back. I hear a whirling noise and Isadora's drones enter the area. They fly over the dead bodies and beam a red light at their faces; I turn to Isadora with a questioning look.

"They are just completing the face recognition scan to identify any outstanding men. It's nearly complete and I've got the clean-up team on the way now," Isadora replies, tapping away on her phone.

"What the hell are those things?" Valentina questions.

"They, are Ida's drones," I reply.

"That one looks like he's got a mini rocket launcher strapped to him. He also look's distinctly like a wasp," Valentina states, pointing to one of the drones.

"Oh, he's Sting. He has a custom mini high-grade missile attached to him and a piston action stinger. That one over there is Bobee, he has a taser attached to him and packs an almighty punch. Then there's Horny who will just be coming through the doors in a minute. He has a built-in mini machine gun, plus a grenade launcher," Isadora informs us animatedly.

Valentina's mouth is agape, as she stares at Isadora explaining her drones as though she's describing a car not a deadly modified robot. Valentina looks over to me, raising her brows in question, to which I just shrug my shoulders in reply. I'm fucked if I'm going to try and explain my nutty sister, I gave up years ago.

"Oh well that explains it then; a Bee, a Wasp and I'd say at a guess Hornet. Just a normal day at the office then, brilliant. Oh, my fucking God, he's a big boy!" Valentina announces comically.

We all look towards the door, as what looks like a giant Hornet flies straight towards us. Fuck me he's the size of a small dog and deadly as fuck. My sister smiles as it heads in her direction. Isadora strokes the thing on its head as it repeatedly bumps its head into her shoulder.

The other drones do the same and she strokes their heads too. I feel like I'm in a parallel universe where this happens every day. Shit, I need a drink.

"I think I like your sister Kai, she's as mad as a hatter but it's endearing," Valentina whispers up to me.

"I don't know whether I should be worried or glad you like her now." I reply.

"Why?" she asks.

"Well, if you two get your heads together we're all done for. But I will warn you, she likes you a little too much after your display today," I reply.

"I'm glad we like each other now; it will make things a bit better with your family I suppose," Valentina replies.

"You don't have to worry about my family, Valentina. I'll sort them out. You will be a part of them soon," I reassure.

"Only until you get bored of me and then I'll be thrown out on the scrap heap." Valentina comments.

I stare at her in shock. If she thinks she can escape me now she has another thing coming. She's mine! Before I can tell her this though my sister interrupts our conversation.

"One man is missing Nikki," Ida announces.

"That would be Steel Eye. He's over in The Victoria Gardens, floor 24," Lev states.

"No. That's where Horny was, making sure you killed him, so he's already accounted for. That means this man is missing," Ida replies, handing her phone over to me.

"Of course, I killed him Ida, what the fuck do you take me for," Lev angrily replies.

"A man. So anyway, where is this fucker?" Ida says dismissing Lev.

Valentina leans over so she can see the photo, then she pulls back giving Luka a worried look.

"Who is it, Valentina?" I ask.

"Konstantin." She replies.

"How the fuck has he slipped the net; I want him found now," I roar.

Pasha approaches me, standing closely to my side but not saying a word until I address him.

"How are my men?" I bark.

"Twelve men dead, eight injured and currently being taken to Victor's. We've secured the perimeter and all the cars are outside awaiting your orders Boss." Pasha reports.

"We have one man missing. Ida will send you the photo and I want the remaining men to scour the hotel and grounds. I want him found immediately, dead or alive. Make sure the clean-up is completed by the team and report back to Lev when you have finished. Then get yourself to Victor to assess your side, you're no good to me dead," I instruct.

"I'm staying here, I'll get the grounds covered while the men search the hotel. I'll also look through the journey footage to see if he slipped the net before they arrived," Ida says.

She sits down on the floor, in between dead bodies, and gets her laptop out of her backpack. She doesn't even look up at me, she's so absorbed in her task. There's no point trying to argue with her when she's made her mind up, so I walk over to Lev.

"Stay here with Ida and Luka, I'll take Valentina to the Grand Emperor Hotel. We can all stay there tonight and sort the organisation out later. Keep me up-dated," I order.

"No worries, Kai," Lev replies.

I turn and walk over to Valentina, who is bending over one of her Papa's dead men. When I reach her, I see her pulling her knife back out of his head, wiping it on his clothes then placing it back in the top of her stockings.

"What the hell are you doing Valentina?"

"I'm collecting my knives Kai."

"I'll buy you some new ones, just leave them."

"I'm not just leaving them Kai; these are my knives! They are custom made to my measurements, weights and blade style. I won't be long."

"I'll get you some more specially made Valentina, come on."

"I said no Kai, I've had these knives since I was thirteen. I'm not leaving without them."

I walk over to her and grab her arm; she looks around at me with venom in her eyes. I grab her around the throat and lean down in her face.

"When I ask you to do something you will do it immediately, do you understand?"

"I said no Kai, N.O. Net. I will be collecting my knives and then we can go. Until I find them, I'm staying. I have five more to find. If you help look, I'll be quicker."

"My Little Vixen, you have too many punishments to count and I will thoroughly enjoy inflicting them tonight. I suggest you don't add anymore to the list with that sharp tongue of yours. I'll help you find your knives, but we have five minutes and then we go."

"Thank you baby."

Valentina tiptoes to kiss me quickly as I take my hand away from her neck. She runs off in search of her knives. I follow her, in my new given position as push over as far as she's concerned.

Whatever spell this Little Vixen has over me is certainly working to her advantage.

We both look over the remaining bodies and manage to find all five knives in time. I grab Valentina's hand and drag her to my car, opening the passenger door and pushing her in. I slam the door, walk around to my side and get in. I look over to Valentina, finally I have her safe in the car, so I can relax a bit. She seems quite restless and hot; she grapples to take her cape off, throwing it onto the back seat.

She rubs her hands down her stocking and looks over at me. I'm unsure what's up with her, until her eyes clash with mine. They are full of desire and lust. Before I have any chance to process the thought, she literally jumps me.

Valentina

All I know is I'm horny as hell. It must be the adrenaline of the fight and the blood. Add the hot as hell grumpy bastard next to me and it was destined to be a lethal mix. I don't know why I do it, but I just throw myself at him in the driver's seat. His eyes go round with shock when I nearly head butt him in the confined space of the car. I manage to straddle him in his seat whilst also elbowing him in the ribs and maybe kneeing him in the thigh. I don't think it's the sexiest moment he's experienced but it's what he's got.

Once I'm straddling his lap, I slam my lips to his and slip my tongue into his mouth. I grab the back of his hair, yanking his head back. Breaking the kiss, I start licking and sucking on his neck, whilst grinding my pussy on his throbbing erection.

I expect him to take over any minute because he's always been the domineering one in the relationship. I'm surprised though, as he leaves his hands on my hips squeezing slightly now and again. He moans when I bite down on the left side of his neck, and it spurs me on. I release his hair and run my hands down his chest, then undo one of the buttons on his shirt. Grabbing both sides of the material, I rip it open, all whilst soothing my bite on his neck with my tongue.

I undo his belt and unzip his fly, then shimmy his trousers and boxers down his arse. He releases my hips to push his trousers down his legs so they slip over his knees, putting his hands back on my hips when he's finished. I take his cock in my hands and kiss his neck then sit back. I look into Kai's eyes and let spit dribble out of my mouth. He watches intently as it falls onto his thick, throbbing cock. Kai's eyes dilate and burn with passion and lust as I rub his pre-cum, and my spit, into the tip of his cock and then down the length.

While he's watching my movement, I pull my knickers to one side and slam myself down on his cock. Fuck me this man is huge, but I manage to seat myself fully on him. His head tilts back into the headrest and he groans deep and sexily. I wiggle a bit on his cock, trying to get myself accustomed to his size. Not really the best idea to slam yourself down on such a big cock, but my horny inner hussy really wasn't bothered about the ratio of tight pussy to horse dick.

I dig my nails into Kai's chest and start to slide my pussy slowly up and down his cock. We both moan in unison as my pussy slowly adjusts to Kai's size. His grip tightens on my hips, but he doesn't force me to go any faster. I've never seen this side of him; it feels empowering to take control for once from such a dominant man in the bedroom.

Looking at Kai, I find his eyes half hooded, watching my pussy slide up and down his cock. His mouth is slightly open and I feel my pussy clench, releasing more juices. Kai's eyes lock with mine and the way his pupils are dilated pushes me to flip out. He's covered in blood and I know I'm saturated in it too; added to the way he's looking at me makes me feel animalistic. I lean down and lick from his collarbone, up his neck and over his cheek.

I put one hand in his hair, grabbing it tightly at the roots and, with the other hand, I squeeze his throat, making sure I'm putting enough pressure on the sides of his neck. This will help me control his breathing, making him rely on me for his next breath. I look down at him and see the pure carnal pleasure in his eyes.

"I'm going to fuck you like you've never been fucked before big boy, would you like that baby?"

"Fucking hell Valentina, what are you doing to me? I've never let any woman take control before, let alone touch me."

Kai pants, trying to hold back. I know he's trying to let me have this moment. I think, in a way, he needs me to have this moment, to show him I'm nothing like those other women. I have no doubt these moments will be few and far between, as Kai's dominant to the bone. So, I need to show him it's hot to give control over occasionally.

"I'm fucking you baby; my pussy is going to milk your cock dry. Then I'm going to clean you up with my mouth."

I start to pick my pace up, riding Kai's cock hard. It's quite difficult in this position as he's so big it feels like he's splitting me in half. A fine sheet of sweat starts to cover my body; the pain I feel as his cock spears me deep and the ache of the stretch fuels my pleasure. Who would've guessed I like equal amounts of pain with my pleasure?

The sound of flesh meeting flesh, and wet slapping due to all my juices, fills the car. It's the most erotic moment of my life; we could be caught in the act by someone at any moment fucking like animals in Kai's car. If someone tried to stop me now though, I would stab the fuckers in the neck. I need my release; I can feel it building in my body to epic proportions. I've never felt so turned on in my life.

"Fuck baby, yes. Your cock feels so good, fuck yes," I groan, throwing my head back in carnal pleasure.

Kai's hands move to grip my arse cheeks. The grip is painful but oh so good. He groans, so deep and guttural that when I look back down at him, I find his head back against the headrest and his eyes closed. I rotate my hips, grinding my clit every time I bottom out on his engorged cock. My pussy starts to flutter with the tell-tale signs of the colossal orgasm that threatens to rip through me at any moment.

"Sorry my Little Vixen but I can't hold back any longer. I need to feel your tight little pussy come around my dick."

Kai starts to piston into me from below, with me still riding him. I reach my hands to the roof of the car, holding on for dear life. We both groan in unison as we build each other to our releases. I can't catch my breath and feel like I'm going to implode at any second. Kai's panting and gritting his teeth.

"Oh, Kai I'm going to come! Fuck me, fuck me harder."

"That's it my Little Vixen, come. Come now!"

I don't know what happens to my body when Kai tells me to come, but it seems to listen. I explode around his cock like a nuclear bomb. I'm spasming, shaking and screaming so hard I'm worried I might break him. Kai ramps up the speed of his thrusts and roars out as we both find release. I feel him pulsating deep inside me, filling me with so much cum that it starts to escape.

I'm that exhausted I collapse onto his chest; we're still moving slowly in tandem. I can hear Kai's racing heart beating in his chest, confirming he's just as affected as I am. I can't believe what I just did, or what came over me. I just know that I needed him. Kai grabs my face and pulls it up to his, his eyes search mine with wonder.

"You are so fucking hot Valentina. My Little Vixen is definitely coming into her own. You're still going to receive a punishment from me tonight though, for not staying in the penthouse. And also for coming out to fight half naked. Fucking hell kotehok, what were you thinking? Then I'll deal with Misha and Luka. I ordered them to keep you safe, not take you on a half-naked killing spree."

"If you want to blame anybody, Kai it's me. If you knew me at all, like the lads do, you would already know I will do what I think is right, and nobody will be able to stop me. This is my fight, Kai; I will not leave you to sort this out for me. Don't expect me to cower in a corner waiting for you to rescue me, I will fight to the death, always."

Kai pulls me to his chest squeezing me so tight I can hardly breath.

"That's what worries me Valentina, I can't lo…" He stops himself from voicing what worries him and brings my face to his again and places a soft kiss on my forehead. "I need you to be safe Valentina. Come on, let's get you back to the hotel."

I look into his eyes, searching for what he really meant to say. I give up, proceeding to climb off his lap and into the passenger seat. I shimmy my dress back in place and put my seatbelt on. Then smiling over at Kai, I snark, "Come on then Kai, show me what this baby is made of."

He smiles back at me and presses the ignition button, revving the engine. I can't help but squeal with delight as we take off at high speed. My excitement is catching, and we forget about our predicament for a while. Just me and Kai in the car, just a moment's reprieve but an insight into a future we desperately want.

Chapter 17

Valentina

We arrived at the Grand Emperor Hotel after Kai really showed me what his Bentley GT Continental can do. I've always loved cars, but Kai's cars are in another league. I know he took me for a longer drive than we needed, as we are now back in the centre of Birmingham.

We enter around the back of his hotel to an underground parking lot. Staff come to greet us and Kai gives them his keys, before coming around to my side and opening my door. He extends his hand for mine and I take it, getting out of the car. He weaves his fingers into mine and we head into the hotel.

My God, if I thought the Enigma was high end? This hotel takes the biscuit. Grandiose is not the word for this hotel. Fuck me, it's like something out of John Wick. I expect Winston or Charon to come and greet us at any second. I close my cape around myself, feeling totally under-dressed for such an establishment. Oh, and then there's the small fact we're both covered from head to toe with blood and brain matter.

A tall, catwalk model heads over to us. She's blonde, figure to die for and beautiful. She's immaculately dressed and has an air of grace that screams high society. She approaches Kai, not even looking at me as though I'm insignificant and places her hand on his chest, kissing him on both cheeks.

"Darling it's been too long. To what do we owe the pleasure of your attendance today? Is it business or pleasure?"

I know what she's offering as pleasure, and I feel like my skin is heating by the second. I don't realise what I'm doing until Kai reaches over and grabs my hand, squeezing it to get me to release the knife I was slipping out from my stocking. I look at him in surprise and he smirks down at me shaking his head. I release the knife and Kai removes his hand to address the woman.

"Amanda, I'd like you to meet my soon to be wife Valentina. Valentina, this is Amanda the Hotel manager. Anything you desire, Amanda will deliver. Please make sure Valentina is treated like the Queen she is while we are here Amanda." Kai orders.

I try to hide the smirk on my face but fail when

Amanda's face drops. I look at Kai and he winks at me, making a goofy smile spread over my face. I look at Amanda who is trying to pull herself together, then a fake smile appears on her face.

"Lovely to meet you Amanda, what pleasure do you have in mind for me today?" I say sweetly.

I can't help it; I know it's irrational but I'm jealous as hell of all these women in Kai's life. Kai squeezes my hand and I look up at him, giving him doe eyes in return, while fluttering my eyelashes at him. This makes him laugh and seems to break Amanda out of her shock.

"It's lovely to meet you too Valentina, I'll just go and get the room key. If you'll excuse me?"

"Play nice Valentina, you can't go around stabbing my female staff."

"She needs to keep her slimy paws off you then Kai."

"Jealousy doesn't suit you kotehok, especially if it's not warranted."

"You've obviously fucked her Kai, and she can't wait to jump back onto your cock."

Kai throws his head back and laughs. It's such a beautiful sight I can't help but smile at him, dampening some of my anger at Amanda slightly.

"I think she would definitely pick up an injury if she jumped on my dick Valentina."

"Haha, very fucking funny."

"I always aim to please."

"Oh my God will you just shut up, what's taking her so long anyway. I'm standing here, with blood all over me looking like Julia Roberts in Pretty Woman. You could've warned me that we were going to be standing in the main reception."

"What would you have done, grabbed a shower on the way?"

"Smart arse."

Kai pulls me towards the reception desk and I look around, but nobody is there at all. It's deserted. Amanda walks out from the back room and hands Kai a key card.

"Everything is ready for you Kai; we hope you have a nice stay. Let me know if you need anything."

"We will do Amanda, please send Misha and my men up to the penthouse when they get here. I do not need to stipulate the privacy needed when they arrive, do I?"

"Of course not Kai. Everything is in hand as always."

"Glad to hear it."

Kai pulls me off toward the elevators, while I give Amanda the death stare as we leave. We enter the lift and Kai presses the button to the penthouse.

When the doors close, I'm encompassed in Kai's boisterous laughter.

"What have you got to laugh about Mr?"

"You can stop giving the death stare, Valentina. She's gone."

"Fuck you arsehole."

I tilt my head to the floor to hide my smile. This man misses nothing. I can't help wondering what he must think of me. Maybe he's regretting even meeting me, with all the trouble I've brought to his life. He should have just gotten rid of me though surely, not taken on this war with me.

When the doors open to the penthouse, they reveal a large waiting room, equipped with chairs, a table and two additional doors other than the double doors in front of us. The penthouse itself runs with the same theme as downstairs; reds, browns, beiges and golds. The old-fashioned charm and elegance that England always has to offer.

"That door is the staff entrance and that door is the exit to the stairway."

Kai points to the door on the right and then left, then he zaps his card on the fob next to the door. I follow him in and look around the open plan area; there at least four seating areas, another huge dining table but, unlike his other penthouse, this one has deep oak fixtures and dark chocolate leather settees. Red cushions and a huge floral display on the oak dining table accent the space.

This room has several doorways branching off in different directions. I don't know whether it's me, but something feels off about this penthouse. I just can't put my finger on it. As I'm looking around the room, Kai drops the keycard on the side table and turns to me.

"Come on Valentina, I'll show you to our room so you can shower. I told Ida to bring some clothes for you when they arrive, so just use one of the dressing gowns for the time being."

"Aren't you showering too?"

"Yes my Little Vixen, but I'll use one of the spare rooms."

My heart drops. He doesn't want to shower with me. I'm trying to figure out why, when he must read my mind and interrupts me.

"If I shower with you Valentina, I can guarantee we will be getting dirtier rather than cleaning ourselves. Go, have a shower and I'll meet you back out here after. We can order some food and talk about your punishments."

Kai's eyes dilate when he mentions my punishments and I can't help squeezing my thighs together to ease my arousal. I should be exhausted after everything we've been through today but I'm far from it. Kai sees my action and smirks at me, turning to walk toward a door on the far left of the room.

"Follow me kotehok."

"Bossy much."

"Always! Get used to it. And less of that sassy mouth of yours before I use it for far more enticing things than talking."

"Yes Sir!" I say cheekily.

"See! much better manners already."

The fucker! I duck my head to hide my smile and follow him through the door. We arrive in what must be the master bedroom. As with the other rooms it's furnished with a dark wooden queen-sized bed, wardrobes, and dressing table. The colour scheme continues throughout, when I reach the ensuite I squeal in delight pushing past Kai.

"If I knew a claw-foot bath would have had this reaction from you, I would have one fitted into every room."

"I can just see it now. Me lying back, submerged in bubbles while your men come in and out of your office for meetings. I may even sing for them as a farewell."

"You sing?"

"Out of all of that, you ask me if I sing?"

"I would kill any man that saw you naked so that's not going to happen. Stop avoiding the question."

I hadn't meant to slip up and tell him I sang because I'm not even that good. I've always sung, while I was in the privacy of my bath or shower though. Nobody has ever heard me sing; my mama had a beautiful voice and used to encourage me to sing with her. After she died I didn't sing for ages, then after a while, I started again when I had privacy and it soothed me. I felt like I had her back with me for a moment.

"Yes, I sing. But I'm no good, honestly."

"Why don't you let me be the judge of that."

"I've never sung with anyone, except my Mama Kai."

"Well now you have me to sing to, so get your sexy arse in that shower and let me hear you sing. I'll go, take a quick shower and will be back."

"Okay."

Kai gives me a quick kiss on my forehead and leaves the room. I look at myself in the mirror and cringe. Bloody hell I look abysmal. Blood covers every inch of my body and my hair looks like I've been dragged through a hedge backwards. I peel off my ruined dress and undergarments, along with my cloak. It kills me to throw them away, but they are well and truly past saving.

After taking far too long figuring out how to use the shower, I stand under its spray, thinking about everything that has happened today. God, it could have gone so differently. And how many more of the people I love is my Papa going to take off me? I love Luka and Misha like brothers and well Kai? I'm falling deeper and deeper into heartbreak. I just can't seem to stop myself even though I know he will never love me back.

Washing my hair I try to think about anything else, other than what a disaster my life is. I think back to singing with my Mama out in the gardens of our estate; she used to prune her roses and sing to me. I gather up the courage and start to sing one of the many songs she sang to me. 'Somewhere over the rainbow' by Judy Garland. My Mama's voice used to sound so haunting when she sang this. At age six I didn't understand why Mama sang that song as though her soul was shattered.

I wash my body while I sing the remainder of the song, with a slight tremor in my voice. When I finish, I wipe away my silent tears and let the shower rain on my face. I let it wash away my heartbreak whilst silently promising my Mama I will get her justice, no matter the cost.

Switching off the shower, I open the door to find

Kai staring at me in awe. He wraps me up in a white fluffy towel and cuddles me to his chest.

"Valentina, that was absolutely breathtaking, you have such a beautiful voice."

"It's nothing compared to my Mama's but thank you."

"Are there any other talents that you are hiding from me?"

I smile, looking up at this beautiful but deadly man.

"No, that's everything in my arsenal."

Kai chuckles at me and helps me dry off, wrapping me in a white fluffy bathrobe which is far too big. I have to turn the sleeves up. I follow Kai out into the main room, and sit on one of the leather settees, as Kai picks up his phone to order the food. He opens a bottle of white wine and offers me a glass, before sitting and sipping his own glass.

Kai

We've eaten our food and polished off the bottle of wine. Valentina is sitting cuddled in a blanket at the end of the sofa watching a film. Lev has reported back and given me a detailed report of events that happened when we left, and they're making their way back as we speak. They haven't tracked down the missing man, but Ida says she'll continue the search from here.

I need to punish Valentina before they arrive, because then I will have calmed my rage down slightly for when I reprimand Misha and Luka.

"Follow me, Valentina."

I get up and Valentina looks at me, a puzzled expression on her face. I ignore her and continue to walk towards my Den here. I checked that everything was in order while Valentina was in the shower and left the door unlocked. I twist the knob and open the door, then turn to see Valentina following me. She stops dead on the threshold.

"What the hell is this room, Kai?"

"It's my Den and from now on, whenever you enter this room; I want you to strip and kneel just inside the doorway. Do not speak until spoken to, I will explain the rules of the room when you are kneeling in the correct position."

Valentina looks up at me shocked, but thankfully listens to my orders and takes off her robe. She folds and places it by the door on the floor and kneels, looking up at me. Perfect.

"This room can either be for your pain or pleasure Valentina, how you act throughout the day will determine which one you receive, maybe a bit of both. You will remain silent unless I ask you to answer a question, you will always reply with your answer then follow it with 'sir.' Do you understand so far?"

"Yes."

"Yes what?"

"Yes Sir."

"Excellent. We will go through hard limits another time as today's punishment will only consist of a flogging. Is that all clear?"

"Flogging?"

"You will see what flogging is in a moment, but do you consent?"

"Why do you have to punish me, Kai?"

"This is your last chance to get this right, Valentina. The next time, I will give no warning and you will be gagged. You really need to ask me why I am punishing you? You put your life, and the life of my men in danger today, Valentina. Amongst other things. Now, I'll ask again. Do you consent?"

"Yes Sir."

"Excellent. Good girl."

I walk over to the cabinet that contains the ball gags and take one out. Even though the thought of Valentina's screams entices me I need to keep her quiet, as everyone is due back any minute. I go to my ropes hanging on the wall and choose four lengths of red.

Placing them on top of the spanking bench I go back to collect a spreader bar. As the spreader bar already has foot cuffs attached, I only have to grab some wrist cuffs. When I've set everything on the spanking bench, I turn to approach Valentina.

Her breathing is rapid and her eyes are dilated, totally focused on the items I've placed on the spanking bench. She will have to learn quickly that I will not tolerate her attention being anywhere other than on me.

"You will look at me and only me until I say otherwise, do you understand Valentina?"

It takes her a few seconds to recognise my voice and pull her gaze away from the bench. Then she looks up at me with trepidation.

"You have one of two choices in this room, Valentina. I will tolerate nothing else. You either give all of your attention to me and only me, or you can look at the floor in front of you. Do you understand?"

"Yes Sir."

"Good girl. Now, the rules. You will give me a safe word that you wish to use to stop everything, slow down or indicate you are okay to continue. The most frequently used is the traffic light system i.e. Red to stop, Amber to slow down and Green is okay. You can choose one of your own or we can go with that one if you're comfortable with it."

"The traffic light system is fine Sir."

"Brilliant, Good girl."

I walk back to the bench and collect the ball gag, then return to Valentina. She tries to keep her attention on me, but I catch her giving looks to the gag. I grab her around the throat and squeeze slightly.

"You've just added yourself five extra lashes for that rule break Valentina, I suggest you concentrate and behave. Eyes on me or the floor."

"Yes sir, sorry."

"Good, now because of that smart mouth of yours and the fact the penthouse will be full of my men at any minute, this time you will be gagged. Normally if I gag you, you will have a hand signal this time, o means okay, two fingers mean stop. But, due to this being a punishment, you will have no get out signal. You will take your punishment, no questions asked. Do you understand?"

"What the fuck Kai…"

"Ten more lashes Valentina, do you understand?"

"Yes sir." Valentina replies with venom.

I let that go, but when she's more experienced in this room, I will pick her up for the slightest waver. It looks like I have a brat on my hands with my Little Vixen and what a delight that will be for my Sadist soul.

Gently, I place the ball gag in her mouth and fasten it at the back of her head. I hold my hand out for her. When she places her hand in mine, I lead her over to the spanking bench. I take her to the end and push her back, so she's bent over exactly to where I want her. The top and side rests are cushioned, covered in leather to ensure no harm comes to her pressure points.

I fasten the wrist cuffs on and thread my rope through the rings, before I attach and tighten them to the bench, immobilising her front half. I would normally have her legs bent on the leg rest, but today I've chosen to place a spreader bar, so I attach my ropes to that. When I've finished, I walk around and take in the glorious sight before me. While I was binding her legs, she'd already placed her head to the side on the surface.

Calmly I run my hand over her back and stand behind her, then squeeze her arse cheeks really tightly.

"Argh" Valentina's muffled screams sooth my anger.

"This is a punishment Valentina, it's to ensure you behave in future. Suck it up princess, as this is going to hurt."

I walk over to the floggers and pick out a particularly cruel one. Its bite will mark her for days and sting like hell. I walk around her body, dragging the flogger over her skin. Her muffled whimpers only spur me on and, when I reach her delectable arse, I bring the flogger down at full force. Valentina's screams are muffled by the gag which makes my dick jump against my fly. Fuck, I'm rock hard already and I've only just started.

Her arse cheeks have reddened nicely, and I can't wait to see what the final result of my torment will be. I bring another four strikes down on the same cheek, then do an additional five strikes on her other cheek. Her voice is going horse with her screams and her arse is bright red. I continue on with another five strikes on each thigh, all the way from her sit spots down to her knees. I know this is particularly painful, but revel in her screams of agony.

I walk over to her face and find drool and tears coating it and my bench. It's a sight that only brings me satisfaction, seeing the evidence of her suffering at my hands only. She will learn to be a good girl or suffer the consequences; she will stop taking risks as I can't have her taken from me. I will not allow it.

"Halfway through my Little Vixen, you are taking your punishment so well. Good girl," I say as I stroke her hair.

She starts sobbing, but this will do nothing to deter me from my actions. I go to her left-hand side and give her five strikes to her back and shoulders. I repeat the same on her other side; by the time I've finished there is not a spot on her that isn't bright red. Delicious, I've been dreaming of what she would look like when I finally got her in one of my Dens. This though, is far more erotic than I ever imagined. I've spanked plenty of women and torture is my specialty, but nobody has even come close to the sight of Valentina now.

I go back down to her arse and I drag two fingers through the evidence of her arousal in her pussy. I swipe over her clit and she bucks from the bench. I rub over her clit teasing her to the point of coming, then move my hand away. Valentina whines around the gag, and I just laugh and suck her juices off my fingers.

Before I bring the flogger down another five times on each of her arse cheeks. Then I give her five strikes on each thigh again from her sit spot to her knees. Once I've finished the last lash, I drop the flogger to the floor and squeeze her arse cheeks viciously. She screams in agony and I revel in her anguish. Fucking hell, I'm feral. I cannot change something that is so deeply ingrained in my soul though.

I make quick work of taking all the restraints off her and pile them up in the corner to be cleaned later. Even though I've taken all the restraints off her she lies sobbing, bent over the top of the bench. I go back over to her and start stroking her hair.

"You did so well with your punishment my Little Vixen, such a good girl for me. It's all over now, so let's get you in the bath to soothe that edible backside of yours?"

"My body feels like it's on fire, you arsehole. I don't think I can move, let alone get in a bath, what the fuck is wrong with you?"

"Everything is wrong with me Valentina, but you will get used to my ways. You have only experienced a punishment so far. Believe me though, when you experience my form of pain with your pleasure, you will be begging me for more. I'll get you some cream."

"I will beg you for no such thing you animal, fuck that hurts like hell."

"It was meant to hurt Valentina, it's a punishment. Learn from it and you shouldn't have to endure one again. This cream should help."

"What is it?"

"Arnica cream."

I go over and squeeze a liberal amount of the

stuff into my hands. I apply it to all the areas I've lashed, which is most of her shoulders, back and arse, plus her legs, then return it to the cupboard. I go over and help Valentina up; she whimpers but eventually straightens.

As we go over to the door, I grab her robe and help her into it, then fasten it around her. I grab her face and place a soft kiss to her temple.

"You have done so well for me Valentina; I can't wait to introduce you to my world."

"What, you spanking the hell out of my arse and legs, then bringing me to the point of coming to only get another beating. No thank you arsehole, how about I beat your arse instead?"

"I'm a sadist Valentina, you will be doing no such thing. I can also tell by how wet your pussy was, that some part of you enjoyed it, when I gave you a punishment just now, and when I used my belt on you in the beginning. You are a masochist Valentina, you enjoy pain with your pleasure. I will show you soon."

"Fuck that shit."

"We'll see."

I open the door and exit with Valentina, knowing she'll have to get used to my kinks, and I can't wait to show her them all.

Chapter 18

Valentina

I'm awoken to an almighty argument and shouting; I jump up in surprise, wondering how the hell I ended up in bed. The last thing I remember is trying to sit comfortably on the sofa while watching a film. I didn't want to talk to anyone as I was sulking. My arse and legs were on fire and I was horny as hell, with no relief in sight.

Kai kept on smirking at my every move to get comfortable and it was pissing me off more. I must have fallen asleep eventually watching the film, as everyone had appeared and they were talking over the events the day. They still hadn't found Konstantin, which worried me as he could now give information back to Papa. I switched off and watched the film, ignoring everyone.

I scramble out of bed, wincing as I sit on my sore

arse. I throw a dressing gown on and march out of the bedroom to see what's going on. I find Ida and Lev trying to hold Kai back, whilst Misha and Luka are sporting a matching pair of red swollen eyes. Fuck me, what the hell?

"What the fuck is going on here?" I shout out in rage.

"My son is dishing out some much-needed punishment, who are you?"

"The Loch Ness fucking monster. Kai, what the hell have you done?"

Kai's Papa just sits there with an annoying look on his face and Kai is panting with rage in Lev's and Isadora's grip. I walk over and stand in front of him, putting my hands on my hips. He looks down at me.

"I've done far less than I wanted to Valentina, they put you in danger," Kai roars at me.

"Don't you dare fucking shout at me you idiot! It was me who wanted to fight. I told you this before you went to pick up Isadora; I will not stand back and let others fight for me. Do not take it out on Bear and Luka do you understand?" I scream right back at him.

"Fucking hell, has anyone got any popcorn. She's sexy when she's mad Brat." A man says lounging on a nearby sofa.

I look at him. I know the use of Brat means

brother, so he must be Kai's brother Dimitri. Fuck me he's gorgeous, with darker hair than Kai but the family resemblance is there. He gets up off the sofa with a lazy smile and holds out his hand for mine. I place my hand in his and he brings it to his lips, kissing the back of it before introducing himself.

"You must be Valentina, it's lovely to finally meet you. I'm Dimitri, Kai's younger but better-looking brother," Dimitri says.

I pause a moment, trying not to be sick in my own mouth with his self-absorbed ego. Fucking hell, what is it with gorgeous men that are full of it? It's such a turn off. I remove my hand from his and wipe it on my robe; fuck knows what Romeo has got.

"You are correct, I'm Valentina. Pleased to meet you, but I'm a little busy here right now so can you sit the fuck down while I knock some sense into your brother, please?" I reply sweetly and turn back to Kai.

Lev and Isadora are smirking at Dimitri, and Kai is still standing between them enraged.

"Kai if you want to blame anyone it's my fault, don't you dare hit them again on my part."

"They had clear orders Valentina; they are my men. And they will be punished for their indiscretions accordingly. This has fuck all to do with you."

"It has everything to do with me Kai, it was me that decided to come down. If they hadn't have come down to watch my back, I may have been in danger. They didn't though, they protected me at all costs," I rage back at Kai.

"They should have stopped you going down in the first place. If they can't control one-woman, what use are they to me?" Kai rages back at me.

"How fucking dare you, nobody controls me, Kai. NO FUCKING BODY." I scream.

"And therein lies the problem," Kai's Papa comments.

"Fuck you arsehole." I shout to his Papa at the same time as Kai retorts with. "Not now Papa."

"What did you want them to do Kai, knock me the fuck out? Because that's what it would have taken to keep me from going down." I ask.

"I should have tied you the fuck up before I left, you are fucking infuriating Valentina. In answer to your question though; no, none of my men have any right to touch you," Kai replies.

"Then there is no problem here, is there? I was always going to fight Kai and nobody would ever be able to stop me. Stop trying," I advise.

"You have to admit Nikki, she's a vicious little thing when she fights. Also hot as fuck. I have a personal copy of her fighting; I may give you a copy if you ask nicely. Dimitri has already ordered one," Isadora states with a wink at me.

"Fuck off Ida." Kai snaps.

I just stand there in shock for a few seconds. My God, who are these people?

"Um, thanks I think." I eventually reply.

"I'll leave it for now but if they ever disobey my orders again, I'll kill them. No questions asked." Kai states.

I let it go for now, but I'll be having words with him later. I walk over to Bear and Luka and check their eyes out. They are swelling by the minute, so I walk into the kitchen, I retrieve two tea towels and fill them with ice from the freezer. I give each of them one to place over their eyes.

"Sit at the table guys, keep that on for at least ten minutes. It will help with the swelling."

"I was a cage fighter Red, I know how to deal with a black eye. Thank you anyway," Misha says.

"I know you do dickhead, but humour me." I retort.

They both sit down and I go into the kitchen to make myself a cup of tea. I feel Kai enter before he puts his arms around my waist.

"Fiery little kotehok today, aren't you?"

"Do you blame me Kai, my arse is on fire. You have also hurt both of my friends for no good reason."

"I'm not going to get into this again Valentina, your arse and their eyes are hurt for exactly the same reason. Deal with it and behave from now on."

"Oh my God, you infuriate me Kai. What the fuck is everyone doing here anyway?"

"We were all discussing security for the wedding when my Papa and Dimitri arrived. It's the dress fitting today and the family meal tonight."

"Oh, for fuck's sake, I have to try a dress on with a sore arse. Then I have to sit down at a meal with your strange family. Brilliant, I can't wait."

"It will be fine my Little Vixen I promise."

"If you say so."

I finish making my tea and exit with Kai, sitting down on a sofa with him. Everyone talks around me but I'm not really in a talkative mood so I just drink my tea.

Once my cup's empty I leave to get showered, then get ready to go for the dress fitting. We all have some breakfast and Sam texts me to say she's meeting us at the dress shop. We all leave and head there in a convoy of cars. There must be at least ten cars in the convoy; I feel like the prime minister or something. I hate all the fuss, but I can understand why Kai is taking precautions. All his family are here so he has to be careful.

We arrive and all of Kai's men form a barrier around the car. Kai gets out first and comes around to open my door. He holds his hand out and I place mine in his to exit the vehicle. I think Kai is going to release my hand once I'm out, but instead he threads his fingers through mine. He escorts me into the shop where all the staff are stood, lined up as though they're waiting for royalty.

They're like statues, until everyone arrives safely in the shop, and the dressmaker we originally met comes over to greet myself and Kai.

"Welcome Mr Filippov and Miss Ivanov. Everything is ready and waiting for the final fitting. I am Grace, as you know from our initial meeting. I would like to introduce Mr Mark Gracey here who is our expert tailor and will be dealing with all the gentlemen in your party today." Grace announces.

"Hello, it's a pleasure to meet you both," Mark says, as he shakes Kai's hand and gives me a peck on the cheek.

"If you would like to follow me gentlemen and we can get started?" Mark asks.

"I'm leaving Misha and Luka with you Valentina; I shouldn't be long," Kai says, as he kisses my forehead.

"They can't come into the dressing rooms, Kai. I think Isadora and I can look after ourselves if we are attacked. I wouldn't have put it past Isadora to have snuck her robots in," I jest, trying to calm Kai's mood.

"They will stay outside, but will be there if you need them. Humour me Valentina," Kai replies.

"Okay, okay. I'm just waiting here for Sam, she won't be long. Then we'll go and have our fitting," I concede.

"She'll be fine Nikki, she has me," Isadora says.

"Yes, that's what I'm worried about," Kai retorts.

"Haha dickhead, move your arse now before I kick you into the middle of next week," Isadora replies sweetly.

I'm liking Kai's sister more and more each day. She's as nutty as they come but she's my sort of crazy. Kai admits defeat and, after a quick quiet word with Misha and Luka, he disappears with his Papa, brother, and Lev.

Grace comes over to us and offers us some champagne, to which Isadora turns her nose up at.

"Don't you have something stronger? I'm going to need it if you want me to entertain trying one of your hideous dresses on. Don't even think of giving me anything with frills or bows; I'll snap your neck in a heartbeat, capisce?" Isadora says with venom.

Grace's face drains of all colour. I'm sure she's

about to pass out at any second. Bloody hell, hurry up Sam so we can get this shit show over and done with. As if my prayers have been answered, Sam bursts through the door all windswept and interesting. Thank the lord.

"She's only kidding Grace, can you get us all some cognac please?" I ask, trying to smooth things over.

"Um. Yes, of course. Give me a moment and I'll be back." Grace mutters rushing off.

"Fucking hell Isadora, you nearly just killed off the dressmaker. If she doesn't come back, I'll kick your arse," I whisper angrily.

"I wish! Why the hell you and Kai thought I would want to wear a dress is beyond me. It better be floor length because I'm wearing my Doc's, I don't give a fuck what anybody says," Isadora rants, crossing her arms.

"Suck it up buttercup and please don't threaten the poor women again. That's if she even comes back," I scold her.

I walk over to Sam and give her a hug and kiss; she's looking wide eyed around the shop.

"Thank God you're here Sam, Isadora has just threatened the dressmaker. She's just gone off to get us drinks and I'm hoping she comes back. What a shit show," I whisper.

"Sorry I'm late. The babysitter was late to look

after Juliet, then I got stuck in bloody traffic," Sam whispers back.

"Never mind babe, you're here now. I want this shit show over and done with already," I reply.

"Hi Sam," Isadora greets.

"Hi Isadora," Sam replies.

The dressmaker, who has a bit more colour in her cheeks than a moment ago, comes over to give us our drinks. We all take them off the tray.

"If you'd like to follow me ladies?" Grace requests.

We all follow her to the ladies' dressing rooms and she directs us to a chaise lounge. We all sit down and sip our drinks; God I need this.

"Okay who's going first?" Grace asks.

We all look at each other and, with no takers, I decide to take the lead.

"I'll go first," I announce.

"Excellent, follow me please," Grace replies.

I give Sam my drink and follow Grace into the dressing room. My dress is hanging on a coat hanger on a hook. It's absolutely stunning and I secretly can't wait to try it on. Grace leaves and I get undressed, before excitedly stepping into the dress, and calling her back in to do the corset up.

"All done, are you ready to show your party?" Grace asks.

"Can you give me a moment please?" I ask.

"Of course, I'll be outside when you're ready," Grace says, then leaves me.

Looking at my reflection in the mirror, I hardly recognise myself. The dress is an ivory silk gown that clings to my every curve. It's embroidered with an intricate lace bodice that stops just above my waist but is repeated around the hem of the trail. It's as beautiful as I remember, and I get tears in my eyes. I wish my mama were here to see me, oh how I wish.

I pull myself together and pull the curtain across, then step out and walk over to the podium to stand on it. Grace goes around me, fussing with the bottom of the dress, then moves away. I take a deep breath and look over to Isadora and Sam. Sam has her hand over her mouth and tears in her eyes, Isadora has a strange look on her face that I can't make out.

"What do you think, Miss Ivanov?" Grace inquires.

"It's beautiful, thank you," I reply.

"What do you think ladies?" Grace asks.

"You look breathtaking, Valentina; the dress is so beautiful," Sam sniffles out.

I look over to Isadora again. God knows what the hell she'll say about it.

"My brother is a very lucky man, Valentina, you

look sensational," Isadora says.

I just stare at her in shock; I think my mouth is hanging open, so I shut it quickly once I realise. I don't think anybody was expecting that reply because even Grace and Sam are staring at her in shock.

"What's the matter with everyone, I can be nice if I want to," Isadora states.

I smile at her and turn to look in the mirror; this is the dress I'm getting married in. I feel overwhelmed so I turn back around and address Grace.

"Okay, I'll take it off now so you can sort the girls out." I state.

"Lovely, it fits perfectly so no other alterations will need to be done. Do you want a veil?" Grace asks.

"No thank you," I reply.

We head to the dressing room and Grace undoes the corset, then leaves me to get out of the dress and put my clothes back on. Once I'm changed, I exit and take my drink off of Sam, downing what's left in the glass. I sit down, waiting to see who's going next. Sam volunteers and heads off to the changing room.

She walks out of the dressing room a short while after, in a pale blue dress with a matching embroidered bodice to complement my dress. At the waist it turns into a flowing silk skirt which falls elegantly to the floor. She looks stunning with her black hair and bronze skin tone.

"You look so beautiful Sam; do you like it?" I ask.

"It's perfect, thank you Valentina," Sam replies.

"Do you have these dresses in children's sizes?" I ask Grace.

"We do, what size are you after?" Grace asks.

"What size is Juliet, Sam?" I ask Sam.

"Oh no Valentina, you don't have to get her a dress, I already have one for her. Thank you for the offer though," Sam replies.

"I'm getting her a dress to match her Mama's, so what size is she?" I demand.

"She would be a two-to three-year-old," Sam responds in defeat.

"I'll go and have a look now, if you'd like to get out of your dress." Grace answers before disappearing off.

"Thank you, Grace," I call.

Sam disappears back into the changing room and comes back to sit down. Shortly after, Grace reappears with a tiny replica of Sam's dress. It's so adorable we gasp at it as she shows us.

"Thank you so much Grace, we'll take that as well," I gush.

"Thank you so much Valentina, it's beautiful," Sam whispers tearily.

"It's my pleasure, she'll look like a beautiful little princess in it," I say as I hug Sam.

"I suppose I'm next, hit me with it Grace," Isadora says, then downs the rest of her drink.

Sam and I pull away from our hug laughing; this is going to be hilarious. I didn't know Isadora hated dresses. Well, I don't know her at all. I would've thought that Kai would have mentioned it though but, knowing him, he's probably done it on purpose.

We giggle to ourselves when Grace exits the changing rooms, flustered after a torrent of swearing from Isadora. I thought I had a potty mouth, but Isadora swears like a sailor. Grace looks as though she's met the devil itself and I think she's counting the seconds until we all leave.

Isadora stomps out of the changing room and stands in front of us, but I can't get words out. She looks stunning. I can't believe she's transformed into a totally different person in the blink of an eye. Don't get me wrong, Isadora is beautiful in whatever clothes she wears. She has a natural beauty I wish I were blessed with. In this dress though she looks elegant and demure, two words I would never have associated with the Isadora I've seen so far.

"Isadora you're breathtaking, you should wear dresses more often. Just wow!" I coo.

"This is the one and only time you will see me in a dress, so don't get any ideas. Do you like it so I can go and rip it off now? I think I'm getting hives just being in it," Isadora rants.

Sam and I burst out laughing at her. God I'm growing to like her more every day. Isadora rolls her eyes at us in hysterics and marches back into the dressing room.

"Don't you dare rip that dress, it's beautiful!" I shout.

"That's what I think of your stupid dress," Isadora replies as she throws the dress out of the dressing room onto the floor.

Sam and I gasp at her but, when we look at each other, we can't help but burst out laughing again.

Chapter 19

Valentina

After we left the dress shop thankfully only Kai and I returned to the penthouse, alone with Misha and Luka of course. We chilled for the afternoon watching a film and relaxing for the first time since we met. I have to say if I could do anything again it would be to have this afternoon with the chilled-out Kai I experienced.

I'm currently adding another layer of my red lipstick in the dressing table mirror and then we're heading out to our meal with his family. I'm not looking forward to it, but it looks like I have no choice. Getting up I grab my clutch from the table and take one last look at myself in the mirror. I'm in a red, silk wrap dress, which sits demurely above my knees, with matching red high heels. My hair is down, in its natural loose curls, hanging to my waist. Happy with my look, I head into the living room and find Kai in one of his signature suits. He looks as delicious as ever and his hair has that messy perfection that men can always get away with.

However, I have to say, no matter how much I love him in his suits, I prefer him in his joggers or jeans… preferably with no shirt. He finishes typing out a message on his phone and takes his time scanning every inch of my body.

"You look sensational, my Little Vixen; I might cancel and keep you all to myself."

"Thank you and that's fine by me."

"Not so quickly Valentina. As tempting as it is, we must go to this meal. I need you to get to know my brother and Papa before our wedding tomorrow. I also need to go to one of my other clubs to sort a few things out. I've organised Sam and Rose to have the night off though, so you can have your friends there to keep you company."

"The night doesn't seem so much of a drag after all, are the girls really coming? Which club are we going to?"

"Empire and yes, the girls are arriving there at ten. Misha and Luka will be staying with you while Isadora, Dimitri, Lev and I will be sorting our little problem out. You need to be on your best behaviour Valentina, do you understand?"

"I've always wanted to go to Empire, but have never really had the chance so it will be fun. Where will your Papa be? And yes, I'll behave."

"Papa will be going to the Imperial Lounge, as he always does when he visits Birmingham."

"What's that?"

"A gentlemen's club to cater for the more… adventurous tastes, let's just say."

"Oh intriguing? You'll have to tell me more on the way to dinner."

"Are you intrigued about my Papa's sexual tastes, my Little Vixen?"

"Ew no, I was talking more about the club."

"If I told you about the club Valentina, I don't think you would be able to look at my Papa again. Now, we need to go or we will be late."

"Spoil sport, I could use some ammunition against him for the third degree he's bound to give me."

"Behave Valentina, keep those claws of your's in tonight."

I smile at Kai sweetly and he shakes his head at me as we exit the hotel. Misha and Luka are waiting for us when we exit. Kai helps me into the car, then gets in on the other side. We make small talk for a bit, but Kai gets a call and I spend the remainder of the drive nervously looking out of the window.

How can so many years of hate and anger be turned into anything else? I think Kai's optimism about this being a bonding event is unrealistic, all his family will see is Mikhail's spawn.

We arrive at the restaurant and Kai helps me out of the car. I take a big breath as we walk into the restaurant. As we enter with Misha and Luka following us, a beautiful brunette hostess approaches us.

"Good evening, Mr Filippov. Your family have already arrived, and have been escorted to your private room. I'll take you to them now. Who is this gorgeous goddess you have with you today?" She asks, much to my surprise.

"Good evening, Jasmin. This is my fiancée, Valentina Ivanov. Valentina, this is Jasmin, her father is the owner here and a good friend," Kai introduces.

"Pleased to meet you, Jasmin," I reply.

"The pleasure is all mine, it's good to see the woman who has finally tamed Kai. He's so annoyingly grumpy that I thought it would never happen." Jasmin says cheekily, winking at me.

I can't resist laughing and Kai grumbles under his breath as Jasmin turns to lead us to Kai's private room. We walk to the left and enter a corridor marked 'staff only.' As we get halfway down the corridor, Jasmin stops and opens the door to the left. We enter and Kai's Papa, Isadora and Dimitri are seated, drinking and talking.

They all look up as we enter; Dimitri and Isadora smile and get up to greet us. Kai's Papa remains seated, sipping his drink and giving me the death stare.

They both give Kai a hug, then Isadora comes over and hugs me. Dimitri follows suit, but pauses to whisper in my ear.

"He'll come around, he's just set in his ways and a grumpy arsehole to boot."

He pulls away with a smile and I smile at him in return. It looks like at least Kai's brother and sister are warming towards me.

We all take our seats, Kai pulling mine out for me and placing me in between him and Isadora. He holds my hand under the table, giving it a light reassuring squeeze.

"It's so lovely to have you all with us tonight, Papa is putting on a special meal for you all. He is hoping to come and say hello soon, can I get anyone a drink?" Jasmin asks.

Everyone gives their drinks orders and Kai orders a Bacardi and coke for me, thank the lord. Jasmin goes to get them and the room falls into silence. This is so uncomfortable, I haven't experienced this since leaving my Papa's house three years ago.

"Fuck's sake, will someone please just say something before I bash everyone's heads together," Isadora threatens.

"Valentina, I'd like to formally introduce you to my family. Firstly this is my Papa, Viktor. Papa, this is Valentina, your soon to be daughter-in-law." Kai announces.

"Pleased to meet you Viktor." I reply softly.

"I wish I could return the sentiment but alas, I would be lying. We need to get this over and done with so I will just be blunt. The hatred between our families has been there for over a century, you are and will always be Ivanov scum. Kai might be willing to give you our name for whatever schemes he is planning, but to me you will never be one of us. Nor will any spawn you try and palm off on my son," Viktor seethes at me.

"Fuck me," Dimitri says, slapping his hand over his face.

"Way to go Papa, charming as always," Isadora deadpans.

"How dare you speak to Valentina like that, I warned you Papa. If you do not accept Valentina, then you will lose me. If I ever hear you call Valentina, or our children 'spawn' again I will kill you," Kai seethes at his Papa.

"How will you ever know they are your children; she will be fucking anything with a dick. I know you won't give up all the pussy you have on offer, so don't even pretend. You have a fuck toy in every establishment you own and countless on speed dial. You've probably fucked twenty plus people since you told me about this charade of a marriage. I thought it was to just get one over on Mikhail and you were just using the bitch," Viktor seethes.

The table shakes and the cutlery and glasses smash as Kai tries to fly across the table at his Papa. Dimitri manages to pull him back and hold on to him, but Viktor hasn't moved. I can't let this carry on and I don't want Kai to fall out with his family, even though I could happily sink a knife into his Papa's throat right about now.

"Kai listen to me, please baby," I say softly, as I grab onto his hand trying to get him to sit back down in his seat.

Kai looks at me and I smile at him, still trying to pull his hand so he will sit. He eventually listens and sits down. The power and anger emanating from his body is electric.

"I'm fine baby, honestly. If your Papa doesn't like me? That does not matter at all to me. I'm used to it; you don't need to fight my battles for me," I say honestly.

Kai shakes his head about to say something again, but I put my finger to his lips stopping him. Turning to Viktor who is still scowling at me, I smile sweetly.

"You've had your say now Viktor, so listen and listen well. I could not give a fuck what you think of me or my Papa. You are probably right about everything you think. This feud you have with my family is not my problem though. If you don't trust me? Fine. Hate me all you want, but don't lose your son over it. Wind your neck in, grin and bear it. You're a big boy. We can play nicely, or I can just stab you in the throat now. Take your pick!" I reply sarcastically.

"How dare you speak to me like that you two-bit whore!" Viktor rages.

"Oh. Shit," Dimitri moans.

"She's a dancer Papa, not a whore for Christ sakes. Why are you judging the daughter for the Papa's sins?" Isadora states calmly.

"Because the apple never falls far from the tree Ida, the sooner this is all over the better. Then Kai will come to his senses and kill the bitch and we can find him someone far more suitable for his stature," Viktor replies.

"Shut the fuck up Papa! I will not be divorcing Valentina; she will be my wife. She is nothing like that bastard Mikhail and I will not have you keep on insulting her. If you don't like it, I suggest you don't turn up tomorrow. Now, if you will excuse us, we will be leaving now." Kai says and stands.

"Kai there is no need…" Viktor starts to say.

"There is every fucking need!" Kai roars.

"Kai it's oka…" I try to calm things.

"It's not okay Valentina, men have treated you like shit all your life. I'm not going to stand by and watch it. You are mine so get used to it, you don't deserve any of the treatment you have suffered," Kai growls at me.

Gobsmacked, I literally just stare at him, wondering what the hell is going on. He's right, men have treated me like shit, a commodity to use. I thought Kai wasn't any different, but maybe I was wrong after all.

"Come on, we're leaving." Kai pulls me up by my hand from my chair.

"Fuck this shit. Papa, if you don't sort yourself out tonight and turn up at this wedding tomorrow? I'm moving to Birmingham too; Kai is right. I can't stand by and let you do this. Kai, I'm coming with you," Isadora states.

"Me too. Papa, you need to think long and hard about this. Put your own family before some bitter old grudge one of your ancestors had. I'm not saying to make friends with Mikhail, God no, but clearly you can see his daughter is nothing like him," Dimitri adds.

Viktor sits there with a shocked look on his face, then quickly hides it with a blank look. He watches as all of his children get ready to leave and I want to scream.

"I'll phone you later to let you know what I'm doing, Kai. I need to think and let off some steam. Have a good night," Viktor finally says.

"Fine. Goodbye Papa," Kai replies.

We all leave the room and bump into Jasmin on the way down the corridor. She looks at us worriedly and I feel so sorry for her, as I can tell she cares about this family.

"Where are you guys going?" Jasmin asks.

"We have to leave I'm afraid Jasmin, apologise to your Papa for us but something urgent has just come up. See if my Papa still wants to eat and just bill the usual card for the entire meal. I'm sorry Jasmin." Kai replies.

"Oh, I hope everything is alright? I'll sort your Papa out, don't worry about the bill. Please let me know if everything is okay later?" Jasmin pleads.

"I will honey, thanks," Kai replies.

Kai kisses her on the cheek and I wave goodbye as we leave, with Isadora and Dimitri following. We all pile into the car and head over to Empire; I have to say I'm glad we left because I couldn't have eaten a thing. I feel sorry for Kai though. Why couldn't his pig-headed Papa keep his mouth shut?

We get to Empire and I'm in awe, I haven't been to many clubs as I wasn't allowed out at Papa's.

Then when I ran away with Luka we had to keep low key, so I didn't go to clubs, I went to a few bars with the girls but not very often.

Empire is a huge Victorian building, with stained glass windows and the most spectacular arched double doorway. Over the top of the doorway is the only place where the club's name is, carved decoratively into the stone above it. When we get out of the car, I'm shocked as I can't hear any music at all. At a glance you would never know a nightclub was here. That is, except for the line of beautiful people winding down the street.

Dimitri and Isadora step in front of us and Misha and Luka follow behind, with Kai's men surrounding us. When we get to the entrance, the door staff part and two of them open the doors to escort us in. That's when the music hits me like a ton of bricks. Loud, pulsating sultry bass, a balm to a dancer's soul.

Kai holds firmly onto my hand as we walk towards a beautiful marble staircase. As I look around, I can't believe this is a nightclub. It reminds me more of an entrance to an opera house. Tall pillars and archways drew my eyes to the high vaulted ceilings adorned with crystal chandeliers. Black and Ivory caress the walls, ceilings, and bannisters in a bold but elegant style.

As we ascend the staircase, leaving the masses

of people who are entering the main hall downstairs, I gasp as there are another three balconies above this one. As we reach the first level, we turn to the left and start ascending the next staircase. I wonder which level we are going to. My answer is the second, as we walk across the balcony and four armed guards are standing outside another spectacular double doorway.

The guards open the doors as we approach and stand aside for us to enter, before closing them behind us. The room is beautiful, or should I say the hall, as it is huge. Directly in front of us is a balcony that must overlook the club, with sliding glass doors to divide it from the room. Which must again have soundproofing of some sort, because the only music I can hear is the haunting tones of Sia's 'Deer in Headlights.'

The decor continues the same as throughout the rest of the club. But in this room, there are couches, coffee tables and chaise lounges scattered around it. A bar is on the right-hand side, currently manned by two staff. To the left-hand side of the room is a small stage.

"Are we expecting entertainment tonight?" I ask Kai with a raised eyebrow in question.

Kai looks down at me with a smirk and raises his hand to softly caress my cheek with the backs of his fingers.

"I have all the entertainment I need tonight

my Little Vixen, so my girls will not be needed tonight," Kai replies.

"Your girls?" I reply coldly.

"Retract your claws kotehok, they are girls who work for the club for special parties. I have my own little dancer now, so what is my need for them?" Kai replies smugly.

"Maybe for our entertainment if you are not willing to share, Brat." Dimitri cheekily mutters.

"If you wish to continue breathing Brat, I suggest you keep your hands to yourself. Valentina is mine and mine alone. That goes for you too, Sestra. After we have finished with our problem, I will get you all the entertainment you need," Kai sternly replies.

"Rose is coming with Sam, maybe you will find her entertaining for tonight?" I suggest.

"Now, now my Little Vixen, do you wish my brother to have his balls chopped off and handed to him on a platter? That may be the entertainment tonight needs after all." Kai smirks at me.

"Why, who is this Rose?" Dimitri questions.

"You wouldn't be able to handle her Brat, she'll eat you alive. She is so far from the desperate deprived housewives who fawn over you," Isadora replies.

"I only use them for the information, you know

that Sestra. Anyway, I've never met a woman who can resist my charms," Dimitri replies.

Kai and Isadora burst out laughing and it's so infectious that I join in. Dimitri looks wounded, but nobody pays him any attention. After minutes of us all laughing at Dimitri, we calm down and take seats on the couches. I sit with Kai, while Isadora and Dimitri sit opposite us. Lev sinks into the armchair to our right. The bar staff come over, asking us our drinks order and then supplying us with them.

The guards that came with us, along with Misha and Luka, stand around the room on guard.

"Can Misha and Luka join us, Kai?" I whisper.

"Of course, my Little Vixen," Kai replies to which, with a single hand gesture, he calls them both over and instructs them to join us.

About an hour passes in no time because we're all laughing and joking with each other. Mainly taking the piss out of Dimitri, but he takes it in his stride. Being an only child with no friends, it's strange to experience the dynamics of them as a family. They bicker with each other all the time, but I can see the deep love they have for each other shine through.

Suddenly I hear raised voices outside the door and then they burst open. Everyone in the room suddenly has a gun in their hand, pointing at the newcomer entering the room. To my surprise though, she doesn't look like a threat that is worth worrying about. Kai groans under his breath and everyone puts their weapons away.

Isadora looks at me and then at Kai. She must know this woman, I can tell by her reaction. Dimitri scrubs his hand over his face and grumbles something I can't hear to Isadora, and she shakes her head. Fucking hell, who is this woman.

"Kai, will you tell these idiots, they said I'm not allowed in. They have never stopped me before, what the hell is going on?" The woman whines.

"Maybe it's because your invitation has been revoked, Nadia." Kai replies coolly.

This seems to ignite a rage in Nadia, as she marches over to us and stands directly in front of Kai's parted legs. She looks angrily down at him and points her finger at him. Kai's answering move is to look up at her with a bored look on his face.

"You do not revoke invitations to me Kai, neither you nor your minions get to do that. One word to my brothers and this little kingdom of yours, will be destroyed," Nadia snaps angrily.

"I think you forget who runs this city Nadia, I suggest you take your sorry arse out of here. You are no longer welcome here or in any of my establishments. If your brothers are stupid enough to show their faces, I'll make sure they are never seen again. Do you understand me?" Kai replies.

Nadia rages and goes to slap Kai around the face. I shoot up from my seat and in seconds have one the hidden knives from my stocking against her throat. My other hand in her hair, pulling her head back against me. I whisper in her ear.

"If you do not wish me to slice this pretty throat of yours open and bleed you out right here, I'd keep still if I were you. Now, you see that man in front of you, the one that you were just trying to lay your hands on? Well, he's mine now and I don't like skanky bitches trying to put their hands on him. Do you understand me?" I whisper.

She tries to nod but this brings her throat into contact with my blade. She stays deadly still and whimpers.

"Yes."

"Very good, so we understand each other. Now, I'm going to take you out of here and you are going to behave. Do not make me ruin my dress with your blood," I instruct.

She whimpers at me which I take as another yes. Still holding on to her hair I remove my knife from her throat and drag her to the door by her hair. She's taller than me so I'm literally dragging her bent over slightly. When I reach the doors, Pasha and the other guard are looking at me in question, but I pay them no notice. I release her but push her at the same time, so she tumbles to the ground.

I nod to Pasha and say, "excuse me gentlemen, just having a clear out."

Pasha surprises me by replying quietly, "you do you, Printcessa," his mouth lifting ever so slightly at the corner in a barely there smile. Some more guards approach and Pasha acknowledges them before taking his leave.

I turn around and leave her sorry arse to the guards, who close the door to deal with her.

"Get me another drink Kai and make it a double."

Chapter 20

Kai

I'm sitting here with a hard-on I can't hide, and my brother and sister are pissing themselves laughing. As I watch my Little Vixen walk back from throwing Nadia out of the room, I'm still in a lust filled daze. The last thing I expected when Nadia went to slap me was Valentina putting a knife to her throat and dragging her out of the room.

The size difference between Nadia and Valentina made it even more comical, as when Valentina dragged her out by her hair, Nadia had no choice but to bend over. My little firecracker is so sexy in her rage, it's an aphrodisiac that I'm finding extremely hard to ignore. I just want to march over to her and bend her over the back of the nearest sofa to fuck the living daylights out of her.

"My Brat, your woman is a walking wet dream if I

ever saw one," Dimitri says.

"You should have seen her back at the hotel when we were attacked, she was hot as fuck. I have a video; I'll send it to you for your wank bank," Ida replies.

"You will do no such thing Ida, stop sending everyone videos of my future wife. Nobody else is allowed to wank over her but me. Fuck me but she's glorious."

"That she is Brat," Dimitri replies.

"Get me another drink Kai and make it a double," Valentina demands as she takes her seat next to me.

"You heard my woman, get her a drink," I shout to the bar staff while grabbing Valentina and placing her straddling my lap, facing me.

"What did I tell you about those claws of yours kotehok?" I ask Valentina.

"These dirty skanks of yours are starting to annoy me Kai, I'll have to stop coming out with you," she replies.

"You will always be by my side Valentina, with no arguments. My wife will never leave my sight so get used to these types of problems. The only reason I'm not taking you to sort out the problem we have tonight is that I want you to have a good time with your friends on the night before our wedding," I state.

"I'm not coming to see one of your fuck buddies with you Kai, it's just distasteful," she informs me.

"I no longer have fuck buddies Valentina, I have you and only you. Get this into that beautiful head of yours. Now get off my lap before I fuck you here in front of everyone," I warn.

Valentina searches my face for any sign that I'm lying but she will find nothing. I mean every word I've said to her, she will be the only woman I ever fuck again. I can't blame her for not trusting me, as that is the way of life for most men in our line of business.

My Papa taught us a different way though, a wife is to be cherished. Loved with every fibre of your soul and never disgraced by sleeping with other women. He idolised our Mama and still does to this day. I know he fights with his demons every time he fucks a woman, I think that's why his kinks have developed into the darker side he now craves.

I'm hoping Valentina will learn to trust me, but I know from her life so far I have a mountain to climb. She will though in the end, she'll eventually learn what it means to be my wife. I'll just need to have patience, which is something I'm not used to, but I'll try for her.

The bartender brings Valentina the drink she requested. She knocks it back in one and hands the glass back to him.

"I'll have another please," she says, he looks to me for verification. I nod and he goes off to fulfil her request.

My phone alerts me to a message; Valentina's friends are here. They are on their way up with my men as we speak. It's a relief as I need to purge my needs in some way, and I've chosen against fucking Valentina in front of everyone. It normally wouldn't bother me in the slightest to fuck a woman in public. Valentina though is different; she belongs to me and only me.

"Your friends are here my Little Vixen, so I should not have to remind you to behave, should I?" I ask Valentina.

"I'll be a good girl Kai, I promise." She replies sweetly back to me.

"Now why do I not believe a word you've just said, you little brat?" I question.

"Because you know me so well Kai. I'll try, that's all I can say," she replies honestly.

"I have a pre-wedding gift for you later Valentina, how you receive this gift is entirely up to you. You can be a good girl and receive it with pleasure or you can be a brat and receive it with pain. The choice is yours, my Little Vixen." I state.

She looks at me with wide, lust-filled eyes and I know I've enticed her enough to try and be a good girl. Before I get a chance to say anything else though, the doors open and her friends are escorted in. She spots them and dives up from her seat, running over to them and hugging Sam and Rose with all her might.

I look over to Lev, who is staring at Sam like the lovesick puppy he is for only her. I can't understand what has happened between them but, from what he has told me, she's not interested anymore. There must be something else though, as whenever I look at her, she's always watching him with a forlorn look on her face. I'll have to get Valentina on the case to find out why she's really holding back from him.

Standing I signal to my siblings that it's time to leave. They get up and we all walk over to the girls.

"Good evening, ladies, please excuse us for a while as we have a meeting to attend to with the staff. Have fun and we won't be long."

"Hi Kai," Rose replies.

"Hello Kai," Sam says.

"Ladies." I respond.

I grab Valentina and kiss her forehead; she sighs quietly then I release her.

"Behave Vixen," I demand.

She smiles up at me, then wanders off to her friends who are sitting where we were before. I walk out of the room and head up to the top floor of the building. I walk towards my office, which is currently being guarded by Pasha and my men.

"How's the side my friend? I tried calling you to check but you didn't answer." I ask.

"Much better Boss, you know me… tough as old boots. I must have been sleeping the pain meds off, sorry," Pasha replies.

"Never mind as long as it's healing, is everything ready?" I ask.

"Da Boss," he answers.

He nods in respect to which I return the gesture, then we walk into the office and through to the holding room or, as it's more commonly known, the red room. The room was given its name because of the copious amount of blood that has been spilled here. I enter first, Dimitri and Ida follow, then Lev enters, closing the door behind us. The room is almost empty, with only a table in the far-right hand corner and a chair in the centre of the room.

Currently the man tied to the chair is Konstantin. He looks calm and watches everyone who enters the room. Lev walks over to the back wall and leans against it as he lights a cigarette up. Dimitri does the same on the right wall and Ida walks over to Konstantin. She runs her hand through his hair, as she walks around him until she arrives at his back. She then grabs a handful of it and tugs his head back viciously.

"What secrets have you got to tell me little pig? Don't squeal them too quickly though, I prefer a challenge when breaking people down, as they try to hold out on me. You see, many prisoners don't get to meet me as I'm a bit insane but as you're such a special visitor, I've been given a day release to make you more comfortable. You may wish, in the end, that one of my brothers were dealing with you, but try and stay for the ride big boy," Ida tells him with venom.

The thing is though, she's not lying about anything she's said to him. Like the rest of us, Ida has been trained in all methods of torture. Unlike Dimitri and I, she enjoys it far too much. So, she's mostly been kept away from that side of the business. Tech became her new release. There is no point trying to get her to back down from this and let one of us do it, I value my life too much.

"Stop playing with him Ida and sort this shit out. I want to get back to my woman some time tonight," I demand.

"See big boy, they want to spoil our fun already; I haven't even started the foreplay yet. Looks like I'll have to skip it tonight and fuck your arse raw, straight off the bat," Ida coos to Konstantin.

She releases his hair and walks over to the table which holds every torture device she could need. As Ida peruses the table, I watch Konstantin in the chair. Since we walked in, I've been assessing his every move. It's key to perfect torture to know what makes your captive tick, what affects them and any little tell they give away in their sessions.

I'd have liked a lot more time with Konstantin but, due to everything we have going on, I need this resolved so we know what tomorrow may bring. Now though, it's the first time I've seen any form of worry in his face. He wasn't expecting a woman and I can tell he's unsure of how to deal with her. He sees me watching him and hides his emotions behind a blank mask.

Ida walks back over and kneels in front of him, holding up the cigar cutter to his right index finger. She slides it all the way down to the bottom of his finger, looks up at him and slices his finger off. He thrashes against his restraints, trying to hold back his scream. This doesn't impress Ida though; she wants his screams.

She quickly moves on to his middle finger, before he knows what's happening as he has his eyes tightly shut, she cuts off his middle finger. He does let out a scream to this one. On and on we go, until he has no fingers left. He's still conscious though so she grabs his face, looking down at him.

"Have you got any secrets to tell me yet big boy?" she asks.

"Fuck you, you psychotic bitch. I'll never give you anything," he replies.

"Oh, goody. Because I would have been disappointed if you caved at the starting line. Stay here while I go and fetch a new toy. Oh, silly me… you're tied down." Ida coos as she gets up from the blood-stained floor and goes back to choose her next torture device.

Next, she comes back with a knife. She grabs his t-shirt and cuts it open from the collar to the gut. She pushes the fabric apart to expose his chest, running the knife across his pecs and abs slowly.

"It's a shame we haven't got more time to get to know each other before I kill you, such a waste of a fine specimen of a man. I do get rather horny when I torture someone and getting off while torturing them is a high you never forget," she says as she starts digging the knife into his skin.

"Spare us from having to watch you fuck the captive Ida, that's not something I want in my memory banks," Dimitri moans.

I couldn't agree with him more. The last thing I want to watch is our little sister kink fuck the captive, but she wouldn't be bothered in the slightest though. As she steps back to survey her work. She has carved Ida into his chest with a kiss at the end. For fuck sake's I may have to try and pull her off the job, I think she may have been spending too much time with her robots.

She bends back down to him though and stabs him deeply in several places, missing the vital organs every time. While she wanders over to the table again, I look over our captive.

"Do you have anything to tell us Konstantin?" I ask.

He takes a few deep breaths and raises his head to look at me, then smirks.

"Enjoy the time you have left with Valentina, Nickolai. Because once her Papa has her back? There will be nothing left of her. She will pay for letting the enemy fuck that sweet pussy of hers, for bringing shame onto the Ivanov name. That is why I will give you nothing you Filippov scum, I will enjoy knowing that my death results in hers," he replies.

I just see red mist; I have never lost control when torturing someone. Never let my emotions lead me into doing anything rash, but hearing Valentina's name mentioned is like a spark to tinder.

Flying across the room I start pummelling his face with punches. I don't stop, I can't stop. Dimitri and Lev try to pull me off of him but it's no use, I'm too far gone in my rage. I continue with blow after blow to his face. They finally manage to pull me back from him. I'm heaving with rage and violence, as I look over the damage I've done. His jaw is badly broken, hanging awkwardly to the side, his face itself is hardly recognisable with the blows I've inflicted.

I shrug their hold on me off and walk over to the table, I pick up the spike I had specially made and walk back over to him. I place it under his chin and lean down to whisper in his ear.

"You tell your boss when he's down in hell with you that I win. I always win. Valentina will bear my name, my children and my family's future. The Ivanov name will be wiped from this earth like the scum it is, no one will ever remember he existed. I've managed to put an end to his family name forever by taking his sole heir to my bed. She is mine and will always be mine, so let him try and take her from me," I roar.

At this, I ram the metal spike up into his brain from under his chin. The life bleeds from his eyes as I watch. I rip the spike out and toss it to the floor as his head slumps forward. Blood pours from the wound under his chin and pools on the floor under the chair.

I march out of the room as the others follow me silently. They know not to talk to me. They now know what Valentina means to me without any words being shared, nothing needs to be said.

"Clean the room and dispose of the body. When you have finished, report back down to my Lounge," I order my men.

"Pasha follow us."

"As you wish, I am but a humble servant." He deadpans, but my mood is too dark to appreciate his humour, so I shoot him a warning look and stalk away.

I walk to the room I keep here for instances like this, I need to clean up and get a change of clothes. So does Ida. It will also give me time to cool down. I go in there and head straight for the shower stripping my clothes off as I go. I stand under the shower with just one thought on my mind. What scheme are they concocting to take my Little Vixen away from me?

I can't help thinking I let my emotions get the better of me, I should have let them torture him more. Got more information out of him, find out if they knew all my properties or where Valentina was. I've fucked up royally and the only thing, other than my family, that they can use against me, is the very thing they are after. Valentina.

They think it's just a vendetta, waring families using assets against each other. They just think I've taken their Queen off the board, using her to get to the King. Which, if I didn't feel the way I did about Valentina, they would be right. I would have made a checkmate move; and their family name would have ceased to exist.

The problem is I care about Valentina deeply, love her even. How fast I've fallen is astonishing, even to me. She has burrowed under my skin, carved her name on my heart and bonded my soul to hers forever. Since the first moment I saw her, not even knowing who she was. She called to me like the true Siren she is. Now, no matter what I do, I'm ensnared by her call.

No, they will never get to Valentina. Over my dead body will they ever take her from me. I haven't much time, but I need to make sure I have all the bases covered from here on out. I know, from what Konstantin said, they are determined to get her back, so something is going to happen. I just don't know what or when.

I get out of the shower thoroughly washed, then put on one of the outfits I have here; black shirt and black trousers. I fold the sleeves up on my shirt and leave three buttons open from the collar. As I head back out into the lounge of the suite, Lev, Dimitri, Pasha and Ida are grouped around the table discussing something. They go quiet when I enter and look at me with worried expressions.

"It's okay guys, I'm under control for now. What I need is information, has anyone got anything new for me?" I ask.

"Brat, you need to chill out for a bit, let's go back to the girls and have a good time. Once we are back in the hotel, we can go through all the security details, ramp it all up for tomorrow then go from there. You will be in a much better frame of mind if you spend some time with Valentina," Dimitri says.

"This is important, Brat. I need to make sure you're all safe as well as Valentina. They will use you all against me and I've brought it on you all," I reply.

"Brat, this war between our families has been ragging for decades. It was always going to catch up with us all, you have done nothing wrong." Dimitri counters.

"Except fall for the one woman off limits, the heir to the enemy's kingdom." I scoff.

"Is my big brother admitting he has fallen in love?" Dimitri asks, somewhat shocked.

It's too late now, the cat is out of the bag. They have a right to know and so does Valentina, but I want to wait to tell her. I need her to know I mean it; she needs to trust me first.

"I am a lost cause, Brat; I have fallen in love with Valentina. She is mine as much as I am hers," I reply solemnly.

"Well, this is truly a celebration indeed, our big Brat is in love. So, it is important to spend tonight with your soon to be wife. Congratulations Brat," Dimitri replies, coming over to slap me on the shoulder.

"Does Valentina know you love her?" Ida asks.

"No and I wish it to remain like that for now, I need her to trust me before she can truly believe that I'm telling the truth," I reply.

"Very well Nikki, I never thought I would see the day you fell in love. I'm really happy for you." Ida smiles, then comes over and hugs me like she used to when she was young.

"Thank you both, but as you can see, it's no bed of roses. It may just be a fight to the death for us all, but I vow to you that, when the time comes for you both, I will be the first by your side. Fighting with you so that you can keep your own love," I promise to them.

"Always," they reply in unison.

"Okay, so let's get back to the ladies, let's make sure they haven't gotten themselves into trouble," I announce.

"I'll hang back Nikki, I want to check over some surveillance and make sure the plans for tomorrow are watertight. Text me when you're on your way out and I'll join you then," Ida replies.

"Are you sure Ida, we can stay and do some with you?" Dimitri replies.

"I'm not alone, I've got Pasha here to help. Besides, I want you to make sure Nikki enjoys himself. He needs to relax tonight, go and entertain the ladies guys." Ida dismisses us.

"You're so stubborn Ida, why don't you wait until later and do it with the rest of us?" I reply.

"Because I will take all the women off you all and have them for myself if I come. You know you lot are no competition for me, they would be putty in my hands. I mean the dick is on short supply unless I want to give Misha's cock another ride, or maybe sample Luka's rideability," Ida retorts.

"Fuck off! No woman can resist my dick, Ida." Dimitri resorts.

"It's not dick the women are after Dima, the things I don't know about how to please a woman, or a man, are not worth knowing. Once a woman has sampled my tongue lapping at her clit, your cock will fade in comparison. Just face it; they love my sort of crazy," Ida replies with a wink.

"Am I just invisible here?" Pasha questions as we chuckle.

"I think I'd break you Pasha, but if you're offering, I may decide to test out the goods," Ida says, smirking at Pasha.

"Think I might have to renege on my offer, beautiful. You'll probably rip my stitches open." Pasha grimaces as we laugh at him.

"For fuck sake's, can we just go and get this party started? I for one need a drink," Lev groans.

"Ida, behave and let me know if you find

anything out," I demand, before leaving the room.

As we get back to where we left the ladies, the guards part and open the doors for us to enter. When we walk into the room, I can only describe it as a hen night on acid. It has changed considerably since we left. There are balloons, banners and giant inflatable cocks bouncing about the room. Bottles of champagne are lying about empty, cocktail glasses half full discarded on the tables.

The music pumps out of the speakers on full blast, the sultry sensual beats of a New Orleans version of 'Seven Nation Army.' Amongst all the chaos of the room, the ladies are nowhere in here and neither are Misha or Luka.

"Where are the ladies?" I ask the bar staff coldly.

"They are changing out the back Sir, they will be on the stage shortly. They said if you come back, that you should take a seat in front of the stage in the chairs provided." The young bartender replies.

"For fuck sake's, what the hell are they up to now?" I grate out, rubbing my hand down my face.

"Well, I'm game. Fuck yes, I could do with a show right about now," Dimitri says as he wanders off and takes a seat on one of the chairs.

"Where the fuck are my men?" I ask.

"Out back guarding the dressing room Sir." The same bartender replies.

I can't for the life of me think about what's going to happen now, I know Valentina she's going to come out here half naked and dance her sexy little arse off all over the stage. It's going to make me want to kill every mother fucker in the room.

Clenching my fists together I walk over sitting in the middle chair, once I'm seated, Lev comes to sit in the seat to the right of me. The chairs are in a row and spread out evenly away from each other. I look over to Dimitri and he looks like a kid in a candy store.

The music stops and my heart starts to throb in my chest, she always has this effect on me. My Siren affects me just from feeling her presence, I haven't even seen her yet and my dick is throbbing in my trousers. My blood feels like it's on-fire, threading through my veins and coating my organs with liquid nectar.

The ladies finally walk out on stage and my heart stutters a few beats. They are all in cream silk fitted bodices with white pearls weaving around their breasts and down the bones in the bodice. They all have matching pants and thigh-high stockings; and their hair is loose and weaving down their backs.

If I weren't besotted with Valentina this would

have ended very differently tonight, as they would have all ended up in my bed. The contrast between Valentina's fiery red curls, Sam's jet-black loose curls and Rose's Platinum blonde hair is astonishing, but captivating nonetheless.

A full spectrum of delicious delight stands before us, but I'm only drawn to my little red-headed vixen in the middle though. My mind and body know the delights and splendour she offers.

They're standing with their backs to us, and each have an ostrich feather fan positioned behind them, covering their arses and backs. The music kicks in. Fuck me but what a tune to pick, it's 'Glory Box' by Portishead. As the intro kicks in they sway from side to side, making their fans flutter.

They bring the fans in front of them, so I get a delicious view of Valentina's edible arse swaying from side to side, an invitation that is incredibly hard to resist. They spin to face forwards, but they have the fans over their faces, so all our eyes are drawn to the thigh-high stockings and delectable panties they have on. I look at my brother and Lev and find they are as enthralled as me, but Lev is captivated by Sam, and Dimitri wipes his bottom lip not taking his eyes off Rose.

They move their fans to the left, fluttering them. All the fans are sideways now, so we only get a full view of Sam seductively swaying to the beat.

They quickly flutter their fans to the right, so we only get a view of Rose. They bring their fan back to cover their own bodies, then Valentina raises hers above her head fluttering it above her as she seductively sways her body. Her eyes are focused directly on mine, and I lick my bottom lip in anticipation.

They close the fans and demurely throw them to the side. Rose and Sam enclose Valentina and start to run their hands over her body. They are all looking at each other as if there is no-one else in the room.

"Fuck me, that's so fucking hot," Lev groans.

"That's the biggest understatement of the year Lev, no wonder you lot don't get anything done here. I'd spend my days playing with these three in my bedroom. It's the most erotic thing I've seen in my life. I'm in danger here of coming in my boxers like a horny teenager," Dimitri moans while adjusting himself in his trousers.

"You think of touching Sam Dima, and I'll cut that fucking dick right off you." Lev threatens.

"Chill man, I have my eyes firmly on that delicious platinum blonde. Those legs go on for fucking miles and will wrap around my waist deliciously while I fuck the living daylights out of her." Dimitri groans while adjusting himself again in his trousers.

I laugh at them both, I don't need to threaten

either of them about Valentina. The fact is, I don't mind them seeing how delectable my Little Vixen is as long as they never act on it.

The girls are now kneeling at Valentina's feet and she looks directly at me, giving me a cheeky wink. She grabs a handful of their hair and proceeds to lean down to give them both a feather touch kiss on the lips.

"Holy shit man, Brat. Your woman is dangerous. She's like a temptress, luring us all to our deaths. Sexy as fuck but what a way to go." Dimitri moans.

"She is that Dima, a Siren whose call is irresistible but also deadly. She could make any man fall to their knees for her. Then they will smile while she cuts their throats," I answer.

"Fuck me, why is what you just said even hotter. Shut the fuck up Kai, don't forget I still have that video Ida sent me to keep me company on the lonely nights," Dimitri threatens.

"Fucking hell, I told Ida not to send you that video, the bitch," I reply.

Any other retort is cut short when I see Valentina get down on all fours and crawl to the end of the stage, while never taking her eyes off me. She prowls towards me like I'm a delicious meal she wishes to devour. The girls follow behind her and Valentina slides off the stage to the floor, going back onto all fours and continuing to crawl towards me until she is in between my spread legs.

Fuck me, at this rate I may join my brother and make a fool of myself. Though, I'm commando, so I have no boxers to conceal the mess I'll make. Sam has crawled over to Lev and Rose to Dimitri, who is currently biting his lip.

Valentina places her hands on my knees and starts to sway deliciously to the music, while running her hands further up my legs to the top of my thighs. I groan and she smiles at me. She teases me by running her hands up and down my thighs, but without going to the place I most want her to.

She stands up and places herself demurely on my lap with her legs either side of me. Valentina pushes my face to the one side and licks a path from my collar bones, all the way up my neck to my ear. I can't help but shudder at the feel of it, then she bites my ear lobe viciously. She soothes the abused flesh by sucking it into her mouth and lavishing it with her tongue. The same must be happening to the other guys as I hear Lev and Dimitri groan.

Valentina's mouth releases my abused flesh and she sits up, placing her hands on my shoulders. She starts to gyrate her sweet little pussy over my erection, rubbing it over and over. She looks down at me while still gyrating her pussy against my dick and starts running her hands over my pecs and down over my abs.

When she grabs onto my belt I hold my breath, thinking she's just going to undo it and grab my engorged dick out, but she doesn't. She throws her head back and leans back, still winding her body on me.

I can't resist any more. I have to touch her, so I run my hands over her stomach, all the way up to her breasts which are trying to escape from the confines of her bodice. I give them a vicious squeeze and grab her extended neck within my palm. I squeeze tightly and bring her body back up to me. Looking into her lust-dazed eyes, I fall. I bring her luscious mouth to mine and kiss her with all the power, passion, and fire I have thrumming through my body.

Her tongue answers back with her own lust and passion and we're lost, nobody else exists but us. My Little Vixen breaks our kiss and climbs off my lap, much to my dismay. They all walk up to the stage sultrily and climb back on it, standing back together in the middle of the stage, Valentina in the middle and Sam and Rose sexily draping their arms and legs against her.

The music then stops and Lev, Dimitri and I start to cheer and whistle at them. Fuck me but what a show. The hottest thing I've seen out of my bedroom with Valentina in my life. Fuck me. If I knew this was the show we would get, I would never have left the room.

The girls bow and laugh at us cheering but I can't resist, I need her close again. I jump up and march over to the stage, jumping up onto it and picking a surprised Valentina up to throw her over my shoulder. The others follow my lead and I carry her over to one of the sofas. Placing her back over my lap I grab her hair and bring her face to mine so I can whisper in her ear.

"Is that my pre-wedding gift from you my Little Vixen?" I groan in her ear.

"Yes Kai." She purrs and shudders when I blow over the shell of her ear.

"What an erotic gift to bestow on your future husband, I could not have asked for a more precious gift from you. I have a pre-wedding gift for you too Valentina, but this gift will be given in private. You will be a good girl for me and behave yourself until I get you back to the hotel." I groan now, licking the shell of her ear.

"Yes Kai." She replies as she shudders against my body, rubbing that delectable little pussy over my erection.

The dam breaks; I have to get her on her own, I need to be inside her. Own her and devour her all at the same time. I stand and throw her back over my shoulder. I walk towards the door, shouting back.

"I'm taking my Little Vixen back to the hotel, get your ladies and hurry up about it."

As I fling open the doors I call to Misha as he follows us. Dimitri and Lev both have Rose and Sam over their respective shoulders.

"Misha, go to my sister and make sure she is safe, let her know we've gone ahead to the hotel and to meet us there. Stay with her until she wishes to return," I order.

"Da Boss," he acknowledges, before walking off towards the stairs.

I march down them with Dimitri and Lev following and my Guards surrounding us. The lower level is packed but people soon part when they see us marching towards them. They stand there, gobsmacked, as we carry our bounty out of the club and into the awaiting cars.

I can't wait to get my Little Vixen home and place my pre-wedding gift around that delicious neck of hers. Even though she will be kneeling at my feet when I place it around her neck, what she doesn't know yet is I'd happily kneel at her feet every day of my life if it meant she stayed with me.

Chapter 21

Valentina

As we walk through the reception area in the hotel people look at us in shock, I mean it's not every day you see three hot as fuck men carrying three half-naked women over their shoulders. I'm quite chilled this time as Kai is deliciously rubbing my arse cheek, but the opposite can be said for Sam and Rose.

Three continuous spanks on the bottom seems to quieten Sam down, apart from a whimper and then a moan when Lev soothes the abused flesh with his hand. Rose on the other hand is like a wild cat, hitting Dimitri with blow after blow on the back. The smile on his face though is telling me he is enjoying the fight Rose is giving.

Rose's language is turning the air blue, and I can't help laughing. Her Birmingham accent was hard to master in the beginning, as she has a dialect that misses out half of the letters in a word, but

I'm cultured now. I have also picked up quite a few words for my own use.

"Put me down ya wanka, ya fuckin knob, why the fuck av ya chucked me over ya shoulder again. I can walk ya know, ya cocky bastard," Rose screams.

Whack, whack, whack three hard slaps on her arse as we enter the lift. She screeches and nearly deafens us all in the process. We all get in and start our journey up to the penthouse apartment of Kai's.

"What the fuck ya doin, slap my arse again and I'll knock ya the fuck out. Ya Tw..." Rose doesn't get to finish her sentence.

Dimitri throws her off his shoulder, pinning her body up against the lift wall. He grabs her around the throat and callously chuckles in her face.

"I suggest you shut that fuckable little mouth of yours my dearest Rose, or I will have you on your knees with your mouth full of my cock in front of everybody in this lift. Do you understand me?" Dimitri warns, his tone laced with both menace and mirth.

"I'll bite the fucka off!" Rose grates out.

"Umm, Brat? Do you have an open mouth gag I can use on my dearest Rose here, she seems to be a bit nippy?" Dimitri asks Kai.

"Well, Dima I don't carry them around on my

person, but I have one in the penthouse that you can use," Kai chuckles back at Dimitri.

"What the fuck is one of those?" Rose screeches.

"You will soon find out my sweet, if that fuckable mouth of yours keeps on spewing out those curse words of yours. Now you have one opportunity to back out, I will drop you off home and you can bath that sore bottom of yours. Or you can be a good girl and stay, be fucked raw by yours truly and I'll drop you off later. Choose wisely my little Rose," Dimitri coos.

The lift stops and we all step out into the foyer. Luka goes and checks the penthouse while we wait for Rose, who is still pinned to the lift wall, to answer.

"Last chance Rose, the lift will be going down any second now," Dimitri warns.

Rose nods her head at Dimitri.

"Words, my dear Rose," Dimitri chastises.

"I'll come with you," Rose mutters.

"You certainly will, and not until I say," Dimitri replies, before releasing her neck and grabbing her hand, pulling her out of the lift.

Luka comes back out of the apartment and gives the go ahead to enter. Kai marches in followed by the rest of them.

"Lev room to the left, last door on the right.

Dimitri room to the right, second door on the left. Do not disturb us for anything," Kai orders, before carrying me off.

I think we are heading to the bedroom, but he marches off in the other direction to the room he showed me last night. His Den. Oh hell. Fuck no.

"Kai, fuck that shit I am not going in that room again," I shout.

"You are my Little Vixen, and you will be quiet and listen to me. Remember the rules of the Den Valentina." Kai retorts, as he opens the door and locks it after him.

He slowly slides me down his body and places me on the floor. I look up at him in question and he places his right index finger over my parted mouth.

"I wish to give you your pre-wedding gift Valentina and this is the place I will give it to you. That though, will be when we are about to leave this room. Before that I have a one-off offer for you," Kai says to me, with an edge of uncertainty to his voice.

"What offer is it, Kai?" I ask.

"Tonight, and only ever tonight, I will let you take control. I will let you do whatever you wish to me in this room. Make the most of this chance Valentina, because this will not be offered again." Kai replies.

I look around the room at the things I have no clue of how to use. I doubt Kai is making the right decision here, giving me free reign with his toys. I look over at the bed though and a memory flashes before my eyes. Umm, I could improvise.

"Kai, does the bed have chains?" I ask.

"Does my Little Vixen want to chain me up?" Kai teases.

"I do, actually," I say, smiling up at him.

He laughs down at me and it's beautiful. No mask, no barrier, just a genuine laugh. He walks over to a cupboard at the far corner of the room. Opening the door he pulls out what look like leather padded cuffs.

"Does my Little Vixen want just my arms chained, or my legs as well?" he asks over his shoulder.

Well fuck, might as well have him at my mercy.

"Legs as well, please," I reply.

"Lovely manners my Little Vixen," he coos.

I shiver at the praise. I have no clue as to why I feel this way with Kai. Why every compliment or praise he gives me matters, but it does. The thing is, I feel no less empowered by the need to please him though.

He finishes getting the equipment he needs from the cupboard and closes it, carrying the things he has selected to the bed. He places them down and flips the ornamental knobs on the top of the headboard over. They must be hollow because sitting underneath them is a metal clip.

I walk over to the bed to get a better look; Kai grabs hold of the clip and pulls on it, revealing it's attached to a chain that must run throughout the headboard. He attaches the cuffs to the clips on either side of the headboard, then walks to the bottom of the bed. I follow and find that there are hidden pockets in the legs of the bed which contain the same clips and chains as the headboard.

I'm flabbergasted. *Who the hell makes these contraptions for him,* I wonder. As Kai finishes up fastening the cuffs to the bottom of the bed I stand there watching, trying to plan what I'm going to do.

"Everything is ready my Little Vixen," Kai says, breaking me out of my thoughts.

I look him over standing there in all his delectable glory, black shirt open about three buttons down revealing a glimpse of his tattooed chest. His shirt sleeves rolled up to display his muscled forearms with bulging veins. His hands are in the pockets of his black trousers, and as I look back up at those ocean-blue eyes of his. I can see humour at my perusal of his body.

"Strip!" I demand.

He smirks at me, but follows my demand and starts unbuttoning his shirt slowly. I watch his hands as he goes and when he opens the bottom button and glides the shirt off his shoulders. His body is a masterpiece, honed to perfection and built for sin.

His hands go to his belt buckle and I hold my breath. He loosens it and smirks at me. I hold his gaze, but can't resist looking down at his hands again as they undo his fly. He just loosens his grip on his trousers and lets gravity take over, sending them puddling to the ground. Fuck me, he was commando. His cock slaps back up against his abdomen.

He toes off his shoes and leans down to pull off his socks. He stands, looking at me in all his naked glory. I take my time looking over his body and then bring my eyes back to his.

"Lie on the bed Kai, I want you spread eagle so I can restrain you," I order.

He smirks at me again but gives no rebuttal to my order. He lies down on the bed on his back and positions himself as I've asked. I go over and pull on the first cuff, placing it around his wrist and buckling it shut, which was easier than I thought. I go around the bed, doing the same with the three remaining cuffs.

Once I'm finished, I go to the bottom of the bed and look over the sight of Kai chained up and at my mercy. Fuck me, but I think I may have just come without being touched. Having such a powerful man, who oozes lethalness out of his pores, laid out for my indulgence is such an aphrodisiac.

There are several things I want to do to Kai that in our short time I have not been allowed to do. The sexual appetite he has awoken in me is astounding, I've watched porn and masturbated daily so have never been shy in my sexual needs. I've just never been drawn to anyone like I am to Kai, never felt the need to untie the weight that was my virginity from around my neck. Until him, Nikolai Filippov, my kryptonite and my death sentence if my Papa gets his hands on me again.

I stand there and start stripping myself out of my bodice, loosening the ribbons that are keeping it fastened at the back, then start weaving them undone. It's quite tricky but I manage. I let it slip to the floor and watch Kai's eyes dilate as my breasts come into view. I caress them with my hands and tweak my nipples, throwing my head back at the delicious pain and pleasure it creates. Kai's answering groan brings my face back up to look at him again, to find him struggling with his restraints.

"What's the matter Kai, do you wish to touch me? Feel my skin tremble under your hands? Feel my pussy flutter as you lick a path down my body to it? Well, this is your chance to feel the pain of not being able to touch what you want. Like the many times you have restricted my hands from wandering over your delectable body while you fuck me. The wanting, the need, all taken away from you." I coo as his face heightens with frustration and need.

I push my fingers into the high waisted panties I have on and start to slowly peel them down my hips and to my thighs, exposing my pussy as I go, then shimmy my body to enable them to fall to the floor. I choose to keep my thigh-highs on and place one foot up on the bed. This opens my pussy to Kai's lust-filled eyes as I bring one hand down to caress my clit, while my other hand tweaks my nipple at the same time.

"Valentina get on this fucking bed and place that pussy on my fucking face, now," Kai grates out, while pulling harder at his restraints.

I laugh at him, but stay where I am and push two fingers into my juicy pussy, fucking myself with my fingers as I continue to pull and tweak on my nipples alternatively. Throwing my head back, I let out a sinful moan and fuck myself faster, feeling my juices run down my fingers the more aroused I get.

"Valentina here, now, for fuck's sake," Kai shouts, pulling on the headboard that much that I think it's going to crack.

I bring my head back up, so my eyes collide with his manic ones, and shake my head from side to side telling him no. Then proceed to remove my arousal coated fingers from my pussy to my mouth placing them on my tongue and closing my lips around them. As I suck my arousal off my fingers, I moan at the taste and lick them clean as I push them in and out of my mouth.

"Argh!" Kai roars.

I watch him with my fingers in my mouth, trying to pull the chains from the bed. Luckily, the restraints make grating noises but do not give into his power.

"Such a naughty boy you are for me, naughty boys must be taught lessons. Naughty boys do not get to come, they do not get to have my delicious pussy smothering their faces," I tease.

"Let me loose Valentina, I've changed my fucking mind. This is torture," Kai begs.

"Uh huh, you don't make the rules tonight, Kai, I do," I taunt.

I climb on the bed and start crawling over his body. I get to his dick and I lick it from his balls all the way up to the tip. Kai stops struggling, bringing his head up to watch me with a tortured moan leaving his lips. I stare at him while I repeat my path several times and, on the last time, I suck his cock into my mouth and take him to the back of my throat, lapping my tongue around his throbbing cock while I slide my mouth up and down as far as I can go.

"Fuck, yes." Kai moans as he throws his head back to the bed.

He starts to thrust his cock down my throat, which I allow for a few times then I take my mouth away, watching the trail of saliva coat his balls and engorged cock. It's throbbing and jumping with need and I just watch it in its plight.

"Fuck, my Little Vixen, put your mouth back on my dick," Kai moans.

"I would have kept it there for longer if you would have behaved Kai, but you didn't, you chose to be a naughty boy. Didn't you?" I admonish.

"I'm not a fucking boy Valentina, I'm a very sexually frustrated man. Now get that mouth or delicious pussy on my dick," Kai demands.

"Oh, you are all man, Kai. But my naughty little boy nonetheless." I coo.

I laugh when he groans at me, then climb further over his body to straddle his chest. I place my pussy right in front of his face but far enough away that he can't get to it. As I trail my fingers down over my breasts and my stomach, Kai watches the path they are taking with ferocious need pouring from his body.

When I reach my destination, Kai struggles underneath me again, but I don't let him deter me from my planned show. I start to tease my pussy lips not yet giving in to my desire to caress my clit, then I slip three fingers into my juicing pussy and start riding myself right in front of his face.

"Valentina, fucking release me now!" Kai roars a strangled plea at me.

I think about placating him and giving him what he so desperately needs, but I remember this is my only chance to do this to him. I have no doubt what he will do to me in return for this, so I must make it worth my suffering.

I ride my fingers faster and faster whilst squeezing and tweaking my nipples, I'm so close to coming. I look down. Kai's eyes are watching me with such need that it evokes my body to thrum with so much pleasure I think I'm going to explode. I bring my other hand down and start strumming my clit whilst still riding my fingers.

Kai roars with lust, trying to get to me and I detonate. My pussy spasms with such an explosive orgasm it ejects my fingers with the power. My body is lost in powerful spasms and I fall forward over a pained, panting Kai. My pulsating pussy is making a beautiful mess all over his heaving chest and I stay laying there for a moment, trying to regain my senses.

When the flutters and spasms finally die down, I push myself up and gently push two fingers back inside my sensitive pussy. I gather as much of my arousal as possible and remove them. They are coated and glistening with my juices, and I place them at Kai's parted mouth. I push them in and he greedily sucks on them and licks them clean, moaning around them as though they are the most delicious thing he has ever tasted.

It's one of the hottest experiences we have had together, and it's only just begun. I remove my fingers and climb off Kai's chest then off the bed. Kai is watching my every move and, when I go over to the dressing gown hanging in the corner of the room, he starts to struggle.

"What are you doing Valentina?" he bites out, whilst struggling to free himself.

I put the gown on and walk to the door.

"Just hang around for a while Kai, I'll be back." I open the door, shutting it quickly with how loud the roar from him is.

I laugh as I rush off to the bedroom. I collect the things I need and then wander towards the kitchen. I grab some ice and the bottle of cognac off the side. As I wander back to the Den with my goodies, I hear banging and stand still, on alert for a moment, until I hear moans and then a feminine scream. I giggle to myself as I try to open the door to the Den with my contraband.

Looks like one of the girls is having fun.

I finally manage to get the door open to be greeted with the grating of chains against wood and Kai's animalist roars. He turns to face me when I enter and his demeanour makes my body flood with arousal. His body is flushed and coated with a fine sheet of sweat. He's frustrated, angry and it is so fucking hot I forget myself lost in the sheer sight of him.

"Where the fuck have you been," Kai roars out at me, whilst pulling at the chains again.

I look at the headboard and see that the wood has split slightly at the top where the chain feeds out. Fuck, that takes some power for that to happen. I'm wondering whether it will hold for the rest of what I have planned for him.

"I needed some things," I reply, walking back over to the bed and placing the bag of ice and bottle of cognac on the bed. I sneak my other item under the bag of ice from out of the gown pocket.

I undo the gown and throw it to the floor, climbing on the bed to straddle Kai's waist. I rip open the bag of ice and choose an ice cube. I look back at Kai, who is panting and gripping the chains restraining him to the bed. I place the ice cube over his nipple and rub in a circular motion, his body jumping at the coldness. Once I've kept it there for a few minutes and it has melted slightly from the heat of Kai's body I remove it, throwing it to the corner of the room. I lean down and lick around his nipple, then suck it into my mouth.

His body bucks underneath me and he moans as I lap at his nipple whilst it's captured in my mouth.

"Fucking hell." He moans in pleasure.

I bite down hard on his skin around his nipple and he roars. When I release his abused flesh, I can see the indentations of my teeth; they have not broken through the flesh, but they will remain for a while.

I give the other nipple the same treatment, getting the same response. I discard the ice cube and pick another one out. This time I run it over Kai's lips then hold it down on his plump bottom lip. Once I'm happy I discard it and crash my lips down on his. Our teeth clash, tongues fighting in a war that neither of us wish to back down from. It's erotic, animalistic and feels so right it sends my body into an overload of lust.

We are forbidden, enemies of a war that has continued throughout the years. Our forefathers have hated, killed, and maimed in the name of this war. Yet we were drawn to each other, we found solace with each other. This war will continue, with us leading the way either as lovers or enemies, but I like the thought of both.

Waring inside the bedroom and standing against the world outside of it. That's how I would like this war to end, but what I want and what happens are two vastly different entities.

As the passion of our kiss threatens to take me under, I must take back control, show Kai I will not be some weak woman that will surrender to his every whim. I break the kiss and bite down hard on his bottom lip, he roars in pain until I release the abused flesh.

"Fuck me Valentina, I need you on my dick. Ride my dick baby," Kai groans out.

"I have other plans Kai," I reply, reaching over for the cognac.

I undo the bottle and take a few gulps; it slides down my throat with a delicious burn. I take another mouthful, replace the lid and lean over Kai's face. He looks up at me and I drizzle a slow stream of cognac out of my mouth. At first it lands on his parted lips, but he opens his mouth to receive the rest of my mouthful. I take another mouthful of cognac and repeat the process.

Giving him one last passionate kiss, which tastes like fire and sin. I slide down his body placing my body in between his spread legs so my face is right over his throbbing cock, which is currently leaking pre-cum. I lick him clean, and he moans, tightening his hold on the chains restraining him. It's so erotic, seeing him struggling with his domineering nature, all his muscles are bulging in his arms and legs.

I open the cognac again and take a small mouthful, I look up at Kai and when our eyes collide, I start to dribble the cognac over his cock and balls. Ravenous for him, I lick him from his balls to his bell end and swallow him to the back of my throat.

"Fucking hell, Valentina, yes baby, fuck me with that talented mouth of yours. Oh Shit." He moans when I swallow him down my throat slightly before my gag reflex kicks in.

I keep my eyes locked with his as I fuck his cock with my mouth, taking him further back as I go, finding it easier the more times I do it. The answering groans from Kai spur me on. It's not an easy feat. Due to how long and thick his cock is as I'm only about halfway down, but I use my hand on the bottom of his cock mimicking the movement of my mouth.

"Fuck yes, Valentina, I'm going to come down that pretty little throat of yours," Kai groans, thrusting to the movements of my mouth.

I continue for a couple of seconds more and, when I feel him tensing, I pull my mouth and hand away.

"What the fuck Valentina, get that fucking mouth back on my dick now." He roars.

I sit there, watching him struggle and his cock pulsates against his stomach, looking for relief only for none to be found. I smile down at him sadistically, enjoying the pained groans and struggle he is granting me.

I wait for him to stop struggling and he's lying there, panting with his eyes closed. His breathing is heavy and his skin is covered with another sheen of sweat. I move up his body and place my pussy over his throbbing cock, sliding it slowly up and over the length of it.

His eyes fly open and immediately go to the view of my pussy sliding up and down his cock. I keep the pace slow, so I can prevent him finding his relief, but purposely keep nudging my clit on his bell end. I put my hands on his spread thighs and, when I feel myself nearly there I pick up the pace, rubbing my pussy over his throbbing cock. Kai groans and thrusts his cock a couple of times which nudges my clit deliciously and tips me over the edge. I come, coating his cock with my juices. I'm panting and shaking from the orgasm and fall against Kai's who is panting, trying to find my pussy again which is currently in the air.

"Valentina, I swear I will rip this room apart in a second if you do not give me your pussy. I do not like being denied my Little Vixen and remember, payback's a bitch," Kai threatens.

"It sure is Kai, what do you think this is? It's not

nice to be left aroused and needy is it, like I was yesterday?" I reply.

"Valentina, it was a punishment, I was left needing just the same as you," he replies frustratedly.

I don't answer him as I'm shocked. He didn't get himself off after, in the shower or something? Instead, he left himself needing just the same as me. It's the last thing I expected to hear off Kai.

Crawling up his body to grab handfuls of his hair I slam my lips down on his. I kiss him with all my wants, needs and desires. For our uncertain future, for a future I wish for and for the gut feeling I have that it will never happen. We have now and that's all that's certain. The rest? Well that's in the hands of the universe.

As I'm kissing him, I slip one hand down and grab his throbbing cock. I direct it to my pussy and slide down to seat myself fully. Even though I'm wet with all my arousal, it still takes some wriggling to take him all. We both break the kiss but stay, panting just over each other's parted lips. I open my eyes and see him watching me with a look that I'm struggling to comprehend.

Slowly I start to sit up, and putting my hands on his chest. I begin to ride his cock, slowly sliding my pussy up and down his length. He starts to add slow thrusts to match my own and we both moan out loud at the feeling.

I dig my nails into his chest and start grinding my pussy over his cock, rocking my pelvis backwards and forwards in a delicious rhythm. Yet another orgasm is building and my pussy starts to flutter around his length. I start riding him faster and he matches my movements.

When I'm about to come again, I reach over and pull my knife out from under the bag of melting ice. I place the knife at Kai's throat and still my movements, Kai's eyes flare and we stare at each other, him questioning and me deciding.

"What are you doing Valentina?" Kai demands.

"Do you trust me, Kai?" I question as I start to slowly ride his dick again.

"What kind of a question is that, Valentina." He thrusts up hard into me and I moan, picking up my pace again.

"Do you know how easy it would be to slit your throat right now? Leave you to bleed out on the bed and make my escape? Take what I need from you and disappear?" I ask.

At the sight of my knife at Kai's throat, my body thrums with desire. It's so erotic, but so wrong at the same time. My pussy flutters and I feel myself building to one almighty orgasm.

"Is that what you want my Little Vixen? To run from me, hide in the shadows for the rest of your life? Or do you wish to stay and be my Queen, in your rightful place by my side?" Kai replies.

I'm lost in my lust, but then his response hits me like a battering ram. He honestly thinks this thing between us is going to work. That we can live happily ever after, ruling together. Two fated enemies, bred with the hatred of each other born from generations past. A happy ending was never meant for us, one of us was always destined to kill the other.

"Why do you want me, Kai? I am just the spawn of the enemy. We were always destined to meet on the battlefield, never in this bed. We were never destined to be lovers or me your Queen." I reply trying to slow down, but Kai's thrusts speed up to stop me.

"Fuck destiny. Fuck everything. Why can't we end this in a way that benefits us? This was our destiny all along, a way of ending this war without bloodshed," Kai reasons.

"My Papa will never let me live Kai, he will make sure I pay for this. You know he will. I'm better off on my own, I always was," I state.

I pick up my pace and shut out all of my conflicted emotions. With my knife at Kai's throat I build us back up, riding Kai's cock with only my lust fuelling me. I concentrate on the knife at his throat and the feel of his cock inside of me. Kai picks up the pace with me and groans with pleasure when I start to flutter around him.

The orgasm crests and I explode in the most euphoric orgasm I've ever had. Amidst my shuddering and spasming around Kai's cock, I hear him roar his release and feel him coating my pussy with his cum. Wave after wave of the orgasm floods my body, so I throw the knife to the side as I don't want to harm him. I never have and never will. I collapse on his chest and just lie there, shuddering and weak in my bliss.

I feel Kai's heartbeat racing in his chest, I feel his cum leaking out of my pussy making a mess of us, but I have no energy to get up. We lie there, for what seems hours but could only be minutes, before Kai speaks.

"You need to unchain me my sweet Little Vixen, no matter how much I enjoy having you draped over my body. I need to clean us up and give you your present. You also need some sleep for tomorrow," Kai says, breaking our moment.

"You spoilsport! I was hoping to sleep right here. I don't think I have the energy to move," I reply drowsily.

"You will move that gorgeous arse of yours and unchain me now, Vixen. You can sleep in a moment," he orders.

I groan but slowly extract his still hard cock from inside my pussy. How the fuck it's still hard I will never know, but I climb off the bed and start unfastening the cuffs. Once I have them all off, he climbs off the bed and grabs me around the throat, pushing me up against the nearest wall and leaning down so his face is inches from my own.

"Maybe I'll change my mind about letting you have me at your mercy my Little Vixen. When you're given free rein to do as you wish, you are a little firecracker indeed. That was the hottest sex of my life. You and your knives Valentina are erotic beyond belief. Now, go to the door and kneel to await my present," Kai orders.

I smile up at him and, when he releases my neck and walks over to the drawers in the far corner, I go over to the door and kneel awaiting him. He walks over to me and hands me a long, rectangular velvet box. I look up at him in question.

"Open the box, Valentina," he orders.

So I do, and gasp when I see what's inside; a titanium choker with a ruby heart the size of a golf ball set in the middle of it. It's beautiful and I'm so overwhelmed I feel tears prickle my eyes. So I try not to look back up at Kai, but he puts two fingers under my chin and lifts my head to look at him.

"Do you like it, my Little Vixen?" Kai asks.

I swallow and try to prevent my tears from escaping.

"It's a beautiful choker Kai, thank you." I reply shakily.

"It's a collar Valentina, not a choker. It is a sign of your submission to me and an indication to every other man that you are mine. Once the collar is on, I'm the only one who can remove it, as I'm the only one who has the key. Do you wish to accept the collar, Valentina?" Kai asks.

Still meeting his expectant gaze I realise, that I have no clue how to submit to a man. I have no experience in sex let alone this kinky shit.

"Kai, I have no experience with this shit, and I would be a terrible submissive. I've watched fifty shades and experienced a flogging, that's how far my knowledge of this kinky shit goes," I reply.

"I have every faith in you Valentina, I will start your training after the wedding. I think you will surprise yourself," Kai reassured me.

"Okay, but remember I warned you I would be rubbish," I scoff.

"I require your words Valentina, address me properly," Kai orders.

"Yes Sir, I accept the collar," I agree.

"Good girl," Kai responds.

He takes the collar from the box and places it around my neck. I hold my hair up out of the way and he fastens it at the back to lock it in place. When he walks back in front of me, I release my hair to fall back down my back.

"Absolutely breathtaking, a true Queen in all her glory," Kai states as he stares down at me.

I only hope what he says comes true, because I have a feeling in my gut that something terrible is going to happen. A feeling I can't shake no matter how hard I try; I can only pray that my Mama is watching over me and keeps me safe.

Chapter 22

Valentina

I swear, any second now I'm going to throat punch this woman, if she tries to add any more blush to my face. I'm tired, hungover and grouchy. Sam comes in and sees me eyeing up the mark-up artist who's going for the blusher brush again. She rushes over and ushers her off before I have time to snap her wrist.

"She's done now, thank you. You can leave. Now," Sam says, grabbing my arm and pulling me out of the chair.

She drags me into the living room, sitting me down at the table with Juliet who is currently crayoning a beautiful fairytale castle. Sam goes off to the kitchen and comes back with a bottle of water and two paracetamols.

"I want you to drink all of that water Valentina, then we need to put you in your dress. Take those tablets, because we're running behind and I don't feel like having my arse kicked by Isadora. She was in a foul mood when she left for the church. She looked gorgeous, but I don't think she was happy," Sam says while fussing with Juliet's dress.

"She's had her make-up done, hair done and is in a dress. What did you expect she'd be like? I'll bet when we see her, she'll have redone her make-up and her hair will be in her usual buns," I reply, taking a few gulps of my water.

"No doubt, sitting on the floor of the church in the dress, on her computer. I don't think, from the sound of it, anybody had any sleep last night. They were planning when I left and were still there when I got back this morning," Sam mutters.

"Yes. I meant to ask you what time you left this morning?" I ask.

"Lev dropped me back about four-ish; Carrie wasn't happy until Lev slipped her a hundred pounds. I had to push her out of the house with how much she was swooning over him," Sam grates.

"Well, was it worth it? I certainly heard somebody enjoying themselves last night," I ask cheekily.

"No matter how much I try to resist that man, I always seem to cave. He's no good for me Valentina, I know that, but he always pulls me back in," Sam complains.

"Haven't you ever thought about giving it a proper chance?" I prompt, intrigued.

"We did in the beginning, but it's a long and complicated story. One we have no time for now. I love him though and I always will, but sometimes love isn't enough, is it?" She replies sadly.

I'm intrigued about their history now and really need to get her on her own, and probably drunk, so I can get her to spill all the details to me. I look over at her and see so much pain in her expression. I wonder why love isn't enough for them. Surely love can conquer all, or is that just in fairy tales.

"Just the big cock drawing you back for another ride?" I say cheekily.

"What is a big cock, Mama?" Juliet asks innocently.

Sam gives me a scalding look and I cover my face, to hide the fact I'm trying to stop myself from bursting out laughing. Fuck me, I forgot about the tiny ears in the room.

"You don't need to worry about that Juliet, it's a big girl's ride that makes you feel poorly after you've been on it," Sam answers.

I can't hold it any longer; I burst out laughing and can't stop. Luka and Misha walk into the room and stare at me in amusement. Sam comes over and clips me around the head, making me laugh more. Shit, I don't think I've laughed so much in my life.

"You're going to ruin your make-up Valentina! Get your arse in that bedroom and get that dress on. I'll come and tighten the corset in a bit," she says, shooing me off to the bedroom.

"What happened?" Misha asks Sam but, before she can reply, Juliet answers for her.

"Mama had another ride on a big cock, but she said it made her poorly," Juliet answers, not taking her eyes off her colouring.

"For fuck sake's I'm going to kill you, Valentina," Sam shouts while Misha and Luka burst out laughing.

I end up snorting and running off to the bedroom in fits of laughter. I go to the bathroom to grab a tissue, trying to capture the tears from my laughter before they escape and ruin my make-up.

A short while later I'm in my dress and Sam has tied the corset without suffocating me. We stand there, looking at myself in the mirror and I can't help the sadness that overwhelms me that it isn't my Mama standing behind me. That both of us had this chance ripped away from us by my Papa.

Sam rubs my back and gives me a kiss on the

cheek.

"You look absolutely gorgeous Valentina; Kai is a very lucky man. I'm so privileged to be a part of this day with you, thank you for letting Juliet and I be a part of your special day," Sam says.

"You're my new family now Sam, I'm just glad you are here with me because I'm nervous as hell," I reply.

"Bollocks, there is nothing to be nervous about. You'll knock them dead, now chin up and come show Misha and Luka your dress. They're pacing a hole in the floor out there, waiting for you," Sam chastises.

I laugh and pull my shoulders back; before I walk out into the living room. Luka and Misha are pacing and then stop dead in their tracks when they see me enter. I do a twirl, not knowing what else to do.

"You look like the princess in my drawing." Juliet cries out.

We all smile at her, and I take a deep breath as Misha walks over to me.

"You look so beautiful, Valentina; you make me so proud. He better look after you or he'll have me to deal with," Misha warns.

"I'm sure he will do, knowing I have my Bear protecting me if he doesn't. I'm so glad to have you here with me today, Misha," I reply, full of emotion.

"I wouldn't be anywhere else Red. Are you happy?" Misha asks me, cupping my cheek with his big hand.

"I'm happy Bear, he makes me happy." I answer truthfully.

"Good, I'm happy for you sweetheart you deserve it more than anyone," Misha says, placing a kiss on my forehead.

"So do you Bear, you'll find it one day," I reply, kissing his cheek.

"It's not meant for me Valentina; I'll just be happy seeing you happy." Misha replies walking away.

I'll make it my aim to make sure that man finds happiness, he deserves it after the life he's had so far. Luka comes over to me then, giving me a hug and kissing me on the cheek.

"Are you sure this is what you want, Valentina? I can get us out of here if you really don't want this?" Luka asks.

"I'm good Luka, truly. It's time for you to pass all this worry over to Kai and start finding your own happiness. Thank you for everything you have done for me, you will never know how much you mean to me Luka," I whisper, giving him a kiss back on the cheek.

"There's plenty of time for that Valentina, let me

have some fun with a few first." Luka winks at me and I laugh.

"That is absolutely true, you have some fun first. But if any of them break your heart, they will have me to deal with. Understand?" I reply.

"Don't you go scaring them away Lena, I do enough of that myself," Luka winks cheekily at me.

"You know I love you and Bear like my big annoying brothers, don't you?" I ask.

"I do honey, and I love you back. Just make sure that man of yours behaves, or he'll have me and Misha to deal with, okay?" Luka replies.

"I will Luka, don't you worry," I reply, giving him a big hug.

Once I release him, he wanders off to find Misha. I walk over to the bar and pour myself a Bacardi and Coke. Bugger the champagne sitting there in an iced bucket, next to the huge bouquet of flowers Kai left for me this morning. I need my go-to drink to take the edge off.

Misha and Luka walk back in, talking as Misha's phone rings. Answering it, he walks off again.

"I need the toilet, Mama," Juliet whines.

"It's okay Sam, I'll take her," I offer and walk over to Juliet, taking her hand to lead her off to the toilet. Before we leave Misha comes marching in, looking angry.

"What's the matter Bear?" I ask.

"The men aren't sure about some alarm going off downstairs, so I'm going to check it out. Luka you stay here with the girls, the guards are on the doors if you need them. I shouldn't be long, so if you all get ready for when I'm back we can leave for the church," Misha says, before he marches off out of the penthouse.

I get that feeling in the pit of my stomach again and I look at Luka with worry.

"It'll be fine Lena, take Juliet to the toilet. Misha will be back soon," he reassures me.

Sam starts wringing her hands worriedly and looking towards the door that Misha disappeared out of. I pull on Juliet's little hand and lead her down the corridor to the toilet.

When we reach the toilet in Kai's bedroom, I help Juliet with her dress as I position her over the toilet to have her wee. She finishes up and washes her hands. Just as we are about to leave the room, an explosion rocks the building. Juliet screams and I cuddle her to me to comfort her.

I hear gun fire outside the penthouse, and start to worry. I look down at little Juliet who is trembling in my hold, and I know I have to keep her safe. I rush her into the closet and push my dresses to one side, placing her as far back as possible. I get on my knees, holding her tear-stricken face in my hands.

"Sweet one, please stop crying. I need you to listen to me, okay?" I plead with her.

"I'm scared," she whimpers back to me, shaking.

"I know you are Juliet, but I need you to be a big brave girl for me, can you do that?" I ask hurriedly.

She nods and looks at me wide-eyed when more gun fire goes off.

"I need you to stay here for me okay. Do not come out until Bear comes in to find you okay. You know Bear, don't you?" I ask.

"Yes, he's like the giant in the fairy tales," she replies, which melts my heart.

"Yes, he is. But Bear is a big friendly giant who will keep you safe, okay? So only come out when you see him, not anybody else. I'm going to help your Mama now, so stay hidden behind my dresses and don't come out until Bear is here. Okay?" I plead.

"Okay, wait for Bear and don't come out," she agrees.

"That's its baby, you're being so brave. Remember no noise, you must keep quiet," I remind her.

"Okay." She sniffs.

I cover her with my dresses and make her a tiny hole she can peak out of. I back away, ensuring that nobody can make out she's there and grab my knife belt with my throwing knives in. I grab my fighting knives and walk over to Kai's drawer. Opening the top one, I find several Makarov's in a compartment. I pick two out and load them with ammo cartridges, then select a few spares and place them in my knife belt.

With one more look at Juliet, I rush out of the walk-in wardrobe. I spot my mobile on the dressing table and stash it down my corset. Quietly, I pull the door open and start to sneak down the corridor. I get to the living room and look around to find Luka and Sam behind the bar, crouched down.

She gets up and starts to run to me as the doors blast open with another explosion. She's about halfway across the room when a gun fires and Sam's face laces with pain. She falls down face first and blood starts to seep on the floor under her. I want to rush over to her to stop the bleeding, but I have to hold myself back.

Luka returns fire and I hear a thud of what must be one of the attackers. He has to duck back down as several guns return fire. I peek around the corner and spot several men entering the room. I fire off a couple of rounds and hit two of my targets then duck back around the corner as I receive returning fire. Shit! How many of them are here?

Luka returns fire again and I look around

the corner, managing to take out another two targets. We take cover again as more gunfire comes our way. Then I hear the tell-tale sounds of a grenade and I run back down the corridor, ducking into another room just as the grenade detonates.

I pull the mobile out of my corset and dial Kai, his phone goes to voicemail straight away. I try another time, desperate to talk to him, but the voicemail hits again. I decide to leave him a message as my time is ticking and I need to get back to Luka.

"Kai. I don't have long baby, but I need you to know this. I need you to know I love you; I've not wanted to admit it to myself, let alone you. We are under attack and I'm not sure I'm going to make it, so I need to make sure you hear me say it to you. I always said we weren't destined for a happy ever after, but know I will try everything I can to get back to you. If I don't make it just know I love you, even in death. Sam has been shot, she's lying face down bleeding and not moving. Luka is trying to fight them off, but there are too many Kai. Juliet is in the walk-in hiding under my dresses. If Misha doesn't manage to rescue her..." I pause when I hear what sounds like a door being kicked open in my vicinity and they are too close to Juliet for my liking.

"I have to go now, Nikolai. If I don't see you again, know I'm safe with my Mama and love you so much." I end the call and throw the phone away.

I open my door and sneak a peek around it. I see two men coming out of the first room on the corridor, so I grab two of my throwing knives and aim at my targets. I throw and get two bull-eyes, right in the middle of their foreheads, before they drop to the floor. Gun fire continues in the living room as I creep out of the door, heading towards Luka.

Creeping to the end of the wall I look around the corner, to find Luka firing back at the gun men. Then he gets shot. He falls back and I cry out, before the gun man can get another shot out. He has one of my knives in the back of his skull and falls forward. I grab my guns and fire, killing the remaining gun men in the room. I run over to Luka and find him unconscious, sprawled on his back.

As I'm about to check the exit wound on the back of his chest, I hear more men enter. I peek over the bar to find the room full of men again. At least fifteen are flooding in. I fire off some more shots before ducking again from returning fire. As I peak over the bar again my blood runs cold as I see Nikon enter the room. I grab one of my knives in my hand. I've run out of bullets; I know I don't have a chance at escaping from all these men.

I can only hope that either Kai has my message

or Bear is on his way back with help. As Nikon walks towards the bar, I get ready with both my fighting knives in my hands. As he reaches me, I dive out and jump on him, toppling him back with my weight and the added wedding dress.

Grappling with him, and slashing at his arms I manage to bury one of my knives deep into his collar bone. All he does though is laugh at me as I'm dragged backwards by my hair and thrown into the waiting arms of two of my Papa's soldiers.

The man that threw me grabs Nikon's hand to help him up. My brows furrow together as I scrutinise his appearance. Why is he not in Papa's tell-tale uniform? He turns to me with a sadistic smile and I gasp, shocked beyond belief. How could he betray Kai like this? I actually liked him.

"What a vicious little hellion you are, Valentina Ivanov. Your Papa will be so pleased to see you again, for he wishes to repay you for the betrayal, shame, something something, dishonour you have brought to your family name and blah blah blah... it was a long speech. If I'm honest, I checked out in the middle and forgot some, but you get the jist of it," Pasha states sardonically.

"Fuck you, you dare talk to me about honour when you've betrayed Nikolai like this? You're scum and I wish I were going to be there when you get your comeuppance," I spit out.

"I have no loyalty to Nikolai whatsoever, I infiltrated his kingdom for a different reason. I have been here for some time and, unfortunately, that path has paid no dividends. Then, my dear Valentina, fell into my lap with double the bounty on your head. I can't understand why your Papa is paying such a price on a disgrace like you. His only heir, opening her legs to the enemy so willingly?" Pasha tuts at me, shaking his head before continuing. "It's quite shocking, how much you have shamed your family name. However, the world will recover."

"If you've chosen to get into bed with my Papa, you're a fucking moron. He will betray you at the flick of a wrist, or kill you when you're of no more use to him," I spit.

"I have chosen no sides; all of this is for my own ends. I'm the best tracker and bounty hunter available... I pick my pay day. I have no allegiances, no family, no links," he snarls. "One day I could be working for someone and the next day I could be killing them," he replies coldly. "Let the monsters kill each other off to their heart's content. Do the world some good and my bank balance a favour."

I'm about to reply when we hear several shots out by the lifts. Pasha grabs me and holds me in front of himself, aiming a gun at my temple.

"Put down your weapon Misha, I know it's you,

I was waiting for you to arrive. I have Valentina here and, if you do not wish her pretty little head to be blown off, I suggest you give yourself up," Pasha shouts.

"Don't do it Bear!" I shout before Pasha pushes the gun into my temple hard, silencing me.

Misha walks in with his hands up and moves over to us. He's looking around, trying to assess the room. I know what he's planning and I can't have him dying on me too.

"Hold him back as we take Valentina to the helicopter, make sure you get Luka as well. Mikhail wants to kill him personally," Nikon states.

"He's dead by the looks of it, or he'll die on the way. We'll be quicker just leaving him and taking Valentina," Pasha contradicts.

"Fair enough, let's get the bitch back to Mikhail," Nikon orders.

"Argh…" Misha roars and all hell breaks loose. I try to get free from Pasha but I'm unable to.

Men go flying across the room as Misha goes on a rampage, like a Viking berserker, in an attempt to stop them from taking me. Nikon raises his gun and I scream so loud it deafens everyone.

"No Bear, please stop," I cry. "Promise me you'll leave him alive if I come with you willingly."

"If you come willingly then yes. It's a deal. Lower

your gun Nikon," Pasha orders, then addresses Bear. "Misha, take some advice from... what is it the kids call it... ah that's it, a frenemy... retreat now and live to fight another day. Dying won't help anyone will it?"

Misha gives a roar of outrage.

"Stick your fucking advise where the sun don't shine, you fucking Judas!"

"Now, now my grizzly friend... let's not make this personal. Where were you all when my entire world was taken from me? I didn't see your glorious boss charging to my aid when I lost my everything. So here I am, a man made by men just like him, taking what's due. Just like he does and not giving two fucks who pays the price for my choices, just like they don't. Men like him don't care when innocent people get hurt. Well, I'm not innocent now, am I? They made me, so they have to live with the consequences of their actions," Pasha spits. "I'm Judas, am I? No, my friend, you have the wrong biblical tale. No... this is an eye for an eye."

"Bear stop, please listen to me," I shout.

Misha slams another two men's heads against the wall with a sickening crunch. He looks over at me with rage filled eyes.

"Stop please, they are going to kill you and I can't have that Bear. Let me go with them and please don't fight anymore. Please find my surprise in the dresses in Kai's walk-in wardrobe, and look after yourself and Kai, Brat," I beg, as Pasha and Nikon drag me towards the door.

"No Red, don't do this. I don't care what happens to me." He roars.

"It's for the best Brat," I say, as I'm dragged away.

The last time I see Bear, he's roaring "Nooo!!" as he fights with at least ten of my papa's men trying to get to me.

As I'm distracted looking at a raging Bear, I feel a sharp prick in the side of my neck.

"Time to sleep, little traitor. Soon you will be reunited with your Papa and I, for one, cannot wait for this to be over," Pasha whispers in my ear. "It's a shame really, I was getting quite fond of you."

I feel lightheaded and woozy. I try to shake my head and blink my eyes to fight the feeling, but fail.

Before I fall to the floor, I'm thrown over someone's shoulder and the last thing I see is the stairs, while the rotors of an awaiting helicopter whir in the distance. All light begins to fade as the darkness takes me, and all I can think about is Kai. What a fairytale we would have made. Fairytales don't exist in our world though; I learnt that when I was little. My King will have to find another Queen to reign by his side.

Chapter 23

Kai

I'm pacing by the church altar. I have this feeling in my bones, and I can't seem to shift it. Dimitri is leaning against the wall with a cigarette, giving no shit's that he shouldn't be smoking in here. My Papa is sitting in the front row with a deadpan expression on his face, as Ida rambles on while typing away on her laptop.

The church is full of the guests that had to be invited today. Politicians, judges, the police chief; basically everyone on the payroll. Also, the family's allied with us, such as the Polish, the Italian-Americans and the Spanish mob. I couldn't give a fuck about any of them being here. The one person I'm waiting for is making me fucking sweat by being late.

I look at Ida again, her hands still on the keyboard. Her face goes pale and she gets up, rushing to the back waiting room. I look at

Dimitri and Lev, signalling them to follow, and we all make our way after her. My Papa see's the signal and gets up to follow us.

When we all arrive in the room, I find Ida sitting at the table, typing away furiously on her laptop. She starts swearing and typing faster.

"What the fuck's going on Ida?" I shout, startling her slightly.

"It's all gone down; everything has gone dark. I'm blind and can't get back into any of our security systems. I've got alarms going off everywhere and I can't track down what the hell is happening." She rambles, still furiously typing away.

"Can you fucking explain properly? What the hell is going on?" I ask again.

"The security system has booted me out, I'm trying to get in the back door as we speak. I should be back up and running in a few minutes but until then. We're in the dark. I have no visuals on the hotel or the travel routes; the camera's set up around the church have gone dark as well," she replies.

"How the hell has this happened Ida? I thought you and Pasha went over all the security details last night. That's what you assured us in the meeting this morning," I demand.

"We did. Everything was in place. I went

through all the security measures with Pasha with a fine-tooth comb. We spent hours putting the implements in place. What the fuck?" Ida screeches.

"What now?" I ask, pissed off to the back teeth of this shit.

"Some fucker has placed a Crypto Locker on my system. Do they think I'm a fucking novice? Wait until I trace you, you fuckers. You'll wish you were never born. Just give me a few minutes and I'll be back up and running," Ida announces.

"Fuck this shit, I'm calling Misha." I announce.

I dial Misha's number and he picks up after five rings, very much to my dissatisfaction.

"Da Boss?" He asks.

"What the fuck took you so long to answer?" I rage down the phone.

"Sorry Boss, all hell's kicking off here. We've got alarms going off everywhere and I can't find Pasha. The men are trying to disable it as we speak, and I've sent guards to the entrances to check they are secure," he reports.

"What the hell are you doing down there? I gave you strict instructions to stay with Valentina," I roar.

I see Lev pull out his mobile and start ringing someone. He isn't getting any joy either. I can see the panic in his eyes and he keeps redialling, desperate to get in contact.

"Pasha called me and insisted I come to investigate as Ida had instructed me to. I started a security check but when I got to the location he gave me, I couldn't find him. I tried calling, but his phone has been switched off. Something's not right Boss and now the lifts are down," Misha reports.

"Get the fuck back upstairs now, I'm going to try and get in touch with Valentina." I roar and end the call.

I dial Valentina's mobile, but nobody answers; I ring at least ten times to no avail. Shoving my phone back into my jacket pocket, I walk over to look at Ida's computer. It's full of code and she has about twenty windows open all over the screen.

I turn to Lev and see him still trying to reach someone.

"No answer?" I ask.

"She always answers her phone, always Kai. Fuck, I knew I shouldn't have left her there," Lev rambles, while still redialing the number and expecting a different outcome.

"Valentina's not answering either, have you tried Luka?" I ask.

"He's not answering. Fuck, something's seriously wrong," Lev mutters.

"Fuck this I'm going back, stay here and I'll let you know what's going on," I announce.

"I'm in, I've got the hotel back but nothing else. Shit. Oh fuck, get my bag I need the controls for my Idabots. The hotel is under siege and there's a shit ton of them," Ida shouts suddenly.

I look at all the screens, searching for the penthouse. The hotel is in chaos. I see my men, lying dead on various screens, and the stairwells are littered with more. How many fuckers are there, and how have they taken my men by surprise like this?

"I'll get it," says Dimitri, breaking into my thoughts as he heads out to the church for Ida's bag.

"It's under the seat...the skull case." Ida shouts, as Dimitri bolts out of the door.

"How have they managed to bypass all of the security measures Ida?" my Papa asks.

"I have no clue Papa. Even with my computer down all of them were still in place. Wait until I get my case, and I'll send Bobee on the hunt; I left him there and brought Horny and Sting with me," Ida declares, as she skips through the screens, trying to find the penthouse camera.

"Where's the penthouse camera's, why the fuck are they not there?" I ask, frustrated.

"It looks like they've been disabled, that's why

I've asked for my case so I can investigate with Bobee," Ida says, distracted.

"Who is this 'Boobie' you keep talking about and what are these Idabots things? I haven't a clue what you are talking about child," Papa asks.

"My drones Papa, I've explained this to you several times. Obviously, you listen to nothing I say," Ida groans.

Dimitri runs back in with the case and passes it to Ida, then gives me a look and signals me to talk. I walk over to him and we stand in the corner, so I can still see what Ida's doing. I don't want to leave the room until she has any information.

"They're all getting restless out there Brat, do you want me to try and smooth things over?" Dimitri suggests.

"I think it would be best, under no circumstances does anybody leave until we have visuals on the outside of this building. The last thing I need is anymore shit hitting the fan." He nods. "There's a shit ton of intruders Brat, they've killed most of my men. I'm going to need to pull resources from the ranks until I can recruit again," I inform Dimitri.

"That goes without question Brat. I have an elite forces team just finished training as well."

"Good!"

"Two squads and three teams of guards. I've been ramping up on recruitment since our last encounter with the Irish. Our numbers are level currently, so the new recruits can come here," Dimitri answers.

Fuck he's kept all this information quiet; I need to polish up on the family Empire. I've been so preoccupied with taking over Birmingham, I'd not had time to check on the motherland. After this mess is sorted, I need to take control and get everything back in line.

"Perfect Brat, go and sort the wedding guests. Under no circumstances are the families allowed to leave the church. I need to locate Valentina." He nods, listening. "Ida needs to get eyes on the outside of this building to make sure it's safe before anyone can leave. The last fucking thing I need is all the families at war because someone dies at my wedding. What a fucking shit show!"

"Don't worry Brat, I will sort everything. You just concentrate on finding your bride," Dimitri promises, before he turns to leave.

"Who the fuck has any news for me?" I demand.

"There's no answer from Misha, Sam, or Luka. I have reports from some of the men outside, of a helicopter landing on the roof. They are trying to gain entry to the building again but are finding problems accessing the entrances," Lev reported.

"They are currently trying to break in and give us

an update, as none of the teams from the inside are answering."

"Fuck, this doesn't feel right at all," I roar.

"How does a task force of men get past my soldiers, and manage to lock up my fucking hotel?" I clench my fists, frustrated. "This screams sabotage and I want the insider found immediately." Lev nods, gritting his teeth in annoyance. "We've missed something big here, and now my bride is in danger from my own stupidity," I roar, slumping into the chair.

"It will be okay Kai; we will sort everything out my child. Keep your head and think about this. Can you think of any of the men that would betray you?" Papa reasons.

"No Papa, all of our men are vetted and only the trusted ones are given high positions in the ranks. The only new one is Luka, but I can't believe he would betray Valentina. He has risked his life on numerous occasions for her. He knows that betraying her now would still lead him to his death by her Papa's hands," I reply.

"I have Bobee live and going up to the penthouse as we speak. There are several dead on both sides in the stairwell, no sign of Misha or Pasha yet on the face recognition," Ida interjects.

"Have you got visuals on the outside of the church yet?"

"I've already gained back control on the entrances and allowed the men access. They're not far behind Bobee. I've just released Horny and Sting out of the window and they're doing recon on the surrounding area," Ida straightens up, typing fast.

"They are compiling a report as we speak. I've left them to concentrate on Bobee and gain access to the hotel."

"Good!"

She nods. "I've also managed to gain access to the hotel opposite the Grand Emperor, to view the roof. The reports of a helicopter are correct and there is currently one on the landing pad of our hotel," Ida reports, while continuing to frantically type away on the keyboard.

I hear a ping on my phone and grab it out of my pocket. It's a missed voicemail so I place it back and rush to Ida's laptop to see the footage from Bobee. The footage is brilliant considering it's a drone. As it reaches the door to the penthouse reception, I wonder how the hell it's going to gain entry. Suddenly a wire shoots past the camera and attaches itself to the door. The wire tightens, the door flies open, and Bobee flies through.

Fuck me the number of bodies scattering the floor is mind blowing; squares fly over the screen and scan the faces of the men within seconds. The doors look like they have been blown off as the drone passes. The penthouse tells the same story, bodies littering the floor; then we see somebody flying across the room and hear a roar coming from within.

We watch as Misha flies across the room and smashes the man's head repeatedly off the floor, smashing his skull to bits. Several other men run towards Misha, but don't get a chance to get to him as several wires shoot out of the drone again. This time they insert themselves into the men's bodies and we watch, captivated as they start convulsing.

"That's my boy, fry the fuckers," Ida shouts gleefully.

"What the fuck's it doing to them?" Lev asks, shocked.

"He tasered the fuckers, but Bobee's voltage fry's your brain," Ida gloats.

"Fuck where's Misha going?" I ask as Misha rushes off somewhere.

"Let me put the mic on," Ida says.

Bobee pans around the room and finds Misha, stumbling towards the penthouse reception. He's holding his abdomen on the left-hand side, and bumping up against the wall.

"Misha, where the fuck is Valentina?" I shout.

Misha's steps falter, but it doesn't stop him on whatever mission he's determined to do.

"She gave herself up so they wouldn't kill me, I have to get to her. Why did she do it? I begged her not to." Misha groans, still stumbling along and pushing through the stairwell doors.

"Who's got her and where are they?" I roar.

"Roof, helicopter, I have to get to her," he says, as he trundles up towards the roof.

Ida taps frantically at the keyboard, which minimises the drone's camera footage and brings up a camera view. It must be the hotel across the road. A helicopter takes off just as she enlarges the image.

"No!" I roar, jumping up.

We see Misha, followed by Ida's drone rush through the roof door. Misha falls through the door and collapses to his knees when he sees he's too late.

Ida switches the footage back to the drones and brings up a small screen on its monitor. A small object shoots past the screen and the little screen shows its trajectory towards the helicopter. The small screen approaches the helicopter and then slams down on the back of the cabin.

She switches the view back to the Bobee and focuses on Misha.

"Get up Misha, honey. You tried your best; we will find her I promise." Ida pleads with a distraught Misha who is slumped on his knees.

I stumble and my Papa guides me to a chair. I'm numb, unable to form a rational thought at the moment.

I hear their voices around me, and just sit there on autopilot. They have my Queen, and it's all my fault. It's her Papa, it must be, and someone on my team has betrayed me.

Once her Papa has her, the clock will be ticking. I know he will punish her for her disobedience. My Queen's life is in the balance. I need to help her believe me, anybody involved in taking her will pay with their lives.

My phone ring's again and I ignore the call from Misha, looking at the icon showing my missed call. I click on it and bring the phone to my ear.

"You have one new voicemail, new voicemail playback," the phone announces.

My blood runs cold when I hear Valentina's panicked voice between the gunfire in the background.

"Kai. I don't have long baby, but I need you to know this. I need you to know I love you; I've not wanted to admit it to myself, let alone you. We are under attack and I'm not sure I'm going to make it, so I need to make sure you hear me say it to you. I always said we weren't destined for a happy ever after, but know I will try everything I can to get back to you. If I don't make it just know I love you, even in death. Sam has been shot, she's lying face down bleeding and not moving. Luka is trying to fight them off, but there are too many Kai. Juliet is in the walk-in hiding under my dresses. If Misha doesn't manage to rescue her…" There's a pause and I'm frantic to hear her voice again. Then, seconds later.

"I have to go now, Nikolai. If I don't see you again, know I'm safe with my Mama and love you so much."

Then nothing. Silence and the voicemail kicks in again. I roar and throw the chair, along with anything I can get my hands on across the room. My phone smashes against the wall and I feel hands grabbing me. I'm not going to sit here any longer, my Queen needs me.

"Kai, you need to calm down and think about this logically, you are no good to Valentina…" I interrupt my Papa's words.

"Don't you fucking dare even breathe her name, do you hear me?" I say, as I point in my papa's face furiously.

"My boy you need to think…" My papa tries again, but this is wasting my time.

"I need to save my Queen that's what I need to do, fuck whatever you think. She means nothing to you, but to me she is MY FUCKING WORLD!" I roar in my Papa's face.

I turn and rush toward the door. Frantic voices

call after me, but I pay them no attention. I walk into the church and ignore all the eyes that are zoned in on me. Dimitri rushes over and I continue walking towards the exit.

"Dimitri, stop him quickly." I hear Ida shout from behind me.

Dimitri tries, but I turn and push him so hard he falls to the floor. He looks at me distraught, but I have no time to reassure him. There's no reassurance to be had.

As I push the doors to the church open, I hear Ida scream "No…" behind me and that's when I see them. I feel the first bullet hit my arm and then another one pierces my stomach, knocking me onto my back. As I lie there, starting to choke on my own blood, I think of my Queen. I see her beautiful face flash before my eyes, and it's as though I can almost reach out to touch her.

I try to lift my arm to touch her smiling face, but I get it about halfway towards her before it drops back down to the floor. I see Ida above me, frantically trying to stop the blood from my wounds.

The last thought I have is for my Queen, my world, my soul's keeper. I made her a promise that I intend to keep 'I'll be waiting, my Little Siren, for we will rule the afterlife together for eternity once you are safely back at my side.'

Chapter 24

Daniil

Time is such a precious commodity in life, for me I wish I could turn back the clock. Right the wrongs that scarred my soul, and made me who I am today. They say time heals all wounds, what a crock of shit that saying is. I treat it as my countdown to the end, some try to prolong the end, I welcome it. My time to others costs money, after all they pay for an impeccable service, but my customer service is debatable.

I blame other men for my woes, which is true, but it is not just them to blame. One man was the catalyst to all of these events, one man I will destroy as soon as I find him. His actions had a butterfly effect on all of our lives, plunging our world as we know it into darkness. I know some of his sins, and they are unforgivable, truly monstrous acts. I also have a nagging feeling the worst is yet to come.

I'm currently at a dead end in my search for answers, but this has by no means been a waste of time. I have one of my chips collected and a shit ton of leads to follow.

The path I'm about to take is wrong but I have no other option. This is how it has to be. She doesn't deserve this, but she's strong, and she'll handle it. She won't forgive it, and I can't blame her, but sometimes you have to do what's best for the bigger picture. She will hate me, they all will, but let them hate me. It's what I need them to do if the next part of my plan is going to work…

To be Continued…

Glossary

Privet - Hi

Da - Yes

Net - No

Brat - Brother

Sestra - Sister

Mama – Mother

Papa – Father

кто ты, черт возьми? Ты дикхед! - *Who the fuck are you? You dickhead!*

Королева - Queen

Kotehok – kitten

Printessa - Princess

Author's Note

Thank you so much for reading The Siren's Call, I hope you enjoyed the story. I'm hoping that book 2 in The Treasured Possession Duet will be out early next year.

I always appreciate your feedback and would be grateful if you could leave me a review on Amazon, Goodreads or social media.

As with all Authors, reviews mean the world to us. They encourage us to strive for more, help us when we are low, and tell us that you love the world's we create for you.

About Tammy

Tammy Bradley lives in England with her Fiancé, Craig, the love of her life and her children. She is the mother of four beautiful girlies; her family means the world to her. She has a crazy Chihuahua and a psycho budgie. She loves a good cuppa, chocolate and sweets. Reading is her main passion along with her love of films. She loves Marvel and Transformers with a nerdy obsession, with Quick Silver and Bumblebee being amoung her favourite characters of all time.

Tammy loved stories and writing as a child, and would often spend time alone with a book or writing pad. She left this behind as she grew up, worked, and started her family with Craig. After a tragic loss in the family, her eldest daughter brought her The Mortal Instruments book set as a gift. The love of reading returned and offered an escape from the devastation.

Hundreds of books later, she finally admitted to her family that her life's ambition had always been to become an Author, but her self-doubt had always stood in the way.

As they say the rest is history, and now Tammy writes dark romance books. Her first book The

Siren's Call is part of The Treasured Possessions duet, a dark mafia romance. This is just the start of her journey; she invites you to come along and enjoy the ride.

Connect with Tammy

Join Tammy on social media. She regularly posts about updates and her next books on TikTok, Facebook and Instagram.

Join Tammy on Facebook

Author Tammy Bradley official fan group – All Sorts

Join Tammy on Tiktok

@authortammybradley

Join Tammy on Instagram

@authortammybradley

You can also subscribe to Tammy's newsletter through her website.

www.AuthorTammyBradley.com